# Gazumped!

Also by the author

*Hot Property*

SARAH O'BRIEN

# Gazumped!

First published in Ireland in 2004 by Hodder Headline Ireland,
8 Castlecourt, Castleknock, Dublin 15, a division of Hodder Headline.
First published in Great Britain in 2004 by Hodder & Stoughton,
338 Euston Road, London NW1 3BH, a division of Hodder Headline.

A Coronet/Lir paperback

1  3  5  7  9  10  8  6  4  2

A CIP catalogue record for this title is available
from the British Library.

ISBN 0 340 83043 3
Ireland ISBN (including Northern Ireland) 0 340 83564 8

Typeset in Plantin Light by
Palimpsest Book Production Limited, Polmont, Stirlingshire
Printed and bound in Great Britain by Clays Ltd

Hodder & Stoughton and Hodder Headline Ireland
Divisions of Hodder Headline
338 Euston Road
London NW1 3BH

# NOTE ON THE AUTHOR

Sarah O'Brien has a dual personality – she is both Helena Close and Patricia Rainsford, two best friends since childhood. Keen writers, they have collaborated on everything from teenage romance to weddings, babies and career paths. It was only a matter of time before they began writing together.

Helena has worked in public relations and journalism and Patricia teaches part-time. Both live in Limerick, Ireland, with an assortment of children, husbands, cats and dogs. *Gazumped!* is the sequel to their first, best-selling book, *Hot Property*.

# ACKNOWLEDGEMENTS

As always we would like to thank our agent, Faith O'Grady, our publisher, Ciara Considine, and all the team at Hodder, both in Ireland and the UK. While we're at it we'd also like to thank Quentin Tarantino, Scooby Doo and the Italian football team.

For the usual suspects

# I

*When you're looking thirty in the eye, as well as getting older, you should be ridiculously successful in your career. You should be dealing with cots and crèches, be intimately acquainted with your nearest DIY shop, and congratulating yourself on managing to hook up with the man of your dreams. Or so my mother and all the best magazines would have you believe.*

*The only thing I'd managed by the time I was twenty-eight was the getting older bit. Instead of conforming to the norm, I was chasing psychopaths, with ex-criminals who were also ex-lovers – not a good plan for settling down. Maybe I had to accept that I, Ellen Grace, lanky Limerick estate agent, was attracted to trouble and chaos the way other women my age were attracted to soul mates and soft furnishings. But you'd never have believed that, the day of the wedding . . .*

I awoke from a fitful sleep and lay staring at the white hotel-room ceiling as I listened to Andrew on the telephone, talking about air conditioning. As snippets of his bad Spanish floated into my sleep- and heat-addled brain, I squirmed with sheer happiness as I remembered the night before. The reflection of the moon on the surface of the sea. The silvery sand of the beach that was almost luminous as it caressed our feet. The mesmeric sound of crickets and . . . oh, my God! . . . what time was it? What day was it? It was Tuesday – that was it, Tuesday. It was definitely Tuesday and there was something about Tuesday, wasn't there? Something important? Oh God! Tuesday was the wedding day.

I jumped out of bed and ran into the bathroom where I gradually managed to focus on my watch and slow down my breathing. Six o'clock. That was fine – unless it was six in the evening, of course, and if it was, then it was too late anyway, and they'd all be standing at the wedding, dressed in their new clothes, waiting for us . . .

'Ellen?'

I looked at Andrew.

'Are you OK?'

I nodded.

'Are you sure?'

'Of course, I'm sure. Why would you think I'm not OK?'

'Well, it might be something to do with the way you ran out of the bedroom.'

I yawned.

'Are you worried about the wedding?' Andrew asked.

'No. It's just I was so hot while I was asleep, and it took me ages to wake up properly and . . . it *is* six in the morning, isn't it?'

Andrew nodded.

'Good. Then we have eleven hours before the wedding, don't we?'

Andrew nodded again.

'Who was on the phone?' I asked.

'I rang reception about the bloody air conditioning, I was awake half the night – the heat was unbearable. They said they'd send someone up to fix it today.'

'That's what they told us yesterday,' I said, turning on the shower and stepping back as it spurted to life. 'We'll be back home before they sort it out.'

'Maybe they'll fix it today,' Andrew said, stepping up behind me and winding his arms around my waist. 'Meanwhile, is that a shower I see running?'

'Last time I looked.'

'I think, in the interests of water conservation, we ought to share the shower.'

He paused to kiss the back of my neck and I groaned softly.

'What do you say?' he asked, brushing the length of my neck with his breath. 'Aren't you impressed by the fact that I'm so environmentally friendly?'

'Well,' I said, pulling him towards the cascade of cool shower water. 'I'm not sure how sincere you are about the environment but you certainly are friendly all right.'

India had already finished breakfast by the time we reached the hotel dining room. She waved and motioned for us to join her at her table. Andrew and I circled the buffet-style table in the centre of the room. We piled our plates with fruit and cheese and bread, and poured enormous glasses of juice before joining her. She smiled like a lantern as we sat down beside her.

'Where's Tim?' Andrew asked.

'Gone for a walk,' India replied, picking a piece of cantaloupe from my plate. 'I just couldn't face it – too hot. I'll go for a swim in a while and that'll have to do me for exercise.'

'You're already working hard enough,' I said, between mouthfuls of deliciously cool fruit. 'Think of it, Ind – even when you're doing nothing, you're doing something.'

I leaned forward and patted the barely visible bump that was swelling under her long, white dress.

India leaned back in her seat and smiled at me. Andrew wiped juice from his mouth with a serviette. 'You're great to come all this way to the wedding when you're pregnant,' he said.

'I wouldn't miss this wedding for the world – I'd fly to the moon to attend it!'

We all laughed. Andrew and I tucked into our breakfast and India sat back in her seat, her hand idly patting her belly. It was so good to be able to sit in silence together like this after all we'd been through. Just doing something as ordinary as sitting in this Spanish hotel dining room, with the early-morning sun streaming through sheer, voile curtains, and normal people eating breakfast all around us, was wonderful in itself.

It was almost impossible to believe that just months

earlier, I'd been mixed up in a whirlwind of crime wars and murder. It was equally hard to believe that I'd also been mixed up with Tony Jordan. I put that thought straight out of my head. Today of all days, I had no intention of thinking about Tony Jordan. I'd spent months with vague thoughts of him nipping at my heels. Where was Tony? Was he all right? Who was he with? Somehow that one was especially distracting for me. But I was resolved: there'd be no more thoughts of Tony Jordan. I was going to focus all my attention on Andrew.

As if on cue, just when I was desperately in need of distraction, the dining-room door opened, and Ruth and Emerson appeared. Ruth was wearing a cherry-coloured sarong, her blonde hair streaked a multitude of shades by the sun, and her skin a glowing amber. Every head in the room turned to watch her as she tottered on some sort of wooden platform sandals to our table.

'Mommy – it's Kylie Minogue and she's having a baby, look!' a chubby-cheeked little girl whispered at the top of her voice. We all laughed as her mother shushed her and gave us an embarrassed smile.

'Yeah, right,' Ruth said, sitting down. 'It's been a while since I looked like Kylie.'

Emerson bent his blond, silky head over Ruth and kissed her on the forehead.

'Way more beautiful,' he said. She smiled up at him

'Run over there and get me a plate of food before I drop down with the hunger.' She paused to wink at him – 'Darling.'

Emerson nodded and headed for the buffet table.

'Jesus, I wish I smoked,' Ruth said, pushing her chair out from the table to make room for her large, round stomach.

'Why?' I asked. 'You never smoked.'

Ruth sighed and nodded. 'I know but I feel so bloody virtuous – no drinking, no running around and staying up all night and . . . and—'

'Stuff like that,' I supplied.

'Exactly. Stuff like that. I'm suddenly a pillar of virtue and I don't know what to do with myself, so at least if I took up smoking—'

'You shouldn't smoke when you're pregnant, Ruth,' India interjected.

Ruth and I both looked at her.

'Sorry,' India said. 'I was just saying.'

'Anyway,' Ruth continued, 'It looks like I won't even have time to take up smoking because the way I feel now, I'd say I'm about to have this baby any minute.'

'Not today, Ruthie,' I squealed. 'For God's sake, not today. What about the wedding?'

Ruth shrugged. 'Might not have a choice.'

'Hold on at least until tomorrow,' I said. 'Otherwise you'll ruin our day.'

'Thanks for thinking of me, Ellen,' Ruth said.

'One day more,' I pleaded. 'I don't think that's too much to ask. If you were any kind of a friend, you'd hang on for one more day after we've travelled all this way for the wedding.'

'What about the wedding?' Emerson said, plonking

a whole platter of food in front of Ruth who set upon it with great energy.

'Just think I might be going into labour . . . miss the wedding—' Ruth said, through a mouthful of nectarine.

Emerson sat on the empty chair beside her and leaned towards her, placing his long, tanned arm protectively around her shoulders. 'Really, love?'

Ruth nodded and swallowed. 'Bloody contractions all night, Em. I told you that.'

Emerson sat back in his chair. 'Braxton-Hicks contractions,' he said with a sage smile, looking around at us. 'Nothing to worry about – false labour – though I think of it more as preparatory labour rather than *false* labour as such.'

'That time Emerson spent filming childbirth practices in South America will come in really handy now,' I said to Ruth, and we both turned to look at him. Emerson blushed slightly and squirmed in his seat. Ruth shook her head and rolled her eyes.

'Well,' she said, patting Emerson's arm. 'I don't know about that but it *is* a fact that that's where he learned his Spanish, which is certainly coming in handy here in the south of Spain. Better than his knowledge of obstetrics anyway – eh, love?'

Emerson relaxed visibly and smiled a wide, boyish smile as he sipped his steaming coffee. His blue eyes flashed in his darkly tanned face as he looked at Ruth, and the tenderness between them was almost palpable. I was glad for Ruth. She deserved somebody

who loved her as much as Emerson did. Ruth grimaced and sat back in her chair.

'Ow,' she said. 'That hurt.'

Emerson reached over and rubbed her naked
shoulders.

'Stop that right away, Ruth Joyce,' I said. 'Put all
thoughts of giving birth out of your head, at least
until after the wedding.'

'Anyway, Ruth,' India said, 'there's no real need
to worry. Chances are that even if you are in labour,
it'll take you eighteen hours or more to give birth.
So you shouldn't have any difficulty getting through
the wedding.'

Ruth was peeling a tiny orange and dripping juice
onto her bump. 'Gee, Ind,' she replied, 'why doesn't
that cheer me up?'

'It cheers me up,' I said. 'Anyway, I have to go
get beautified for the big day. What are you doing,
Andrew?'

'I think, Tim and I are going snorkelling at
twelve.'

'Have a lovely time and don't drown,' I said,
leaning across the table to kiss him. 'See you later.'

At the beauty salon, as well as having my hair done,
I had a manicure and pedicure. I even let a tiny,
fine-boned Oriental woman, who made me feel like
Arnold Schwarzeneggar in a dress, give me a Swedish
head massage. I was delighted we had come to Spain
for the wedding, I thought, as she manipulated my
scalp until I was almost ecstatic with relaxation. It

was somehow right to be here – all friends, all together and – for once – all happy.

I lay back in the leather salon chair and thought for the umpteenth time how lucky I was. Everything was so good between Andrew and me that sometimes it was hard to remember all the time we had spent apart. Hard to believe it was real. One thing was for sure – I'd learned my lesson. From now on, I was going to appreciate what I had and not always look to see if there was something better beyond the horizon.

After all that had happened, here I was, in a beautiful Spanish village with golden sands and azure Mediterranean water, and Africa a mere shout away. And as if that wasn't enough, I was here with Andrew and my dearest friends. It was all so perfect, I might have cried, except that I was just too bloody happy to cry.

After I left the beauty salon, I went shopping and bought two handbags and a pair of red leather shoes, and then I went back to the hotel. Somebody had fixed the air conditioning, so the air in the room was like a refreshing dip in the ocean. I looked at the clock beside the bed: 3.30. That was great – plenty of time to get ready. On the dressing table stood a note from Andrew.

Back after snorkelling – I didn't drown. Tim and I have to go and sort out some work stuff – need to find a fax and a computer. Don't worry, I'm dressed and ready – I won't be late. See you there. Love, Andrew

Kicking off my sandals as I read the note, I threw myself down on the bed. The clean, white sheets were like a balm on my hot skin. I hoped Andrew wasn't going to be late for the wedding now. Bloody work! It's always a problem when you mix your personal and work lives, isn't it? Not only was Tim Gladstone married to one of my best friends, he was also the owner of Gladstone and Richards Auctioneers – for whom Andrew and I worked. Which made him our boss. Still, working while we were here in Spain was ridiculous. It would be very embarrassing if Andrew was late for the wedding.

My body ached with exhaustion and sank deeper and deeper into the bed. I'd close my eyes for just one minute, I thought. Just a little cat nap to refresh me. Just forty winks before I showered and put on my dress and make-up and made my way through the hotel to the beautiful garden booked for the wedding.

We'd looked at it the night before, Andrew and I. Very pretty. A tall, arching fountain splashing water gently onto white marble pebbles. A series of bowers, like a tunnel, twined with huge red hibiscus flowers, trailing green ivy and purple wisteria. A fairytale garden. Just the place for a fairytale wedding.

As I drifted into unconsciousness, I saw Andrew standing in that garden, waiting for me. Tall and handsome in his cream linen suit, an hibiscus flower in his buttonhole, and a broad smile stretching his beautiful mouth across his beloved face.

# 2

The dream of getting married in the garden paradise was so enjoyable that I tried to ignore the bell that was ringing somewhere outside. A church bell, I told myself as my dream filled up with bells. School bells. Sleigh bells. Doorbells. Telephone bells. Telephone bells?

'Oh shit!' I said, leaping onto the floor. I grabbed the telephone receiver.

'Hello?' I said in a slow, sleepy voice. I coughed. 'Hello?' I repeated.

'Ellen!'

'Ruth?'

'Where are you? It's twenty to five, for God's sake, and you're supposed to be here.'

'OK,' I said, struggling to order my thoughts. 'Calm down. I'm coming. Is Andrew there?'

'Of course, Andrew is here. Where were you? Were you asleep? We've been ringing and ringing the room. Andrew and Tim just got here and I was about to send Andrew up for you.'

'OK, OK. I'm on my way. I won't be long, I promise.'

'You'd better not be.'

'I won't. Are you still in labour?'

'Not this minute. Come on, Ellen. I can't believe you.'

'I'll be right down.'

I dropped the receiver back onto its cradle and ran into the bathroom. I looked in the mirror at the bird's nest that was my hair. Oh dear God! After all that time at the beauty place. What exactly had I been doing with my head while I was asleep? I turned on the shower and jumped straight in, not even waiting for the water to heat up. Oh my God! I was going to be late! I couldn't believe it.

Having towelled myself dry quickly, I plastered my face with make-up and manipulated the hairdryer, praying that my hair wouldn't go bananas as it usually did when I needed it to behave. I almost laughed as I remembered my earlier plans of plaiting some of the beautiful flowers from the wedding garden into my hair before the ceremony. Now I'd be lucky if my hair didn't drip down my back for the rest of the afternoon.

I shook my silk dress free from its tissue-paper wrapping and didn't even stop to admire it before pulling it on over my head. Then, grabbing a huge silver slide, I wound my hair into a knot and pinned it in place. I looked in the mirror. I still looked as if I'd been asleep all afternoon, but I'd have to do. I shoved my feet into stiletto sandals, and ran out the door. I was going to be killed. How could I have done something like this? What would everybody say? What would Andrew think?

The hotel lobby was full of newly arriving visitors who all stared as I whizzed past them, out the door and around the side of the building to the wedding garden. The important thing was that I was there, I told myself. It would have been good if I had looked less like a one-woman disaster area, but at least I'd be there on time. I looked at my watch. One minute past five. OK – almost on time.

'Ellen,' India greeted me, as I appeared in the tunnel of vegetation that led to the fountain-loud centre of the garden.

'Ind,' I gasped.

'Here,' she said. 'This way. Everyone's waiting.'

We cleared the final flower bower and there in front of me were all the other members of the wedding party, all waiting for me. The sight of them together made my eyes fill with tears, but the look on Ruth's face soon evaporated any sentimentality. I ran to where she stood.

'You look lovely,' I said. And she did. Ruth was dressed in a full-length, white, silk shift dress with delicate pastel-coloured embroidery around the neck and along the cuffs of the wrist-skimming sleeves. Ruth looked at me with wide, blue eyes. She blinked slowly.

'I almost sent Andrew up to break down the door,' she said.

'He has a key,' I replied.

'Oh, Jesus! Always an answer. You know what I mean.'

And I did. Andrew came and stood beside me,

looking pretty much as handsome in that cream linen suit as he had in my dream.

'You look beautiful,' he whispered. 'Are you OK?'

I nodded, still looking at Ruth.

'I'm sorry I'm late,' I said, leaning forward to kiss her cheek. 'Will we get going?'

Ruth stared at me and I wondered if she was going to cry. She could be odd like that – you could never be sure quite how she'd take something. Then she nodded and smiled a wide, beautiful Ruth smile.

'We'd better start,' she said, grabbing Emerson by the hand. 'I'm determined to be married before this baby puts in an appearance, and, to tell you the truth, I'd say that'll be any time now.'

Andrew kissed me on the cheek and went to sit beside Tim Gladstone who waved and winked at me. India and I stood side by side behind Emerson and Ruth. A short, dark-haired woman, with the beginnings of a fine moustache, pronounced the beautiful-sounding Spanish words. And so, Emerson Burke and Ruth Joyce were married in that fragrant, flower-filled garden, with India and me as witnesses, and Tim and Andrew as guests.

As soon as the ceremony was finished and the kissing and hugging had begun, Ruth let out a shout and stumbled forward.

'Oops!' I said, catching her in my arms.

She looked up at me. 'Ellen.'

'I'm sorry I was late,' I said.

'It's not that. I think my waters just broke.'

'Oh God!' I screamed. 'Emerson! Ambulance! Now!'

Emerson paused for one millisecond to look at his new wife. 'But—'

'Emerson,' Ruth muttered between deep breaths, 'forget Braxton-Hicks – think 999.'

Emerson nodded and ran towards the hotel.

The Registrar of Marriages helped me to carry Ruth to a seat, and Andrew and Tim clucked around like two hens about to lay eggs. India and I sat on either side of Ruth, holding her hands. Ruth inhaled deeply.

'Fuck!' she said, leaning forward. 'Fuck, fuck, fuck!'

She looked at India and me, and we all began to laugh. Tim and Andrew looked at us as if we'd lost our senses, but that made us laugh louder.

The ambulance arrived within minutes, and India and I kissed Ruth before she was whisked away. We stood in silence, in front of the hotel, watching as the ambulance drove off. Andrew put his arm around me.

'You OK?' he asked.

I shrugged. 'I can't believe it.'

He nodded. 'It's a bit of a surprise all right – when was the baby due?'

'Not that,' I said, tutting loudly. 'For God's sake, Andrew! She's been saying she's in labour all day. I mean, I can't believe Ruth is actually married.'

'Oh,' he said. 'Why?'

I shrugged. 'I don't know. Because she's Ruth, I guess. Good-time girl *extraordinaire*.'

Andrew laughed. 'I don't think it's all that surprising. Ruth is a lot more sensible than she looks.'

'She always liked you,' I said.

Andrew shrugged. 'See, I told you – a rock of sense. Just one thing.'

'What?'

'Why did she get married today if she thought she was in labour?'

'That one's easy,' I said. 'Ruth's adopted and she's always had a bit of a thing about it. Not that the Joyces weren't great parents – they were and she loved them to bits and was heartbroken when they died—'

'I never knew she was adopted.'

'Yes. She told me once if she ever had a baby, she'd make damn sure she had two parents there to raise it. Mind you, even I didn't realise quite how determined she was.'

Andrew touched my face with his hand. 'Will you marry me, Ellen Grace? We can't let Ruth and Emerson have all the fun.'

I stared into his eyes and concentrated on how the sultry Mediterranean air made his hair slightly curly.

'I love you, Andrew,' I said. Because it was true and it took my attention away from the horrible feeling that was growing in the pit of my stomach.

He kissed me gently on the lips, 'I love you too, Ellen. Is that a yes?'

We were interrupted by India who had just walked over to us. 'Oh, my God!' she said. 'I don't believe it – I'm going to be an auntie.'

I hugged her hard, grateful for the distraction from the ridiculous feelings that were flooding me. It was just a proposal after all. A declaration of love. There was nothing wrong with that. I loved Andrew madly. I hugged India again.

'Auntie India,' I said. 'Sounds like a political movement.'

'Very funny. I hope Emerson didn't forget his camera in the rush.'

'Why?' Andrew asked.

'Well, he's hoping to film the birth.

I laughed. 'I hope he forgot it.'

India looked at me in surprise. 'Why?'

'Well, because I'd say he'd be safer filming bare-knuckle Gypsy fights than coming at Ruth with a camera while she's in labour!'

India laughed and made a face.

'Come on,' I said, leading the way through the flower-fragrant bowers. 'Let's go eat the wedding feast that Ruth and Emerson have already paid for, and then go to the hospital and see if Baby Burke has arrived. We can bring Ruthie a doggy bag.'

Ruth had a baby boy. Fair-haired and sallow-skinned like his father, with his mother's enormous blue eyes. Ruth displayed him to us as soon as we walked into her hospital room.

'Oh my God!' India whispered. 'Look at my beautiful nephew.'

'He really is beautiful,' I agreed.

'Of course,' his mother said.

'Was it hell?' I asked as India and I settled onto the end of Ruth's bed.

'Hell on wheels,' Ruth said. 'Have an epidural, India. I was almost ready to pop when we got to the hospital so it was too late to have any drugs. Still, it was short – as torture goes – and look what I got.'

Ruth cradled the baby in the crook of her arm and kissed the top of his head.

'What are you calling him?' I asked.

'Not sure yet, but I'll be picking the name – no offence, India, but you Burkes have strange taste in names.'

We all laughed. As well as India, and Ruth's new husband, Emerson, there were three Burke sisters – Isis, Saffron and Venus – and two brothers – Lake and Palmer.

The baby gurgled and his eyes began to close. Ruth looked at him with such a smitten expression on her face that I had to smile. Andrew was right about Ruth – all a façade, that good-time-girl stuff. Sitting on a rubber cushion in a Spanish hospital bed, she looked happier than I'd ever seen her. We sat in silence for a few seconds, all lost in our own thoughts.

'Christ!' Ruth said, suddenly, breaking the silence. India and I looked at her.

'What?' I asked, alarmed by her tone. 'What is it?'

'I forgot about it because I was in labour – Tony and Wolfie – when I was being wheeled through the hospital to the labour ward, I saw Tony and Wolfie.'

'No, you did not!' I said. 'How could you see them?'

'Tony Jordan?' India asked. 'Here?'

'He can't be here,' I said, my heart flipping at the thought. I forced myself to be calm. But if he was here, at least it meant he was safe.

'Why not?' Ruth asked, 'They have to be somewhere, don't they? They're not in Ireland – why not Spain, Ellen? Didn't you tell me that Tony said he might be going to Spain?'

It was true – I had told her that. But that night was so confusing. After all, a gang of drug-dealers was trying to kill him. 'Yes, he mentioned Spain all right . . . but he can't be here . . . how do you know it was them? Did you talk to them?'

Ruth laughed. 'I was otherwise occupied and they were walking away from me down a corridor. It looked like Tony had his arm in a plaster cast, now that I think of it.'

'Which would explain what they were doing in the hospital,' India suggested.

Ruth nodded. 'Exactly.'

'But you didn't talk to them – so you don't know for certain that it was them?'

Ruth rearranged the baby and kissed his head again. 'I know for certain that it was Wolfie, Ellen. And I'm pretty sure Tony was with him – who else would it be?'

'It could be anybody – they had their backs turned and you were in labour, Ruth.'

Ruth shook her head and pursed her lips. 'I think I'd recognise Bobby Wolfe, all things considered. There was a time – before my reincarnation as a respectable woman – when let's just say I would certainly have recognised any part of Wolfie by touch, never mind sight—'

'Stop!' India squealed. 'Too much information! I believe you.'

Ruth grinned. 'OK, but how about you, Ellen? Do you believe me?'

I shrugged.

'Take my word for it,' Ruth continued. 'Bobby Wolfe has probably the best ass I've ever seen in all my life. And God knows I've seen a few. I'd know that ass anywhere, Ellen – so I *am* one hundred per cent positive that it was him.'

'Oh my God!' I said. 'Well, Ruth, if it's the ass-recognition test, how can I doubt you?'

Ruth winked and looked straight at me. 'Damn right. But it doesn't matter anyway if Wolfie and Tony are here in Spain – does it, Ellen?'

I shook my head. 'No, of course not. Why would it matter? I'm just curious, that's all.'

We were silent for a few minutes before I continued. 'You might meet him while you're here, Ruthie – if it *is* him. How will you feel about that?'

'About what?'

'Meeting Wolfie?'

Ruth laughed and snuggled her baby. 'That's really not a problem. I think you could safely say that Wolfie and I got everything we wanted out of our time together.'

'How much longer will Emerson be on location with the Romany Gypsy documentary?' India asked.

'Another three or four months, anyway. I'll tell

Tony you were asking for him if I meet him. Will I, Ellen?'

I looked at her and she stared hard at me. I love Andrew. I love Andrew. I love Andrew. I repeated the words like a mantra over and over inside my head. And it was true – I did love Andrew. But, somehow, Tony Jordan was like a plant rooted deeply in my heart. I could see that Ruth knew that. She smiled.

'There's just something about those two guys, isn't there?' India said. Ruth and I turned to look at her in surprise.

'Wolfie and Tony Jordan, I mean,' she said, smiling.

'We know *who* you mean, but *what* do you mean?' I asked.

India shrugged. 'They're like exotic birds or impossibly high heels – really, really lovely to look at, exciting and you'd love to own them, but . . . I don't know – not meant for ordinary living.'

Ruth laughed. 'You're mad, India Burke, and now that my son is related to you, I'm praying it's not hereditary.'

'I'm right though,' India said, looking at me. 'It's like hot property – that's what it's like – beautiful, expensive, in demand, but not a practical alternative for most people in the long run. Too much risk involved when all is said and done. Isn't that right, Ellen?'

I smiled and nodded, and the talk turned back to babies. But my mind remained with this new turn of events. India was right about Tony. And I didn't even miss him – well, mostly I didn't. I couldn't understand why I was so rattled to hear that he was in the vicinity. It made no sense. It particularly made no sense because I so wholeheartedly agreed with India.

'There's only one thing about Tony and Wolfie that I want to say,' Ruth said, suddenly turning the conversation back and getting my complete attention. I looked at her. She handed the baby to India who was delighted to hold her new nephew. Then she rummaged in her bedside locker for a small mirror and a red lipstick which she applied at leisure as if she wasn't mid-sentence.

'What?' I asked impatiently.

Ruth pulled out a mascara wand and began to coat her eyelashes. 'India is right – they *are* very risky and that's not a good thing. But you have to hand it to them – risks or no risks, it may be worth it, because – in every sense of the word – they provide one hell of a ride!'

I laughed. India tutted. Ruth winked. The baby made a squelching noise and the door opened and our three men tumbled into the room, carrying flowers, chocolates and a bottle of champagne. Real life, I thought, as we toasted the baby's arrival, drinking from paper cups. Real life was good and safe – and happy as well – and that was what I wanted. Wasn't it?

# 3

After all the high drama at Ruth and Emerson's wedding in May, life was pretty calm for the rest of that summer. Which suited me fine. Andrew and I settled down in his large, red-brick terraced house. We went to work at Gladstone and Richards. We shopped and ate and visited our families.

Andrew's parents had moved to Donegal as soon as Andrew had grown up and left home, so we didn't get to see them all that often. Which made me happy. I was as terrified of Andrew's tall, strident mother with her talk of *decorum* and *etiquette* as I was annoyed by his father who seemed to play golf twenty-four hours a day.

But they were Andrew's parents so I kept my opinion to myself. And anyway, I was no one to talk about mad families. Andrew visited my parents without complaint and even ate my mother's cooking as though it was real edible food. I felt the least I owed him was a little containment of my feelings about his folks.

Apart from my nephew, Kieran, the very nicest relative that either of us possessed was Andrew's three-year-old daughter, Katie. Katie visited our house to be with her dad every Sunday. In addition, Andrew also called to her mother's house to see her at least twice a week.

Katie seemed to have managed to inherit all the best genes from both of her parents, being as dark and handsome as her father, and as fine-boned and delicate as her mother. Apart from the fact that she was related to Andrew, it had to be said that Katie was also a very entertaining person in her own right, and she and I had quite a good time watching *Toy Story* every time she came over.

I really admired Andrew's devotion to Katie. In fact, I often boasted about him and how he'd moved back to Ireland to be with his daughter even though he had no relationship with her mother. Katie was the product of a one-night stand. 'What a guy!' my female friends and acquaintances would say when I bragged about what a new man my boyfriend happened to be. Yes, indeed. What a guy. It never occurred to me that that might be the very rock upon which I'd perish.

I simply luxuriated in my life with Andrew that summer – our cosy routine of work, food, sex and lots of laughing. And to be honest, it wasn't just a cosy routine – it was a lovely routine. But still, I couldn't quite shake the feeling that there was something missing from my life.

Ruth, Emerson and their baby, who they'd named Paddy, moved back from Spain in mid-August. They bought a lovely, though basic, cottage in County Clare, with money Emerson had earned from his

Romany Gypsy documentary. I laughed when Ruth told me how much he'd earned.

'No way,' I said. 'For a film about Gypsies running around boxing and singing?'

'I swear to God,' Ruth said. 'I find it hard to believe myself but seemingly my husband is a great artist, and *Stateless Happiness* is a work of art.'

'Stateless happiness?'

'It's the name of his film. Everybody loves it.'

'And do you love it?'

Ruth grinned. 'Well, let me put it like this. I think it's a fine film and I love the fact that it has earned us enough to buy a house. What more can I say?'

Nothing. The look on her face and the aura of contentment she exuded said it all.


September that year started with a bang. Or, to be more accurate, a phone call from Tim Gladstone at three a.m. on 1 September. I answered the phone, desperately trying to stanch the flow of neurotic fears that accompany midnight telephone calls. Who was dead, dying, injured, kidnapped?

'Hello?' I managed to say.

'Ellen?'

'Yes?'

'Tim Gladstone here. Sorry to disturb you. I hope you weren't asleep?'

'It's OK, Tim. Is everything all right?'

'Oh dear – I see that it's 3.14 a.m. – I'm sorry, Ellen. You must have been asleep. How thoughtless of me, I didn't even look at my watch. Lost track of time—'

'Tim? Is everything all right? Is India OK?'

'Oh yes, India's fine. Thanks for asking. I'd say she might be asleep now because I went for coffee after I left her. Well, when I say coffee, I mean that horrible stuff you get from those big machines – vile. And expensive considering it's dishwater.'

'Tim,' my anxiety was about to blow its top. I swallowed hard. 'Tim, why did you call, if you don't mind me asking?'

'I didn't say? Oh, I'm sorry. I meant—'

'Tim?'

'India's had the baby.'

'Oh my God! When? How? Is she OK? What is it? Is everything all right?'

Tim's soft laugh filled the earpiece of the telephone. 'Tonight – about an hour ago. We have a beautiful daughter, Alyssa, and she is just fine. They're both just fine – no, they're better than fine – they're wonderful. Both of my girls.'

'Oh, Tim.' My eyes filled with tears and I couldn't speak for a moment.

'Well, sorry to disturb you, Ellen. I had no idea of the time.'

'I'm delighted you called. Give my love to India. Tell her I'll be in to see her and the lovely Alyssa tomorrow.'

'Will do. Goodnight.'

'Goodnight, Tim . . . oh and Tim?'

'Yes?'

'Congratulations, yourself – Daddy.'

Tim laughed and hung up. I slid back into my warm bed beside Andrew.

'Who was that?' he mumbled sleepily.

'Tim. India had a baby girl – Alyssa.'

'That's great news – everything OK?'

'Fine. Everything is just fine.'

I snuggled closer to Andrew's sleepy back and wound my arm around his waist.

'We must get one of those ourselves sometime,' Andrew said.

'A baby?'

'Uh-uh,' he said, his voice slipping back into sleep. 'What do you think?'

I burrowed my face into his back and he fell asleep. As I drifted towards unconsciousness, I thought about babies and friends and love and happiness, and I wasn't sure what to make of any of it.

I went to visit India and her beautiful new daughter first thing next morning. I didn't stay long as I had a busy day lined up, and anyway, ecstatic as India was, she was also exhausted. I was just sitting into my car in the hospital car park when my mobile rang. Foolishly I answered without looking at the screen.

'You were supposed to call to confirm the time.' My mother's voice sang into my ear.

'I forgot,' I said. The time? What time? The time of what? 'India had her baby and I sort of forgot everything else.'

'India had her baby? That's wonderful. What did she have?'

'A baby girl.'

'Oh, Ellen, isn't that lovely? They must be delighted.'

'Thrilled.'

'You'll be next. I met Ruth in town last Thursday. Isn't baby Paddy adorable?'

'Adorable.'

'Your day will come,' my mother said, getting all super-sensitive on me.

'I know,' I said, wanting to move the conversation along and away from topics I was trying to avoid thinking about, not to mention talking about.

'Alison just rang.'

'Great,' I said. 'That's great.'

I dearly love my sister, Alison, but she's so perfect, she always makes me feel inadequate. She and I are so different, it's a real stretch to believe we're related at all, let alone sisters. I'm five foot ten, dark-haired and more than a little on the lanky side. Alison is petite, blonde and pretty like an American cheer-leader.

I'm a happy-enough estate agent, while Alison is an upwardly mobile teacher tipped for the principal's post. I have dithered and fumbled and generally mismanaged my relationships since the onset of puberty. Alison, on the other hand, had a succession of suitable boyfriends, culminating in her eventual marriage to Dermot – a nice if boring rugby-playing doctor from somewhere in Co. Wicklow. There is the fact all right, that she did give birth to my favourite person – my two-year-old nephew, Kieran. It suited me that Alison lived in Dublin as it spared me being continuously reminded of my shortcomings. The only downside was that I hardly ever got to see Kieran.

'Look, Ma, I'd better go. I'm in traffic and not supposed to be talking on this thing. See you later.'

'OK, love. I just wanted to check that six tomorrow week was still all right?'

'Oh sure,' I said, having no memory of making any arrangement with my mother.

'That's great,' she said. 'I'm just doing a lamb roast – I know how much Andrew likes that. Don't tell him, though. It'll be a nice surprise when he sees what we're having for dinner.'

'Oh, I won't tell,' I said, grinning. 'Andrew loves surprises. Got to go. Talk to you later.'

I started my car and drove out of the hospital car park so that I could convert into truth the lies I'd just flogged my mother. Poor Andrew, I thought as I pulled out in front of a silver Mercedes and flashed my most seductive smile at the portly male driver. I'd have to break it to Andrew gently that we were having dinner at my parents'. It didn't matter much anyway. We could always get a Chinese on the way home as we usually did after being subjected to one of my mother's inedible concoctions.

I checked my list of appointments which was propped behind the gear stick, and saw that I had a day of viewings all in the same part of town – Hollyfields. Hollyfields was a medium-sized, reasonably settled estate of houses that had been built by the local authority in the late 1950s. Nowadays,

Hollyfields was quite des res, as we say. An un-crowded estate with large, green areas and plenty of trees, it was also within walking distance of town. For the average young couple desperately trying to cobble together enough money to buy a house, it was affordable. Not to mention the fact that the houses were comfortable and spacious when compared to the new houses on offer in the same price range.

There was a spate of selling up in Hollyfields just then. I figured it was the age of the estate. Most of the original residents had died or were elderly and had moved into nursing homes or gone to live with their children. And the word on the street (or at least the word in auctioneering circles) was that the huge green area behind Hollyfields – where traditionally the kids from the estate had played – was zoned for development as a hotel and leisure centre.

There wasn't as much as a sod turned in the devel-opment yet, and I didn't see how it was ever going to happen. The green area itself was enormous and fell very prettily down towards the river. But unless you wanted to reach it by boat, there was no real access to the site. Notwithstanding the rumours, I didn't anticipate having any trouble shifting a couple of houses in the area.

The first house I was to show was number 14 – *Sacre Coeur*. As I pulled up outside it, I saw the burned-out remains of a beautiful period house. I knew this was Acorn House, a Georgian mansion that had been uninhabited since the late 1960s. I'd read about the fire in the paper a couple of months before and, if I remembered correctly, there was a suggestion of arson.

I got out of the car and made my way to the front door of *Sacre Coeur*. When I pressed the doorbell, it played the opening bars of 'Greensleeves'. A stocky woman in her sixties opened the door so quickly when I rang the bell that I suspected she must have been waiting in the hallway.

'Yes?'

'Mrs Hegarty? Hello, I'm Ellen Grace from Gladstone and Richards—'

'About time,' the woman of the house said, buttoning a moss-green Aran cardigan. 'I'm going down to Sheila Fahy's while you people are traipsing around my house.'

'Great,' I said, as she pushed past me in the doorway. 'Mind if I wait inside?'

But Mrs Hegarty had already gone out through the newly painted but creaky garden gate. I walked into the house and closed the front door behind me. Somehow, even though I had worked as an estate agent for going on seven years now, I still managed to feel like a burglar whenever I was in somebody's house alone. I walked tentatively around to familiarise myself with the place before the clients arrived.

Three small bedrooms, a bathroom, kitchen and sitting room. All immaculately clean and well cared for. After my tour, I went into the small sitting room to wait for my clients. The room was papered in one of those textured wallpapers, and painted a cool shade of mint green. There was a tall, mahogany sideboard covered in ornaments, and an over-stuffed pink velour suite with heavy, roped-back curtains to match. At least there was no corpse on the sofa. Not like two years earlier when Andrew and I had found an old man shot through the head in the front room of a house we were showing. That wasn't something I'd forget in a hurry.

Apart altogether from corpses, there was something about being in a stranger's house. It made me feel as if the householders were, somehow, vulnerable and exposed, allowing people to view their home in a judgemental way. Still, it was my job and, for all my weird musings, it was a job that I loved.

I paused in front of a group of family photographs clustered together, proudly, in ornate frames, all along one wall. Two smiling, gap-toothed First Communion girls and four serious-looking boys brandishing their First Communion prayer books like shields. A whole row of wedding pictures. Two graduation pictures. Six or seven fat, blond babies and an old, hand-coloured wedding photograph of a woman I took to be Mrs Hegarty herself on her 'big' day. I thought I remembered someone telling me that the woman of the house was a widow, so that meant that the skinny young man in the pinstripe suit was already dead. They looked so happy, laughing together, arms entwined on their wedding day, I wondered if it had stayed like that and if she missed him now. Mind you, she was a formidable woman, so he might be enjoying the rest as he waited for her to catch up with him.

I studied the sepia face of the bride in the photograph, and wondered why it was that I didn't seem to have the same warm feelings about getting married that everybody else had. The whole reason Andrew and I had broken up in the first place, three years previously, was that I'd bolted when he'd proposed. Then he'd asked me again, in May, when we were in Spain at Ruth's wedding, and I'd managed to avoid giving him a straight answer.

I wanted to say, 'yes', and be delighted at the prospect of marriage. But something seemed to prevent me from taking that step. It wasn't that I didn't love him – even the first time he'd asked me, I'd known that I adored Andrew Kenny. It was something else and I couldn't put a finger on it. I'd just have to pull myself together though, or I'd end up a bitter, lonely old lady on Sally Jessy Raphaël's show, bemoaning her life as a commitment-phobe.

The doorbell rang.

'Mr and Mrs Dawson?' I said as I opened the door.

Two teenagers stood in front of me on the doorstep. The boy was tall – about six two. His right eyebrow was pierced, and his shortish blond hair was gelled to stiff obedience. He was smoking a cigarette which he extinguished as soon as he saw me, grinding the butt with a pristine white trainer.

The girl was fresh-faced and pregnant. Her long, blonde hair was scraped back off her face and tied up ien a high, bouncy ponytail. She didn't look a lot older than the little girls in the Communion photographs in Mrs Hegarty's sitting room but she must have been a little older to be pregnant, I supposed. She was almost wearing a short white T-shirt and low-rise combats that separated to show the smooth skin of her swelling belly.

'Sorry,' I said, thinking that these must be Mrs Hegarty's grandchildren. 'Mrs Hegarty has just popped down the road for a few minutes.'

'Roxy Dawson,' the girl said, stepping forward on her platform sandals to shake hands with me. I shook her hand and stepped back into the house. The teenage couple followed me.

'Can we have a look, so?' the boy said, more to his companion than me.

'Sure,' I said. 'How about we start at the kitchen, Mr Dawson?'

'Pa,' he said.

'Pa?'

'My name. Pa O'Brien, but don't call me Mr O'Brien – nobody has called me Mr O'Brien since they were telling me I was expelled from school.'

'Oh, right, great . . . Pa . . . I'm Ellen Grace. Sorry about that. I forgot to introduce myself.'

'No worries,' Pa said, pumping my hand. 'Listen, do you mind if I skip the house and have a look out the back?'

I shrugged and gestured towards the back of the house. 'No problem at all, Mr . . . Pa. Go right on through. I think the back door is open.'

Pa nodded his thanks and disappeared into the kitchen. I turned to look at Roxy, who was waiting patiently at the foot of the stairs.

'So?' I said. 'Would you like to have a look around?'

Roxy smiled and nodded, and I gave her a quick tour of the downstairs. Then we started up the stairs. As I followed her, I watched her ponytail bob with each step and tried to guess her age. We walked in a companionable silence through Mrs Hegarty's three bedrooms and bathroom. Roxy opened the built-in wardrobes and assessed their storage potential knowledgably, like a woman twice her age with a houseful of kids. When we'd finished our tour, Roxy and I stood on the landing.

'It's very well cared for, isn't it?' I said.

Roxy nodded and folded a stick of chewing gum into her mouth. 'It's nice. Very clean and bright.'

'Yes, and I'd say your husband will like the back garden. These houses have huge back gardens – seventy feet long or more.'

Roxy vigorously chewed her new gum. 'Pa isn't my husband – he's my boyfriend – the baby's father.'

'Oh, right, sorry,' I said.

'No problem.'

'OK, then. Will we go back downstairs and have a look around?' I said.

Roxy nodded and smiled, and though she may have looked like a child, I certainly felt as unsure as one. I started down the stairs, pointing out the high ceiling and original hall tiles and abundance of light. Pa appeared at the bottom of the stairs at the same time as us.

'Great garden, Rox. You'd want to see it, man. It's like a field. Angel and Buffy'll love it.'

Roxy looked at me and smiled. 'His dogs.'

I nodded.

'And there'll be more than enough room to fence off part of the garden for Angel and Buffy and still have plenty of room for Shakira and Shania,' Pa continued

'Great,' Roxy said, 'let's have a look.'

'You certainly keep a lot of dogs,' I said, following them into the garden and glad to be ahead of the game for once. 'Do you breed them?'

Roxy shook her head and smiled a patient smile. 'Shakira and Shania are my other kids. Shakira's five and Shania's almost three.'

'You have two children and you're . . . you're—' I blurted out before I could stop myself.

Pa laughed. 'She's an awful slapper, that one.'

'That's not what I meant,' I said, my face beginning to burn with embarrassment. 'I mean, you're just so . . . young-looking to have three children.'

'Thanks,' Roxy said, rubbing her belly, and looking at me with eyes that were far older than the rest of her face. 'I'll take that as a compliment.'

'I meant it as one,' I said, recovering my composure a little.

'We're very interested in the house. Aren't we, Pa?' Roxy said.

Pa nodded. 'Definitely. You have to see the garden, Rox. It's massive and there's loads of room at the side of the house – we can build an extension for when the girls and himself get older.'

I said nothing, I had no intention of putting my foot in it again.

'It's a boy,' Roxy said, looking at me as if she could read my confusion. 'They told me last week out in the Maternity when I had my scan.'

'That's great,' I said. 'Do you have a name for him?'

'Well,' Roxy drawled, 'I was thinking of Enrique. What do you think?'

'Very nice,' I said. 'Unusual. God, is that the time? I'm afraid I have another appointment in a few minutes, so—'

'There's just one thing I want to ask,' Roxy said.

'Yes?'

'The burned-out house?'

'Yeah,' Pa said. 'See the state of that place. What's that about?'

'It was burned down a couple of months ago, I think,' I said.

'On purpose?' Roxy asked.

I nodded. 'Looks that way, though they didn't arrest anyone for it. Whoever owns it will probably have to demolish it. I'll check it out for you.'

'It's just that it looks a bit raw and I'd be afraid one of the girls might go in and it'd collapse on top of her or something,' said Roxy.

'I can find out for you,' I said. 'They must be doing something with it. I think they might be trying to develop the area at the back.'

'And what are they going to build there?' Pa asked. 'More houses?'

I shook my head. 'I don't know for sure but I think I read that they were talking about putting a hotel and leisure centre there – would you mind that?'

'No way,' Pa said. 'Will there be a pool an' all in it?'

'Probably,' I said.

'Deadly.'

I looked at Roxy. 'I'll have to wait and see exactly what they're planning,' she said.

I smiled at her. 'I'll find out about it as soon as I can and let you know. Is that OK?'

'Grand,' Roxy said, looking at her watch. 'I need to get going. I have to pick up the kids. You have our number and we have your number, and your name is Ellen, isn't it?'

I nodded. 'Ellen Grace. Just ask for me if you want anything.'

'Right, so,' Roxy said holding out her hand towards me. We shook hands and I felt a sudden rush of liking for this child-woman who was running her life so capably.

As I drove through Hollyfields to my next appointment, I thought about Roxy Dawson and Mrs Hegarty and India and Ruth and everybody else who seemed to be making a much better fist of life than I was.

# 4

My mother deposited the white platter bearing the steaming lamb roast in the centre of the table.

'Da-da!' she sang, triumphantly.

I looked at my brother, Will. He and his girlfriend were sitting directly across from me at the table. The girlfriend – Shannon– was a tiny fine-boned individual who looked even smaller sitting next to my lanky brother. It was obviously a very serious relationship if he was subjecting her to the rigours of our mother's cooking.

Shannon had a dainty, heart-shaped face, blanched completely white by some Goth-type foundation. Her lips were painted plum, her hair was bobbed and dyed coal black and her big, green eyes were ringed with heavy, black eyeliner and festooned with thick mascara. She was a very serious-looking girl who was studying philosophy at the same college that Will attended. But serious as she was, she was obviously very taken with my brother. Her face lit up every time they made eye contact, and a beautiful smile transformed her. I poked Andrew in the ribs on one such occasion to show him the 'aw' factor, but he was talking with my father about cars and just held my hand and ignored the silent communication.

Will was leaning back in his chair, his long, skinny arms folded across his *Pulp Fiction* T-shirt, chatting under his breath to Shannon. There was something different about Will. I studied him closely, trying to figure out what could have changed. OK, he'd added a few more bars and rings to the assortment of metal that pierced his face and ears. And he had a good smattering of stubble across his chin and neck – obviously the beard was shaping up – but somehow it didn't seem to be that. Then I realised.

'You're letting the hair grow,' I said.

Will ran a hand across his sueded head. 'You get tired of having to shave it all the time. Such a drag. I'm thinking of letting it grow long, altogether. Less work, what do you think?'

'Love and honour of God!' our mother exclaimed. 'What next? Eat your dinner, William. It might give you some sense.'

I grinned at Will and he crossed his eyes and smiled at me. My mother handed my father the carving knife and motioned for him to do the honours. Dad let out a tiny sigh and stood up, eyeing the roast lamb as if it was an opponent to be defeated. That would be a pretty accurate description of one of my mother's dishes. There wasn't a doubt in my mind that that roast was going to be as tough as old boots. My father hacked valiantly as my mother took her place beside him at the table.

'Pass me your plates,' my mother said.

We did as we were bidden.

'So, Andrew, how's work these days?' my mother asked, passing him a plate of leather strips.

Andrew smiled his thanks. 'Great, Phyllis. Busy at the moment. Aren't we, Ellen?'

I nodded as I took the plate of rubber lamb my mother handed to me. I piled the rest of the plate with lumpy potatoes and half-cooked carrots – at least I had a fighting chance of eating some of that. I smiled at Shannon who was eating her way serenely through a plate of vegetables. Apparently she was a vegetarian. I thought I might chat with Will later about the rest of us telling our mother we'd become vegetarians so that at least we might be spared the meat she cooked.

'How's college, Will?' I asked my brother who was employing the same trick as me with the vegetables. We were old hands at surviving our mother's dinners.

'Great,' he said. 'Is that the phone I hear?'

I shook my head. Running out to answer the phone mid-meal was one of the tactics in our repertoire of dinner-avoidance. 'No, Will,' I said, smiling a mean smile. 'You must be hearing things. Eat up now quickly before your food goes cold.'

Will made a face at me and spooned some lumpy mash into his mouth.

'How's the band, Will?' Andrew asked, smothering his lamb with mint sauce to kill the taste. I grinned at him.

'Terrific,' Will said, his face lighting up, in spite of the food. 'We're going to enter the Battle of the Bands, this year.'

My mother tutted and we all looked at her. I

noticed that my father had managed to avoid giving himself any meat and was hurriedly doing the 'piling the plate with vegetables' thing.

'You'd think, William, that you'd take your studies seriously, now that you're in college,' she said.

'Ah, Ma,' my brother said. 'I can't take them much more seriously than I do – I keep telling you that.'

'Those bands are no good,' my mother said, cutting her lamb as if it was a real piece of edible meat. We all watched her, fascinated, as she chewed and never seemed to notice that there was anything wrong. I glanced at Andrew who was valiantly chewing and studiously avoiding all eye contact with me.

'What exactly is your objection to Will's band?' I asked.

'Well, for one thing, didn't it get him kidnapped last year?'

'That was nothing to do with the band,' Will spluttered.

My mother pulled herself into a huff. 'Well, as far as I remember, you were kidnapped when you were coming out from one of those gigs you're so mad about.'

Will snorted with exasperation.

'Ah, now, Phyllis, you're getting mixed up,' my father said, crossing his knife and fork on his plate as if he'd eaten his fill. I knew that trick as well.

'Was William at a so-called gig on the night he was kidnapped?' my mother asked imperiously.

My father nodded. 'Yes, but it was Ellen they were after. Don't you remember? It wasn't really anything to do with Will at all. It was kind of an accident. Wasn't it, Ellen?'

I swallowed a lump of half-chewed meat and it felt as if it was spraining my oesophagus on its way to my stomach. Still, I didn't care. It was gone off my plate so I was making progress.

'Kind of,' I said. It had been to do with the guys who were after Tony Jordan. They'd thought I was involved with him and had wanted to kidnap me but Will had tried to stop them and they'd taken him instead.

'Love and honour of God!' my mother said, blessing herself. 'Exactly how that makes it all better is beyond me.'

'It doesn't make it better,' I said. 'But it means it hadn't anything to do with Will's band – that's all we're saying. Isn't that right, Will?'

We all looked at my brother who was mouthing something like *I'll tell you later* to Shannon.

'Sure,' he said.

My mother laid her cutlery along the side of her empty plate. 'All I know is that if you were at home, studying, William, none of that could have happened, could it? Now. Who's for dessert? I made a beautiful dessert. Ann Morrison told me about it when I met her in the hairdresser's on Tuesday. It's a Moroccan dish, actually.'

'Moroccan? That sounds lovely,' Andrew said. Liar, I thought.

My mother smiled and nodded. 'She had it at her sister's fiftieth and described it to me, and I made it especially for tonight as you were all coming round. So, hurry up now and finish up your dinners and I'll dish out the dessert.'

My mother stood up and walked to the draining board where she began to scoop some unidentifiable gloop into glass bowls. We watched her with morbid fascination.

'Maybe she used loads of sherry or brandy or something,' Will whispered.

'Hopefully,' I said.

'Moroccan?' Andrew said. 'Muslim. No alcohol.'

'Shit!' my father said and we all turned to look at him. He shrugged and looked around him as if someone else had said it.

'Ah, well,' I said. 'We've probably eaten worse.'

'Kidnapped?' Shannon asked, so we all turned to look at her. She blushed through her inch-thick white make-up.

'Sorry,' she said. 'It's just so . . . odd and I just . . . wondered—'

'Later,' Will said, leaning over to kiss her papery white cheek.

'Now!' my mother announced triumphantly as she placed a tray on the table and began to hand glass dessert bowls to everyone. A gelatinous brown substance shivered from side to side in my bowl as I took a deep breath and grabbed my dessert spoon.

'I'm thrilled really with how it's turned out,' my mother was saying as she sat down and tucked into her dessert. The rest of us were still working up the courage. 'Mmm. That really is a most unusual taste, isn't it? Come on, everybody. Get started. What do you think, Shannon? Do you like it?'

Shannon's green eyes opened so wide they took up half her face. 'Oh, yes, lovely, Mrs Grace. Very unusual.'

'I'm glad you like it. Turmeric. You'd never think of it for a dessert but I think it gives it that extra something. Don't you, Ellen?'

'Definitely,' I said. 'It gives it something extra that most desserts don't have all right.'

Will grinned and swallowed. 'You said it. Listen up, everyone, I have an announcement to make.'

We all looked at him, glad of an excuse to stop eating for a few seconds. Will looked at Shannon and she smiled at him.

'Shannon and I are engaged,' he blurted out, looking directly at me.

'What?' I said.

'Shannon and I are engaged,' he repeated, still directing his comments at me.

'To be married?' I asked, struggling with the meaning of the words that were coming from my brother's mouth.

Will nodded and put his arm around Shannon's tiny shoulders. She smiled at me. I wished they'd all stop looking at me.

'Love and honour of God!' my mother said from the other end of the table. That worked. Everybody looked at her instead of me. She pushed her chair out from the table and slowly stood up. We all continued to watch her as she picked up her half-full bowl of dessert and emptied the remains into the pedal bin. Will looked at me quizzically. I shook my head. How the hell was I supposed to know what it meant? Did he really think I was going to be able to second guess our volatile mother when she'd just been told that her nineteen-year-old son was engaged to be married? She walked to the sink and began to wash her bowl meticulously.

'You're not . . . it's not . . . you know,' my father said.

We all looked at him then. He fumbled in his pocket and took out a packet of cigarettes and lit one.

'It's just, you know, I was wondering, Will. I know these things happen and the two of you are young and—'

Will and Shannon were staring uncomprehendingly at my father.

'Pregnant,' I said. 'Dad is asking if Shannon is pregnant, Will. Sorry, Shannon – if you're pregnant.'

'No way,' Will spluttered, as if the very thought that he'd contemplate having sex was too shocking for him to bear. I looked at him and raised my eyebrow so high I'd have given Elvis a run for his money. Will shrugged sheepishly and looked down at his dessert.

'I'm not pregnant,' my brother's fiancée began, 'but Will and I love each other and we don't intend to get married for a while – until we finish college and stuff – but we decided to get engaged as a way of showing the world how we feel about each other. It's just like, you know, engagement is like a public statement, isn't it?'

She looked at Will and he nodded so hard I thought his peach-fuzz head was going to fall off.

'That's all,' Shannon continued. 'We want everybody to know how we feel about each other, like, you know—'

By the time Shannon had finished her speechifying, my mother was standing at the end of the table, drying her hands on a tea towel that advertised Killarney beer.

'You're too young to get married,' she said.

'We know,' Shannon agreed.

'But not too young to be in love so we're not too young to get engaged,' Will said. 'And we *are* engaged. Show them your ring, Shannon.'

Shannon held her dainty left hand up to the family to display a delicate gold Claddagh ring.

'It's lovely,' I said.

'See the way the heart is turned?' Will said. 'That means the wearer's heart is taken. See – mine's the same.'

Will held up his long-fingered left hand and, sure enough, there on his ring finger was a matching Claddagh ring.

'And you're not planning on getting married for a long time, is that it?' my father asked.

'That's it, Dad,' Will said.

'Sure, what harm so?' our father said. 'What harm, Phyllis?'

My mother nodded but didn't speak.

'You can be bridesmaid, Ell,' Will said.

'What about Alison?' I asked.

'I'll ask Alison as well – both of you can be brides-maids. Shannon is an only child.'

'Thanks,' I said.

'Congratulations,' Andrew said, standing up and leaning across the table to shake hands with the happy couple.

'Thanks, Andrew, thanks.' Will pumped Andrew's hand enthusiastically. 'I really appreciate it, man.'

'The best of luck to both of you,' Andrew continued. 'And may you be very happy together. Sure, you'll have plenty of time to save for a new hat, Phyllis, before these two get married, won't you?'

Andrew looked at my mother and smiled warmly.

'I suppose,' she said, trying to return his smile.

'The outfit you wear to our wedding will have gone well out of fashion by the time Will and Shannon tie the knot,' he said, pausing briefly to pat me on the shoulder. This time my mother smiled broadly and nodded as if she understood what Andrew was saying.

'Tea? Coffee?' she asked.

'Great.' 'Lovely.' 'Thanks.' We chorused, delighted that Mam seemed back to her food-and-beverage-supplying self. That was a good sign.

Andrew sat back down beside me and I kissed him.

'Well done,' I whispered.

He smiled and I thought how much I loved him and decided to run out and buy a stack of bridal magazines to plan my wedding to this marvellous man.

# 5

The following Friday morning, as I got ready for work, the telephone rang. It was Ruth.

'Morning, Ellen. Lovely, sunny autumn morning, don't you think? The sky is blue. The leaves are beginning to turn beautiful shades of brown and gold and red—'

'Stop it! It's 7.30, for God's sake – too early for me to like any kind of a day. Is everything all right?'

'Fine. Fine. Just calling to chat.'

'At this hour?'

'Thought I'd catch you before you had to leave to conquer the Everest of the property market.'

'It's the crack of dawn.'

'No, Ellen. It isn't the crack of dawn – I saw the crack of dawn and it was hours ago.'

'Paddy.'

'Yes, indeed. My lovely son decided he'd had enough sleep at about 5.30 – goo-ing and gaa-ing and feeding like it was going out of fashion until I finally relented and got up.'

'Why didn't you make Emerson get up?'

'He's in Cork on a job all this week.'

'Poor Ruthie. So you're all alone in the wilds of County Clare.'

'Well, not alone. I have Paddy and the two dogs to keep me company, but none of them are exactly great conversationalists.'

'Do you want me to call out this evening after work? I think I'm finished at four today. Hang on a minute. Here's Andrew. I just need to check that there isn't something urgent we have to do tonight.'

I patted Andrew's shapely rump as he walked by. 'Where are you off to so early?'

He smiled at me as he picked up his briefcase. 'I've a meeting with Lee Properties at nine and I have to swing by the office first.'

'Will Davina Blake be there?' I asked, scowling.

Andrew grabbed me around the waist and kissed me long and hard. 'Where?'

'At the meeting, Andrew. Where do you think? That ex-girlfriend of yours still works for Lee Properties, doesn't she?'

Andrew laughed and kissed me again.

'She was never really my girlfriend,' he said, as he nuzzled my neck.

'Could have fooled me,' I said.

'And if she were at that meeting, what difference would it make? I wouldn't even notice.'

'Well, unless you were struck blind, I think you'd have to notice – the woman is a goddess.'

'Who? Who?' Ruth's voice was calling from the ignored telephone receiver in my hand.

'Davina Blake,' I said into the mouthpiece. 'Stop eavesdropping on my conversations.'

'Then stop snogging while I'm still on the phone,' Ruth shouted. 'Get a room.'

'We have loads of rooms, O jealous one. Do we have to go anywhere tonight, Andrew?'

He shook his head, which dislodged his neatly combed shower-damp hair. I ran a hand across it and rearranged it.

'I'm going to go out to see Ruth after work, so.'

Andrew nodded and smiled. I made kissing noises at him. 'See you later.'

He kissed me as he walked past. 'Looking forward to it.'

'OK, Ruth,' I said, returning to the telephone as Andrew's broad, navy-suited body disappeared from our kitchen. 'I'll come out to you straight after work. I'll be there before five. How about that?'

My cat, Joey, strolled past, and I leaned down to rub his stripy back. Joey looked at me and then walked on over to his dish of food.

'Oh, Ellen, that would be brilliant – can't you come to dinner while you're at it?'

'Why, Ruth – did you learn to cook?'

'Well, no, but I thought I should ask – I'd love to see you, and there's some stuff I want to talk to you about. Nothing bad, now, before you jump to conclusions. Just some things I want to run by you.'

'Tell me now! Tell me now! Tell me now!'

'No. You'll just have to learn to wait – deferred gratification as they call it in the parenting books.'

'You're not going to tell me about parenting stuff, are you, Ruth? I mean, I love Paddy, but the theory is a bit boring for someone without kids.'

'So, go and get some kids! And no – it's not that anyway. I'll tell you tonight. The only problem about the parenting stuff is that I need to warn you – I gave India some of my books.'

'You did not!'

'Sorry – she would have bought them anyway. What could I do when she asked? Refuse?'

'I don't know, Ruth. You could have told her the were useless or dangerous or something. India loves theories – we'll never hear the end of the parenting theories.'

'She can talk to Emerson. All those Burkes are the same – he loves that kind of thing.'

'And we'll ignore them while they talk about babies? Sounds like a plan, Ruthie. Anyway, I'd better go and get ready for work. See you this evening, and please don't cook, I beg you. I'll pick up some ready-made dinners on the way so we'll just have to pop them in the oven or the microwave. You do have a microwave?'

'This is me we're talking about – of course, I have a microwave. Otherwise we'd be dead of starvation.'

'Great stuff. Do you want anything else?'

'No, thanks. See you later, Ellen.'

'Bye, Ruth.'

I hung up and went to the kitchen window to see what the weather was like. It was a hell of a lot duller in Limerick than the magnificent day Ruth had described four miles away in Cratloe. In fact, it looked as if it was about to bucket rain. I tried to decide what I'd wear as I made my usual breakfast of cocoa and toast. I had a lovely new cream angora sweater that I'd bought the week before, and I was just looking for an excuse to wear it. The weather had been a bit warm up to this but I was sure there was a cold snap on the way – so, what the hell!

By 8.40, I was dressed in my new cream sweater and a short, rust faux suede skirt. Very autumnal, I thought, especially as I was also wearing a pair of low-heeled, pointy-toed, rust suede shoes that I adored and which also happened to perfectly match my skirt. I was pretty impressed with myself and sure that any clients I had would be equally knocked out by my fashion sense.

I crawled through the morning traffic with the window of my pink Hyundai open to counteract the effect of the angora sweater. A statuesque African woman in a bright yellow dress took my attention. She was standing at a bus stop holding a beautiful baby in her arms. Watching them together as the mother snuggled her baby close made me realise – yet again – that everybody seemed to have a child except me. Even Andrew had one. My feelings about children were a bit confused. I'd thought I was pregnant the previous year and that had truly been one of the scarier moments of my life. In fact, it had probably been *the* scariest time in my life, especially as I hadn't had even the semblance of a father for the imagined sprog.

I shuddered even remembering. I'd never forget it – it was more terrifying than being chased by the hooded drug-dealing thugs who had kidnapped my brother, shot an old man and wanted to kill Tony Jordan, and, possibly, me. Yes, it was definitely way more frightening than any of that.

I don't like to think too much about things – a fact that is probably obvious from the mess I tend to make of my life. So, once I'd found out I wasn't pregnant, I had tried to put the whole thing out of my head. But as far as I was willing to reflect, I was beginning to think that old Mother Nature was turning up the heat under my broodiness.

There was a part of me that found something very appealing about the notion of having a version of Kieran in my life. I sometimes watched Andrew with Katie when she was over in our house, and even I could see that there was something special about their relationship. Katie loved her dad – that was obvious. But when I looked at Andrew's face while he was with his daughter, I couldn't help thinking that love was an understatement for what he felt for that short, chubby, dark-haired little girl. Not a good idea, Mother Nature, I thought, as I swerved to avoid a tall African man on a bicycle, especially as I was so ambiguous about marriage and commitment to begin with. It was too much work trying to figure it all out, so I decided I wouldn't bother.

Molly was typing diligently as I pushed open the double glass and oak doors of Gladstone and Richards Auctioneers, Estate Agents and Valuers.

'Morning, Molly. Have you got my list of appointments for today?'

Without missing a beat in her typing, Molly pointed a long, blueberry-coloured talon at a typed list on the reception desk.

'Mine?' I asked.

She nodded, still looking only at the computer screen as her almost black nails flew across the keyboard with supernatural speed.

'Thanks,' I said, waving as I made my way across the open-plan office to my desk. I was impressed that Molly – though ignoring me – was at least not downright insulting to me. When I thought about it, I realised that Molly was almost civil to me these days. She didn't really like me much – nothing personal, she just didn't really approve of people who weren't rich or powerful. And I wasn't either of those.

Well, that wasn't strictly true. Molly O'Sullivan liked men even if they weren't rich and powerful. For heaven's sake, Molly even liked Ryan, the gangly, pimply faced, back-stabbing junior in our office. I myself hated Ryan Ferry with a hatred that was of operatic proportions. I had good reason not to like him as he'd tried to steal a sale from me the previous year, but Molly loved him because – well, she just couldn't help herself where there was testosterone involved.

I made myself a mug of coffee in the tiny hallway that passes for a staff kitchen at Gladstone and Richards, and then plonked myself in front of my desk. The offices occupied the whole bottom floor of two three-storey Georgian buildings. As soon as you walked up the front steps and in through the doors, you were greeted by a curved beech-wood desk, decorated by the lynchpin of the organisation – our receptionist and secretary, Molly.

Then there was a huge, bright, open-plan office, separated from the general public by a six-foot-high wall of glass blocks. Ryan, Andrea and I each had a desk in this area. Tim and Andrew had their own offices which were situated at the front of the building looking out onto the street. The management very kindly supplied employee parking in a car park that was accessed through a laneway that ran along beside our end of terrace building. The only downside was that there was no back entrance to our premises, which meant that Molly could track all our comings and goings. I switched on my computer, picked up my e-mails and sipped my first cup of office coffee of the day. It tasted like sand and water but it relaxed me in an odd way – there was something sort of comforting in its familiar, horrible taste.

I glanced at my list as the e-mails downloaded, and saw that my first appointment was at eleven o'clock. I was scheduled to show Roxy Dawson Mrs Hegarty's house in Hollyfields again – which reminded me that I'd better see if I could rustle up any information regarding the burned-out shell of Acorn House. I sipped my coffee and tried to think who I could call. I could try the Planning Office but they might want me to go through' 'channels' and I didn't have time. So, who? If only I had some hot-shot journalist friend who knew everything. Or, indeed, a solicitor friend who worked a lot in property and basically knew everything there was to be known in this town. I picked up the phone and, checking that the new number I had was correct, punched in the digits.

'India?' I said as soon as she picked up.

'Ellen? How are you?'

'Great, just great. More to the point – how's the new Mammy?'

'I'm fine – we're fine, but having a baby is a lot more work than I'd ever imagined, Ellen.'

'I'll bet, sure she's only a week old, isn't she?'

'Eleven days.'

'All right – eleven days. Anyway, she's probably a bit of a tearaway already, like her mother.'

'I used to listen to women going on and on about babies and how hard it was to get everything done, and I always thought it was just a question of organisation.'

'And it isn't?'

'Not really. Alyssa is great but she seems to have a mind of her own as far as eating and sleeping are concerned. Everyone – my mother, Ruth, everyone – says that's normal. And it might be normal, Ellen, but I don't know what I'm going to do. It takes me half the day to get the two of us dressed. I don't see how I'm ever going to be able to go back to work or do any normal things ever again.'

'Get Tim to help.'

'Tim does help – he's really, really great – but he's not much better than me. The two of us are like people trying to thread a needle while wearing a pair of gloves.'

I couldn't but laugh at the picture that conjured up.

'It's not funny, Ellen.'

'I know, I know, but it'll improve. I'm sure it will. If there's anybody who can lick this mothering job, it's you, Ind.'

'Do you think?'

'I think. Now can I ask you a professional question?'

'Please do, though I think the hormones may be affecting my mental capacity.'

'In which case, you'll still be cleverer than most people.'

'Thanks, Ellen. You really are a pal.'

'I speak the truth. Now, listen here to me, girl. Do you remember Acorn House?'

'The one that went on fire?'

'That's it.'

'So?' India said.

'So who has responsibility for it?'

'Well, it belongs to a development company – I can't think of their name. Do you remember the big dinner we all went to last year?'

'Where you met Tim?'

'Exactly. And you were with Tony Jordan and Ruth was with Wolfie.'

'Imagine that's only a year ago.'

'Imagine. Feehily and Sloane were there because we were doing the legal work for the company,' Feehily and Sloane was the company India worked for.

'So what was the name of the development company?'

India sighed. 'I just can't remember.'

'I need to know what's happening with Acorn House, Ind. We're selling a house near it and the people have small children and are worried about living beside a derelict house.'

'I'll make a few phone calls, if you like. There's probably a demolition order on it if it's a health-and-safety hazard, but I'll find out for sure.'

'You're an angel, India Burke.'

'It'll give me something interesting to do while I breast-feed in my pyjamas.'

'Thanks a million, Ind. Talk to you later.'

'Bye.'

I hung up, delighted that India had offered to investigate for me. India Madeline Burke – the most meticulous and conscientious person on the planet. Roxy Dawson could hardly have had a better person gathering information.

I was glad to be showing her the house again. It was a nice house and good value as houses went these days. I was hoping she'd manage to raise the money to buy it. Mind you, I couldn't imagine giving that young woman a mortgage if I were a bank manager. I think if her pert little-girl face had appeared across a desk from me looking for a mortgage, I'd probably have burst out laughing. It would have been like Will asking for a mortgage, really.

Thinking of that reminded me that my baby brother was engaged. God above! What was the world coming to? Andrew's spin on the situation was to stay calm and not make too much of a fuss in case it caused Will and Shannon to become galvanised in their romanticism and run off and get married straightaway. I thought he was completely correct – calm was the thing, all right.

I opened my mostly junk e-mails and scanned them for interesting bits and pieces. As I was trying to sort through them, Ryan's pimply face appeared in front of me.

'Ellen, how are you this morning? May I say that that jumper really suits you?' he said, sounding as sincere as a cheating boyfriend on Jerry Springer. 'What is it? Mohair?'

'Cat hair,' I said, not looking up. 'What do you want, Ryan?'

'Tim was in at 8.30, same time as me. I like to get an early start, get the paperwork out of the way for the day before I go into the field. Anyway, we got to talking – he showed me pictures of his baby daughter. Beautiful. The mother is a friend of yours, isn't she?'

'She is, Ryan, and she's also a person, not a brood mare – what do you want?'

'Well, I didn't realise your friend was married to Tim and—'

'So you thought you'd be nice to me for once as I'm so well in with the boss. Is that it, Ryan? Just slither back to whatever hole you crawled out of and stop annoying me if you don't have any business to discuss.'

'There's no need to be rude, Ellen. I was just going to ask you about the Reval franchise.'

'What about it?'

'Aren't they sending over one of their top men at the weekend?'

'Yeah,' I said. Gladstone and Richards was getting into bed with a huge American property company, and some big shot was coming over. Wasn't I the one who was to book the man's hotel? Why had I offered and not just let Molly do it? Still, it was done now and I had to do it or lose face with Molly. I made a quick note to myself on a post-it and stuck it on my computer.

'It'll be very interesting. You know what they say – a new broom sweeps clean,' he said.

'What the hell is that supposed to mean, Ryan? Did you get a new book of clichés from Santa last year?'

Ryan smirked. 'We'll see. That's all I'm saying, Ellen. We'll see.'

I wanted to punch in his I-know-something-you-don't–know expression. Instead, I stood up. Kicking back my chair like an extra in *NYPD Blue*, I gathered up my papers and hefted my ton-weight of a leather satchel onto a protesting shoulder. 'If you'll excuse me, some of us have work to do.'

Then I walked away in what I hoped was a fair impersonation of Clint Eastwood in *The Good, The Bad and The Ugly*. I was so cool, I could almost hear the music playing and, of course, I was looking particularly good in my lovely sweater – even if it was making me sweat a bit more than normal.

# 6

Roxy Dawson was already sitting on the garden
wall outside Mrs Hegarty's house when I arrived.
I had a key to let us in because Mrs Hegarty
was away. Roxy jumped off the wall as I pulled
my car to a halt in front of the red garden gate.
With her high, swinging ponytail, she still looked
about twelve, but I couldn't help noticing that her
face was pale and there were dark rings around
her eyes.

'Roxy,' I said as I approached.

She smiled. 'Hi, Ellen.'

'How are you?'

'Fine, fine – a bit tired, that's all.'

'It's hard work being pregnant.'

'Do you have kids yourself?'

I shook my head. 'No, but my two best friends
just had babies, so I know all about it. When is your
baby due again?'

'Two weeks.'

'Not long so.'

Roxy laughed a soft laugh. 'That's easy for you
to say.'

'I suppose. At least you'll have some of the house-hunting out of the way before the baby puts in an appearance.'

'Hopefully.'

'Molly said you wanted another look at the house?'

'If that's OK.'

'That's no problem.'

I walked ahead of her along the narrow garden path and opened the front door to let us in. A powerful smell of synthetic jasmine hit me in the face like a slap with a wet cloth.

'Oh, God,' Roxy said, behind me and I hoped she wasn't going to throw up. I turned to look at her and she smiled her energetic smile as she waved her hand in front of her face to disperse the fragrance.

'Would you like to have a look around on your own? I know people often prefer that – less pressure.'

'That'd be great.'

'I'll wait in the kitchen for you.'

'I won't be too long.'

'Look, Roxy, take your time. I'm in no hurry.'

Roxy smiled again and started up the stairs as I went into the kitchen. I stood for a few minutes looking out the window at the back garden. Pa was right – it was huge. You'd never find a house built in any town nowadays with such a long garden. And, though it wasn't exactly the type of garden that was ever going to appear on a TV show, it was a relaxing, pleasant sort of place all the same. Most of the garden was devoted to a healthy-looking green lawn, with a couple of trees dotted along the sides and a bed of exuberant roses showily demonstrating their beauty before the first frosts.

I looked around Mrs Hegarty's kitchen, with the shining countertops and the everything-in-its-place look. She really was a fabulous housekeeper. When I thought of the corners of rubbish – old clothes, shoes, books – at home, I figured that Andrew and I could do with taking a leaf from Mrs Hegarty's book. During the summer, I'd read a book on feng shui and de-cluttering. I'd told almost everybody I met about it while I was reading it, but it was now just another piece of clutter in our lives.

I opened Mrs Hegarty's fridge and had a surreptitious peek inside, but thought better of actually stealing any of her food. I was starving. As soon as Roxy was finished, I was going to head for the cake shop at the edge of the estate and buy myself a big, fat cream cake of some description.

I was tired, really. Tired and hungry and wondering more than anything else how to keep my mother calm in the face of Will's engagement . . . was that my name I heard? I listened but couldn't hear anything so I walked into the hallway.

'Roxy?' I called up the stairs.

'Ellen. Ellen could you come here, please?' a very strained version of Roxy's voice answered.

I ran up the stairs.

'Roxy?'

'In here.'

I opened the door of what was obviously Mrs Hegarty's bedroom. Roxy was sitting on the edge of the eiderdown-covered bed. Her face was pale and haggard and her ponytail seemed to have slipped to one side.

'Ellen,' she said, closing her eyes as she paused mid-sentence to take a long, deep breath. 'My waters have broken.'

'What? As in what happens when you're about to have a baby?'

Roxy nodded as she released small, panting breaths through pursed lips.

'But they can't have – you're not due for two weeks – you just told me.'

Roxy shrugged. 'Well, what can I tell you, Ellen?'

She gave me a twisted half-smile and then focused on a spot on the wall behind me as she began her breathing again. I walked over and crouched down in front of her. The floor and bed around her were stained and wet. Mrs Hegarty would have a fit.

'Come on, Roxy. I'll bring you to the hospital.'

She shook her head and her slipped ponytail danced in my face as she groaned and bent forward. 'Too late.'

'What?'

'Too late. I can't walk. I'm having him.'

'Having him? Who? The baby? In Mrs Hegarty's bedroom? You can't be having a baby here with nobody competent to help. Come on, Roxy. It'll be all right. I'll take you to the hospital. Just try to stand up.'

Roxy looked up at me then. Her eyes were wide and frightened but in them was a determination like

I'd never seen before. 'I can't go anywhere, Ellen. This is my third baby, and I promise you, he's almost here.'

'He can't be.'

'He is. I'm going to lie down here and you're going to have to help me.'

'Me?'

'Just do as I say, OK?'

I nodded like a six-year-old taking instruction from an adult.

'Call an ambulance,' she said.

'Call an ambulance,' I repeated.

Roxy gave a small whelp of pain and I rooted in my handbag and pulled out my phone. I punched in 999.

'Emergency services,' a woman's voice said. 'Which service do you need?'

'She's having a baby – here, right here and right now and I'm the only one here and we need an ambulance right away.'

'OK. I'll put you through.'

'But . . . but—'

'Ambulance service. Can I help you?'

'Jesus! I already told the other woman – Roxy's having her baby and we're in Mrs Hegarty's house and I'm the only one here and I have to tell you they didn't cover delivering babies when I was in college studying the property market.'

'We'll send somebody straight away. Where are you?'

'Mrs Hegarty's house.'

'And the address?'

'OK, the address – 14 Hollyfields, and its called *Sacre Coeur* – it's on a plaque outside the door.'

'14 Hollyfields? We'll be there as soon as possible.'

'How long is that?' I asked, panic rising in my throat.

'As soon as possible.'

'Shit!' I said. 'Look Roxy, I'll be right back. I just need to run down and open the front door for the ambulance people.'

I left the room and tore down the stairs. I opened the door wide, put on the latch and ran straight back to Roxy. By the time I got back, Roxy had set herself up on Mrs Hegarty's bed. She was lying down, half naked, her face as white as the pillows she was propped up on, and twisted by the exertion of pain. Her breath came in short bursts as she bore down, and her ponytail flipped wildly from side to side.

'Shit,' I said again – if I wasn't mistaken, that was a baby's head I could see appearing. Roxy looked up at me as the contraction receded, and the terror in her eyes was like a neon sign.

'You'll be just fine,' I said, sitting at the end of the bed, deciding it was about time I started acting like a grown-up.

Roxy's eyes filled with tears. 'I'm scared.'

I took her hand and squeezed it. 'There isn't a thing to be scared of, Roxy. You're doing great and the ambulance is on its way and everything is going to be just fine. I promise you.'

Roxy nodded and tried a smile but another

contraction interrupted and took her attention. Little and all as I knew about the process of childbirth, even I had a feeling we were really in business this time.

'Ahhhhhhhragh!' Roxy roared, and a small, blood-and-slime-covered body slid onto Mrs Hegarty's white eiderdown.

'Oh my God!' I said, instinctively reaching forward and catching the baby. He squirmed in my hands, and I clutched him close. 'It's a boy, Roxy. It's a boy.'

The baby looked at me with Roxy's knowing eyes. Then he opened his mouth and roared like an ass. I looked at his blood-streaked face, enthralled by this miraculous tiny person.

'Is he OK?' Roxy asked.

I nodded. 'I think so. Look, he's lovely and he's roaring, and that's a good sign, isn't it?'

Roxy extended her hands and I gave her the tiny boy. She took him – trailing umbilical cord, flailing limbs, wailing protestations and all – and folded him, tenderly, into her arms. Kissing his head of matted black curls and muttering to him, she examined every part of him.

'He's gorgeous, and look at the colour of him – he looks like he just came back from Spain,' I said.

Roxy laughed. 'Oh Jesus! I don't believe it.'

'Don't believe what?'

But she never answered me as the sound of heavy footsteps on the stairs took our attention. A heavy-set middle-aged man ran into the room, followed by a willowy, blonde nurse.

'Well, well,' the man said as he approached the bed. 'I see our work here is already done, hah, Lisa?'

The blonde nurse walked past him to Roxy and gently stroked the baby's head.

'Look at this lovely little fellow,' she said in an English accent, sitting down on Mrs Hegarty's bed beside them. 'Hello, young man. How are you? You gave us all a bit of a shock arriving suddenly like that. When was he due?'

'Two weeks,' Roxy answered.

'Well, he's obviously an impatient lad. Well done to Mummy and helper for giving him a hand into the world.'

Roxy grinned at me and I winked.

'I think he deserves the credit,' I said. 'We didn't really do anything.'

'Speak for yourself,' Roxy said, smiling.

'Sorry – Roxy did loads as well. It's just that I didn't do—'

'You were great, Ellen,' Roxy interrupted. 'I couldn't have managed without you.'

'I'm sure that's true,' the blonde nurse said. 'And look at his lovely tan. Where's Daddy from?'

'Limerick.'

'I mean originally.'

'Limerick.'

'Oh,' the nurse said. 'A touch of jaundice, maybe. Nothing to worry about. Now, Madam, if you wouldn't mind stepping outside. We just need to cut the cord and clean up a little.'

I nodded. 'No problem.'

I left the room and made my way down the stairs. I could hear baby Enrique wailing, and I fancied that he was protesting at my absence. I stepped into the front garden and saw that it had turned out to be the lovely, sunny autumn day that Ruth had described. In what felt like milliseconds, Roxy and Enrique and the ambulance crew appeared. Roxy waved wearily at me as she passed. Her ponytail had slipped completely down to the nape of her neck.

'I'll come and see you later,' I said.

She nodded again and cuddled the baby closer. I stood and watched as Roxy and her baby were loaded into the ambulance and driven away. Maybe I should go back into the house and clean up. I looked at my watch. A quarter to twelve. God Almighty! I'd delivered a baby. Ohmygodohmygodohmygod! I fished out my appointments list. That was good – I had another appointment in Hollyfields at twelve – 2 Cratloe Crescent, Hollyfields. I'd easily make it. The house was only a couple of streets away, so I could leave my car and walk there. Which is exactly what I did.

As I walked to Cratloe Crescent, I tried to think how I was going to explain the state of Mrs Hegarty's bedroom – especially to Mrs Hegarty. Maybe I'd call Molly after I'd shown these clients around. Molly was the one who generally employed cleaners for the firm.

A couple in their late twenties were parked in a red Fiesta outside 2 Cratloe Crescent when I came along. I rapped at the window and a soft-looking woman with blond-streaked hair turned her head to look at me. I waved.

'Ellen Grace,' I said to the closed window, and smiled my winning smile. The woman tapped the man beside her on the arm and he looked at me as well. I waved again. He smiled a nervous smile and waved back. Suddenly the engine of the Fiesta started and the woman banged down the door buttons. Before I could say another word, the car had pulled away and was driving at speed up the wide street. I stood looking after them. Maybe I'd been mistaken? Maybe they weren't my clients.

I looked around but there was nobody else in the vicinity. It had to be them. So what was that about? Bloody weirdos. I leaned against the garden wall and waited five minutes just in case somebody else came along, but I knew they wouldn't. I was in the business long enough to recognise waiting clients when I saw them. All I could conclude was that I was glad not to have been alone in a house with that pair.

I gave up waiting and headed back to Mrs Hegarty's house to collect my car. Just as I turned the corner, I heard my name.

'Ellen?'

I looked up and there in front of me was Angela Maunsell. Angela Maunsell – my mother's seventy-one-year-old cousin who also just happened to be my ex-neighbour and friend.

'Ellen, love, are you all right? Are you hurt? What happened?'

'Hello, Angela. I'm fine. How are you?'

'But what happened? Where did you come from?'

I shook my head. 'What do you mean? I just came from Cratloe Crescent – around the corner there. I was supposed to show a couple a house and they just looked at me and drove away. Bloody weirdos.'

'Did they hurt you?'

'Well, no – unless you mean my feelings and then I suppose the answer would have to be yes. Why would they do something like that?'

Angela peered into my face. 'You are all right, aren't you?'

'Fine, but—'

'So why are you covered in blood? Is someone else hurt?'

I looked down at my new cream angora sweater and saw that the front of it was covered in blood.

'Oh my God!' I said, lifting my hand to my face and noticing blood streaks along my palm as well. 'Is there blood on my face as well?'

Angela nodded. 'All along one cheek.'

'Do you think that might be why that couple drove away?'

Angela nodded again.

'I delivered a baby.'

'What?'

'I swear to God, I did, Ang – I was showing a client around a house and she just had the baby there and then before the ambulance arrived, and I don't know if you'd call what I did delivering him, but I sort of caught him when he was born.'

'That would explain the blood all right. Well done, Ellen, well done!'

'Thanks, Ang, but I don't think I did much, and Mrs Hegarty will have a fit when she sees the state of her white eiderdown.'

'Alice Hegarty?'

It was my turn to nod. 'I'll get cleaners in but I'd say she'll have to burn the eiderdown.'

'Don't mind her. I'll talk to her.'

'You know her?'

'Since she was going to Irish dancing classes at the Mechanics Institute. I used to go with her. Pudgy knees. Alice Walsh – that's her own name – she always had pudgy knees. All the Walshes had the same knees but at least on the boys it didn't look as bad. Where is she now? Is she at home?'

I shook my head.

'I'll talk to her later on, so. Don't worry about it. That woman lives to clean. She'll be delighted with the challenge of getting the stains out of the eiderdown.'

'Really?'

'Really. I know Alice Hegarty. Don't worry about it.'

'Thanks, Angela. How are you, anyway? Are you well?'

'Dragging the devil by the tail. Now, why don't you call up that Molly one who works with you and tell her what happened and go on home before you scare anybody else away?'

I nodded.

'Good girl,' Angela said. 'But tell me first – how's the family?'

'Grand.'

'And that handsome boyfriend of yours?'

'Fine as well.'

'Good stuff. Off you go now and call your one, and go home.'

'Thanks, Ang.'

Angela patted my arm and it was only when I saw that she was power-walking away that I realised she was wearing a work-out outfit, complete with a head-band that would be worthy of a TV tae kwon do instructor.

I sat into my car and called Molly who was more than happy to reschedule my appointments once I told her I was frightening off the punters. I drove home and headed straight for the shower, not sure whether to consign my new cream sweater to the bin, give it to Roxy as a souvenir of her son's birth, or drop it in to Alice Hegarty to throw into the same Daz challenge as the eiderdown.

As soon as I was showered and dressed, I called the hospital to check on Roxy and the young fellow to be told that they were both-doing-fine-thankyou-verymuch.

After that, I rang Ruth who was delighted to hear I was arriving earlier than expected. I dropped in at the deli to pick up some ready-assembled lasagnes, a bundle of Italian breads and a plastic bowl of ready-made salad. Then I pointed my car out the Cratloe road.

# 7

Ruth, Emerson and Paddy lived less than four miles from Limerick but their idyllic cottage was up a series of winding roads that brought you to the edge of a magnificent – if hilly and remote-feeling – wooded area. The cottage was a renovated traditional Irish cottage and, although it had a slate roof instead of thatch, it still had all the charm of the original: bumpy, white-washed plaster; a row of small, green-framed windows; and the obligatory pink roses climbing around the front door. Ruth, with Paddy in her arms, opened the door of the cottage as soon as she heard my car slither over the gravel in her front yard.

'You need to get rid of that gravel,' I said, kissing them both hello.

'You need to get rid of the baldy tyres on that heap of junk,' Ruth said, hugging me. I took Paddy from her arms. He really and truly was a most beautiful baby. Paddy's skin was a gentle honey colour; his eyes were the same clear blue as his mother's; and his hair was blond and curly and starting to become plentiful. He was exactly like a cherub.

'You could exploit this child and have him do

commercials so that you and Emerson could retire,' I said, cuddling him close. Paddy smiled a lopsided smile at me before grabbing hold of my hair and pulling.

'Ow,' I said, disentangling his fingers. 'When did he learn to do that?'

Ruth smiled. 'Isn't he clever? He's been doing that for over a week, now.'

'You must be so proud.'

'We are, and his father has the reels and reels of film to prove it,' Ruth said, leading the way into the kitchen. 'Why are you here so early, anyway? Pulling a sickie?'

'You have no idea,' I said, handing her the bag full of food as I settled myself with her lovely – if grabby – son. 'Put on the oven and heat up this lot. I'm starving and I've loads to tell you.'

So Ruth heated up our dinner, which we wolfed down, even though it was only three o'clock in the afternoon. I told her of my midwifery and then she fed Paddy who fell asleep. With Paddy in his Moses basket, sleeping like the baby he was, we went into the sitting room with our coffee.

'I have something to tell you,' I said.

Ruth looked at me. 'You're pregnant?'

'No, fool. But I've decided to get married.'

'About time.'

'Andrew proposed in Spain.'

'I know. India told me. *You* never told me though, you sneaky bitch.'

'I know. I'm sorry. I should have told you. But it's

such a big commitment and you know me and commitment, Ruth. Anyway, it's not like we set a date or anything.'

'So now you have?'

'No, but we will, and sooner rather than later. I think at long last I've finally stopped being scared of marriage.'

'I'm glad to hear it. Andrew Kenny must be the most patient man in Ireland. You've been stringing him along for years. What does he have to say about this forthcoming marriage?'

'I haven't told him yet – I think I'll tell him this weekend.'

Ruth looked as if she wasn't sure whether she believed me or not. But I was resolved. I had never been so positive of anything in my life. I loved Andrew Kenny with all my heart and I was going to marry him and live happily ever after.

Ruth and I slid into a companionable silence. I was slumped on the cushion-covered sofa and on the verge of dozing off to sleep like Paddy when I remembered the phone call.

'What is it you promised to tell me?' I slurred sleepily from between the cushions.

'I'll tell you later.'

'No,' I said, propping myself up on one elbow as curiosity woke me up. 'Spill the beans now.'

Ruth was sitting on a fashionably battered armchair, her feet curled in under her slender body, her usually meticulously made-up face scrubbed clean, and her blonde hair pulled back into a ponytail. The overall effect was to make her look almost as young as Roxy Dawson.

'Tell me,' I repeated.

Ruth chewed her bottom lip and looked at me. 'I had a call from this woman at the adoption agency.'

She paused and re-arranged her ample bosom. 'Bloody breast-feeding – I keep forgetting to close my bra. Do you know, I went to the shop in the village last week with my tits waving around the place like balloons?'

'I'd say the male population of Clare will be sending Paddy thank-you cards. But go on – what did the woman from the adoption agency want?'

Ruth shrugged. 'My mother wants to see me.'

'Oh my God! Your birth mother?'

Ruth nodded.

'So when are you going to meet her?'

She shrugged again. 'I don't know.'

I looked at her and she seemed so small and fragile – like a hurt child, curled into the big armchair – that my eyes filled with tears. I swallowed hard as I realised.

'*Are* you going to meet her?'

Ruth looked down at Paddy who was snoring softly in his Moses basket at her feet. 'I don't know.'

'What does Emerson think?'

'He says I should do whatever I feel is best.'

'And that is?'

'I don't know.'

Ruth and I sat in silence for a few minutes as I struggled to think of the right thing to say. Most of the time, I'm not great at saying the right thing. No – that's an understatement. The truth is that most of the time, I say exactly the wrong thing.

'How do you feel about it?' I asked finally, as I really wanted to know what was creating the bruised expression on my friend's face.

She looked at me, her eyes glassy with tears. 'I don't know – angry, I guess. I can't stop thinking – well, who the hell does she think she is? Do you know what I mean? She gave me away when I was three days old and now, twenty-six years later, she thinks she can march back into my life as if everything was just dandy and we can take up where we left off—'

Her voice trailed away and she began to cry. For a few seconds, I was shocked. Ruth never cried. Well that's not true either, but she wasn't a big cry-baby like me. I jumped up from the sofa and sat on the arm of her chair and hugged her. Her thin shoulders shook with emotion and, for an instant, holding my friend reminded me of holding Roxy's newborn baby. Weird. Eventually Ruth's tears subsided and she blew her nose.

'Sorry, Ellen.'

'Don't be sorry. It's fine. Are you OK?'

She nodded and blew her nose again. 'I can never understand where all the snot comes from, can you?'

I slapped her arm and walked back to the sofa. 'That's disgusting, Ruth Joyce.'

'What do you think I should do?'

I shook my head. 'I'm with Emerson on this one, I think you should do whatever you want to do – can you tell the agency you don't know if you want to meet her yet?'

Ruth nodded. 'I suppose.'

'Maybe you should do that? It'd give you some time to think about it.'

'Maybe. That's a good idea, actually, Ellen.'

'Don't sound so surprised. I do have good ideas sometimes.'

'I know, but be honest – not often.'

'Very funny, Ruth.'

A sudden rustling caused us both to look at the Moses basket. Paddy blinked his big blue eyes and cooed softly. Ruth bent forward and picked him up. He squirmed with obvious delight and she hugged him close.

'The only thing is,' I said, watching the mother and baby tableau, 'she probably didn't just casually give you away. I'm not saying anything but it was probably horrible for her as well.'

Ruth nodded. 'I know but it still feels like that.'

We sat there together, then, the only sounds a far-away cow lowing and the slurping sound of Paddy having a quick feed. As soon as he was sated, Ruth sat him up and winded him.

'Let's go for a walk,' she said.

I frowned at her. I was sort of back in the snoozing mode.

'Really,' she said, standing up. 'There's a beautiful lake just over the hill and it's still quite warm out.

Get up, Ellen. You'll enjoy it and you can always sleep later on.'

I rose, groaning, to my feet. Ruth bundled Paddy into a jacket and then strapped on a baby sling and slid him inside. By then, it was almost five o'clock, but the sun was still shining and it was quite warm. Though it was autumn and the air had that distinctive smell of soft soil and fallen leaves, the weather was still warmer than it had been for most of that summer.

We walked across Ruth's gravelly yard and a short distance up the road before she led me over a wall and through a small wood. As we emerged from the wood, I saw an upwardly sloping field dotted with cows.

'Cows,' Ruth said, before I could ask.

'How do you know they're not bulls?'

'Take my word for it, Ellen – they're cows, and they're not even slightly interested in us.'

I took her word for it and we waded through the long meadow grass and clover and wove our way through stepping-stones of cowpats. And all of that before we even began to climb the hill.

I thought of complaining as we walked up the steep incline but as Ruth was carrying Paddy and hardly even breathing hard, I felt like too much of a wimp to draw attention to myself. We reached the top – me panting, Ruth and Paddy composed – and my breath was further taken away by the view. The other side of the hill seemed to unroll down to a large, still lake that lay like a giant mirror at its foot.

'Oh my God!' I said, 'Look at that.'

Ruth grinned. 'Told you you'd love it.'

'It's beautiful,' I said but that was so inadequate a description that I felt sort of frustrated. 'I mean, really, Ruth. It's unbelievable. Amazing. Fabulous.'

'Save your breath for walking,' she said, winking at me as she trotted down the hill to the lake.

I followed, almost able to keep up with my friend now that we were going downhill. As we came close to the lake, I could hear the gentle sound of lapping water.

'This is incredible,' I said, feeling guilty that my voice was disturbing the still air. 'I could live here.'

Ruth laughed. 'No way, Ellen. You're a total townie.'

'I know, I know, but there's something about this place. I really could live here, Ruth.'

'Well, buy a house, girl. I could do with new neighbours.'

Paddy had been lulled back to sleep by his mother's walking, so Ruth and I sat on a large, flat rock and just stared across the lake. Two swans glided effortlessly past, not deigning to look in our direction, and a pair of magpies fought over something at the edge of the water. As we sat, mesmerised by the still atmosphere around the lake, a tall figure crested the hill on the other side and walked towards us. We watched in silence as the figure came closer and closer. It was a man. A tall man in a green coat. Just as I began to think I recognised him, Ruth gasped.

'Well, fuck me!' she said. 'If it isn't Tony Jordan.'

# 8

The sight of Tony Jordan walking towards us felt so surreal, I was suddenly certain that I was dreaming. There was no way that he could be here, at the side of a lake across the hill from Ruth's house. It wasn't possible. Tony Jordan had left Limerick a year ago because Robert White and his cronies were trying to kill him, so how could he be here now?

I decided that if I sat really, really still, it would all pass away and I would wake up and discover that it was just another ordinary day. Andrew would be asleep beside me in the bed. Joey would be snoring his puffy cat snores at my feet, and I'd be feeling for the alarm clock so that I could hop it off the wall to stop it ringing. I'd wake up and discover I hadn't delivered Roxy's baby, and Ruth's mother wasn't looking for her, but most of all that Tony Jordan wasn't standing, smiling, twenty feet away from me.

'Oh my God!' Ruth was squealing in my dream. She jumped up and ran to Tony Jordan and hugged him hard.

'Ruth,' he said, obviously delighted to see her. 'And who is this?'

Ruth beamed, fit to burst. 'Paddy. This is my son, Paddy.'

Tony's face melted as he stroked the top of Paddy's curly head. 'He's lovely, Ruth – at least the part of him I can see is lovely. Is he asleep?'

Ruth nodded. 'Just like his father – likes to sleep with his face in a pillow of bosom.'

Tony laughed.

'Oh my God, Tony!' Ruth squealed again, squeezing his arm. 'It's great to see you, and you look fantastic. How have you been?'

'You look terrific yourself. Being a mother suits you.'

'Thanks. Oh, it really is good to see you, Tony. I can't believe it.'

'It's great to see you, too,' Tony said, looking straight at me. I looked away.

'So,' he continued. 'Fill me in on all the scandal.'

'Well, I'm a respectable married woman now, hard as that might be to believe.'

'And who's the lucky guy?'

'Emerson Burke – India's brother.'

'Wolfie'll be gutted.'

Ruth grinned. 'How the hell *is* Wolfie?'

'He's great. And how are you, Ellen?'

I started at the sound of my name. If this was a dream, it was beginning to take on a life of its own. Ruth and Tony were looking at me. I looked back at them. Ruth was right. Tony did look great. His olive skin was tanned, and his black hair was longer than I remembered, and curled slightly around his beautiful neck. A sprinkling of designer stubble accentuated the shape of his jaw.

As he looked at me, he smiled, and his brown eyes were as bright as I remembered, and still had that nameless quality about them that made me catch my breath. I wanted to touch him so badly I could hardly bear it – which is the effect Tony Jordan has had on me since the first day I met him – but if he was a dream, I couldn't touch him, and if he was real . . . well, if he was real, I didn't dare.

'How are things with you, Ellen?' Tony said, going for a minor rephrase.

I looked at him for what seemed like ages. Then my mouth opened and the words came out by themselves.

'Where have you been?' I asked, like a scared five-year-old.

Tony moved closer to where I was still sitting on the rock. 'Spain. Portugal. Alaska.'

'Alaska?' Ruth echoed.

Tony laughed but never took his eyes off me. 'I'll tell you about it sometime.'

'Oh,' I said.

'And you?'

'Here. I've just been here all the time. Well, not here as in *here* here – on this rock by the lake – but still here.'

Tony grinned and his hand reached forward towards me as if to touch my face, but then he rubbed his head and looked at the ground.

'That's great,' he said, staring at his feet as they scuffed a patch of grass. 'Here. How's Andrew?'

'He's good,' I said, remembering Andrew. 'Really good.'

'That's great.'

'Isn't this some place?' I said then, and I could feel my face gearing up to throw me into motor-mouth. 'I mean, I never even knew this lake was here. Ruth lives just over that hill there – imagine that! She and Emerson bought that lovely little cottage past the wood, and at first I thought it was a mad place to live but then today she made me come here for a walk and I couldn't believe it when I saw it. I never saw any place like it, did you? I could live here. I was just saying it to Ruth before you came along – wasn't I, Ruth? I really could live here.'

'I do – I live here,' Tony said, interrupting my verbal diarrhoea and lifting his head to look at me.

'Oh,' I said.

'Where?' Ruth asked. 'This is excellent – that means we're neighbours. Have you seen the other neighbours, Tony? Where do you live? Is it far?'

Tony turned his head to look at Ruth and pointed back up the hill we'd seen him walk over. 'That's my house there.'

We both looked at the large, red-brick house he was pointing towards. It was a double-fronted traditional-shaped house, with tall, white windows and a slate roof.

'You can see the lake from your house,' I said.

Tony nodded but for some reason was still looking away from me.

'Would you like to come up and have a cup of

tea?' he asked. 'Wolfie's above and I know he'd love to see you.'

'Well—' I began.

'Great,' Ruth interrupted. 'I'd love to see Wolfie as well. Have you anything nice to eat up in the mansion, Tony? Ellen and I already ate our dinner – we were starving and we couldn't wait – but now I'm starving again after the walk.'

'I'm sure we'll find something for you,' Tony said. 'Will we go up?'

'Sure,' Ruth said, and she and Tony fell into step and began to walk in the direction of his house. I walked along behind them, slowly losing my conviction that this was a dream, and struggling to deal with the deluge of emotions. I would never have believed that seeing Tony Jordan again could have had such a devastating effect on me. When he'd left, we'd parted on good terms, with him expressing regret and me pretty certain that Andrew was the man for me. So what was this all about? All this wanting to touch him and plaintively asking him where he'd been? I was embarrassed by myself – not that that was unusual, but still. . .

The only explanation I could think of for the way I was feeling was the trauma of delivering Roxy's baby. That must be it. That was really quite traumatic for me and had thrown me off balance, so that now, when I met Tony, I was . . . vulnerable. It would pass. It would have to pass.

The driveway that led up to Tony's house was so large that it had more gravel than a lot of Spanish beaches. As we crunched our way towards the house – Ruth and Tony chatting, me bringing up the rear – the huge, mahogany front door opened and Wolfie stood framed in the doorway. Luckily it was an enormous doorway that could accommodate his size. Wolfie looked precisely the same as when I'd last seen him. He was still the same six foot six tall, three foot wide, shaven-headed, goatee-toting Wolfie he'd always been.

Ruth squealed and ran up the steps and threw her arms around him. Wolfie let out a shout and picked her and Paddy up, and then put them back down as soon as he realised that Paddy wasn't a rucksack. Tony and I followed Ruth, in silence.

'Jesus, Ruthie – a baby!' Wolfie shouted, a massive grin spreading across his face.

Ruth laughed. 'Jesus, Wolfie – a baby! This is my son – Paddy Burke.'

'And Ellen!' Wolfie said, stepping towards me to enfold me in a crushing hug. I laughed and hugged him back.

'It's great to see you, Wolfie,' I muttered into his chest. Because it was great.

'And you, Ellen. You look terrific. How have you been?'

'Good, and you?'

Wolfie let out a loud laugh. 'Well, we're alive. And considering everything, I'd say that means we're doing good – eh, Tone?'

Wolfie laughed again, and Paddy let out a yelp as the commotion had woken him up.

'You've frightened the child, Wolfie,' Tony said.

'Oh God! Look, sorry – I didn't mean to frighten him.'

Ruth laughed as she extracted Paddy from his sling and turned him around towards us. 'Don't mind Tony. Paddy's like his mother – he's not afraid of anything.'

Paddy blinked his blue eyes sleepily at us and wriggled in his mother's arms.

'Ah, Ruth, look at him,' Wolfie said, smiling. 'Hello, small fella. How are you? Did you see him, Tone?'

'Yeah. He's a cracker.'

'Like his mother,' Ruth said.

'Just like his mother,' Wolfie agreed, winking.

I looked from person to person as they spoke but said nothing. I was still numbed at the shock of seeing Tony. However, the estate agent in me was obviously more robust and couldn't help noticing the broad, elegantly proportioned hallway with its mahogany table, exquisite marble tiles and tall picture windows, full of plants.

'You promised us tea, Tony Jordan,' Ruth said.

'Indeed I did. Come on.'

We followed Tony through the wide hallway and down a staircase that led to a huge, warm basement kitchen, complete with Aga and gigantic table.

'Take a seat,' Tony said as he and Wolfie immediately, and as if by prior agreement, set about slicing bread and making sandwiches and tea. Ruth discreetly fed Paddy as she sat in a high-backed chair by the Aga, and I fidgeted with a loose end on a rattan tablemat.

'Ellen delivered a baby today,' Ruth said all of a

sudden. Everybody stopped what they were doing and looked at me. Ruth grinned. I smiled awkwardly and pulled at the unravelling mat.

'Not your baby?' Wolfie asked.

Ruth threw her eyes up to heaven. 'You've obviously never been around anyone who ever had a baby, Bobby Wolfe. Do you think I'd be hopping around the countryside if I'd had a baby a couple of hours ago? It was a client's baby. Wasn't it, Ellen? What did you say her name was again? Lola?'

'Roxy,' I said.

'That's it, Roxy. Great name, isn't it? Ellen delivered Roxy's baby all by herself – I call that a great day's work for an estate agent.'

'Fair play to you, Ellen. Fair play,' Wolfie said.

'Not Roxy Dawson by any chance?' Tony asked.

I looked at him. 'How did you know?'

'Well, I didn't, but it isn't everybody in Limerick is called Roxy – I know her mother well. Kitty Dawson, Wolfie.'

'Kitty Dawson's child just had a baby?'

'Her third baby,' I said.

'Her third?' Tony and Wolfie chorused.

I nodded.

'And you delivered it?' Tony said.

I nodded again.

Tony smiled at me and I wanted to slide onto the floor under the slab of pine table in front of me. 'I always knew you'd be a great woman to have around in a crisis.'

I shrugged because I had lost my powers of speech

as Tony and I had become, somehow, locked in looking at each other. He let his hands drop to his sides, and I knew I should look away, but I just couldn't seem to convince my eyes of the same.

'A boy or a girl or can you tell at that just-born stage?' Wolfie asked.

Ruth laughed. 'Of course you can tell. A boy – wasn't that what you said, Ellen?'

I nodded and forced myself to look away from Tony.

'Enrique,' I said, and looked back to where Tony had been standing, but he was gone. His back was turned to me as he chopped something or other on a board.

'Sorry?' Ruth said.

'Enrique – that's what she's calling him.'

'She must have been in Spain like us – eh, Tone? It's amazing the number of Enriques in that place – we must have known half a dozen of 'em at least, didn't we?'

'We did,' Tony said, swivelling around with a plate of sandwiches in his hand. 'Here we go – food.' He put the plate on the table.

Wolfie poured the tea and then he and Ruth kept the conversation going for the rest of the visit. I sipped at a cup of tea. I couldn't eat – everything tasted like sawdust in my mouth. I was as polite as I was capable of being but I made sure not to look at Tony again for the rest of the visit. Not that it mattered. I could still feel his presence without ever looking at him. He was like a fire radiating energy that I couldn't ignore, no matter how hard I tried.

# 9

Andrew brought me breakfast in bed the next morning. I smiled gratefully and then put the tray on the floor and shoved my head under the duvet. Andrew laughed and pulled the quilt away from me.

'You'll be late,' he said as he leaned over and kissed me.

'It's Saturday,' I said, and started to kiss him back.

'You promised.' He was lying beside me now, running his hands up and down the length of my body.

'I'm delivering,' I said and jumped up and knelt over him. He laughed and shook his head.

'Spencer Alexander the Third, Ellen.'

'Holy shit!' I said and jumped out of bed, landing on the breakfast tray. I shook cornflakes from my feet as I searched for clothes. Andrew lay on the bed watching, a smile playing on his lips.

'Help me,' I said as I threw on a pair of combats and a grey sweater that had once been green.

'You promised you'd do it. Don't wear the combats. There's a big hole in the leg.'

'If you loved me, you'd go to the airport,' I said and rooted in the pine wardrobe for something else to wear.

'No way, Ellen. Dermot got me a ticket for the match and they're like gold dust. And anyway, you promised.' He was still smiling as he lay, hands behind his head, watching me hopping around the room in a bra and thong.

'Bastard!'

'It'll be fine. Spencer Alexander the Third will probably be a really nice guy. His flight is due in around two o'clock. Did you book the hotel room for him?'

I stopped dressing, remembering with horror the yellow post-it I'd stuck to my computer screen.

'You're not serious, Ellen – you forgot, didn't you?'

I nodded. 'Well, I was busy delivering Roxy Dawson's baby, you know.'

Andrew grinned. 'We'll never get a room for him now, not with this rugby match on in the city. I'll ring around and try, but I'd better make up the guest bed, just in case.'

I pulled a black sweater over my head and stepped into tight black jeans.

'No way am I spending my weekend with an American who might eventually own half the company we work for,' I said, looking at my reflection in the mirror.

I could see Andrew behind me on the bed, grinning from ear to ear.

'You look like a Bond girl in those clothes. Cool.'

'Do Yanks like Bond girls?' I asked and went to pick up the overturned breakfast tray.

Andrew grabbed me and wrestled me onto the bed. 'I don't know, but what I do know is that he'd better keep his eyes off this Bond girl,' he whispered as he began to kiss me.

I was late and it was Andrew's fault. The Bond girl sex had cost me half an hour, and the search for the keys of Andrew's beemer had taken another hour. I ended up booting my way to Shannon Airport in my old pink Hyundai, while Andrew sorted out hotel rooms and lost car keys before Dermot picked him up for the match.

I hadn't a clue what this guy looked like, but Tim Gladstone had given me a placard with his name written in bright orange magic marker. Spencer Alexander the Third. He sounded old, fat and rich. I pulled into the short-term car park and ran towards Arrivals with my stupid placard. I checked the bulletin board and was delighted to see that the flight from New York had been delayed. I'd have time to grab a coffee and call Andrew about hotel rooms.

I sat down on an orange plastic chair in the waiting area, noticing, as I threw the placard on the ground, that the writing was exactly the same colour as the seat. I drank my coffee quickly and rang Andrew. No answer. The bloody match must have started. I debated whether I'd ring India and see how she and Baby Alyssa were doing, but decided that Tim might answer the phone, and I'd have to explain about the severe lack of hotel rooms. I closed my eyes instead and enjoyed the warm sun streaming through the huge glass windows. I drifted into a delicious dream about me and Pierce Brosnan and Andrew.

'Excuse me. That's my name on the floor,' a voice said in an American accent.

I opened my eyes, expecting to see Pierce Brosnan. Instead I saw Matt Damon, or his doppelgänger. This was the most gorgeous-looking man I'd ever seen, and I wondered what he was doing in Shannon Airport, talking to me. I sat there, speechless, on the orange chair, gazing up at him. He looked like someone who had walked straight out of an Armani ad. His golden blond hair was streaked with shades of honey and beige, and he wore it long, almost rakish – I bet my new ultrabra that it cost a small fortune to get it that way. He wore a black cashmere sweater and grey trousers and was carrying a matching grey jacket neatly over his arm.

'I didn't mean to wake you,' he said, grinning. 'But that does look like my name on the placard at your feet.' He ran an elegant hand through that thick, luxurious hair.

I stood up and smiled at him.

'I'm Ellen Grace, from Gladstone and Richards. I'm sorry. I should have been standing over there with all the other placard people, but I got some coffee and . . . have you been waiting long?' I asked, hoping that even if he had, he wouldn't say it.

'Fifty-two minutes exactly,' he said, glancing at a sleek silver wristwatch. Gucci – I could see the G on the strap.

'Oh,' I said. 'Lucky so that you saw the placard.'

'Very lucky. Very lucky indeed.' He stared at me.

He had the most unusual eyes – a kind of green with curly eyelashes.

'Nice placard,' he said.

I looked down at the lurid orange letters and noticed that the placard had somehow acquired a shoe print while I was asleep. Was he serious?

'Oh,' I said.

'Yeah, well maybe everybody wouldn't like it but I love it.'

I couldn't decide whether he was trying to be funny or was actually serious – so I smiled back and changed the subject.

'There's a huge rugby match in Limerick today, so we'd better go now before the traffic—' I shrugged at him instead of finishing the sentence. He grabbed a suitcase at his feet and I grabbed the placard, but then changed my mind and threw it on the chair. He gave me a curious look and followed me out to the car park.

As we approached the lurid pink glow of my Hyundai, I wished with all my heart that we'd found the keys to Andrew's lovely silver beemer. I opened the boot and nodded at him to throw his suitcase in, then walked around to the driver's door. He came around to open the passenger door, and then I remembered that the lock on it was busted. And that the passenger seat was broken, so that it lay permanently forward like a collapsed deckchair. This was turning into one shit day. He shook the door handle in an attempt to open the door. I got out and pushed back my seat so that he'd fit into the back of the low-slung coupé.

'That door is kind of stuck, and so is the front seat, so you'll have to get in the back through here,' I said. 'Sorry.'

He nodded, then came around and began to climb into the back seat. I had the best view ever of an almost perfect bum, and I wished I had a mobile phone that took pictures so that I could send one to Ruth. He looked ridiculously large in the tiny space that was the back seat, and his knees almost hit his chin. I smiled at him in the rear-view mirror, and he gave me a weak, scared-looking smile.

We made slow progress back to the city, and the stilted efforts at conversation didn't help. But I managed to steer the subject away from hotel rooms until we hit the outskirts of Limerick. Then Spencer Alexander the Third asked me directly.

'Do you know anything about my hotel? Those long flights really make the muscles seize up. It does have a gym, doesn't it?'

I nearly crashed into the red Hiace in front of me.

'Hnmm,' I said and concentrated very hard on the stalled traffic. My mobile phone rang at that moment. Great – Andrew to the rescue. I rooted in my bag and answered before the traffic moved again.

'Hi.'

'Hi, Ellen – bad news.'

'Don't tell me,' I said. The traffic began to shift and I tucked the phone under my chin.

'Can't get a hotel room for love or money. Oh, and Joey peed on the guest bed just before I left for the match.'

'I don't believe you,' I said.

'Yep. But it's not all bad news, love. Munster are winning and I cleaned up the pee. See you later.'

I threw the phone on the floor on the passenger side and smiled in the mirror at Spencer. I was starting to sweat with the stress of it all, and I prayed that Joey had made only a small pee. We finally pulled up outside our red-brick semi on the Ennis road.

'Here we are,' I said brightly, getting out of the car and bounding up the drive before you could say Yankee Doodle.

At least Andrew had tidied the place up. I heard Spencer coming into the kitchen behind me and decided that now was the time to come clean.

'All the hotels were booked out because of the rugby match and . . . well . . . you'll have to stay here for a day or two . . . and, well . . . that's it, really—' I said and smiled at him and shrugged. He truthfully was a beautiful man. His face was showing the first signs of a very sexy five o'clock shadow. Jesus! I had to stop admiring him like this.

He smiled tightly at me.

'Something might become available,' I said. 'But then again, maybe not. Those Gloucester supporters love the craic so they'll probably make a weekend out of it.'

'Oh.'

'Would you like something to eat or drink? Tea, coffee, maybe?'

'Freshly brewed coffee would be real nice.'

'No problem,' I said, but it was a lie. I had a vague

recollection of an old bag of ground coffee in the back of some press. I got out the coffee machine anyway. And then I had a brainwave.

'You must be very tired – jet lag, all that stuff. Would you like to go to bed?'

Spencer Alexander the Third did a double take and stared at me in shock.

'Not with me,' I said quickly, and I could feel my face turning bright pink.

'I know,' he said laughing. 'I was just kidding.'

I laughed too like a demented hyena.

'I'll show you your room and you can freshen up,' I said. I had heard that in a movie and it seemed like the right thing to say.

I showed him to the guest room, hoping he wouldn't notice the cloying scent of air freshener and faint cat pee.

'Would you mind if I skipped the coffee, Ellen? I could do with a couple hours' shut eye.'

'Not at all,' I said, trying not to sound delighted. 'Have a good rest. We can chat later.'

I left the bedroom with a quick wave and returned to the kitchen, started the coffee brewing for myself, and rang Andrew.

'Come home this minute.'

'Hello, Ellen, and how are you?'

'Andrew, I mean it. Come home or I'm leaving you today.'

'I trust our American colleague has arrived safely.'

'Home, now.'

'I'm just going for a pint with Dermot and—'

'Now,' I said and hung up. I poured myself a big mug of coffee, which didn't taste too bad considering its age, and settled into *Hello!* magazine. Andrew arrived home just as the phone rang.

'Hi, Ellen.' It was Ruth.

Andrew nuzzled the back of my neck. I pushed him away and glared.

'Hi, Ruthie. How are you?'

'I'm fine except for having to put up with screaming babies.'

Andrew was standing behind me with both his arms around my waist. He started to kiss my neck again. It felt good.

'I've never seen that baby crying yet, Ruth Joyce,' I said. Andrew nibbled my ear.

'Just checking about tonight, Ell. We'll be over around eightish – how's that?'

And then I remembered. The previous day, when I was at their house, I'd invited Emerson, Ruth and Paddy for dinner. Mind you, at the time, I hadn't reckoned on having bloody Spencer Alexander the Third staying.

'No problem. That's great, Ruth. There's another guest coming, though. Remember I told you that an American franchise company was buying into Gladstone and Richards? Well, their man in New York is staying here for a couple of days.'

'In your house?'

I pushed Andrew away. Here he was kissing and canoodling and we had a dinner to organise.

'Set the table,' I said.

'Who, me?' said Ruth.

'Why?' asked Andrew.

'No, Ruth – I was speaking to Andrew who spent the afternoon in Thomond Park while I minded our American colleague.'

Andrew had started to empty the dishwasher.

'Why is the Yank staying in your house?' Ruth asked.

'Long story – I'll tell you tonight.'

'Why am I setting the table?' Andrew asked. I waved at him to shut up.

'So, what's he like?' asked Ruth.

'Who – Andrew? Same as he ever was. Actually, I think he's getting a tiny bald patch on the back of his head.' Andrew threw a dishcloth at me in response to this.

'No, you eejit. The American.'

'Well he's . . . he's . . . American.'

'Brilliant, Ellen, brilliant! I'd better run. See ya tonight, girl. Jesus! I wish I could have a few drinks! This breast-feeding is no fun.'

I laughed. 'It won't be forever.'

'Feels like it. Bye, Ell.'

I hung up and looked at Andrew, who was putting away clean dishes.

'Ruth and Emerson are coming for dinner – what will we do?'

'Feed them, I'd say,' he replied, opening the fridge.

'And Spencer Alexander?'

'Him too. Where is he, anyway?'

'In bed. What will we do?' I asked again and could

feel the beginnings of a very major panic attack starting.

'We'll go shopping. I'll cook and you ply everybody with wine. It'll be grand,' Andrew said, coming over to kiss me.

# 10

As soon as our guests arrived, I grabbed Ruth and dragged her into the kitchen, supposedly to help with the cooking.

'You look brilliant,' I said as I checked all the pots. It seemed that Andrew had everything under control. Ruth wore a black satin top with a deep cleavage. 'Did you have a boob job?'

She laughed. 'One of the few advantages of breast-feeding,' she said and poured me a glass of wine from the bottle on the countertop.

'You might as well drink if I can't. So, what's the sca? Where's the American and what's his name, by the way?'

'You'll never guess.'

'I give up – tell me.'

'Spencer Alexander the Third,' I said and the two of us burst out laughing.

'I don't believe you!'

I guffawed and nodded my head at the same time.

'What's he like? A cigar-chewing middle-aged property tycoon?' asked a still-giggling Ruth.

'The opposite.'

'Handsome?'

I nodded vigorously.

'Very handsome – like Tony Jordan handsome?'

I nodded with even more energy.

'On a scale of 1 to 10?'

'Thirty-five. Armani-ad handsome.'

Ruth's eyes widened and she shook her head in disbelief.

I laughed. 'Don't get all excited, Ruth. You're a married woman.'

I gave her a quick recap of my day while I checked the food yet again. Then Andrew stuck his head around the door to tell us that Spencer Alexander had finally come downstairs.

We followed Andrew into the dining room, which looked great, bathed in the warm glow of candlelight and table lamps. A coal fire glowed in the Georgian fireplace. Andrew had opened the doors between the sitting room and dining room, and the space looked fabulous. Baby Paddy was asleep on the aubergine couch, like a beautiful rare accessory.

Spencer Alexander the Third was standing with his back to us, in deep conversation with Emerson. He turned around and smiled, and I thought I heard Ruth give a little yelp. He had a dazzling smile, with perfect, even, pearly teeth. His hair was still damp from showering, and he hadn't shaved. He wore lovely cream linen trousers and a coffee-coloured sweater that flattered his super-fit physique. He looked sexy, dishevelled and smart – all at the same time.

'Spencer, this is Ruth Joyce, Emerson's wife, and you met Ellen already,' said Andrew.

'I'm delighted to meet you,' said Spencer. He took Ruth's hand, the smarmy bastard, and kissed the back of it. Ruth giggled like a schoolgirl.

'Ellen,' he said and nodded at me. I smiled back at him. Andrew went to the kitchen with Emerson and we sat at the dinner table. Spencer poured a glass of wine for me and fizzy water for Ruth, who watched Spencer with total concentration

'So, how's Limerick treating you, so far?' asked Ruth finally, in a breathy star-struck voice.

'Gee, it's really hard to say. I only saw the airport and this house so far. Although I did see quite a bit of the airport,' he said, looking at me. Ruth giggled and I threw her a *don't-make-a-show-of-me* glare.

Andrew and Emerson returned then, with the pasta first course. Spencer Alexander was pleasant and witty throughout the meal, and, by the time we'd finished our steak main course, even Andrew had succumbed to his charms. I couldn't believe how clever and well-informed he was. I mean, he'd even seen some of Emerson's films, which was more than I had.

'I'll get some more wine,' I said as the conversation moved to films and great directors – all foreign, all with unpronounceable names. I escaped to the kitchen and opened two bottles. I downed a glass and carried the bottles into the dining room. Paddy had woken up and was sitting on his daddy's lap. 'How cute are you, Paddy Burke?' I said, as I put the wine on the table.

'He's adorable – I love babies,' said Spencer.

'Are you . . . do you have any yourself?' asked Ruth as she took Paddy from Emerson.

Spencer Alexander the Third looked directly at her. 'I wish. I just split up with my partner, so I'm in the process of adapting to being single again. What about you, Andrew? Any patter of tiny feet on the horizon?'

'I have a little girl, Katie. She's almost three.'

'Cool. Where are you hiding her?' Spencer asked, looking at me.

'She's not . . . I'm not the mother,' I said.

Spencer looked embarrassed. 'I'm sorry. I just assumed that . . . sorry.'

'It's fine,' said Andrew. 'You'll see her tomorrow – she usually spends her Sundays with us.'

'All this talk of families reminds me that I heard you two were going to give us a day out very shortly,' said Ruth, grinning.

I tried a smile in the hope that she'd shut up.

'Ellen just has to name the day,' Andrew said, looking directly at me, a small smile curling the corners of his beautiful mouth.

'Come on! Come on! I dare you!' Ruth said. 'Name the day, Ellen. Do it now. It'll be like one of those dating shows.'

Everybody looked at me expectantly and I wanted to answer, but somehow I just couldn't. Instead, I jumped up and started to pour wine into empty glasses, but all the while I could feel Andrew's eyes on me. What the hell was wrong with me? Because I was so preoccupied, I didn't notice until it was too late that Spencer had put his hand over his glass –

and I poured red wine all over his hand. It dripped like blood onto the white tablecloth, and then onto his cream linen trousers.

'I'm really sorry. Here, let me help,' I said, and started to wipe his crotch with a table napkin. I stopped suddenly when I realised what I was doing. Looking directly into his eyes, I noticed they were flickering with amusement. Ruth broke the silence that had descended on the table.

'Take off your trousers and put them in the wash straightaway, Spencer,' she said.

Spencer stood up. 'I'll run upstairs and change. It's no problem.'

Andrew, Emerson, Ruth and Paddy all looked at me at once.

'It was an accident. You'd swear I'd shot him in the crotch or something,' I said defensively.

Emerson laughed. 'Ellen, you're so funny sometimes – really you are.'

Andrew looked away.

'Dessert,' I said and ran to the kitchen. I stood at the counter, fidgeting with my wine glass.

'You're something else,' said Ruth who had followed me into the kitchen and closed the door.

'Ruth, please,' I said and took a huge gulp of wine.

'Ellen, please. What was that about?'

'I don't know what you mean.'

'Yes, you do, Ellen, and it's very unfair.'

'On me?'

'On Andrew. What is the matter with you? How could you embarrass him like that?'

'It's your fault, Ruth.'

'I beg your pardon?'

'How could you bring up something like that in public?'

'I didn't know it was a secret. You told me, Ellen – just yesterday in my house – that you had decided to marry Andrew.'

I started to load the dishwasher.

'I don't know how you could have humiliated him like that in public,' she continued

I slammed the dishwasher door shut and grabbed my glass and gulped more wine.

'I didn't mean to humiliate him.'

'Then why did you do it?'

I shook my head.

'Is it something to do with Tony resurfacing?' Ruth asked.

'No way, Ruth. Don't be ridiculous.'

'Are you sure? There was definitely something going on between the two of you yesterday.'

'I don't know what you're talking about.'

'Yes you do. Look, Ellen, it's simple. Do you love Andrew?'

'I . . . He's the best thing—'

'Yes or no. Simple question. Just cut to the chase for once, Ellen Grace.'

'I love him,' I said and looked straight at her.

'Do you?'

'Yes, I do.'

'Marry him so. You did tell me yesterday that you had decided to marry him. Did you tell him?'

'Not yet, but I will, Ruth. Get off my case.'

'Do it soon.'

'I will,' I said. 'But you know me – it's always the finer details that catch me out. Like choosing which shoes to wear or picking a shade of lipstick.'

Ruth looked at me. 'Don't worry – it'll all be grand. Now, what's for dessert? Yes, yes, yes! Chocolate fudge cake. Come on – let's bring this in to the boys. Jesus! Spencer's something else to look at, isn't he, Ellen?'

I nodded and cut wedges of chocolate cake.

'Best eye candy since Jude Law in *The Talented Mr Ripley* . . . and he's really funny, isn't he?'

'I suppose.'

'Wait until they see him in the office on Monday – there'll be a cat fight over him. I mean, gorgeous, funny, probably rich *and* available. Hard to believe really.'

'He's not that good-looking, Ruth.'

'You're getting old, Ell – the eyesight is always the first thing to go.'

'And you shouldn't be eyeing anyone, Mrs Burke.'

'Eye candy, dear. I can appreciate the goodies without sampling them.'

'Slut,' I said and began to pour cream on the thick wedges of cake.

'He did look like you'd shot him in the crotch though,' said Ruth, and we both laughed as we carried the plates into the dining room.

# I I

It was late when I awoke the next morning. Andrew was gone and I curled up in bed, enjoying the comfort. Joey had commandeered Andrew's space and eyed me gravely, tail wagging.

'Piss in this bed and you're one dead cat,' I said, and he blinked calmly in response. I could hear *The Tweenies* on the television downstairs and I remembered that Katie was coming for the day. I smiled and jumped out of bed, eager to see Andrew's lovely little girl. I threw on jeans and a T-shirt and hurriedly brushed my teeth. As I walked downstairs, I heard a woman's voice in the kitchen. It was Linda, Katie's mother, and she sounded upset. I felt like I was eavesdropping, so I opened the door.

'Hi,' I said, too brightly, and walked over to Andrew. He was standing by the sink, arms folded, head down, and I knew straightaway that something had happened. He kissed me on the cheek, and I tried to make eye contact with him, but he just stared at the floor, scuffing a piece of grime with his foot.

'Hi, Ellen, how are you?' said Linda. She was holding a coffee cup in her hand.

'I'm fine. I'll . . . look, I'll just go and say hi to Katie.'

Neither of them acknowledged my departure.

'Katie!' I said as I went into the living room.

She was sitting on the floor with her back to me, her beloved Buzz Lightyear beside her.

'Ellen,' she yelled as she stood up and ran into my outstretched arms. I lifted her up and kissed her cheek. She looked at me with Andrew's clear, grey eyes.

'Buzz's leg broke but Mammy glued it with supergoo and I did a picture for you but the dog ate it. Can we go to McDonald's for our dinner?'

'We'll see, honey. You got bigger in just one week. Look at the size of you,' I said as she climbed down from my arms and pulled me down on the floor with her to watch TV.

I wondered where Spencer was as I watched *The Tweenies* with Katie. Joey had put his head around the door but ran when he saw her. He had too many recent memories of being nearly strangled by her.

'Can we watch *Toy Story*?' she asked, as the Tweenies sang their goodbyes. This was our regular routine. Me, Andrew, Katie and Buzz Lightyear and our favourite movie in the world.

'Sure,' I said and went in search of the DVD. I heard Linda leaving as the movie started. I kissed Katie on the top of the head and went into the kitchen. Andrew was standing by the French doors, staring into the garden. I went and stood behind him and put my arms around his waist, silently cursing Ruth for dropping me in it the night before. Andrew was obviously very upset about the scene at the dinner table. For all I knew, he'd just confided in Linda about it.

'OK?' I asked.

He said nothing. I leaned into him and stretched up to kiss the back of his neck. No response. Damn Ruth!

'Where's Spencer?' I asked.

'Jogging,' he replied and extricated himself from my grasp. 'Don't worry about Spencer. I gave him a key, and Tim Gladstone is collecting him later. He'll be fine.'

He turned around and caught my face in both his hands and kissed me hard on the lips. 'I love you,' he said and left the room.

I stood there in the kitchen, trying to sort out my head. I was envious of Linda and the relationship she had with Andrew. I knew this was completely irrational because they had to have some kind of relationship for Katie's sake. But sometimes I felt excluded. It all made my head hurt. Or else I had a hangover.

Katie and I watched *Toy Story* while Andrew spoke on the phone in the kitchen. I couldn't hear what he was saying but I thought the whole thing was very odd as I was certain he was talking to Linda and she'd only just left our house. As the credits of the movie rolled up and Katie and I sang along with the sound-track, Andrew came into the sitting room.

'How about Treasure Land for the afternoon?' he

asked, attempting a smile though his face was drawn and tired.

Katie clapped her hands together and cheered.

'Treasureland, treasureland, treasure. We all going to treasure land,' Katie sang, clearly ecstactic at the prospect of spending her day rolling around in a sea of plastic coloured balls. I hated the place and figured it was about as adult unfriendly as it was child friendly. It was noisy, and all the seats were plastic, as indeed were the coffee cups – and the food they served. I made a face at Andrew.

'I need to visit Roxy in hospital,' I said.

Andrew nodded. He didn't smile, just nodded.

'It's just that I did deliver Enrique on Friday and today is Sunday, and with Spencer and dinner parties and all that stuff, I haven't even managed to get a minute to go see her. And I should, I think.'

My voice trailed off as I looked into Andrew's serious face and he nodded again.

'Do you mind?' I asked.

'Treasureland, treasureland, treasureland,' Katie chanted, now adding choreography as she wiggled and danced around the sitting room.

Andrew shook his head, and this time he smiled, though it still looked a little strained. 'Not at all. Why would I? I'll buy a stack of newspapers, and Katie can run around to her heart's content. It'll be fine. You go and see Roxy.'

'OK, if you're sure.'

'Of course, I'm sure.'

I kissed him. 'OK then. I believe you. When are you going to go to Treasureland?'

The mention of the name jiggled Katie out of a short pause in singing.

'We love Treasureland, every day we love it,' she began.

'Now?' Andrew suggested.

'Good idea,' I said. 'I'm not sure that we can listen to too much more of that song.'

Andrew swept Katie up in his arms and nuzzled her head. She squealed with delight.

'See you later,' he said, winking at me as he headed for the door, his giggling daughter slung over his shoulder in a fireman's lift.

Katie waved wildly at me as they left the room and all the way down the driveway to the car. Then we blew kisses at each other until Andrew's car had disappeared from sight.

As I drove to the hospital, I tried not to remember the cringe-making scene at dinner the night before. Why had Ruth had to say that? Why couldn't she have just let me deal with it in my own time? Why was I so reluctant to marry Andrew? I arrived at the hospital before I had to think too deeply about any of it. I was glad.

As I didn't really know Roxy Dawson very well, I wasn't too sure what to bring to her, so ended up with an armful of sweets and magazines and fizzy drinks, and a card with a baby boy being transported by a flock of storks. Surely something would hit the mark?

The hospital was buzzing with activity when I arrived. Visitors crowded along the corridors with arms as full of rubbish as mine. Old people, teenagers, children, exhausted-looking men and even more exhausted-looking women in dressing gowns strolled past me as I searched for Roxy's ward.

She was in a private room that was so full of flowers I wasn't sure it was a bedroom when I first opened the door. Bouquets of roses competed with bouquets of carnations and gigantic mixed bouquets. Baskets of flowers vied for space with 'It's A Boy!' banners and balloons and teddy-shaped floral arrangements.

'Ellen!' Roxy said as soon as she saw me in the doorway.

She was propped up in bed on about six white pillows, looking more like a little girl than ever, in her satin pyjamas.

I kissed her flawless cheek and dumped my offering on the bed.

'You shouldn't have,' she said, ripping open the card and adding it to the hundred or so that hung over her bed.

'How are you feeling?' I asked, standing up to have a peek into the metal cot positioned on the far side of the bed. 'And how's himself?'

I walked around the bed towards the cot to admire the swaddled infant, smiling to myself as I got close enough to see Enrique's shock of black, curly hair protruding from the cotton blanket. He was lying on his side, sleeping soundly and making small, grunting noises that sounded like a faraway tractor. One hand was folded up against his downy cheek, and . . . that couldn't be right.

'He's great,' she answered. 'Brilliant. But as you can see there for yourself, he's black. Well, more brown than black really, but definitely not white.'

I turned my head to look at Roxy – too surprised to pretend. 'But I thought—'

'That Pa was his father? So did I.'

'And?'

'And so did Pa.'

'Oh my God! How is Pa . . . you know . . . taking the surprise?'

Roxy sighed and, as usual, I thought that the look in her eyes belied her childish appearance. 'Well, it was a bit of a shock at first – even to me. You know, it takes a few hours to go really brown after you're born, though I could sort of see from the start that he was dark – darker than the girls. Could you see that when he was born?'

I shook my head. 'Not really. Except for his hair. Mind you, Roxy, I got such a fright when he arrived, I mightn't have noticed if he was purple with green spots.'

Roxy smiled, leaned over and pulled the blanket away from the baby's face, and we both stared at him.

'He's totally beautiful,' I said, as she stroked her index finger along the curve of his plump cheek.

'He is, isn't he? Shakira says he's the colour of toffee,' she said, briefly looking away from the baby to glance at me. 'You're probably wondering what happened.'

'It's none of my business, Roxy.'

'Well, you did deliver him.'

'More like caught than delivered.'

'Still. You see, I'm only with Pa since New Year's Eve.'

'Look, there's no need—'

'I want to tell you.'

Roxy touched the baby's tiny hand, and his fist opened and wrapped itself around her finger. He wriggled his shoulders and smiled in his sleep – or, at least, it looked to me like a smile.

'He's having a nice dream,' I said and Roxy nodded.

'I was well pregnant by the time I found out – more than four months according to the scan, and I was sure it was Pa's. We both were.'

Roxy paused.

'Pa and I were mad about each other, so we weren't upset or nothing. We were glad to be having a baby together.'

'I suppose.'

'I'm not really a slapper, you know, though I can see it looks like I am.'

'I never said—'

Roxy smiled and shook her head, and her pony-tail bounced high in the air. 'I know, but I'm not a fool and I know what it looks like – twenty-four-year-old with three kids, different fathers. Shakira and Shania have the same father, by the way – Teddy

Hannon – he's in jail since last year but we were already finished. He's a fool. I married him when I was eighteen – we broke up after Shania was born.'

'My God!' I said. I found it all a bit hard to believe.

Roxy shrugged. 'I know it sounds bad but—'

'It's not that – you're twenty-four? You look about twelve and you're twenty-four.'

'Thanks.'

'No, really – I mean it as a compliment.'

'I know – thanks. What was I saying?'

I shook my head. 'Something about somebody being in jail?'

'Oh right, Teddy Hannon – don't remind me of that waster. Anyway, that's all there's ever been – Teddy Hannon and now Pa – well, OK, there was Enrique's father as well, but I didn't think anything about that. It was nothing and I always use protection – drunk or sober. I have two girls to raise, so I have no intention of getting diseases.'

I looked down at the magnificent baby boy in the green blanket. 'Well, nothing works all the time, I suppose.'

'Except that I thought the . . . the—' Roxy scrunched up her face as she was searching for a word.

'Contraceptive failure?' I offered.

Roxy laughed. 'That's one name for a burst condom I suppose! Anyway, I thought that the *contraceptive failure* was when I was with Pa not . . . not the other guy. I met him at a Christmas party. He was a Yank from Tennessee – I remember that much. And he was fucking fine. Really, Ellen, you should have seen him – Will Smith would look like Jimmy Magee beside him.'

'Sounds pretty nice.'

'He was gorgeous but I can't even remember his name. It was just one of those things, and, less than a week later, I met Pa and that was that.'

'Love,' I said.

Roxy shrugged.

'What did Pa say when he saw Enrique?'

Roxy's eyes filled with tears and she picked up her baby and cuddled him close. 'I told him about your man, the Yank, and that I didn't know I was already gone when we met, and he didn't say anything – just left the room and I haven't seen him since.'

'Oh, Roxy,' I said.

She shrugged and bit her lower lip. 'I have my baby and, even though he was a bit of a surprise, I wouldn't swap him for a thousand men. Look at him, Ellen.'

'I am looking and he is something else – he's like a baby in an ad on the telly. He's really, really beautiful.'

Roxy sniffed and smiled determinedly. 'He's a great boy. We'll be grand – me and the girls and Enrique – we'll be just fine. We'll buy that house off you—'

'Still?'

'Definitely. You didn't think Pa was the one with the money, did you?' Roxy laughed at what was obviously an absurd idea.

I shook my head but it was a lie. The truth was, I hadn't really thought at all.

'Anyway, I've told the girls all about it, and they're up to high doh with excitement about our new house and our new baby. And they're all that matter to me anyway.'

'You're some woman, Roxy Dawson,' I said and I couldn't resist giving her a hug. She hugged me back, and Enrique mewled but slept on.

'Thanks, Ellen. Thanks for everything.'

'For nothing. When will they discharge you?'

'Tomorrow morning.'

'And do you need somebody to drive you and Enrique home?'

Roxy shook her head. 'You're very good but we're grand. My mother is picking us up. She has the girls and she'll bring us all home to our flat. Did you find out anything about the burned-out building next door?'

'I have someone investigating as we speak.'

'Great. And do you mind me asking if there are any other offers?'

'I don't think so but it is a popular place, Hollyfields.'

'I'll call you as soon as I can.'

'Don't worry,' I said. 'I'll let you know if anyone makes an offer on it. Anyway, I'd better be off. Take care of yourself and this little guy.'

I turned when I got to the door. 'Do you know something, Roxy?' I said.

'No, what?'

'It's Pa's loss. He's a fool to let a woman like you go.'

'Thanks, Ellen. Take care.'

'See you.'

Later that evening, as I lay beside a sleeping Andrew after a lacklustre session of lovemaking, I felt a knot of fear in my stomach. What was wrong with Andrew? He'd told me he was fine, but I wasn't an idiot – I could see that something was bothering him. It had to be the dinner party. I couldn't bring myself to ask him directly. I turned over in the bed and burrowed into my pillow. I was upset that he was so distant but, in a way, that wasn't what was truly niggling at me.

I rolled onto my back and Tony Jordan's face popped, unbidden, into my mind. No way. No way was I having that. Tony Jordan was a lovely episode from my past and that was where he was going to stay. I heard Spencer letting himself in and climbing the stairs and I wondered where he'd been all evening. But musing about Spencer's activities didn't succeed in distracting me from thinking about Tony Jordan.

I forced myself to replace all thoughts of him with Roxy Dawson. There she was preparing to set out on a scary journey through the world, all alone with her three babies. It was a pity about me really, I thought, as I drifted off to sleep. Worrying about nothing. I didn't know when I had it good.

# 12

Molly was enthroned at her desk when I reached our offices the next morning. She had a mirror perched on top of her computer and was applying mascara with great gusto to already perfectly made-up eyes.

'Ellen, you're early – what's up?' she asked, waving her mascara wand in my direction.

'Good morning, Molly, and how was your weekend?' I asked, smiling sweetly at her. Molly on a Monday morning was very hard to take. She was applying lilac eye shadow now, exactly the same shade as her nails.

'Well, what's he like? Spencer Alexander the Third? He has such a great name. Shame about his . . . well . . . his reputation,' she said, never taking her eyes from the mirror.

I knew better than to ask what she meant although I was bursting with curiosity. Spencer Alexander was too good to be true. He probably had a dozen wives or else was some kind of serial killer. They had a lot of serial killers in America. I smiled sweetly again. 'Coffee, Molly?'

'Why, thank you, Ellen. I think I will,' she said.

I escaped into the tiny kitchen and put on the

coffee maker. I could hear all the Gladstone and Richards minions arriving as I busied myself with the coffee and searched for clean mugs. Tim Gladstone stuck his head around the door.

'Ellen, there you are! Thanks ever so much for looking after Spencer. Lovely person, isn't he?'

I smiled and nodded.

'Nice of you to decide to give him the old Irish hospitality treatment.'

'No problem.' I didn't know whether that was Andrew's line or Spencer's.

'Anyway, he'll be around for the next few days, and I want you to show him the ropes, so to speak. You can take him out on the job with you, Ellen – he wants to be right at the coalface, as he says himself.'

'I'm sure that can be arranged,' I said.

'Where is he, by the way?'

'Andrew's bringing him in.'

'Great stuff.' Tim patted me on the shoulder, then yawned and rubbed his eyes.

'Tired, Tim?' I asked, as I poured coffee into two fairly clean mugs.

'I sit with India during the night feeds. We believe breast-feeding should be a shared experience.' He smiled at me and spooned sugar into his coffee.

'Lovely,' I said as Tim waved and headed for the office. I found another clean cup and made coffee for Molly, then followed him out of the kitchen just as Spencer made his grand entrance. A hush fell over the open-plan office and I could have sworn a halo of light enveloped him as he flashed his dazzling smile at everyone. Or maybe he had highlights and he was standing in the path of the sun. He looked out of place – like seeing Brat Pitt in the Credit Union.

Tim did the introductions, and I thought Andrea, the junior, would faint with pleasure when Spencer Alexander kissed her cheek. I could see that he'd already acquired a little fan club and he wasn't even in Limerick five minutes. I went back to my desk, and checked my work diary for the day. I had two viewings in Hollyfield and three in the city centre. I hoped I could sneak off and leave Spencer with Andrew or Tim. My private phone line rang.

'Hello?' I said and continued reading my diary.

'You'll never guess, love!'

'Angela, how're you doing? I meant to call yesterday but . . . what won't I guess? Is there something wrong?'

'No, the opposite. Ellen, I'm doing it! I'm tying the knot!'

I nearly dropped the phone in surprise. 'Angela, what are you talking about?'

'Ralph proposed last night. He did the whole works, Ellen – down on one knee, a solitaire engagement ring. Can you believe it?'

'Who is Ralph?'

'My boyfriend, Ellen. I met him at the salsa dancing classes. He's a great little mover.'

I was speechless for a few moments.

'Do you mind me asking you, Angela – how long do you know him?' I eventually asked.

'Twenty-four days and five hours.'

'Three weeks?'

Angela laughed. 'We can't all wait around like you, love. We're hoping to marry as soon as possible – have things legal and above board, if you know what I mean.'

I turned a bright pink. There was no way I was going to discuss sex with my seventy-one-year-old friend and ex-neighbour. Jesus! What next?

'Angela, look, there's another call coming in. I'll call during the week and we'll crack open a bottle to celebrate, OK?'

'Brilliant, Ellen, and we can plan my hen night while we're at it. Cheerio, love.'

I took the next call.

'Hi, Ellen.'

'India, how are you? How's Alyssa?'

'She's fine. Ruth told me all about your midwifery.'

'Jesus! Can you believe it? I don't know how anybody does it. I'm not sure I'm up to ever being on the producing end of childbirth.'

India laughed. 'It's different when it's you, I promise. Anyway, Alyssa is asleep for once, so I did that investigating about Acorn House for you.'

'Brilliant. It's the same girl, you know – the one whose baby I delivered – Roxy Dawson.'

'Oh, right. I didn't make the connection. OK, this is the story so far. Sarsfield Properties own the land behind Hollyfields – the land that runs down to the river. It was rezoned five years ago as commercial instead of green. There was huge controversy at the time with the usual claims of backhanders. Sarsfield Properties bought it last year.'

'Who exactly are they?' I asked.

'Mainly Foncie and Majella Ryan – they also own that huge new shopping centre in Plunkett Street.'

'The one that's supposed to be going bust?'

'The very one. So, money is tight, and that land behind Acorn House must be put to some use. But there are a few problems in the way.'

'Such as?' I asked. I had the office to myself now and was sitting back with my feet on the desk. A bad habit I'd learned in college.

'Access to the site. There's only that small lane, and they need a wider road to run up to the hotel.'

'So what does that mean?'

'Well, the original plan was to demolish Acorn House, which came as part of the package. Then An Taisce put a preservation order on the place—'

'Which conveniently burned down,' I said.

'Exactly. And I'm sure that they were positive that everything was fine until the residents' association started more trouble. Now they've taken the whole thing back to An Bord Pleanála. They want Acorn House to be rebuilt because of its listed status. And the real drama is that the planning permission for the hotel runs out next May.'

'Oh my God! They'll never rebuild Acorn House,' I said.

'They might. It's happened quite a lot recently. I know of a number of cases in Cork and Dublin where dodgy planning permissions have been revoked.'

'Go away – you're not serious.'

'Yes I am. The grapevine says that the residents have a decent chance and Sarsfield Properties will not be happy with that.'

'Are Sarsfield Properties dodgy?' I asked.

'Well, technically legit, but I'd say they could have shady connections, and if they're compelled to rebuild Acorn House, who knows what will happen? No access – no leisure centre.'

'And in the meantime, what about the burned remains of Acorn House? Will they make it safe?'

'City Council is cordoning it off – literally as we speak.'

'That's good – Roxy'll be pleased. So that's it?'

'Pretty much. One other thing, Ellen.'

'What?'

'Sarsfield Properties have a silent partner.'

'Who is it?'

'No idea – not any of the obvious people otherwise there'd be talk.'

'I need to go here, India. Thanks for everything – you've been brilliant.'

'I know. Just call me Sherlock Holmes from now on. Bye.'

Just then, Andrew buzzed me to come to his office for a meeting with Tim, himself and Spencer. Everybody was seated around Andrew's small conference table. I sat down next to Spencer. He had taken off the jacket of his camel-coloured suit and had rolled up the sleeves of his shirt. Showing off the old tan and biceps to the fan club, I thought as

I sat down beside him, returning his toothy smile in the process. I had a feeling it was going to be a long day.

We had been in the meeting almost two hours when Andrew's phone rang. It was on speaker and we could all hear Molly's voice.

'Andrew, excuse me,' she said. 'There's somebody in reception to see you.'

Andrew rolled his eyes. 'We're really very busy here. Who is it, Molly? Can't it wait?'

'It's Linda,' Molly said. 'She says it's urgent.'

There was dead silence at the table.

'Go on, Andrew. We're almost finished here. Ellen and I will wrap it up,' Tim said.

Andrew glanced at me, excused himself and left.

Tim took Spencer out to lunch and I begged off, pleading mounting paperwork as my excuse. I wanted to get it started as I had tons of viewings over the next few days and, more importantly, I wanted a break from Spencer. Nice and handsome as he was, he was still a job of work for me, and I was glad to have Tim take over.

I persuaded Ryan go to McDonald's for takeaway, and tucked into a Big Mac at my desk, trying not to drip ketchup on my laptop. Ryan munched noisily on his burger at the desk opposite me.

'Did you hear?' he asked after he had demolished his food.

I looked at him.

He took a mouthful of his Coke and smiled his reptilian sly smile. 'Did you hear about Spencer

Alexander the Third? About his . . . well, let's just say his colourful history?'

I wanted to know but I didn't stop working. I really didn't want to fuel the office rumour mill. After all, I had been its mainstay on many an occasion in the past. But I felt sure I was right about Spencer – he was probably some mad, perverted psychotic, kinky type. Whipping and bondage, or serial killing.

'Ryan, get a life.'

He laughed. 'Saint Ellen of Limerick!'

'Nope. Just sick and tired of rumours and character assassination, actually.'

'Not rumours, love. Molly heard it from the horse's mouth. From his Personal Assistant in the New York office of Reval, in fact. Bet you're dying to know, aren't you?'

I resisted the urge to throw my half-finished can of Coke at him.

'No, I don't want to know anything about Spencer Alexander the Third's private affairs, or anybody else's for that matter. Unlike you, Ryan, I have a life and I don't need to pry into other people's to get my kicks.' I gave him a mock smile. 'Now, I'd really like to do some work, if you don't mind.'

'You were much better fun when you hung out with gangsters and drug barons,' he said, laughing.

I refused to rise to the bait. He had no right to be dragging up the past like that, and anyway it wasn't true. I might have been mixed up with gangsters and drug barons but they weren't my friends or anything like that. Except for Tony Jordan and he was a good gangster and a great ride.

We worked in silence for a few minutes, the only sounds being the click of computer keys, and Ryan's weird nasal breathing. I thought I had shut him up for good but then he started again.

'Are you even a tiny bit curious about Spencer Alexander?'

I didn't answer, just kept working. As far as I was concerned, the subject was closed.

'You should be, you know,' he said, and I stopped typing and glared at him.

'I overheard a conversation between him and Tim Gladstone, and he refused to stay in the Clarion – said your house was great.'

'I don't want to hear this rubbish, Ryan.'

'It's true. Andrew invited him to stay on with ye. Be careful, Ellen. Watch your—'

'Oh shut up, Ryan. You're such a large pain in the arse,' I said and headed for the kitchen for a caffeine hit. Ryan was such a fool.

But I had to admit that, in spite of my protestations, my curiosity about Spencer Alexander was definitely aroused. And when he returned to the office after lunch, I tried hard not to stare at him or blurt out any inappropriate questions about his private affairs.

Andrew still hadn't returned from his meeting with Linda by the time Spencer and I left to show some new penthouse apartments in the Steamboat Quay area. As poor Spencer climbed out of the rear of my Hyundai, rubbing his back, I wondered what could be taking them so long.

The penthouse apartments were gorgeous. There was one, in particular, with a roof garden overlooking the city, and it had a small hot tub in the corner. The prospective buyers had just left, highly impressed with the apartment. I felt confident we'd get an offer on it soon, and the stakes were high. The commission was excellent on a property of this calibre, not to mind the trophy value of such a sale. Excellent for the portfolio, as Andrew would say.

I was standing by the wall of the roof garden, admiring the view, when Spencer joined me.

'This property really has the wow factor, Ellen. I think I'm in love with it. I wonder is that hot tub connected up. Cool! Let's have some fun – let's get in!'

I nearly passed out. I wished I had let Ryan tell me what was being said about this man. Maybe he really was a serial killer? Although I'd never seen a serial killer as good-looking as this one. Except that didn't help at all because I'd never seen a serial killer ever.

'You're a terror, Spencer,' I said and laughed in a strangled hysterical way.

'I'm serious. Just look at the view of the river. Imagine sitting in a hot tub, warm bubbling water, both of us together, feasting our eyes—'

He stopped mid-sentence and gave me a piercing look. I was bright red at this stage.

'. . . on the river,' he continued, still looking intently

at me. I was mortified. The hairs at the back of my neck were standing and I couldn't speak even if I had wanted to. 'You and me in that hot tub when we should be working – way to go.'

There was dead silence.

'Not!' he said and mock punched me in the arm. 'And you Irish say Americans have no sense of humour!'

'Ha, ha, very funny,' I said, relief rushing through my body that I wasn't going to be murdered and be the lead story on Sky News.

'I want it,' he said then, and leaned over the wall, looking down at the swirling River Shannon below.

I didn't know what he meant so I ignored him.

'It's the longest river in the British Isles,' I said.

'British Isles?' Spencer said. 'I didn't realise I was in Britain.'

'Don't be smart. That's just the old name for it – the way they taught us at school.'

He laughed and looked directly at me. He looked so like Matt Damon, it was almost uncanny. And he was even more handsome, if that was possible.

'This apartment, Ellen. I want this apartment, and I'm going to have it. I need a whole change of direction, and Limerick looks good to me.'

'What about your job and New York and stuff?' I asked.

'A job is just a job, and New York is just another overcrowded city. You're so lucky to live in a place like this, where people have time to catch up on real life.'

'I'm not sure you know everything about Limerick just yet.'

'I know what I see and I like it. Life in New York is like a read-through for a movie. You do all this stuff – work, eat, sleep, spend money.'

'But don't you go to the Hamptons at weekends?' I asked.

Spencer grinned. 'Not everybody can go to the Hamptons.'

He was getting way too philosophical for me. But he looked really cute when he was being serious.

'I'll handle the sale if you like,' I said.

He laughed and put out his hand and stroked my face. I jumped back a foot.

'Don't do that,' I said, and rubbed my face as if he'd struck me.

'I'm sorry. I don't know why I . . . I didn't mean to do it—' he said. His expression was that of a small boy caught stealing.

I had just been getting to like him. Ryan's warning earlier sprang to mind. *Watch your—* but I hadn't let him finish. What would he have said? Watch your back? Watch your valuables? Watch your virtue?

# 13

India and Tim took Spencer out to dinner that night. Andrew and I were invited but we declined. I was tired and I'd had enough of Spencer and his charming ways for one day. Anyway, Andrew was still very withdrawn, so I cooked us his favourite pasta dish for dinner. Afterwards, we brought our wine glasses into the living room, and sat in silence. Eventually I decided to ask him directly what was bothering him.

'Are you sick?'

'No? Why?' he asked and sipped his wine. He was sitting on the couch and I was stretched out, my head on his lap. I had finished my wine. I couldn't bear this tension any longer. Regardless of the consequences, we were going to have to do my least favourite thing and have a discussion.

'Well, it's just . . . just that you're kind of . . . odd . . . since yesterday—'

I'd said it. I'd actually said it straight out. I looked up at him, but I couldn't see his eyes, only underneath his chin. He needed a shave.

He stroked my hair. 'Oh, don't worry, it's nothing. It'll work out. Anyway, I've booked us a table at Tosca's, for tomorrow night, eight o'clock.'

'Great,' I said, happy to take his word that everything was fine.

I sat up and poured myself another glass of wine. Andrew put his arm around me and kissed my cheek.

'What about Spencer?' I asked. 'Are we bringing him?'

'It's fine. He and Tim are going to look at some property in Lahinch, and then they'll have the obligatory round of golf and dinner at the club. They'll be gone for the whole day.'

I nodded and smiled.

'I love you,' he said, his grey eyes serious.

'Right back at ya,' I said and smiled.


Somehow I struggled through the next day. The more I though about it, the more uneasy I was at the prospect of dinner with Andrew. Why were we suddenly going to a posh restaurant anyway? Maybe it wasn't all about the scene at the dinner party in our house? Did he have bad news? Maybe Andrew and Linda were running away together and he wanted to break the news to me? I knew it was unlikely, but stranger things had happened in my life in recent years.

What could it be? Maybe he was being offered a partnership with Tim. I knew that the other partner, Bob Richards, had retired years ago and that Tim had kept the name on a kind of product-recognition basis. But then that wouldn't really make sense either, as Tim was hoping to come under the franchise umbrella of Reval. Then I had an appalling thought

– maybe Andrew was in line for some huge job, but it would mean him moving away.

My heart started to thump and my computer screen went all blurry. Jesus! What would that mean for us? But then I smiled and my breathing slowed down as I realised that that mad idea was a complete non-starter. There was no way on God's earth that Andrew Kenny would move away from Katie. He was a hands-on dad and I was really proud of him for that. He had already returned from London on her account, hadn't he? So whatever was about to unfold would happen right here in good old Limerick. I decided to ring Ruth before I left the office.

'Hi, Ruth! It's me.'

'Hi, Ellen. Hang on a tick until I put this baby down – Jesus, he weighs a ton! Now, that's better. How's Spencer?'

I laughed. 'Slut!'

'Always, probably to my dying day. So, what's the story?'

'Nothing much. Except everybody's getting married and Andrew and stuff.'

'Oh, Ellen, can't you do better than that? Andrew and *stuff*? What stuff? What's going on?'

I sighed. 'There's something going on with Andrew and he won't tell me what it is and and we're having this dinner tonight at Tosca's and I'm all nervous and confused and stuff—' My voice trailed away and baby Paddy started roaring down the phone. I felt like joining him.

'So, what's the problem? Everything will be fine,' Ruth said.

'How do you know everything will be fine?'

'Because Andrew Kenny loves you, that's how. Look, ring me tomorrow. I'd better see to Paddy before he busts a blood vessel. Oh, Ellen, who's getting married?'

'Angela Maunsell is—'

'I don't believe you.'

'I swear.'

'Oh my God! Look, I'd better go here. Ring me tomorrow, Ellen. Bye.'

Tosca's was crowded even though it was a Tuesday night, but Andrew had managed to get a great little table in the far corner of the elegant restaurant. I'd made a huge effort with my appearance and wore an aubergine-coloured fitted dress that had maxed out my credit card for what seemed like an eternity. It was Andrew's favourite and I could feel his eyes on me as we sat down. I smiled at him and began to read the menu.

'You look . . . you look stunning tonight,' he said, still not taking his eyes off me. I was beginning to feel a growing confidence about the night.

'You don't look too bad yourself,' I said. This was a huge understatement. Andrew always looked terrific – one of those people who wakes up in the morning looking as if he spent the night in a hair salon. I, on the other hand, wake up looking like someone who spent the night in a storm.

The waiter came to take our order and I smiled at Andrew as he poured wine.

'I love this place,' I said.

'Yeah, it's really nice.' He looked at me intently, his eyes dark in the candlelight. He reached out and covered my hand with his.

'You look amazing.'

'Candlelight, Andrew. It hides a multitude.'

I was secretly delighted though that he thought I looked amazing.

'Ellen, I have something . . . I need to talk to you . . . I have two questions—' He stopped talking as the waiter came with our food. Both of us had decided to skip starters and just have a main course. The plates of food looked like works of art.

'Incredible! These dinners could win the Turner Prize,' I said.

Andrew laughed. 'Katie could win the Turner Prize for her surreal portraits of Buzz Lightyear.'

Both of us laughed then and began to eat our food. I wondered what the two questions were. The waiter poured more wine and we ordered chocolate fudge cake and fresh cream for dessert. Soft French music played discreetly in the background. The wine was making me feel relaxed and happy. And it was making Andrew look dead sexy. I'd give him a good seeing to when we got home. That's if we didn't have to babysit Spencer.

'Two questions, Ellen. If the answer to the first question is yes, then the second question is almost irrelevant.'

He smiled across at me.

'I hope they're easy questions,' I said, trying to keep the conversation light-hearted.

He smiled and put his hand into his pocket and drew out a small, black velvet box. My heart somersaulted. I reached for the wine and hurriedly poured myself a glass. I took a huge gulp.

He opened the box, then took my hand and slipped the most beautiful delicate ring on my finger. It had just one tiny, exquisite stone, a perfectly formed diamond – totally understated and so like Andrew. Tears filled my eyes and I prayed that my mascara wouldn't run down my face and make me look like Courtney Love.

He held my hand tightly after he had put the ring on my finger and locked eyes with me.

'Ellen Grace, love of my life, will you marry me?'

A tear rolled down my face and he reached over and wiped it away with his thumb.

'Yes,' I said, choking back the tears. He grinned like a schoolboy, and leaned over and kissed me on the mouth.

'And will you move to Austin, Texas, with me and live happily ever after?'

I laughed. 'Stop messing, Andrew.'

'I'm serious. I've never been more serious in my whole life,' he said, his face giving credence to what he was saying.

My heart started to pound so loudly that I thought the people at the next table could hear it. My head was beginning to hurt and I clung to the fading hope that this was all a big joke.

'Austin, Texas?'

Andrew nodded. 'Linda and Jack are moving there for his work. There was talk of this for a while but I didn't want to say anything until it was definite. And until I'd sorted out work for us as well. That's where Spencer came into his own.'

'Spencer?'

'He says Reval in Austin are very enthusiastic about offering both of us employment.'

'Who, you and Spencer?'

He laughed softly. 'You and me, Ellen. It'll be great. A new start with a great company, and we'll be able to come home three or four times a year, and we'll be near Katie – that's so important to me, to see Katie growing up—'

I put both my hands in the air to stop him talking. 'Andrew, this is all a little sudden, isn't it? I mean, Austin, Texas, is . . . like . . . thousands of miles away. I don't know. It's just all so sudden. And anyway, Linda's husband is probably just on contract or something, and they'll be coming back home in a year, and we'll be stuck in Texas—'

Andrew lowered his head and examined his hands.

'Don't you think I've looked at all the possibilities? It's permanent. Trust me on that. Where *is* this going, Ellen?'

'You tell me, Andrew,' I said and tears began to sneak down my face. I wiped them away with a table napkin.

'Two questions, Ellen. If the answer to the first is yes, then what's there to be upset about? I really think it would be great for us.'

I said nothing and fiddled with the napkin.

'I love you,' he said, then, and reached for my hand again. 'I want us to be together. I don't care if we're in India or Japan or Liscannor as long as we're together and I can see Katie and be a part of her life. I'm her daddy, Ellen. She needs me.'

'I need you,' I said.

'So, does that mean you'll go?'

'I need more time—'

'More time? I asked you to marry me last May in Spain. Every time I raise the subject of marriage, you run a mile. It makes me think sometimes that you don't really love me at all.'

'That's not true. I love you, Andrew. You know it.'

'Do I, Ellen? Do I know that you love me? That you really, really love me? You've just indicated that you don't want to share your life with me, so how can I believe you love me?'

'That's not true. You're twisting everything. I—'

'Will you marry me and move to Austin, so that I can be with my daughter?'

'It's not as simple as that. There's a lot more to consider—'

'Consider this, Ellen. Will you marry me and move to Austin, Texas, so that I can be a father to my little girl and a husband to the woman I love?'

He was staring at me but I dropped my eyes and played with the chocolate cake in front of me. My mind was in turmoil. I was almost sure about the marriage bit – as sure as I could be anyway – but moving to America was another story altogether. I wished with all my heart that none of this was happening.

'Your silence speaks volumes, Ellen.'

I looked at him, at his handsome chiselled features in the dancing candlelight. Tears filled my eyes again and I bowed my head as I spoke. 'Can't I have more time, Andrew? Don't I at least deserve that?'

He laughed and shook his head. 'You've had all the time in the world. There is no time left, Ellen. We love each other, we go. It's not rocket science, just simple logic. I need an answer.'

'Tonight?'

'Now.'

'Oh, Andrew, don't.'

'Don't what? Don't make you face decisions? Don't make you face commitment? That's your problem, Ellen. You can't commit to anything on a long-term basis. You don't love me, not really.'

He picked up his dessert fork and then threw it on the table.

'I'm going to Austin, Ellen, with or without you. I'm going to Austin to live and work and raise my girl, and it will be sooner rather than later, so there is no time to kick this to touch or analyse it. Now, are you coming with me? Can you just answer that simple question?'

'I . . . there's so much to think about – it's a big decision.'

'They have lots of planes in America. You're not going to prison, just to another country.'

'It feels like going to prison, you know – no friends or family—'

My voice trailed off as I saw the hurt expression pass over his face. His eyes seemed to harden then and I kicked myself for my big mouth.

'I'm sorry, Andrew. I didn't mean the marriage would be like prison. I meant—'

He waved at the hovering waiter, to get the bill.

'If you loved me, you'd stay, Andrew. You'd think of a way for us to stay – Katie too.'

'If you loved me, you'd go, Ellen. You'd be happy to go. Welcome to the real world – Katie's going and that means I am too. I think you should stay here. Know why? You don't love me. You probably never really did. Not fully anyway, and certainly not like I loved you.'

'Loved?'

Andrew laughed quietly. 'Remember this, Ellen. You called the shots here tonight, not me.'

'You're trying to rush me into something that—'

'Something like marriage?'

'No, like moving thousands of miles away.'

'So, you'd marry me if we were staying in Limerick but not if I have to move away? Funny kind of love, Ellen, don't you agree?'

'You're twisting things again.'

'Not at all. Let's get out of here. There's nothing left to say.'

He got up and paid the bill and went for our coats.

I sat there, paralysed, knowing in my heart that I had lost something. Or, worse still, that I had thrown something away. And I knew for certain now that a ride tonight would be out of the question.

# 14

Andrew didn't sleep in our bed that night. He was gone to work by the time I got up the next morning. Spencer came into work with me, his body nearly doubled in the back seat of the car. I answered his small talk in monosyllables. I parked in the office car park and locked the car, forgetting about poor Spencer altogether. He banged on the car window to get my attention, and I opened the door for him.

'Want to talk about it, Ellen?' he asked as we headed into the office.

I shook my head. 'Thanks anyway, Spencer,' I said and pushed open the door. He patted me on the shoulder and the gesture almost made me cry.

Andrew was chatting to Molly as we came in, and he nodded at both of us and continued talking. I ran to the haven of my desk but tears were beginning to flood down my face. Ryan and Andrea looked at me enquiringly and I made for the toilet.

I threw up. Long and hard – and noisily judging by the looks I got from my colleagues when I re-appeared in the office.

'Coffee, Ellen?' Ryan asked with his customary smirk.

'Shut up, Ryan,' said Andrea. 'You OK, Ellen? Can I get you some water?'

'I'm fine, thanks, Andrea,' I said and pretended to work on the mound of files on my desk.

I rang Ruth as soon as Andrea and Ryan had left the office.

'Hi, Ruth.'

'Hi, Ellen. Perfect timing. Paddy's just gone down for his nap and I'm here with my decaf watching Jerry Springer. Jesus! That guy's so bad, he's good. Never realised it until now.'

'You never saw it until now, Ruth. He's an old favourite of mine – kind of addictive, isn't it?'

'You said it. So, how did dinner at Tosca's go? Romantic, I bet.'

'Oh, Ruth.' I started crying into the phone.

'What is it, Ellen? Don't tell me. Another dead body? Or did you deliver another baby?'

'Oh, Ruth, my life is over . . . what will I do?'

'Tell me what's wrong for a start. What happened at the dinner?'

'Andrew's leaving.'

'I don't believe you.'

'It's true.'

'Why? Where? Where is he going?'

'Austin, Texas – he has a job and all—'

'You poor thing. Look, where are you now?'

'Work but let me tell you what happened—'

'Andrew Kenny – I never thought he'd . . . I'm coming over. Emerson's here to look after Paddy. I'll meet you in Café au Lait in, say, half an hour?'

I told Ruth the whole story over hot chocolate and blueberry muffins. It took me almost twenty minutes to give her a blow-by-blow account of exactly what had been said. When I'd finished, she said nothing, just looked at me.

'So,' I said, when I could bear the silence no longer. 'What do you think?'

Ruth shrugged. 'Does it matter what I think?'

'Of course it does – you're one of my best friends. I desperately need your advice on this one. This is a biggie.'

Ruth shook her head. 'I won't even start.'

'What do mean?' I asked.

'On the phone, you led me to believe that Andrew had just decided to leave. Now it turns out to be a whole different ball game.'

'You didn't give me time to finish—'

'I know, but isn't it interesting how you began – *Andrew is leaving*. Andrew is leaving for a very good reason – the most important reason in the whole world. And do you know something, Ellen? I've nothing but respect and admiration for the man.'

I started to cry. 'Don't you think I know that?' I said as the tears gathered force. I wiped my eyes with the sleeve of my cream jacket. Ruth rustled in her handbag and passed me a baby wipe.

'Mascara – there on your face,' she said and poured more tea.

I wiped my eyes but tears filled up again instantly.

'Why is going such an issue, Ellen? Can you just answer that?' she asked as she spooned sugar into her tea. 'I'd follow Emerson into the bloody Amazon if I had to, so what's the problem?'

I started really crying now, and other customers were beginning to stare at us.

'I . . . love him . . . it's just . . . I don't know, Ruthie . . . what am I going to do?' I said between sobs.

Ruth reached over and held my hand. 'Do you really love him, Ellen?'

'He is . . . I do . . . I really do—'

Ruth shook her head and tightened her grasp on my hand. 'Then, if you really love him, if you're absolutely sure of it, don't shoot yourself in the foot – just go with him.'

I nodded miserably. 'I love Katie too. I can't imagine life without them – I just can't.'

'You can be with them if you want, Ellen. The ball is completely in your court. And all this talk about more time – I think Andrew is dead right about that. It's simple. If you love him, you'll go.'

She patted my hand as she spoke. I smiled at her through my tears, glad I had her as a friend. Then I noticed something odd.

'Ruth, your T-shirt. Did you spill something on it? Tea maybe?' She had two round, wet patches, exactly where her nipples were.

'Fuck it anyway! Bloody leaking again. Welcome to Joyce's Dairy – fresh milk on tap.'

Both of us giggled.

'I'm trying to wean Paddy,' she said as she folded her arms across her damp chest. 'There's another week in it, and by God we'll paint the town red then, Ellen.'

'Definitely, and thanks for everything, Ruth,' I said as we gathered our things to leave.

'For nothing. Hey, you *are* paying the bill – you know that,' she said and we both laughed again.

India rang as soon as I got in from work that night.

'Hi, Ellen. Ruth rang me.'

'Thought she would,' I said as I kicked off my high heels and sat on the couch in the living room. Joey appeared from behind an armchair and pounced onto my lap, rubbing his stripy body against me. It felt comforting and familiar.

'Can you talk? I mean, is—'

'Is Andrew here? No. He's driving Spencer Alexander to the airport.'

'Good, because guess where I am! Outside your door with takeaway Chinese from Fortune City.'

'Fortune City? I'm coming out to get you, girl,' I said and ran to the front door. India was already out of her car.

'What do you want to carry? Chinese food or babies?' asked India as she reached into the car and took out baby Alyssa in her car seat. She was asleep and had one tiny hand tucked under her chin. Her hair was dark, like India's, and she had the most gorgeous little rosebud mouth. I burst out crying as I took the handle of the carry seat.

'Oh, Ellen, nothing is ever as bad as it seems,' said India, her hands full of Chinese takeaway cartons. 'Come on. Let's eat, and we can have a bloody good cry too if we feel like it,' she continued as she walked up the path towards the house.

We put the food out on the countertop and sat on stools in the kitchen. Baby Alyssa slept obligingly in her seat, her beautiful face resting on her chubby fist. 'She's absolutely divine and I want her,' I said as I piled plates with chicken fried rice and chow mein.

'Not so divine at three o'clock in the morning,' said India, tucking into her food.

I hadn't eaten all day but the food tasted like plastic in my mouth. My appetite was gone again.

'Not hungry?' asked India as she spooned more fried rice onto her already overloaded plate, 'Breast-feeding certainly gives you an appetite like . . . well, like you really, Ellen . . . under normal circumstances.' We both laughed at this.

'Did Tim tell you anything? He must have known what Andrew was planning.'

'No. He knew I'd tell you, I'd say. Ruth filled me in.'

'Did she give you the whole story?'

'More or less. I don't know what to say, what advice to give you. Ruth says it's all quite simple – you love him, you go – but . . . I know you, Ellen, and life is never simple. Whatever you do, you're going to lose something.'

Tears coursed down my face as India spoke.

'I feel like such a selfish bitch, India. You've no idea,' I said, sobbing.

'I understand. And at least you're honest about it all, and that's so important. Because no matter what decision you make, if you're absolutely honest with yourself, then it'll be the right decision for you.' She reached over and took my hand.

I grabbed a tissue from the countertop and wiped my eyes.

India looked at me and laughed.

'I know,' I said. 'The Courtney Love look.'

India laughed again and shook her head. 'Worse than that – the Ozzy Osbourne look.'

I smiled. 'I don't think I can go, Ind.'

India nodded. 'Then that's OK, as long as you're sure.'

'But that's the problem. One minute, I'm certain that I can't live without Andrew and Katie. And the next minute, I try to picture myself showing houses to Texans, and I know in my heart that it'll never happen. I know, Ind. I just know it's not me.'

The baby stirred and began to cry. India went and picked her up. Alyssa was wearing the tiniest denim dress I'd ever seen, with pink daisies embroidered on it. She wore matching pink tights and the most exquisite suede booties.

'Oh my God! Her shoes – I love them,' I said.

'Can I sit on the couch to feed her? It's just I need support for my back.'

'No problem. Do you want something to drink? Go into the living room and I'll bring you some juice,' I said and rooted in the fridge for orange juice.

I poured orange juice for both of us and joined

India on the couch. The baby was snuggled into her mother's breast and I could hear gulping noises.

'They work anyway,' I said, nodding at India's chest. India laughed. 'Definitely.'

'Andrew hasn't talked to me since the argument.'

'What do you mean? Is he ignoring you?'

'No, but he's avoiding me. And when he has to talk to me, he's polite but just so removed. Civil but strange. It hurts.'

'He hurts, I'd say, Ellen. It's just his way of coping.'

'I wish I could change everything. Make it the way it was six months ago. This is all just too hard.' I stroked Alyssa's dangling pink leg.

'Can I ask you a question?' India said. 'Tony Jordan?'

'What about him?'

'I heard you and Ruth met him the other day, and maybe there's still something there for you.'

'No way!'

'Don't fly off the handle – I'm only asking.'

'No way, India. Absolutely no way.' I looked directly at her.

She shrugged. 'OK.'

I took a drink of my juice.

'So, tell me all about poor old Spencer. How did he cope with all the turmoil of the last few days?' India asked.

I laughed. 'I've no idea. What did you make of him?'

India switched the baby over to her other breast. 'Lovely person, actually. The more I saw of him, the more I liked him. He's very witty. He's coming back for a year – did you hear that?'

'No.'

'Tim told me this morning. He's going to set up the Reval franchise in all the major Irish cities.'

'Good luck to him. I heard he has a colourful history – Molly had the low-down as usual and Ryan tried to tell me, but I wouldn't give him the satisfaction of listening.'

India laughed. 'He's old money, I know that. That's if old money exists in America. And Tim says he's brilliant at his job, but that's as much as I know. Except he's one good-looking man.'

'Jesus! Between you and Ruth, Spencer would want to be careful. What is it – post-pregnancy hormones or something?'

'No. Just pure unadulterated lust.'

'India Burke, that's so unlike you.'

India shrugged. 'What would Ruth call him? Sex on legs? I must say for once I totally agree with her. By the way, did she do anything else about her birth mother? I didn't want to ask her on the phone.'

I shook my head. Alyssa stopped feeding and burped.

'Ruth's having a think about it. It's the timing more than anything for her. I mean, she just had her first baby and she gets this phone call about her mother. It's a tough one.'

'It'll work out, Ell. All of it. Your stuff too,' said India, handing me a well-fed Alyssa, who looked drunk after her snack.

Andrew came home late. India had just left and I was tidying up the kitchen when I heard the key turn in the door. My heart did a little flutter when he came in. He stopped, as if surprised to see me.

'Hi,' I said. 'There's some wine open. Do you want a glass?' I started to pour two glasses before he answered. 'Did Spencer make his flight? I presume he did because he isn't with you.' I had my back to him as I spoke but I could feel his eyes boring into me. The radio was playing Van Morrison's 'Brown-Eyed Girl', and when I handed Andrew the wine glass, he turned up the radio without taking his eyes from mine. I felt a huge lump form in my throat and I took a gulp of the ice-cold wine to try and clear it.

Andrew didn't speak. He just stood there, sipping his wine. When the song finished, he put down his glass, took off his jacket and loosened his tie. He smiled at me – a beautiful, sexy Andrew special. Christ! Why was my life so fucked up?

I smiled back at him and took two steps closer. He had a tiny piece of fluff in his hair and I reached out my hand before I could stop myself, and stroked the fluff away. He closed his eyes and I let my hand trail down his face, tracing with my fingers his eyebrows, his eyes and nose, then his lovely full mouth. He started to moan. I caught his face and began to kiss him hard on the mouth.

'No,' he said as he stepped away from me, hands in the air like he was being arrested. 'I can't do this, Ellen. I can't.'

I walked to him and put my head on his chest. He still held his hands in the air like a prisoner.

'No, Ellen, no way. I don't want casual, meaning-less sex – not with you. I wanted other things with you. Goodnight.' He picked up his jacket and left the room. I stood there in the kitchen, tears streaming down my face. The only thing I seemed to be good at lately was crying.

# 15

It all happened quickly after that. It was as if the kiss speeded up the whole process and Andrew just wanted to be gone. He came home late on Thursday night and went straight upstairs. I could hear him moving about in our bedroom and I wondered what he was doing as he hadn't slept there since Monday. I climbed the stairs with Joey in my arms and stood in the doorway watching him.

'Hi,' he said without looking up. He had a large suitcase open on the bed and was filling it with his clothes.

'Are you . . . moving . . . moving in with friends? Because if you are, then I'll go . . . because it's your house—'

He stopped piling shirts into the suitcase. 'I'm flying out to Austin tomorrow,' he said, and for the first time made eye contact with me.

'Oh.' I swallowed hard so that I wouldn't start to cry.

He shrugged and went back to his packing. 'You can decide what you want to do with the house. If you want to stay here, that's fine. We can sort out something with the mortgage.'

'I couldn't stay here – you know that.'

'Suit yourself. Tim said he'll look after everything anyway. If you don't want the house, he'll put it on the market for me.'

'You shouldn't sell it,' I said and let Joey down from my arms.

Andrew looked at me then. 'Why not, Ellen?'

'You might need it again, when you come back. You could rent it until then.'

He stood up straight, with two pairs of boxer shorts in his hand. 'I won't be coming back,' he said. 'I'm cleaning out my closet now, Ellen, in the physical and emotional sense.' He threw the shorts into the suitcase and walked to the locker at his side of the bed. I stood there for another while, watching him pack books and clothes and personal belongings. It was as if, with every item that went into the case, he was extricating himself from our life together.

'What time are you leaving?' I asked in a small voice.

'Does it matter?' he replied and fell silent.

I walked away and heard him answer my question as I went downstairs. 'Tomorrow evening at six.'

I went to work the following day with my heart so heavy it felt like somebody had tied concrete blocks to it during the night. I tried to smile at people, but my sadness made me feel as if I was underwater and I couldn't understand the simplest conversation, let alone engage in it. I rang our home number a few times but hung up before Andrew answered. At lunchtime, I couldn't resist any longer so I rang his mobile.

'Ellen.'

'Hi.'

'What's up?'

'Nothing . . . I—' I fell silent and he let the silence continue. 'I just . . . wanted to say . . . I wanted to say goodbye.'

'Goodbye, Ellen.'

'Goodbye,' I said and hung up, dropping the phone on my desk. Tears streamed down my face and I was glad that everybody had decided to go out for the usual Friday office lunch. Instead of eating, I bawled my eyes out. When the others returned to the office, I had reapplied my make-up to cover my corpse-like face, but I felt empty and tired.

I showed some houses for the next couple of hours and was sure that the clients couldn't wait to get away from me before I slit my wrists in front of them or threw myself from the roof garden of one of the penthouse apartments. Being sad was a full-time job.

I got back to the office around four o'clock. When I walked into reception, I almost fainted when I saw him. He had his back to me, but there was no mistaking those broad shoulders or the way his hair curled slightly as it met his neck. He was talking to Tim, and the conversation stopped as he turned around to face me. He smiled.

'Ellen.'

I looked at this gorgeous man with his incredibly sexy smile. It was as if somebody had pressed the pause button on my life and everything was frozen. I couldn't move and I tried to speak but no words would come. Then I dropped my handbag on the floor, and this seemed to kick-start the world. I glanced at Molly, who was watching us with fascination.

'I'm just on my way to the airport, so I dropped in to say goodbye,' he said.

'Oh.'

Tim gave a polite little cough. 'Andrew, I'll speak to you on Monday or Tuesday. How's that, old chap?' he said and shook Andrew's hand vigorously. 'Best of luck in your new home.'

Andrew smiled and said more goodbyes as he headed for the door. I followed him. A taxi was waiting by the kerb.

'So, this it,' he said.

I nodded and looked into his face. He was drawn and tired and, though I didn't want to see it, I knew there were tears in his eyes. And I knew it was all my fault. He was standing so close to me, I could smell his aftershave – a scent as familiar to me as my own perfume.

'Oh,' I said. Jesus! Was that all I could manage?

'Goodbye, Ellen,' he said then and quickly kissed me on the cheek before hurrying into the waiting taxi. I stood there on the footpath, watching Andrew disappear out of my life forever. Tears started to flood down my face, and my heart had acquired another couple of concrete blocks.

I would never survive this – it hurt too much. Even the alternative couldn't be as bad as this. The last thought seemed to galvanise me. What the fuck was I doing, standing here crying when I could be with Andrew if I really wanted to?

Energy raced through my body and I ran back into the office to grab my handbag from the floor. Molly gave me a startled look but I just took the bag and ran back out. I raced to my car and jumped in. As I made my way through slow Friday traffic towards the airport, I felt almost happy again.

I reached the airport with plenty of time to spare, and I parked my car and walked towards Departures. Andrew's face flashed before me, followed by a parade of faces that reminded me of a *This is Your Life* special. There they all were – Ruth and India, Will and Alison. Mam and Dad. Joey. Kieran and all the babies. Tony.

I could feel tears streaming down my face again. As I reached the glass doors of the building, I turned on my heel and sprinted back to my car. I got in and bawled my eyes out, searching my bag for tissues. I was such a fool, coming out here and then running away again. It was typical bloody Ellen. I blew my nose and then bawled all over again. Indecisive, selfish, impossible to please, afraid to be with some-body, afraid to be alone. There was nothing about myself I liked except my taste in shoes. If my life was hard, it was my own bloody fault.

I started the car once I'd composed myself. I'd made my decision. Now I would have to live with the consequences. My life with Andrew Kenny was over, and I'd just have to get on with it. I watched the air-port disappear in the rear-view mirror as I swallowed another gush of tears, and wondered how the hell I was going to live with the hurt. More than that, how was I going to live with the hurt I'd caused Andrew?

# 16

The weeks following Andrew's departure passed in a blurry flash of tears, loneliness and pot noodles for one. The house just wasn't the same. In every silent room, there was a reminder of our life together. His beer remained untouched in the fridge. Some of his clothes still hung in the wardrobe. At the start, I used to take them out and smell them. But after a while, the Andrew smell was well gone, replaced by the musty smell of unworn clothes.

That first weekend without Andrew was the hardest. I took all the phones off the hook so that I could cry to my heart's content. I sat on the couch looking at the phone, tears streaming down my face, and then I thought that maybe he might ring from America and he wouldn't be able to get through, so I ran around putting all the receivers back on the hook. Then I sat on the couch, wrapped in a duvet, watching the phone for another couple of hours. Nothing happened.

I made cocoa and came back and resumed my position in front of the phone. It rang suddenly and I spilt hot cocoa on my legs in my rush to answer. I glanced at the caller display. It was my mother and

I couldn't face talking to her. I let the phone ring out and began to doze off on the couch, Joey curled up at my feet. I dreamed about phones, which wasn't surprising, and Daniel Day Lewis, which was. I don't know what put it into my head – maybe it was the toned body of Daniel – but I awoke from my dream knowing what I should do. I should ring Tony Jordan. Simple as that.

I scrambled for my mobile phone before I could change my mind and looked up his name in my phone book. And there was his number in Cratloe. My heart did a little samba in my chest as I punched in the numbers. Just as it started to ring, I disconnected and threw the phone onto the couch as if it was a bomb about to explode. Joey looked at me calmly, though I suppose a cat couldn't really tell if you'd become unhinged. Jesus! What was I turning into at all?

Then my mobile rang from behind the cushion and I picked it up, thinking that Andrew had finally got in touch.

I pressed the answer button without glancing at the screen to see who it was.

'Ellen, is that you? Did you—'

Tony. He obviously had caller display as well. I held the phone away from me and switched it off. Jesus! Why did I ring Tony at all? What *was* I thinking of? And really, if I was to ring anyone, it should have been bloody Daniel Day Lewis. That definitely was my worst night.

My family and friends were terrific during those first weeks, but part of me wanted all of them to stop fussing and just leave me bloody well alone to lick my wounds by myself. My mother brought over food which I unceremoniously dumped once she'd left. Alison phoned all the time, trying to persuade me to come up and stay with her in Dublin, with promises of shopping trips. But I was in a place where even retail therapy couldn't help me.

India and Ruth minded me like they were job-sharing the task, but even those two couldn't make me come back to the land of the living. Angela Maunsell and her new fiancé, Ralph, called with wine and flowers and chocolate. Ralph was this sprightly seventy-year-old man, with the body and energy of someone much younger. He had a tan to die for and could do a hundred press-ups without sweating. This last piece of information really impressed me, and he even demonstrated in my living room to cheer me up.

It was Angela who sorted out my accommodation problem. I was anxious to move out of Andrew's house and I felt in my heart that once I had left all the memories behind, I could make a fresh start in a new place of my own. I could begin to live the life that I seemed destined for – lots of noodles, no husband, no children and no sex. Angela found me an apartment right next door to her. It was where I had lived before I moved in with Andrew, but my apartment then was on the other side of Angela's. So it felt now like my life was going backwards, with everything reversed to boot.

I moved out of Andrew's house four weeks and one day after he left. It was a beautiful autumnal

Saturday morning, with blue skies and multicoloured foliage. Tim Gladstone had arrived earlier with a large van, and we filled it up with my meager possessions. Most of the furniture was Andrew's, and anyway, my apartment came fully furnished, so I didn't need or want his stuff.

I took one last walk around the house while Tim drove my things to the apartment. The rooms looked big and empty and sad, and I walked from one to the other with Joey in my arms. The familiar tears came then, hot and sudden and plentiful, and I stood at the French doors to the garden, bawling for Ireland.

'Ellen,' a voice said from behind me.

I turned around to see Ruth and India standing there, with a baby each, and they both came over and each put an arm around me. We stood in a silent circle for a minute. The only sounds were me sniffling, the babies gurgling, and Joey squealing to be put down. I dropped him on the floor before he could take somebody's eye out.

'Come on. I brought takeaway cappuccinos and pecan plaits from Café au Lait,' said Ruth. 'Hold Paddy, and I'll get them from the car.' And the hair-pulling Paddy was thrust into my arms.

'Thanks for coming, Ind. Tim's been great – moving all my stuff. It's—' I said, my voice trailing off.

'It's hard – that's what it is.'

Paddy made a grab for my hair again. 'I've heard nothing. Has Tim been talking to Andrew?' I didn't want to ask baldly but I couldn't resist the temptation of just one tiny morsel of information about Andrew's new life.

India shrugged and jiggled Alyssa on her hip. 'Just the usual. He's settled in. He likes the work. Katie started kindergarten and loves it.'

I bit my nail and Paddy made a grab for that too. 'Did he . . . did he, you know . . . ask about me?'

'Oh, Ellen, don't do that to yourself. He's not going to ask Tim about you. He's an Irishman. He's not going to ask anybody about you.'

I smiled in spite of myself and Ruth caught me smiling as she came into the kitchen.

'A smile, Ellen Grace. I forgot you could do that.' She put the coffee and pastries on the countertop and sat on one of the high stools.

'Glad rags tonight, girl,' she said to me and took a large bite of pecan plait.

'For what? My first night in the new apartment with Joey?'

'Nope. My first night on the town since I became pregnant, which, incidentally, seems like a hundred years ago,' said Ruth.

'Paddy's weaned?' I asked, holding Paddy away from the steaming cups of coffee.

'You got it in one, sister. We're going out if I have to drag you kicking and screaming. What about you, India? Are you on?'

'Spencer Alexander arrived back in Limerick last night so I'd say we'll be having dinner with him.'

I'd temporarily forgotten all about Spencer's imminent return, although I'd heard nothing but talk about it in the office all week. He was going to be on the interview panel for the big reshuffle at Gladstone and Richards. Andrew's old job as Area Manager had to be filled. But I was interested in Spencer for one reason and one reason only – he might have heard from Andrew. He might even have met him.

'Bring him along after dinner,' I said. India and Ruth looked at me with big, round, surprised eyes.

'You mean you'll go without a fight?' asked Ruth, reaching for a wriggling Paddy.

I passed the baby over to her and smiled in response.

'I'm definitely coming so,' said India. 'But it may be late and I probably won't be able to stay long. This lady never sleeps for more than an hour at a time.' She stroked her daughter's downy head.

'Is Spencer staying with you?' I asked India.

'No, he'd get no sleep in my house. He's booked into the Clarion for a few weeks. Apparently he's looking to buy one of the penthouse apartments you showed him, Ellen.'

I remembered that day and it seemed like a lifetime ago. That was way back when I had a life.

'We'll go to the River Club. I haven't been there in yonks,' said Ruth. 'Jesus! I can't wait to have a few drinks. It'll be like old times – just us girls living it up.'

I nodded but I knew in my heart it would never be like old times. Ruth and India had men and babies and homes. I, on the other hand, was going backwards, losing men and children in the process.

I settled into my new apartment in no time, which

wasn't surprising, seeing as how I'd lived there before and knew where everything was except now it was all in reverse. I kept turning the wrong way to the bathroom, and opening the wrong doors. It was disconcerting but kind of funny as well. Joey wasn't much better at the reverse thing and cried to go out at the wrong window.

After I'd unpacked my belongings, I rang out for pizza – I was getting tired of noodles by now. As I ate my food, watching Jerry Springer, it felt like I'd come full circle. Angela Maunsell and Ralph called in just as I was about to hit the shower for my night out with Ruth.

'Hi, love. We're just on the way back from the gym. Did you settle in all right?' asked Angela as she swept into the living room, with Ralph in tow. They were both dressed in co-ordinating tracksuits, complete with his and hers baseball caps. Ralph looked like a man who could climb Mount Everest, jogging and drinking ten pints of Guinness at the same time, and Angela wasn't far behind in the fitness stakes.

'Hi, Angela. Hi, Ralph. Ang, you look terrific. Whatever happened to your blood-pressure problem?' I asked.

The previous year, Angela had ended up in hospital – interrupting my very first sexual encounter with Tony Jordan in the process.

'All nonsense, Ellen. Nothing a good man couldn't sort out,' she said and winked at Ralph. He put his arm around her shoulder and kissed her cheek. I wanted to throw up, but smiled instead.

'Coffee?' I suggested.

'No coffee – bad for the metabolism. We're going next door to make smoothies and then we're off to the salsa night in the Glentworth. Would you like to come, love? Ralph's nephew will be there and I've told him all about you already. A lovely boy – isn't he, Ralphie?'

'A lovely boy,' agreed Ralph.

'I'm sure he is,' I said. 'But I'm going out tonight with Ruth and India.' Angela Maunsell fancied herself as a matchmaker and I knew she'd have a queue of what she considered to be suitable boyfriends lined up for me, now that Andrew was gone.

Angela patted my arm. 'Good girl. That's exactly what you need – a good night out. You can put it all behind you from now on. This is a new start, love – a whole new start,' she said as she and Ralph left.

'Goodbye, Angela. Goodbye, Ralph,' I said, looking at the closing front door of my apartment. This didn't feel like a new start at all. Instead it felt like I'd been here before. Many times. It felt like Groundhog Day.

# 17

I had arranged to meet Ruth in the River Club at eight o'clock. I wore the outfit that I'd last donned on the fateful night when Andrew had proposed to me. I also wore black suede stilettos in which I could barely walk, but which gave me loads of confidence. They were worth the pain, or so I thought at the beginning of the evening.

I stood outside the heavily embossed doors of the River Club at exactly eight o'clock, regretting the fact that I'd arranged to meet Ruth here rather than at my place. I felt as if I was wearing my whole sad life like a sign on my back. As soon as I walked into the club, conversation would stop and everybody would read all about me. I was just about to turn around and go home when somebody grabbed me from behind. I screamed.

'Take it easy, you eejit. It's only me,' said Ruth.

I turned around and there she was, decked out like her old unpregnant self, except her chest looked even better endowed.

'Jesus, Ruth! Some cleavage! Even Jordan would be envious of that,' I said. She looked fantastic, in a skintight, low-cut camel-coloured top and brown suede skirt with fringing at the hem.

'Jordan had a few dates with a surgeon for hers, love. Mine is all my own work, with a small bit of help from Paddy! You look lovely, Ellen – that colour really suits you, and I love the black pashmina.'

'I couldn't find my coat. It's probably still packed away somewhere. You look . . . unbelievable,' I said again, because she did.

Ruth opened the door of the River Club and nodded at me to follow her. 'Am I too slutty?' she asked as we made our way to an empty booth at the far side of the room. The club was quiet at this time of the evening, as if taking a breather before the Saturday-night revellers came in droves.

'You, slutty? No way,' I said in mock disbelief and we both laughed as we sat down and ordered drinks from the waiter. My shoes were killing me and I bent down and felt around my ankle. Blood. I rubbed it into my tights with my other foot.

We ordered beers, and the alcohol slowly started to numb my bleeding heel and my broken heart. I gulped back the bottle of Bud and waved the empty bottle at the waiter.

'You mean business, tonight, Ellen. I'm playing catch-up already,' said Ruth, taking a long swig from her bottle.

I laughed. 'Did you do anything else about your birth mother?' I'd meant to ask Ruth about this, but, with all the Andrew stuff, I'd totally forgotten.

Ruth shrugged and took another swig of beer. 'She wrote again to the Agency, asking to meet with me, but I don't know . . . I've still got really mixed feelings about it all. Part of me is dying with curiosity, you know, just even to see what she looks like, what colour eyes she has, do I look like her . . . but another part of me thinks my life is just fine the way it is.'

'I know. You might meet her and it'll all be grand or you might meet her and she could be a total lunatic that could invade your life.'

Ruth laughed. 'Yeah, something like that. Anyway, how are you?'

I looked at my nails and tears welled up in my eyes. 'OK. The new place helps a bit. At least I'm not expecting Andrew to walk in the door at any minute.'

'Guess who was asking about you?'

'I've no idea,' I said, hoping against all odds that it was Andrew, even though he was in Texas.

'Tony Jordan. I met that gorgeous hunk of glorious wonderful sex on legs in the local shop in Cratloe last week. I swear, Ellen, every woman in the shop stopped and stared at him – grannies and all!'

I laughed. 'I believe you. What did he say, anyway?'

'Oh, just that I looked fantastic and how was I and that if I ever got fed up of Emerson, that he was only a hop, skip and jump away, and he winked when he said jump—'

'Slut. No – slapper, Ruth Joyce, that's what you are,' I said, laughing hard.

Ruth looked straight at me. 'He asked about you.'

I shrugged.

'I mean he really asked about you – all interest and concern.'

'Did you tell him about . . . what happened?'

Ruth shook her head. 'Not exactly.'

'What does that mean?'

Ruth grinned. 'Well, I did happen to mention that you had moved back into your old apartment building.'

'Bitch.'

'So you don't want to know what he said so, I suppose?' Ruth said.

'No, I don't. Yes, I do. What did he say?'

'He didn't *say* much, but he certainly asked enough questions.'

'Like what?'

'Oh, just which apartment, how long ago, did ye sell the house on the Ennis road?'

'How does he know where Andrew and I lived?'

Ruth shrugged. 'He just did.'

'You shouldn't have said anything, Ruth.'

'Well, it could have been worse. I could have told him all the details. I must admit, I nearly did, though. It's very hard not to tell Tony Jordan something when you're looking into those chocolate-brown eyes. Jesus! I'd confess anything to him, true or not! I'd say he's great in bed – he oozes sex.'

'Slut!'

'So you're not going to expand on the subject for my entertainment?'

I reddened and Ruth laughed. 'He must have been good if you're getting embarrassed thinking about it.' Ruth called the waiter over.

'Two Slippery Nipples, please, and a bowl of

cashews,' she said and smiled sweetly at him. He looked about twelve and totally besotted by the charming Ruth.

'What in the name of God is a Slippery Nipple?' I asked as the waiter scurried off to get our order.

Ruth laughed. 'It's the most gorgeous drink in the world. Don't worry – you'll love it. By the way, Ell, are you applying for Andrew's job? Tim was telling me last week about the reshuffle.'

Our drinks arrived and I took my first sip of Slippery Nipple. It was delicious. 'Yes, but I don't know if I want it.'

'Ah, for fuck's sake, girl – cop on! You should go for it. You're the senior estate agent in the company. You'll definitely get it – no question about that.'

'Well, it's an open competition. I know that because I saw the ads in the newspapers weeks ago. And I don't know if I'm up to all that competing stuff. And anyway, do I really want the responsibility of Area Manager?'

'No, but you really want the beemer that goes with it.'

'You have a point there. The old Hyundai is on its last legs,' I said and we both laughed.

Just then, India arrived and made her way through the bar, which was fairly crowded by now.

'Hi, girls. You both look terrific,' said India as she plonked herself down on a vacant chair.

'You look pretty good yourself,' I said, and she did, in a simple tailored suit with a mandarin collar and flowing lines. 'That suit is so classy.'

India pretended to fall asleep.

'Tough day?' asked Ruth.

India nodded. 'Spencer Alexander arrived and Alyssa screamed through dinner and the fridge decided to defrost all by itself and . . . oh, I don't know . . . babies and breast-feeding and no sleep—'

'Poor India. Hey, where is Spencer anyway?' I asked.

'The loo. He was so anxious to leave our house, he didn't even ask to use the bathroom! And he seemed very keen to meet you two. Poor man – he doesn't know what he's in for, drinking with the Dynamic Duo.'

'Have a Slippery Nipple, India. It'll do you the world of good,' said Ruth, waving at her besotted waiter. He ignored all the other tables and was at Ruth's side before you could say 'cleavage'.

'I'll just have juice. I am still breast-feeding, you know,' said India. 'Here's Spencer now.'

We all looked at Spencer, picking his way through the crowd and searching the bar for us. India waved at him, and he smiled and made his way towards our booth. And, I swear, every woman in the place followed his progress. He was stunning-looking in a dark suit that made his shoulders look ten feet wide. He wore a simple dark T-shirt instead of a formal shirt and tie. His hair was a multicoloured palette of blonds through to brown, and his smile was a brilliant Daz white.

'Oh my God!' whispered Ruth. 'Oh my God, give me strength to resist temptation tonight.'

I gave her a kick, just as Spencer reached us, and we stood up in unison to greet him. He smiled his dazzling smile and kissed me first.

'Ellen, you look . . . amazing, you really do,' he said and kissed me lightly on the cheek. I was surprised at how my body reacted to this tiny chaste kiss. Jesus! I was worse than Ruth. I watched as he kissed Ruth's cheek.

'So, what are you having to drink?' he asked, eyeing our already half-empty glasses.

'Slippery Nipples,' I blurted out. He looked at me with cat-green eyes that crinkled at the corners with amusement.

'Slippery Nipples it is, then,' he said, nodding at a passing waiter. He sat down on a vacant tub chair between Ruth and myself, and I was conscious of his long, lean legs right next to mine. I could have sworn I felt heat from them, and I moved away a fraction. Ruth and Spencer began to talk, and India eyed me like Judge Judy, over the rim of her juice glass.

'What?' I muttered.

India sipped her juice and smiled at me, tilting her head sideways, as if she'd asked me a question and I'd refused to answer.

'What's up?' I repeated.

She shrugged and winked at me.

'Stop it,' I said, and glanced over at Spencer. He was still engrossed in conversation with Ruth.

'Why not?' whispered India. 'Not handsome enough?'

I laughed and took a handful of cashew nuts. 'No. Just stop it – you're making me feel guilty and I haven't done anything.'

'Not yet, you mean. He's spent the whole evening asking about you.'

'Stop it, India. He'll hear you.'

India smiled and shook her head. 'No he won't. They're in deep conversation. So, what do you think?'

'Of what?'

'Don't be coy, Ellen. He's a lovely person and great-looking.'

'It's . . . just that it's . . . you know—'

'Too soon after Andrew? It's been weeks now, Ellen, and you need to start living your life again.'

'I know that. Did he mention anything about . . . Andrew? Did he say anything about him – meet him, maybe?'

India examined my face and at that moment I knew what it must feel like to be questioned by her in court. It was as if she had a lie detector built into her eyes.

'I refuse to supply information of that nature to you, on the grounds that it will stop you from living your life,' she said, smiling.

'Let me make that decision for myself,' I replied, and drank the last dregs of my cocktail. I called the waiter and we ordered more drinks. Spencer's leg had moved, or else mine had, and they were touching again. I didn't move away this time, and neither did he. It felt lovely, and my heel wasn't even hurting any more. I surreptitiously examined his profile as he spoke to Ruth. He was gorgeous, in an all-American, clean-cut, chiselled-out dishevelled sort of way. Very handsome and very sexy. He turned around and caught me staring.

'Hi,' I said and waved at him. I was such a daw.

He smiled and had that amused look in his eyes again. I turned around and started talking to India again – a kind of motormouth talk about the first thing that came into my head. I rabbited on for a full five minutes until India's mobile rang. I figured she was glad as it shut me up. She answered and stuck a finger in one ear as she tried to listen over the hum of the crowd. I looked around at the sea of people jammed into the bar and wondered how many of those laughing people had survived a broken heart. India hung up.

'I've got to go, people. Tim is at his wits' end with Alyssa. She won't drink anything from a bottle and has mistaken his ear for a nipple.' She smiled as she put on her jacket and searched the floor for her handbag.

'Ellen, I'll ring you tomorrow. See you Ruth, Spencer,' she said and turned to leave.

'I'll walk you to your car,' offered Spencer.

'No need,' said India. 'I know every criminal in town on a first-name basis.'

Spencer laughed but got up anyway.

'I insist,' he said, and took India's arm as they walked away.

'What a man, what a man, what a man, what a beautiful man,' sang Ruth.

'Jesus!' I said.

'Butterballs,' said Ruth.

'What?'

Ruth called a passing waiter and ordered double rounds of vodka shots and butterballs, which turned out to be a weird, beige-coloured drink in small glasses. Ruth held one of the shots up and drank it back in one go. She winked at me and picked up the beige drink.

'Butterballs – Bailey's and butterscotch – to die for,' she said, and drank that back as well. I followed her good example and, by the time Spencer arrived back, I was an expert Butterball drinker.

He sat between us again, and Ruth rolled her eyes and did a mock swoon behind his back. I giggled and Spencer gave me a quizzical look.

'Goldenballs,' I said, nodding at the drinks on the table. Ruth guffawed and Spencer smiled.

'I'll take that as a compliment,' he said, and Ruth laughed even harder.

'Butterballs, Ellen, Butterballs,' she said, still laughing.

The lights flashed then for last drinks and I couldn't believe how quickly the time had passed. I must have been having fun in spite of myself. We ordered a last round of drinks but Ruth declined, yawning as she did so.

'I'm knackered, lads. I'm going to head home,' she said and asked a hovering waiter to call a cab for her.

'I'll come with you,' I said, and bent to pick up my pashmina from the floor.

'No way. You and Spencer had better finish that last round of drinks or we'll get a bad name,' she said.

The waiter came to tell her that the cab had arrived, and Ruth kissed us both and left. Spencer leaned close to me, his mouth inches from mine. I thought he was going to kiss me, and I felt a huge rush of desire. He leaned even closer, staring into my eyes. I could smell his lovely Butterball breath. He stretched up his hand and stroked my cheek. He then held out his hand and I could see something tiny in it.

'Cashew nut,' he said. 'On your cheek.' He smiled and I laughed and downed another Butterball in one go.

They were beginning to clean up the bar and almost everybody had left by now.

'Feel like another drink?' Spencer asked, slipping his jacket on.

'The bar is closed, and I think it's coffee I need right now,' I said, standing up on shaky stilettoed feet.

'I know where we can get really good coffee,' he said, and took my arm as we walked out of the bar.

'You know Limerick better than I do so,' I said, 'because there's nowhere for coffee at this time of night.'

The cold night air hit me. It felt good and stopped my head from spinning. Spencer stopped walking and put his hands on my shoulders.

'The Clarion – my hotel – does great coffee,' he said. He had that amused look in his eyes again.

'I just want coffee. Nothing else.'

He smiled and kissed me chastely on the cheek. 'Your wish is my command. Let's go.'

I meant it, I really did. There was no way I was going to have sex with the new guy in our office – no siree. And certainly not with a broken heart and a belly full of Butterballs and Slippery Nipples.

I felt as if everyone was watching as I waited in the lobby of the Clarion while Spencer got his key at reception. I sat on a red sofa, trying to look sober, but my head was spinning again. I needed coffee and lots of it. I looked over at Spencer, who was laughing with the pretty blonde receptionist. He had taken off his jacket, and his T-shirt clung to him in a very sexy way. He ran his hand through his hair as he talked to her, and he looked like somebody who had walked straight off a catwalk in Paris. Jesus! He was gorgeous. He walked over to me and I stood up and smiled at him.

'You OK?' he asked and put his arms around my shoulders. I could see the receptionist craning her neck to see what was going on. I gave her a little wave, unknown to Spencer, and then I caught his face and kissed him hard on the mouth, right there in the lobby, in front of the whole world. An electric current of sexual desire raced through my body, and my head began to spin again. Jesus! What the fuck was I doing? I pulled away and wiped my mouth.

'I didn't mean that. It was . . . I'm sorry . . . I'm going home . . . bye,' I said and ran for the revolving glass door. Spencer caught my arm.

'Ellen, it's OK. No harm done – the opposite in fact. Come up to my room, and we'll have coffee, and I'll take you home then.' He held my arm lightly and smiled boyishly at me.

'Just coffee, Spencer. I feel a bit drunk.'

'So do I, Ellen. We'll have some freshly brewed coffee and watch the river for a little while. How's that?'

I nodded, and he caught my hand and walked towards the lift. This was a bad idea, I knew that my body was in sexual overdrive, and not even a broken heart could stop it now. But maybe, just maybe, the coffee would do the trick.

His room was a double with a panoramic view of the river and the city. Spencer threw his jacket on the bed and went to the bathroom. I stood at the window, looking out at the view. I kept saying over and over in my head, *no sex, no sex, no sex*. It seemed to work, and when Spencer came out, I felt I had everything under control.

He came and stood behind me. 'I'll order the coffee. Want anything else?'

I turned around to face him. 'No,' I said. His hair had fallen over his eyes, and I reached up to fix it.

'Yes,' I said then, and kissed him on the mouth. He kissed me back, gently but provocatively, slowly and tantalisingly. I wanted to scream. Instead, I pulled up his T-shirt and ran my hands over his naked torso. He stood back and took off his T-shirt, never taking his eyes from me. I sat down on the bed and watched as he took off his shoes and socks.

He then opened the belt of his trousers, and dropped them on the floor. I kicked off my stilettos, and admired him standing there in front of me in Calvin Klein boxer shorts. He finally took those off and knelt in front of me and began to strip me. He had trouble with the tights where the congealed blood had made them stick to my heel. When we were both finally naked, he leaned over me and kissed me. Slow, teasing kisses that I could have spent the rest of my life sampling.

'What a woman,' he whispered as I climbed on top of him.

'What a man, what a man, what a beautiful man,' I sang and I meant it.


I awoke suddenly, Andrew's body glued tightly to my back. I opened my eyes, and my head began to pound straightaway. The room was in darkness, and I raised my head a little to look at the sleeping Andrew. Except it wasn't Andrew at all. It was Spencer, my new boss. Jesus! I'd just had sex with my new boss. I crept back under the duvet, terrified of waking him. What was I going to do? How was I going to sneak out without disturbing him?

I waited a few minutes, and then I inched my way to the edge of the bed. I was just preparing to get up when Spencer flung his arm out, and it landed on my back. He pulled me back towards him. I pretended to be asleep and let out a little snore to make it more believable. His hands began to explore my body and I let out a little groan of pleasure, and then I stopped.

What was I turning into at all – queen of the slappers? I lay there in the bed like a corpse, hoping he'd go back to sleep. And he did, after what seemed like an age.

I finally crept out of the bed, almost vomiting when I stood up. My head felt as if it was going to explode, and I rooted in the tangled mass of clothes on the floor for mine. Spencer groaned from the bed and I dived onto the floor so he wouldn't see me if he did wake.

I finally found my bra, dress and shoes, but my thong and pashmina seemed to have gone walkabout. I stuck my head under the bed to see if they were there, and, at that moment, Spencer started talking in his sleep. I kept very still, waiting for him to calm down. But the talking got louder and more animated. I could make out some of it . . . *I love you, Tiffany. I love you, Babe.* Who the fuck was Tiffany? It finally tapered off into soft murmurs and I came out from under the bed, still knickerless.

I dressed myself while sitting on the floor, and gave up on my missing clothes. When I stood up, my whole body swayed with the effort. I tiptoed to the door in my high heels and managed to get out without waking Spencer. I literally ran to the lift, as if I'd just escaped from prison.

Having left the silent Clarion, unsure of my exact whereabouts, and feeling drunk, I was about to call a cab to take me home to the Ennis Road. Then I realised that I didn't live there any more. I lived in town now, not ten minutes from the Clarion. And I lived alone.

I began to walk down by the Quay. I checked my watch – 7 a.m. The sun was just rising and the river looked lovely in the streaky pink light of dawn. My head hurt and bits of last night started to rise to the surface of my consciousness. The clearest memory was of great sex, and I blushed at the images that came rushing back. Jesus! Spencer must think I was some kind of sex maniac. I consoled myself with the fact that he was fairly lust-crazed himself, and a thrill raced through my body as I remembered. And then, for no good reason at all, I thought of *Toy Story* and Katie, and I started to bawl my eyes out.

A car slowed down behind me. I didn't want to look back in case it was a madman, but, as it pulled up beside me, I realised that it was a taxi. I wiped my tears with the sleeve of my dress and quickened my pace. It could still be a madman posing as a taxi driver – I'd seen the movies. My heart began to thump in my chest and I broke into a run. The car speeded up and the driver rolled down the window.

'Ellen, is that you?' The madman-cum-taxi driver asked. How the hell did he know my name? I decided to risk stealing a glance at the driver and I recognised him straightaway. It was Ralph, Angela Maunsell's boyfriend.

I stopped my frantic running. 'Ralph, what are you doing out at this time?'

Ralph pulled up beside me. 'What happened, Ellen? You look upset and . . . here . . . jump in. You must be frozen with no coat, I'll run you home.'

I climbed into Ralph's warm car. He kept staring at me as he started the engine.

'Is there something wrong with me?' I asked and flicked down the mirror on the sun visor. I nearly died when I saw the thing looking back at me. It looked like a reject from *The Rocky Horror Show* – too grotesque to be in the cast.

'Jesus!' I said.

'Good night?' asked Ralph.

'Does it look like it?' I said.

'You're not that bad, Ellen. I've seen worse in my line of work.'

I laughed. 'Not worse than this.'

We reached our apartment block in no time.

'Thanks, Ralph. I really appreciate it. I never knew you drove taxis.'

'I do. I take the graveyard shift – I only need two hours' sleep, so it's perfect.'

'Oh . . . two hours – is that all?' I asked as I climbed out of the car, 'I'll need two weeks' sleep to recover from last night.'

Ralph laughed. 'Isn't it great to be young, free and single?' he said as I closed the car door. He pulled off into the streaky pink Limerick dawn and I went home. Being young, free and single was a lot of things, but at that moment, *great* was not one of them.

# 18

I woke early on Monday morning, my body finally recovered from the adventures of Saturday night. I'd slept for most of Sunday, with the phones off the hook. I had the hangover from Hell to deal with, and that was a full-time job, best suffered alone.

I showered and dressed for work and gave myself a stern talking to while I ate a breakfast of toast, bananas and cocoa. The Spencer thing was nothing really – just an accident, something to be forgotten about. I'd go into work today and be the essence of efficiency. From now on, I was going to put all my energy into my career. I was done with relationships for the foreseeable future. Men were just not worth the trouble. The only problem with that was that I'd miss the sex. But I'd work something out.

Despite stopping for takeaway cappuccinos, I got to work early. As I put the tray on Molly's desk, I prayed Spencer wasn't in yet so that I'd have time to prepare a face to meet him publicly.

'Morning, Molly. Have a cappuccino. Are we the only ones in so far?' I asked as I put sugar in my coffee and stirred.

She bent her head sideways and looked me up

and down, as if I was some stray dog that had wandered into the office.

'Ryan has been here for the past hour,' she said and sniffed, giving me the stray-dog look again. 'He's preparing for the interviews on Wednesday for the Area Manager's job.'

'Wednesday?' I said, 'First I heard of it.'

'Well, I did leave a memo on your desk, Ellen. Now, if you didn't bother to read it, then what can we do with you?' She did a little tinkly laugh before picking up her coffee cup.

I laughed too and walked towards my office.

'Good night, Saturday night?' she called after me, and I stopped walking. How did she know about Saturday night?

'Brilliant,' I said without turning around to look at her.

Ryan was at his desk, and I nodded at him and dumped my handbag on the floor. I switched on my computer. Roxy Dawson had bought Mrs Hegarty's house in Hollyfields and she was due to move in this week. I wanted to make sure that everything was in order. Roxy had paid cash for the house, and, though I was bursting to know where a 24-year-old had got her hands on that kind of money, I couldn't think of a way to ask. After my past experience with drug dealers, I was inclined to be a bit suspicious. Though I was fond of Roxy and felt positive her money was legit. Still.

I sat down and began to work. Ryan was leaning back in his chair, staring at me, hands behind his head, a smirk on his thin lips. It was unnerving, especially on a Monday.

'What's your problem?' I asked, without stopping work.

He let out a soft, evil, little chuckle.

I looked at him. 'What's that about?' I said.

He laughed again. 'I heard there's a great view of the city from the Clarion.'

I nearly died, and I could feel my whole face beginning to turn bright red. I kept working.

'I heard, actually, that there's a really good view from room 305, sixth floor.'

Bastard! What did he do with himself every weekend – stalk his colleagues?

'Why? Were you up there, Ryan?' I asked, not looking at him.

'No, but two people from our company were. Now, what do you think of that?'

'I think you should mind your own business, and get a life,' I said and headed for the kitchen.

I walked straight into Spencer as I swung open the door into reception. My mortification was now complete, and I mumbled something without looking at him as I ran for the kitchen. I made coffee in an effort to calm myself down. Jesus! What a bloody start to the week. Spencer arrived then, his body blocking my exit. I still couldn't make eye contact with him.

'Ellen, I have your wrap and stuff in my car. I'll—'

'It's fine, keep it, keep the lot. I need to go. I've loads on today. I'm running behind already—'

'Ellen, I really enjoyed Saturday night.'

My face turned scarlet again. 'Oh, right,' I said, grabbing my coffee and pushing past him. Molly called me as I ran into reception, looking for some safe place to hide.

'Telephone, Ellen. I transferred it to your phone,' she said, and examined me again.

I went into the office, glad to see that Ryan was gone. I picked up the phone.

'Hello, Ellen Gr—'

'Ellen. At last I caught you. Where did you disappear to yesterday? I left about a hundred messages for you.'

'Hi, India. I'm sorry. I slept all day.'

'Late night, Saturday?'

I laughed.

'Tell me. Come on – tell me all the sordid details before Alyssa wakes.'

'I can't talk right now.'

'How convenient is that?'

I laughed again. I was getting embarrassed. Christ! I'd spent the whole morning the colour of Heinz tomato ketchup.

'Look, Ind, I'll talk to you later. I really need to go and do some work.'

'Fine, but I'll be calling you later for all the details.'

I groaned, said goodbye and hung up, then dropped my head onto the hard surface of the desk. I heard someone approach.

'Go away,' I said. 'I'm dead.'

There was no reply.

I looked up. Spencer was standing in front of me, holding a brown paper bag.

'Your wrap, and your . . . things,' he said, putting the bag on the desk. He stood there, looking at me. I still had my head on the desk. I sat up and looked at a spot on the wall just behind him.

'Thanks,' I said and rustled some files. He didn't move. I started to blush again. I hid behind my computer and began tapping the keyboard.

'I wonder if . . . could we go for a drink sometime?' he said. I stopped and looked at him. He was more gorgeous than I remembered. He smiled at me.

'A drink mightn't be a good idea,' I said.

He laughed. 'OK. Coffee would be great. How about coffee?'

'Coffee would be an even worse idea, don't you think?' I said, laughing now, too.

'You're funny, Ellen,' he said, shaking his head.

'I'm also right. Maybe coffee in a public place – how's that?'

'Kinky but I'm definitely interested,' he said.

I threw a string of paperclips at him. 'Cheeky,' I said. Molly stuck her head around the glass-block partition.

'Somebody to see you, Spencer. About the vacancies. I've put her in the conference room.' She smiled at Spencer like her life depended on it.

Spencer leaned towards me. 'Catch you later,' he whispered, winking.

Molly stayed by my desk, fiddling with some papers.

'Very attractive, isn't he?' she said as she shuffled papers into tidy bundles.

I shrugged and searched in my diary for Roxy's phone number. I'd forgotten to charge my mobile during my hangover from hell.

'You'd wonder why he's still unattached, wouldn't you?' she said, finding another wad of papers to tidy.

'You might, Molly. I don't.'

Molly laughed. 'Now, Ellen, we all know you like him.'

I glared at her. 'You know more than me so. Molly O'Sullivan, Psychic Phenomenon.'

'Sarcasm does not become you, Ellen. You'll never get a man with that smart attitude of yours.'

I narrowed my eyes and gave her my best dirty look.

'Spencer seems to have no problem getting the girls though. He's been engaged six times – imagine that!' She lowered her voice. 'And he left four of them at the altar. Not all together, mind – four different weddings. Now, there's a young man with a problem,' she said and swanned away, her bum wiggling in her too-tight skirt.

Spencer Alexander wasn't a serial killer after all, just a serial fiancé. A runaway groom. Not that I cared a damn about Spencer except that the sex was great – I had to admit that much.

Ryan came back to his desk and began to pack his leather briefcase. He picked up a fat, yellow file. 'Mustn't forget my portfolio,' he said, looking at me. 'Not much point having lunch with your broker if you forget to bring your portfolio.'

I threw my eyes up to heaven. Ryan's 'portfolio' was probably full of Lotto tickets and takeaway menus. He picked up his bulging briefcase and left the office.

I rang Roxy. Pa answered the phone. I was surprised that he was back in her life but I said nothing.

'Hi, Ellen,' Roxy said as she took the phone. 'I hope you've good news for me about moving. This flat is driving me cuckoo.'

'Hi, Roxy! How would Wednesday be? I talked to the solicitor on Friday and everything should be sorted by then.'

'You're brill, Ellen, you are. Will Pa go in and collect the key or what?'

'No – I'll meet you over there with it.'

'Brilliant.'

'I'll see you Wednesday, around ten?'

'Perfect.'

I hung up the phone and sorted out my work schedule for the day. I also sorted out my messy desk and found Molly's memo about the interviews for Andrew's job. My appointment was for twelve o'clock. I'd be well finished with Roxy by then. I couldn't believe that Ryan had had the cheek to apply for the Area Manager's position though. Now that would be a nightmare – Ryan as my new boss. And there was a bigger nightmare to think about. How would I look Spencer in the eye as he interviewed me?

# 19

I was half an hour early for my appointment with Roxy Dawson. I sat in my car outside the house in Hollyfields, sipping my takeaway coffee. Even though I had mixed feelings about going for Andrew's job, I still wanted to do my best at the interview. I'd dressed carefully that morning in a taupe trouser suit I'd bought at a Brown Thomas sale. I wore my high-heeled slingbacks, which I loved and my feet hated, and a small matching handbag that would barely hold a tampon.

The sun shone but it was a cold day. I noticed that Acorn House was cordoned off – the people at City Council offices had kept their word. There was a narrow laneway between Acorn House and the small, detached bungalow that stood next to it. You could see straightaway the dilemma facing Sarsfield Properties. They would need one house or the other to widen the laneway.

My mobile rang and interrupted my thoughts.

'Hi, Ellen.'

I hadn't spoken to Ruth since Saturday night, and had forgotten to return her call on Sunday.

'I meant to ring you back, Ruth, but it's been hectic.'

'Yeah, sure. I thought you were dead.'

'I was on Sunday.'

Ruth laughed. 'That makes two of us. So?'

'What?'

'So, what's the story?'

I laughed. 'There is none.'

'Yeah, right. I was talking to India, you know. What is wrong with you that you fucked your boss, Ellen?'

I went red. 'What?'

'You and Spencer on Saturday night.'

'It's none of your business, Ruth.'

'Yes it is, Ellen. You're my friend and I feel responsible. I should have stayed and made sure you got home OK.'

'I'm a fully grown-up woman, Ruth. Didn't you notice?'

'You were drunk. Very drunk and on the rebound.'

I lost my temper. 'You were well able to drink and ride in your single days, Ruth Joyce. And I bloody well know what's wrong with you – you're just jealous,' I shouted into the phone and disconnected the call. I put my head on the steering wheel and took deep breaths. I couldn't believe Ruth. Marriage and motherhood had turned her into a nun.

I looked up as a removal van pulled in behind me, followed by a red Hiace van. Roxy and her entourage had arrived. I wondered if the greyhounds were in the removal van or in the Hiace. My phone rang again as I got out of my car. I waved at Roxy as I answered.

'I don't want us to be fighting with each other.'

It was Ruth. I said nothing.

'Ellen?'

I didn't answer.

'I'm just worried about you, that's all. I mean, Andrew's only gone a few wet weeks, and I know you – I know you still care about him. Fuck it, Ellen! You still love him. Let's be straight about it. And having sex with the first available guy isn't going to help you.'

Tears had welled up in my eyes and I blinked them away. Andrew Kenny would never make me cry again.

'I'm well over Andrew, Ruth, and it's time I moved on. That's what India says and she's right,' I said as I watched Roxy climb out of the van. Pa had the back door of the Hiace open, and his greyhounds made a sudden choreographed leap from the van. He snapped two leashes on them.

'I need to go here, Ruth. I don't want to be fighting either.'

'I know that. Look, we'll talk soon. Bye,' she said and hung up. I put the phone in my pocket because it wouldn't fit in my tiny girlie bag, then I waved the key to the house at Roxy and Pa. The removal men had got out of their lorry and were lighting up cigarettes while sitting on Roxy's wall.

'Today's the big day,' I said as I approached Roxy and Pa. He held her hand and held the dogs' leashes with the other. She looked small and pale and beauti-ful in the watery October sun. She smiled at me and let go of Pa's hand, and enveloped me in a huge bear hug that belied her small frame.

'Jesus, Roxy! I only sold you the house – I'm not paying the mortgage for you!' I said, laughing.

'Thanks, Ellen. Thanks for everything. The house, Enrique, everything. You will be his godmother, won't you? This is just the best day ever – I'm so over the moon. Pa will tell you – I'm just the happiest woman in Limerick.' She smiled at Pa.

He smiled back, and I'd swear the greyhounds were smiling too.

'OK, let's do it,' I said and handed the key to Roxy. She took it and then clasped Pa's hand and walked up the path, dogs leading the way.

They stopped at the red front door. Roxy was jumping up and down, like a little girl without a skipping rope. She put the key in the lock.

'Hold it. Hold it,' said Pa. I thought he meant the key.

'What?' asked Roxy.

'I have to . . . like, you know . . . carry you, like, over the threshold,' he said shyly.

Roxy threw her arms around him and kissed him.

'You're a howl, Pa. Here, Ellen – hold the greyhounds while I get carried over the threshold.'

I took the dogs while Pa swept Roxy into his arms and opened the door. They began to kiss when they were inside, Roxy still perched in his arms. The kissing got passionate so I tried to give them a little privacy, but Buffy and Angel, the dogs, had other plans. They began to howl like the Hounds of the Baskervilles when they saw their master and mistress in an intimate embrace. Everybody laughed, and Pa put Roxy down.

'I'd better go,' I said as Pa took the dogs from me.

'No way, Ellen,' said Roxy. 'Not without a cuppa. I've teabags and milk and stuff in a box in the van. We'll let the men move in the stuff and we'll drink tea. I think that's a great idea,' she said, and winked at me as she went out to the van for the tea things. I checked my watch – 10.30. I had loads of time before my interview at noon.

Roxy returned with the box, and we stood in the kitchen while the kettle boiled on the gas stove.

'Where are the kids?' I asked, suddenly remembering Roxy's little army of babies.

'My mother is minding them until we get the place sorted. I'd never manage otherwise.'

The kettle whistled and Roxy started to make the tea. I watched Pa in the back garden, playing with the dogs. Roxy poured tea into two Teletubby mugs. The removal men had started to bring furniture and boxes into the house.

We drank our tea and watched the men work. An elderly man came into the hall, carrying an old-fashioned standard lamp with a bright green tassled shade. He looked way too old to be a removals man.

'He should be thinking of retiring,' I said to Roxy. She looked and her face broke into a smile.

'Come in, come in. Meet Ellen,' she said to the old man, and she walked out to the hall to take the ugly lamp from him. 'A present from my grandparents,' she said nodding at the lamp.

'Oh, it's lovely,' I lied, thinking that the old man was her grandad.

'This is my new neighbour, Maurice McMahon,' Roxy said. 'He lives in the bungalow next door. This is Ellen Grace, Maurice – the estate agent who sold me the house.'

I shook his hand. It was small and wrinkled but the handshake was firm.

'Delighted to meet you,' I said.

'Pleased to meet you, too. I just called to see if you needed anything, Roxy, love.' His face was wrinkled and weatherbeaten but he had twinkling blue eyes that were full of life and kindness. I liked him instantly.

'Have a cup of tea, Maurice, while you're here. Maurice is chairman of the residents' association, Ellen. We met at a public meeting last week. I saw it advertised in the paper and, as we were going to be moving in, I went along.'

'Oh, that's nice,' I said.

Roxy nodded. 'The residents are trying to stop the leisure centre going in behind us. We want it kept as a green area for the children.'

'It's only right the kiddies have somewhere to play,' Maurice said. 'They can stuff their bloody leisure centre. We're happy with what nature provided there.'

'That's right, 'Roxy said.

'And they can forget about knocking Acorn House as well,' Maurice continued, his face getting redder as he warmed to his subject. 'I'll tie myself to the railings sooner than let the bulldozers come in and knock a listed building.'

Roxy patted him on the arm. 'I'll stand by you all

the way, Maurice. Don't mind that shower – they're only interested in making loads of money.'

Maurice nodded his head vigorously. 'They picked the wrong man if they think they can buy me out with their dirty money. Sure, I've no need for money at my age. There's just me and the pigeons.'

Roxy opened the back door. 'Come out the back and I'll show you where they want to build it, Ellen. You won't believe how close it is to our houses.' Maurice and I followed her out.

Buffy and Angel were tethered to the washing line and they started howling when they saw Roxy. She patted their heads as she passed them. We walked to the end of the garden and looked over the low wall. Roxy pointed to a spot where the rear wall of the leisure complex would be. Maurice tutted and I followed suit. It was pretty near.

'We'll stop them if it kills me. The decision about Acorn House is due on Friday, and that'll put a nice spanner in their works. And that's only the start of our campaign – mark my words,' said Maurice, his finger pointing at me. I wanted to tell him that I wasn't the one building the leisure centre.

All of a sudden, I remembered the interview. I checked my watch: 11.30 already. Jesus! I'd have to boot it back to the office.

'Roxy, I need to dash. We'll talk soon. See you, Maurice,' I said, turning and running through the garden, and out the side gate.

I jumped into my car, and drove out of Hollyfields as fast as legally possible. Every traffic light in the city conspired against me, and I swore and sweated as I crawled through the city traffic to my destination.

There was a really strange smell in the car that I hadn't noticed earlier that morning. I looked around the floor of the car while I was stalled at yet another red light, expecting to find a six-month-old apple or banana, but all I could locate was a stick of chewing gum and a pair of black tights. I finally reached the office with exactly a minute to spare. I locked the car and forgot about funny smells as I raced in to face my interview.

Molly stood behind her desk and put her hand up as soon as she saw me.

'Wait,' she ordered.

'For what?' I asked, still heading towards Tim's office.

'For me to tell you it's your turn,' said Molly, smiling sweetly at me.

I smiled back. 'No problem, Molly. Have you any particular place you'd like me to sit?'

She narrowed her eyes and pointed at the chairs outside Tim's office.

Just then, a small woman with long copper-coloured hair came in to reception. She looked like the Cailín Bán and wore the most beautifully cut suit I'd ever seen. It was the colour of olives and was lovely with her rich red hair. She approached Molly at reception.

'Hello. I'm here for a job interview with a Mr Tim Gladstone and a Mr Spencer Alexander,' she said in a bright, happy voice. I was fascinated by her hair, which had a thousand shades of red, and hung down her back in perfect curls.

Molly checked her diary. 'You must be Nicola Behan. You're a little early, but there's no harm in being early – that's what I always say. Take a seat next to the other interviewee,' she said and pointed Nicola in my direction.

So I was an interviewee now, was I? Nicola smiled as she sat down beside me and crossed her legs demurely. She had a small heart-shaped face with huge green eyes and creamy white skin. I could picture her in an Irish-dancing costume. I smiled back at her and was about to start up a conversation when I realised that maybe it wasn't a good idea to be talking to the competition. Nicola sniffed the air then and started looking at the floor as if she'd lost something.

'Did you drop something?' I asked and began scanning the floor too.

'No, I didn't, but there's a really odd smell. Do you get it?' she asked.

I sniffed the air. There was a weird smell and I was just about to agree with her when Tim's office door opened.

'Ellen, if you're ready?' said Spencer, ushering me into the room. Ryan came out, smirking at me as he passed. Bastard, I thought, as I went in and sat down. Tim and Spencer sat behind Tim's large oak desk, and I sat in front of them, smiling nervously. I hoped my motormouth wouldn't take over – a thing that always happens if I get nervous.

'Ellen, we know all about you already. We'll just skip the interview and have coffee!' said a smiling Spencer, and I laughed – a horrible high-pitched laugh with a hysterical ring to it. The sun streamed through the window in front of me, and the air seemed stuffy and cloying. There was that smell again. What the hell was it? Tim Gladstone needed to get himself a new cleaning company.

Tim asked a few perfunctory questions about my work and experience, and I answered, my voice totally dissociated from my brain. On autopilot. But it seemed to be all right – I didn't see any horrified looks on their faces. The room was getting stuffier and that bloody smell was nauseating me. I was sweating like a pig by now. But apart from that, it all seemed to be going fine. Until Spencer joined in.

'So, what do you like to do in your spare time?' he asked but his eyes had that amused look with which I was becoming very familiar.

An image of Spencer and me, naked and rolling around the floor of a bedroom in the Clarion, sprang into my mind.

I blushed. 'Em . . . em . . . t'ai chi,' I said, wondering how that had come out of my mouth.

Spencer's eyes widened in surprise. 'T'ai chi? I've been practising t'ai chi for the past ten years. I took it up while I was at college, and I must say I fell totally in love with it. So, what style do you practise?'

'Em . . . em . . .' I said.

'Cheng style or t'ai chi ch'uan?' he asked, steepling his fingers and looking straight at me.

'The second one,' I said.

Tim was sniffing the air.

'Good choice,' said Spencer, smiling at me with his perfect American teeth. He was wearing a plain white T-shirt inside a charcoal-grey suit, and he managed to make the ensemble look dead classy. He began to sniff the air too. I decided to join in and all three of us sniffed together. This was turning into one weird interview. Then a horrible thought began to dawn on me. Was that the same smell that had been in my car earlier?

'Oh, shit!' I said.

'Precisely,' said Tim.

Spencer nodded. 'Dog shit to be exact. Well done, Ellen. It must be on somebody's shoe.'

I hid my feet under the desk while Spencer and Tim checked their shoes. Sweat was running down my back at this stage and I could have kissed Tim when he shrugged and called it a day.

'That's about it anyway, Ellen,' he said, standing up and offering me his hand. Spencer and I stood too and we all shook hands. I could have sworn that Spencer winked at me. I literally ran out of the office, and through reception, stopping only when I was outside on the pavement. I scraped the shit off my shoe, using the edge of the kerb, and cursed Buffy and Angel's healthy bowels as I did so.

# 20

The successful candidate for the Area Manager's job was to be announced on Friday afternoon, and I was feeling confident despite my mad interview. I mean, I was the senior estate agent and I'd done some really good work in the past year. And so what if Nicola Behan was better-looking than me – Gladstone and Richards weren't a lookist employer. They'd given Ryan a job, for God's sake, and he had a face like the back of a bus.

I was greeted by Molly as I breezed into reception.

'Hi, Ellen. All excited, are we?' she said, patting her Viking blond hair, which was welded into place with iron-strength hairspray.

'So excited I think I'm going to burst,' I said, rolling my eyes as I kept walking. Ryan was already at his desk, peering over the top of his laptop like a rat in a cage. I gave him a wave without making eye contact, plonked my handbag on my desk, and switched on my computer.

'D-day,' said Ryan.

I didn't answer.

'D-day. I think I'm in with a good chance,' he said.

I still didn't respond. I was becoming an expert at ignoring Ryan.

'But then again, I didn't sleep with one of the bosses,' he said.

I rose to the bait like a rabid dog.

'What did you say?' I asked and walked around to stand in front of him, my hands on his desk. His eyes dashed furtively around the room, looking for an escape.

'Nothing . . . I—'

'What the fuck did you say? Come on, Big Boy, say it to my face,' I said through gritted teeth. Just then, my phone rang, and I walked backwards towards my desk without taking my eyes off Ryan.

'Hello, Ellen Grace here. Can I help you?' I said into the receiver, still watching Ryan. He was getting ready to bail out of the office and I can't say I blamed him. Murder was definitely an option if he stayed near me. I put my hand over the mouthpiece of the phone.

'Ryan,' I called. He turned around. 'Don't forget your portfolio, asshole.'

The day dragged despite my efforts at work. When work failed, I rang everybody in my phone book, including my mother. At 2.30 exactly, I was summoned to Tim's office, where he and Spencer shook my hand and congratulated me on my appointment as Area Manager.

Tim showed me to my new office – which of course was Andrew's old office. It felt a bit weird.

As soon as he left, I sat down on the leather swivel chair behind the modern beech desk, and savoured my success. I felt a fleeting pang of sympathy, followed immediately by a wave of exaltation. Ryan didn't deserve the job anyway. I did. Or maybe I didn't, but at least it might take my mind off everything else. I hadn't wanted to admit it to myself all along, but getting this promotion was important to me. I wanted the challenge of the Area Manager's job and really, if all the other parts of my life were crap, I could clap myself on the back about work. At least that was good.

The following night, I was going to meet Ruth, Emerson, India and Tim for a celebratory drink at the Met, a new bar in the city centre. I really didn't want to go – I mean, hanging out with your married friends is such a sad way to spend a Saturday night, but they all insisted that I had to mark the occasion of my promotion. I had a sneaky feeling that Spencer would be there also. As I showered, I decided that if he was, I wouldn't touch a drop of alcohol. There was no way on this earth that I'd sleep with him again. No way – no matter how good the sex was.

I was searching my wardrobe for something to wear when I heard a vaguely familiar voice coming from the living room. If I wasn't mistaken, that was Roxy's neighbour, Maurice McMahon. But what was he doing in my apartment? I realised then that the voice was coming from my TV, and I ran into the room in my underwear to see what was happening.

I couldn't believe my eyes. There in front of me on the telly was Maurice McMahon, flanked by Roxy Dawson and her children. Roxy held Enrique in her arms, and the two little girls were standing by her side.

'I knew we'd win, and this isn't just a victory for Hollyfields Residents' Association, or even for the children of the area. This is a victory for children everywhere. It's up to us to preserve their heritage, and Acorn House is part of that. We look forward to seeing it rebuilt,' he said looking directly at the camera, and not the interviewer.

'And what about the proposed leisure centre? Are the residents still objecting to developing that land?' asked the interviewer.

'That should never have been rezoned, and we'll fight to the end to have it overturned. The planning permission for the leisure centre runs out in a few months' time, and they needn't think for one minute that they'll slip that by us again. I'll use my last breath to object to that planning permission being renewed. Anyway, these modern leisure centres – I mean, what's wrong with what God provided?'

'So, what you're saying is that the residents will do everything in their power to stop this development?' the interviewer interrupted.

'Over my dead body will a sod be turned on that green field. As far as I'm concerned, those bloody speculators can go somewhere else to make their dirty money—' The camera cut suddenly back to the interviewer, just as Maurice was gathering pace.

'So,' said the journalist to camera, in her tinny,

newsy voice, 'Acorn House – a listed building which was burned down in an arson attack last year – must be rebuilt by the owners and cannot be levelled. That was the decision made by the Planning Authority yesterday, much to the delight of the residents here in this quiet Limerick suburb.'

The camera panned once again to Maurice, Roxy and the children. Roxy smiled seductively at the camera – she looked great. Maurice had his hand up in the air, waiting to speak again. The camera settled on the two little girls.

'The owners of Acorn House, Sarsfield Properties, were unavailable for comment this evening but a source said that they were considering legal action. This is Claire O'Hare, for TV7, reporting from Limerick.'

I stood there watching the familiar faces fade and another news story replace them. So the residents had won after all. The times certainly were a-changing. I went back into the bedroom to continue my search for the elusive perfect outfit. I settled on my almost worn-out little black dress. I tried it on and either I'd grown or the dress had shrunk. But if I stood up like a statue for the whole night and didn't raise my hands above my waist, it would just about fit.

I arrived at the Met at exactly eight o'clock, my punctuality surprising even me. Ruth and Emerson were already at the bar, and as I made my way towards them, I noticed the Spartan décor and dim lighting. Emerson ordered drinks, and Ruth and I admired each other's shoes. We both agreed that mine were the coolest – high pointy-toed ones that you could kick ass in.

'Tell me where you bought them and I'll give you my life savings,' said Ruth, standing back to have a better look.

'You'd need a torch to see them in this light,' I said. 'What happened? Didn't they connect up the lighting yet, or maybe it's a power cut?'

Ruth laughed. 'New trend in bar design, I'd say,' she said and sipped a long aqua-coloured drink.

'What? Drinking in the dark?' I said, and took my fizzy water from Emerson. He had his hair tied back in a ponytail and wore faded blue jeans and a black leather jacket. He looked like an overdressed Californian surfer.

'Irish people have been drinking in the dark for centuries, Ellen. My friend, Tomás Ó Brádaigh, made a fabulous short about it a couple of years ago. Let's see, what was it called? The name will come to me,' said Emerson.

Ruth and I rolled eyes at each other.

'Lights Out, Time Up, Have Ye any Homes to Go To?' said Ruth and we both laughed and Emerson smiled.

'Funny, Ruthie, funny,' he said and kissed her on the back of the neck. I looked away and felt like a big huge gooseberry.

Then Ruth jumped off her stool and caught me by the hand.

'Come on, I want to show you something,' she said and made her way through the dim-lit room, dragging me with her. We came to a set of double doors at the rear of the bar. Ruth pushed open the doors.

'Surprise!' a chorus of voices screamed. The small room was filled with my family and friends.

'Oh my God, Ruth, you sneaky bitch!' I said as well-wishers surrounded me. My mother and father came up and kissed and hugged me.

'I'm so proud of you – Area Manager – imagine that!' said my mother.

Next, Will arrived. 'So, Ell, are we in the money now?' he asked, bending his head to kiss me on the cheek.

'Well, isn't she a great girl all the same?' a voice said from behind me. Angela Maunsell with a smiling Ralphie in tow. They were joined by India and Tim. By now, I felt as if I was the star attraction at the Eurovision and I had forgotten my song. Somebody had put a drink in my hand and I began to sip cold white wine. Spencer came over, looking great in ripped blue jeans and a body-hugging T-shirt that looked like the clingy strip worn by the Italian football team during the last World Cup. In my opinion, that Italian lycra number complete with footballers should have been X-rated.

'Ellen, I'm so happy for you,' said Spencer as he kissed me on the cheek. He smelt lovely.

'Thanks,' I said and stopped myself in the nick of time from kissing him on the mouth. I was beginning to think I really was a sex maniac.

'Well done, you deserve it,' he said, smiling at me.

He was too handsome for his own good. No man should be walking around with a face and body like that – there should be some kind of law against it.

'Thanks,' I repeated.

'Would you like another drink?' he asked then.

I looked at my wine glass and realised I'd gulped down the whole glass while Spencer was talking to me.

'No, I'm fine,' I said.

Spencer gave me a puzzled look. 'Sure?'

'Positive,' I said. No way was I having alcohol when this man was in close proximity. Just then, Ryan came along with a girl in tow.

'Congratulations,' he said and offered me his hand.

I shook his limp, damp hand and smiled at him and his female friend. She was tiny – under five feet – with copper-coloured hair and dark brown eyes. She was very pretty. What was she doing with Ryan? Was there a scarcity of single available men in Limerick?

'This is Vanessa Ryan,' said Ryan. 'Vanessa – Ellen Grace and Spencer Alexander the Third, my work colleagues.'

Vanessa gave me the once-over and nodded her head curtly at me.

'Nice to meet you, Vanessa,' I said, offering her my hand. 'Thanks very much for coming.'

Vanessa smiled a narrow smile. 'No problem, delighted,' she said, and I thought I could detect an English accent.

'What part of England do you come from, Vanessa?' I asked.

'England?' Ryan said laughing. 'Vanessa is from Limerick. Her family are probably the foremost property developers in town, Ellen. You'd imagine you of all people would know that. As Area Manager, you're going to have to gen up on this type of thing.'

'I'm working on my portfolio as we speak, Ryan.'

'You can laugh at my portfolio, Ellen. But when I'm a millionaire before I'm thirty, I think the smile will be on the other side of your face.'

'Whatever, Ryan,' I said. 'Very nice to meet you, Vanessa.'

Vanessa sniffed and looked me up and down once again. From the expression on her face, I could see that I'd obviously failed some kind of girl test. She turned her attention to Spencer.

'You're not Irish,' she said to Spencer and did a giggly girly laugh. Ryan stood there watching, his rat face twitching with pleasure.

'I'm from New York,' said Spencer.

Vanessa put a tiny, dainty hand on his arm. Her nails were painted a rich russet, which matched exactly the colour of her skintight dress. 'I thought you were from California – you have that tanned, sunny look about you.'

Was she coming on to Spencer? She reminded me of someone but I couldn't quite put my finger on it. Spencer stood there, looking at her hand on his arm.

Ryan coughed. 'Ellen is the girl I was telling you about, Vanessa. Remember? The girl that had all the problems with the drug barons last year?'

Spencer looked at me, his eyes round with disbelief.

Vanessa gave me the same round-eyed look but her hand remained on Spencer's arm.

'What was your boyfriend's name – the one who ran off to Spain before the cops or the drug barons could catch him? Tony something—'

'Soprano . . . Tony Soprano,' I said.

Spencer laughed. Vanessa didn't. She dropped her hand from Spencer's arm and took a couple of steps away from me.

'And there was the kidnapping and the letter bomb. That letter bomb could have wiped out Gladstone and Richards. It was delivered to our office, Spencer, with Ellen's name on it.'

'It was only a small bomb,' I said. 'Don't exaggerate, Ryan. I've seen bigger fireworks than that bomb.'

Spencer laughed again. 'Isn't she fantastic? I just love this woman – she sure isn't boring.'

'A thrill a minute,' I said.

'Absolutely,' said Spencer, suddenly serious. 'I couldn't have put it better myself.'

He looked at me and for a split second I thought he was going to kiss me. I was vaguely aware of Ryan and Vanessa watching the two of us.

'Excuse me. Gotta go and mingle,' I said in a voice that was too loud and happy. I waved at them and ran to the furthest corner of the small room, where I hid behind a large plant and shook my head to clear it. Jesus! Spencer was something else, and I knew now how he had made all those women in America fall in love with him. He made them so crazy for sex that they lost all sense of reason. Jesus! I'd have to be careful. There was no way I'd fall in love with him or anything stupid like that, but I'd have to do something about the sexual attraction I felt in his presence.

And bloody Ryan, telling him all about the stuff from the previous year. Then it came to me – who his girlfriend reminded me of – Molly. She was like a young Molly. I wanted to go home but I couldn't walk out on my own celebration. It was going to be a long night.

# 21

I arrived at work on Monday morning and sat at my old desk first by mistake. Then I went into my new office and sat down on the black leather swivel chair, slightly overawed by my new surroundings. I laid my head on the cool beech desktop and closed my eyes. I felt tired even though I'd slept for the whole day on Sunday, and I'd got home reasonably early on Saturday night. For once, I'd stuck to my guns and hadn't touched a drink after that initial glass of wine.

But, even sober, I could see that Spencer was as gorgeous as ever. The only other person who had ever had that kind of effect on me was Tony Jordan, and that had got me into trouble. I sat up and swivelled in my fancy new chair. I'd just realised something. Men with that kind of sexual charisma are big trouble. It's like you have to pay the price for being that attractive, so trouble stalks you. The phone rang and interrupted my Monday-morning musings.

'Ellen? Is that you?' I recognised the voice.

'What's up, Roxy? You sound upset.'

'Oh, Ellen.' She faltered and began to cry.

'Roxy, tell me what's happened. Are you OK?'

'Maurice. Maurice McMahon, in the house next door to me . . . they smashed all his windows last night and the kids woke and . . .Ellen, did I make a big mistake buying this house?'

Cold fingers of fear crept up my spine.

'Who, Roxy? Who smashed the windows?'

'I don't know. They didn't wait around to say hello. They wore balaclavas and drove off on a scooter. Pa was going to follow them but I said no, we'd call the guards.'

'Was anybody hurt? Is Maurice all right?' I asked.

'He's fine, just upset and scared, but he won't admit to the scared stuff.'

'And what did the guards say?'

'Oh, that they'd look into it, but it was probably just kids.'

'Kids in balaclavas on scooters? I don't think so, Roxy.'

'I know – I said the same thing to the guards. And we were on telly on Saturday night and Maurice thinks it had something to do with that. Something to do with Sarsfield Properties – remember that shower?'

I was inclined to agree with Maurice but I didn't want to frighten Roxy. She was scared enough as it was.

'Look, Roxy, you did the right thing – ringing the guards. They'll get to the bottom of it. Wait and see,' I said, trying to convince myself as well as her that this was true.

'They've promised to keep an eye on the place,

but still . . . it could have been petrol bombs instead of rocks, and my kids—'

'Roxy, stop that kind of talk. Hollyfields has always been a really nice quiet area. This is just a once-off thing. I know it is. Look, do you want me to call over later?'

'No, I'm fine, Ellen. Really I am. I just wanted someone to tell me I didn't make a huge mistake.'

I hoped she hadn't either because I couldn't help feeling responsible. I mean, I'd sold her the house. If something did happen, I'd never forgive myself. 'Roxy,' I said, 'who was the guard you dealt with last night?'

'I can't remember his name but the detective handling the case rang this morning.'

'What's his name? Maybe I should talk to him,' I said and searched my handbag for a pen.

'Her name,' Roxy corrected me. 'Her name is Detective Hilary Thornton.'

I laughed out loud. My old friend Hilary, who had sorted out all the letter-bomb, drug-baron /crime-lord problems last year. She'd just love a phone call from me.

'What's funny?' Roxy said.

'Nothing. I know Detective Thornton, and she's the best, Roxy – she really is.'

'That's great, Ellen.'

'And Roxy?'

'Yeah?'

'You didn't make a mistake. That house of yours is a gem . . . trust me.'

'I do trust you. Bye, Ellen.'

'Bye, Roxy.'

I hung up the phone. Poor Roxy, I'd have to ring the detective at some stage today and put her straight. I settled into a morning of tedious paperwork. God I hated that stuff and there seemed to be twice as much of it with my new job. Still, there was no avoiding it. I took a break at one and had a light lunch in a nearby bistro. I was having forty winks at my desk after lunch when there was a knock at my door. I jumped.

'Come in,' I said as I straightened up in my chair. It was Tim.

'Ellen, Good afternoon. How are you?' He sat gracefully on the edge of the desk.

'I'm fine, Tim. How are you? Good weekend?'

'Great. Alyssa actually slept for two straight hours last night.'

'Really?'

'Anyway, look what I have!' He dangled a set of keys in front of my face.

'The beemer,' I said.

'Correct – just arrived back from the valet service.'

'Brilliant, ' I said but my heart squeezed at the thought of driving Andrew's car. It's my car now, I told myself. Get over yourself, Ellen.

'Enjoy it,' he said, and dropped the keys into my open hand. He rose to leave.

'One other thing, Ellen. The filing cabinet in the corner has a combination lock and I don't know the number. Molly says the only person who knows it is Andrew. There's his work number – they're about six hours behind us in Austin, so you should be able to catch him now.' Tim smiled and turned towards the door.

My heart had started to pound really loudly and I looked at the scribbled number in my hand.

'Tim,' I said, holding the piece of paper in the air.

'Yes, Ellen?'

'I was thinking . . . wondering . . . if maybe you could ring . . . or maybe Molly—'

'I don't think so, Ellen,' he said, his hand on the door handle. I could almost hear him thinking that it was time I grew up and faced the consequences of my actions, but he didn't say it – he didn't have to. 'It'd be better if you rang,' was all he said before he left. I stared at the door.

Then I stared at the telephone. I picked up the receiver before I changed my mind and pressed zero for a direct line. I heard the dial tone and began to dial, hoping that Molly wasn't her usual efficient self and that the number was wrong. But the phone on the other side of the Atlantic rang nearly straight-away. My heart began to pound and I almost screamed when a woman's voice answered.

'Good morning. Reval Properties. My name is Lynn. May I help you?' The voice at the other end had a strong Texas accent.

'Yes . . . may I speak to Andrew Kenny, please? Though I'm happy to leave a message if he's busy,' I added, letting out a nervous squawk of a laugh.

'I'll put you straight through. Thank you for calling Reval.' Her voice was breathy and false.

'Hi, Andrew Kenny here.'

I nearly dropped the phone, and sweat dripped down the back of my neck.

'Hello?' his voice said again. Tears sprang to my eyes, and I blinked them away. I bloody well wouldn't cry.

'Hi, it's me.'

'Ellen?'

I studied the door in front of me.

'Yes, remember me?' I said, trying to joke but regretting it instantly. I was sure he could hear my heart pounding.

'Hello, Ellen. How are you?' he asked, but in his formal voice. The joke was a bad idea.

'I'm fine, brilliant actually. I've just been made Area Manager and things really couldn't be better.'

'Congratulations.'

'Thanks. How's Katie?'

'She's great. She's really settled in quickly.'

I blinked back more tears and resisted the urge to ask the obvious question – did he miss me?

'Sorry to disturb you. I'm sure you're very busy. The reason I rang was to get the combination number for the filing cabinet in your office which is now my office—' I stopped my motormouth, to take a breath.

'Oh.'

'Anyway, I need the files and stuff, so can you remember the number? If you can't, we'll have to get a locksmith to bust it open, or maybe India will know a good thief—'

'One three nine nine – Katie's birthday – the first of the third, 1999.'

'Oh, OK. That's fine, so.'

'Glad I could help.' His voice was cold and distant. 'Anything else, Ellen?'

My heart felt as if somebody had done a dance on top of it.

'No. Thank you for your help, Andrew. Goodbye,' I said and dropped the phone into its cradle as if it was suddenly too hot to hold. Jesus! What a first day this was turning out to be. I fought back tears again and willed Andrew's voice out of my head. Had I made a mistake? How was I supposed to live without Andrew?

There was a knock on the door. 'Come in,' I said in a high, squeaky voice.

Spencer came into the office looking like a male model as usual.

'Ellen, you look like you've settled in,' he said, as he pulled out the chair opposite me, and lowered his long body into it in one swift movement.

'Baptism of fire, I'd say,' I said and smiled at him. I must say, you could do a lot worse on a Monday than look at that face across the desk from you.

Spencer drummed the desktop lightly with long tanned fingers. 'Why, what's the matter?'

'Oh, I sold a house to a young mother a few weeks ago and the house next door was vandalised last night. She's really upset over it.'

Spencer shrugged. 'Sure, but it's not your fault, Ellen. You didn't do it, did you?'

I laughed. 'I know, but I like her and I'm worried for her – that's all.'

'I understand.'

'And I had to ring Reval in Austin to get the combination of the filing cabinet.'

Spencer looked straight at me. 'That was hardly in the same ball park as your distraught friend. The Reval people are lovely, but how do they know the combination?'

I examined my nails. 'Andrew.'

'Oh, I see. I could have done that for you. I was speaking to him last night myself.'

I looked up from my nails. 'Were you?'

'Yeah, just work stuff really. And I spoke to Claudia as well.'

'To whom?' I asked, trying to keep my voice steady.

'Claudia,' said Spencer, smiling at me. 'She's Andrew's counterpart in Reval Austin, and it seems she and Andrew—'

'That's good,' I said. 'That's great. Andrew must be settling in well. I'm delighted for him. Now, did you want something in particular, Spencer?'

Spencer straightened up in the chair. 'Oh, right. We have a project that needs some hands-on input and I was wondering if you could suggest a candidate?'

'What project?' I asked. I wouldn't let myself think about Andrew and the Claudia one. Jesus! He didn't waste any bloody time, did he?

'Holiday homes in the outer Hebrides. It sounds kinda crazy, Ellen, but I like the idea. It's funky and the place is beautiful.'

'There's no harm in sending someone out for a look. Although it's not a great time of the year to be up there.'

Spencer laughed. 'I'll say! There were huge storms there all last week.'

I clicked my fingers in the air. 'Don't worry – I know the perfect person for the job.'

'Who?'

I winked at Spencer and picked up my phone. 'Molly, could you ask Ryan to come into my office, please?'

Spencer smiled. I laughed out loud. I loved my new job.

# 22

On Wednesday night, I was sitting in my apartment, eating noodles, cuddling Joey and watching a stupid movie about a little girl, with blonde curls and a horrible illness, who had lost her dog. It was the dumbest movie I ever saw and still it was making me cry like the rain. Just as the little girl was whisked off to hospital in an ambulance and the dog tried to follow and got lost, the telephone rang.

'Ellen?'

'Ruth.'

'Have you still got that pink fairy outfit?'

'Why? Stuck for a disgusting marital fantasy costume? There are magazines and websites for people like you.'

'Oh my God! My friend has been taken by aliens and they've left someone who thinks she's hilarious.'

'Come on! I'm tired and watching a dumb movie, and OK, I may be a tiny bit cranky, but my personal life is ruined, so I'm entitled.'

'Well, I won't even begin to go down the road with that one so I'll stick to why I rang you.'

'Why exactly *did* you ring me, Ruth?'

'We're having a Halloween party. We've been

meaning to have a housewarming party and then we thought we'd have a baby-welcoming party.'

'Lovely,' I said. 'Really, your social plans are thrilling.'

'Shut up – what was I saying? Oh yeah, well we just couldn't manage to get our act together with those but now I'm determined – we're having a party on Saturday night.'

'This Saturday?'

'Yes, ma'am. This Saturday, and, as Friday's Halloween, I thought what a great chance to have a costume party.'

'Oh my God! A costume party? Where a load of adults dress up in stupid clothes and act like kids?'

'No, Ellen. That's an ordinary party. This is a party where a load of adults pretend to be someone or something else and have great fun.'

'I hate them.'

'And I love them and it's my party and I'll dress up if I want to.'

'But forcing it on your guests . . . that's just being a bad hostess.'

'Pity about you.'

'But I don't have anything to wear to a costume party.'

'Which brings us back to where we started. See if your mother has that fairy costume stashed away – the one you wore to Eleanor Finnegan's party years ago.'

'God almighty! We were eighteen and I looked like a fool.'

'No, you didn't. You looked lovely – for a five-foot-ten fairy. So go and find that or – I don't know, El – find something else, but get your weird rags on and come to my party.'

'I don't suppose I have a choice?'

'No.'

'Didn't think I had but thought I'd check anyway.'

'Look, Paddy is waking up. I can hear him starting to sing. See you Saturday – in costume.'

'But it's Wednesday.'

'Bye, Ellen.'

The phone went dead and I turned the sound back up on the TV. The hero dog was lying, as stiff as a board at the side of a lake. Beside him, the tiny girl with badly drawn circles under her eyes, and a white nightdress, cried pitifully beside him.

'Yeah, yeah, yeah,' I said to the TV, standing up from the couch. '

'He's not dead – he can't be. He's the hero of the movie, for God's sake! They called it *Rascal's Wisdom* after the bloody dog. What kind of a name is that for a film, anyway?'

I pointed the remote control and flicked. The TV went satisfyingly silent. I stood there and stared at Joey as he lay curled on the warm spot of the sofa I'd just vacated. Why couldn't people be more like cats? I knew I could be happy just sleeping and eating, and I was definitely equipped with the sexual inclinations of a tomcat. It looked like a pretty attractive package to me. All the angst of being a person was really not worth it. The telephone rang again.

'Ellen?'

'Hello, India.'

'Did Ruth call?'

'Yep.'

'What are you wearing to her party?'

'Oh God, India – don't.'

India laughed. 'You'll enjoy it – stop moaning. I'm thinking of going as Cruella DeVille – my mother has a coat that would be just ideal and I have this spotted baby-gro that I could put on Alyssa so she'd be like a Dalmatian and—'

'What about Tim?'

'Oh he can be the side-kick guy – I can't remember his name. Do you know it? The guy in the cloth cap and brown overall – what's his name?'

'No idea.'

'Come on, Ellen. Get into the spirit of it – it'll be good for you.'

A shrill baby cry and some electrical feedback made the phone reverberate in my hand.

'What's that screeching noise?' I asked.

'Alyssa's awake. I have to go.'

'No, India, not that – even I can recognise a baby's cry. What's that electrical noise?'

'Oh, just feedback from the baby monitor. I have to go. See you Saturday.'

The phone went dead in my hand and I went to my tiny galley kitchen and stuck two slices of bread in the toaster and boiled the kettle to make cocoa. I was starting to grow fond of my new apartment but I wasn't sure I was ever going to get totally used to how everything was backwards.

As I waited for the toast to pop, I realised that I was starving and that I hadn't eaten anything apart from noodles in ages. In fact, when had I last had a proper meal? I couldn't remember, but I was pretty sure it must have been sometime before Andrew left. Now, though, at least I was hungry, and surely that was a good sign. It couldn't be good for me to subsist on toast and cocoa and noodles. I'd have a proper dinner, for once. That would make me feel better.

I strode the one-and-a-half steps across my kitchen to the fridge and removed the Chinese takeaway menu stuck to the door with an Eiffel Tower magnet India had given me a couple of years before. Just as I was perusing the delicious-sounding selection, the telephone rang again. I tutted and sighed and considered ignoring it but finally couldn't, so I grabbed the receiver off the hook.

'Yes?'

'Ellen, hi.'

'Spencer?'

'Yes. Sorry to call you so late.'

'It's only nine, Spencer.'

'OK, great. I'm a little worried about something and I was wondering if I could run it by you?'

'Sure, sure. No problem. What's wrong?'

'Well, I was just speaking with India on the phone and she said that Ruth had asked her to invite me to a costume party on Saturday night.'

'Oh don't worry about that,' I interrupted. 'Just get India to tell Ruth you're ill. I'll tell her if you like – she'll get over it.'

'No, no, it's not that. I'd love to go to Ruth's party. It's just I was wondering if you knew of any good costume-hire store?'

'What?'

'You do have them in Ireland, I presume. Stores where you can hire costumes? Like for theatre and stuff?'

'Yes, we do have them, Spencer, and I'm warning you now that if you do the *pigs-in-the-parlour-do-you-have-these-sophisticated-things-in-your-quaint-country* routine, I will have you quaintly beaten with shillelaghs.'

Spencer roared with laughter into the phone. 'OK, OK, calm down. That's not what I meant. I just thought you might know of someplace good – save me searching. Local knowledge, that kind of thing, Ellen, that's all. So? Do you?'

'Do I what?'

'Know of a good costume-hire emporium?'

'I don't even know what an emporium is, Spencer. I suggest you check the *Golden Pages* – it's the yellow book by the phone.'

'I'll do that, thank you very much.'

'No problem. I'm happy to share my local knowledge about telephone books. It's the least I can do for you blow-ins. Anything else?'

Spencer didn't answer for a few seconds.

'Spencer?'

'I was . . . just wondering if you're going to be at Ruth's party?'

'I have no choice. Take another piece of local advice

and never, ever annoy Ruth Joyce if you can help it. Don't be fooled by that innocent girlie exterior. Ruth is like Napoleon – small but deadly. I sometimes call her Ruth-less, but never to her face because I'm afraid.'

Spencer laughed again. I was impressed with myself. Usually nobody laughed so heartily at my jokes. Either I was getting funnier or else. . .

'I like Ruth,' Spencer said.

'Me too,' I said. 'After all, she is one of my best friends.'

'She's very nice – just like everybody else I've met since I arrived,' Spencer continued, his voice dropping at least two octaves. My heart squeezed in my chest.

'Ooops!' I said. 'Gotta fly, Spence – my dinner is burning. Talk to you tomorrow at work.'

Spencer barely had a chance to say goodbye before I hung up. I stared at the silent phone as if it had offended me. I had had nothing all evening but phone calls that disturbed my peace and relaxation. Maybe I should get rid of my phone altogether. Then I'd have some peace and quiet. Except that I couldn't call up for food. Which reminded me. . .

I ran back to the kitchen and retrieved the take-away menu. Barbecued spareribs and chicken chow mein looked like they might make a good dinner. I rang the number and placed my order, then threw the cold toast in the bin and made a mug of cocoa.

I shouldn't have had sex with Spencer. It was a bad mistake. Not the sex – the sex was great – but it's not a great idea to get involved with someone you're going to have to look at every day at work. How many times did I need to make that particular mistake before I learned my lesson? Why couldn't I have left Spencer – and well enough – alone? Who would it be next? Ryan? I laughed out loud at that thought. Slug boy. Yeuch!

The doorbell rang just as I finished my cocoa. I paid for my food and carried the damp, fragrant paper bag back into the kitchen. Then I dumped the contents of the cartons onto a plate, poured myself a glass of Montana and padded back over to the couch. Joey raised his head and looked at me as he smelt the food.

'I might leave you some, if you're good,' I said, winding noodles around my fork. My God! It was delicious! I found an old episode of *Murder She Wrote* to watch as I devoured my dinner. It tasted so good, I just knew it couldn't be nutritious. Still, it was probably more nutritious than noodles and toast, and the wine was certainly vying with cocoa in terms of getting into my Top Ten.

For the first time since Andrew had left, I managed not to think about him for almost an hour. Not great, but still progress. If I could just keep away from complicating factors like Spencer, then who knew? Maybe I'd be able to straighten out my life.

# 23

I awoke the following morning and decided that even though I hated the idea of Ruth's stupid costume party, if I had no choice but to go, I was determined not to look like a complete idiot. I planned to do some research and find someplace that could rent me a flattering costume. Surely there was something elegant and interesting that I could wear? Maybe I could be a vampire? That might be OK, especially if I could be all sort of vampish and sexy. Better than a giant fairy anyway.

With that in mind, on my way to my first appointment – which was to show a suite of offices in the centre of town – I gave the shoe shops a miss and bought a bag of fake blood capsules in a joke shop.

'They melt in your mouth,' the small elderly man behind the counter said. He was wearing a turquoise satin shirt and striped pants, and had a comb-over that looked like someone had spray painted his head with steel-grey paint. On second thoughts – maybe they had.

I smiled. 'Like M & Ms?'

'Sorry?' he raised his bushy eyebrows and stared at my chest which was at his eye level.

'Melt in your mouth – not in your hand?' I said, weakly.

'Don't hold the capsules in your hand,' he said, shaking his head at my ignorance. 'Never do that. Keep them in the bag. It's more hygienic. There are millions of bacteria on your hands – do you know that?'

He glanced briefly up at my face and then returned his eyes to my chest. 'Put a capsule in your mouth and let the enzymes in your saliva break down the gelatin coating, and then just let some of the saliva trickle out of your mouth – very effective.'

'Great,' I said, grabbing the plastic bag of fake blood off the counter. 'Thanks a million. Bye.'

I dashed out the door into the warm, sunny autumnal light. 'Bloody weirdo,' I said, chucking the bag of blood capsules into the bottom of my handbag as I looked at my watch and realised I was about to be late for my appointment.

I showed the offices to a tall, red-haired woman and a short dark man who looked like a stereotypical Mexican in a spaghetti western. She was a physiotherapist and he was a doctor and was Australian, not Mexican. They were planning to open a city-centre healthcare business – maybe to offer painkillers and exercises to those injured in the many gyms that dotted the town. Or else to offer medical and physiotherapy services to the poor of the inner city. My guess was the former.

I finished showing the offices and was strolling through the sunny streets back to Gladstone and

Richards when I saw Roxy coming out of a shop. She was wearing a white track pants and a baby-blue long-sleeved T-shirt, and her blonde hair was pulled into its usual high ponytail.

'Roxy,' I said, as she walked past me. She started and looked around.

'Ellen. Jesus, Ellen, I never even saw you there.'

Roxy's eyes were bloodshot and ringed with dark circles.

'You OK?' I asked. She shook her head.

'Someone broke into the house,' she said.

'Oh my God! When?'

'Yesterday, while we were at my mother's.'

'And did they take anything?'

Roxy shook her head again. 'They busted up the sitting room – smashed our new wide-screen TV and wrote . . . stuff.'

Roxy's eyes widened and two glistening tears slid down her flawless cheeks.

'Oh, Roxy,' I said, taking her arm. 'Look, there's a coffee shop over there – let me buy you a cup of coffee. How about that?'

Roxy nodded but didn't speak as the two original tears became a constant flow. I held her elbow and propelled her into the coffee bar to our left. I sat Roxy at a small, round aluminium table in the corner and bought us two large cappuccinos and two fat blueberry muffins.

'Now,' I said, plonking the tray on the table in front of her. 'Tell me.'

Roxy had stopped crying and was tumbling a

sachet of sugar between her fingers. 'There isn't anything else to tell,' she said. 'That's it. That's what happened. Someone broke in, trashed the place and wrote the stuff.'

'What stuff? What do you mean, "wrote the stuff"?'

Roxy sighed and sipped her coffee. 'On the wall behind the TV. Whoever broke in used one of Shakira's markers and wrote stuff about Enrique.'

'Baby Enrique?'

Roxy nodded.

'But what could you write about a baby? I'd say he might be a bit young to have collected enemies,' I said.

'Monkey baby,' Roxy said, pausing to wipe her mouth as if she'd accidentally eaten something horrible. '*Fucking slapper bitch with her monkey baby* – in red marker.'

'Oh my God!' I said. 'Who would do such a thing?'

Roxy's face clouded over and she crumbled the edge of her muffin. 'Teddy Hannon – he's out of jail since last week.'

'Teddy Hannon?'

'My husband. Shakira and Shania's father.'

'Oh right,' I said. 'Why would he do such a thing? I thought you said you finished with him years ago?'

'I did – nearly three years ago, after Shakira was born. He wasn't too happy though.'

Roxy filled her mouth with muffin and took a long slug of coffee.

'In what way "not happy", Roxy? Was he crying

and saying he loved you or was he threatening and stalking you?'

Roxy swallowed. 'That one. I had to get a restraining order to keep him away and then he went to jail and I thought I was grand – that he'd forget us after a while . . . but now the fucker is out again.'

'Why would he do something like that to your house, though?' I asked.

Roxy shook her head and shrugged. 'Because he's a mad bastard? I don't know. Why do mad bastards do what they do?'

'Good question,' I said. 'But how would Teddy Hannon even know where you live now? You've moved house.'

'You'd be surprised,' Roxy said. 'This is a small town.'

'I don't think it's that,' I said, as the pieces began to fall into place. 'I saw you and Maurice on TV last week, by the way – you were great, Roxy. You look good on TV – maybe RTÉ will offer you a job.'

Roxy gave a weak smile.

'Anyway,' I continued, warming to my subject. 'I think the break-in is something to do with the residents' committee.'

'But they asked me to be on the committee – well, Maurice asked me. I don't think Annette Downes likes me but I don't think she'd break into my house.'

'No, Roxy – not the committee itself, but because you're on the committee. I bet the break-in was to do with the hotel and the planning permission and all of that.'

Roxy's eyes widened. 'Oh my God!'

'Think about it,' I said. 'Acorn House was burned down – that's the only way to get rid of a listed building, by the way. But it didn't work – now it has to be rebuilt and all because of the residents' association. Maurice is already a well-known opponent of the hotel and he's had his windows put in, and then you're on telly and, a couple of days later, your house is trashed.'

'Oh my God!' Roxy said, again.

'Makes sense, doesn't it?'

'I don't know.' Roxy looked doubtful. 'It could be Teddy Hannon.'

I shook my head. 'I bet it isn't. Why would he bother? What's in it for him?'

'I don't know, Ellen, but he is one mad fucker so he could have any sort of an idea in his head about me.'

'But can't you see what I'm saying? Doesn't it make more sense for it to be something to do with the planning permission and all that?'

'Yeah, yeah, I see it all right. Maybe you're right. Jesus, I hope you are.'

Roxy smiled broadly and a tiny amount of colour seeped into her cheeks. 'I know it wouldn't be great but I'd really prefer if it was something to do with that.'

I laughed and took a long drink from my luke-warm cappuccino. 'You'd prefer to think a whole load of powerful businessmen – crooks most of them, by the by – were trying to intimidate you? You can't be serious.'

Roxy covered her face with her hands for a couple of seconds and then looked straight at me. 'I'm completely serious. Teddy Hannon is probably the scariest person I've ever met.'

'In what way?'

Roxy's eyes lost focus as she disappeared back into herself for a few seconds. 'He just is,' she said, at last.

'Why was he in prison?'

'Assault. He beat the crap out of a guy in a pub who said United were useless.'

'Typical,' I said.

Roxy shook her head. 'Nothing typical about Teddy Hannon. Anyway, I think you might be right about the break-in, though.' She smiled suddenly and finished her coffee in one long gulp. 'I'd better be off. Pa has to bring one of the dogs to the vet at two.'

'How is Pa, by the way?'

'Great. He stayed up half the night painting the sitting room. I think he was more upset than I was about the things on the wall about Enrique.'

'Did you tell the police?' I asked.

'We did.'

'Good.'

Roxy stood up. 'Thanks, Ellen. I'd better get going.'

I stood up as well. 'Hold on a minute. Would you like a lift home? My car is just down the road, at work, and I'm on my way to a meeting – I can drop you off, if you like.'

Roxy smiled. 'If it's not too much trouble.'

'No way. I'd be delighted to show off my new car.'

'Ah, Ellen – don't tell me you got rid of that lovely pink car.'

'Sarcasm is the lowest form of humour,' I said, as we emerged back onto the street. 'I have a new job – I'm Area Manager.'

'Congratulations.'

'Thanks. But most importantly, I also have a company car – the Gladstone and Richards Area Manager's BMW.'

'Very cool,' Roxy said, grinning.

'Well, it is, except that even though it's a brand-new car, the last person who had the job was my boyfriend, and he's gone to America, so the car kind of reminds me of him.'

Roxy patted my shoulder. 'Life is shit.'

'You said it,' I agreed. 'But still, you might as well have a nice car to drive you through the shit. Look.'

We walked through the gates of the car park of Gladstone and Richards and I was pointing out the gleaming navy BMW, and Roxy was murmuring her appreciation, when I heard my name being called. Roxy and I both swivelled round.

'Hey!' Spencer said as he reached where we were standing.

'Hello, Spencer,' I said.

Spencer pushed some silky, blond hair behind his ear and grinned.

'Lovely day,' he said.

'Yes, indeed,' I agreed, squirming slightly under his gaze. Then I remembered. 'Spencer. This is Roxy – my friend.'

Spencer stuck his tanned hand forward.

'Nice to meet you, Spencer,' Roxy said as they shook hands.

'Roxy?' Spencer said, training all his attention momentarily on Roxy. 'I know that name.'

'Probably reminds you of a cinema or something,' Roxy said, laughing.

Spencer laughed as well and shook his handsome head. 'No, no, it's not that. I know! Didn't Ellen deliver your baby?'

Roxy smiled broadly. 'Yes, she did.'

They both looked at me.

I shrugged. 'I keep telling you – I sort of caught him, that's all. No biggie.'

Spencer's face seemed to glow with something I truly didn't want to see. 'Capable and modest as well,' he said.

'Not really,' I said. 'Look at the time. Didn't you say you were in a hurry, Roxy?'

'Well—' Roxy began.

'And I have to get to that Miller and Harris meeting. Did you need to talk to me about something, Spencer?'

Spencer shook his head and smiled slowly. 'Not really. Just wanted to say hi. I'd better get back indoors. Nice to meet you, Roxy.'

'And you, Spencer.'

Then he waved a hand and loped back into the office building. I pointed the key at the car and popped the door locks. 'Let's get going,' I said.

Roxy looked as if she was about to say something

but instead she sat into the car. I started the engine and drove out of the car park.

'He's a fine thing and he seems to be a very nice man,' Roxy said eventually, as if she could read my thoughts.

'Mmm,' I said.

'And he seems to like you.'

'Oh my God! Don't say that, Roxy,' I said, groaning loudly. 'He's just very polite. Yanks are way more polite than Irish people.'

'Mmm.'

'No, really,' I continued. 'I have no interest in him – or any other man at the moment, Roxy. I just broke up with my boyfriend – I told you that and I . . . I . . . well, my heart is a bit mangled. I have no intention of getting involved with anybody right now. Well, in fact, I was thinking maybe never again – you know yourself.'

'Yeah, I know.'

'So, you see, he's just got very, very good manners.'

'I believe you, Ellen – thousands wouldn't.'

'Ha-ha.'

I pulled the beemer to a halt outside Roxy's house. 'I see Maurice had his windows replaced,' I said.

'He did.'

'Looks good,' I said.

'It does.'

The front door of Roxy's house opened and Pa emerged with a sleeping Enrique draped over his shoulder. He waved and smiled at us and then went back inside, leaving the door open for her.

'I'd better go,' she said.

I nodded. 'Give me a ring and let me know how things are.'

'I will. Thanks, Ellen.'

'No problem.'

Roxy got out of the car and closed the door. She waved a hand at me and then, as if suddenly remembering something, tapped on the window. I slid the window open with the electric control by my elbow.

'What is it?' I asked.

'One thing.'

'What?'

'I think the Yank has it bad.'

'Shag off, Roxy!'

Roxy winked and her ponytail flicked to the left. 'See you later, Ellen. Bye.'

I drove away immediately and filled the car with talk radio to take my mind off what Roxy had said. I had no intention of entertaining the idea of Spencer Alexander the Third having a notion of me. What we'd had was a fling. A one-night stand. And we were both adults and he knew the rules as well as I did.

I went to my meeting with Miller and Harris – the crankiest women in town. They were sisters and owned a shopping centre that Gladstone and Richards let on their behalf. Sometimes I thought if we rented the units to Tiffany's and Harrods, they'd still manage to complain. Tim Gladstone had advised me once to employ the nod-and-smile technique with Miller and Harris, and that was exactly what I did as they reamed off their litany of whinges. 'The-rent-is-late-the-caretaker-is-stupid-who-do-those-tenants-think-they-are?' they said – or words to that effect. 'I know, I know,' I said, as I nodded and smiled and let it all wash over me. The only good thing about my meeting with the terrible twins was that it kept at bay all unsavoury thoughts about Yanks.

On my way back to the office, I had to pass close to my parents' house. As I got near, I was suddenly gripped with the unshakeable belief that my mother would know if I passed close by and, 'couldn't even be bothered to drop in to say hello'. So, resigning myself to bad coffee and even worse cake, I pulled up outside my childhood home. I'd stay for only a few minutes – just long enough to placate the ma. Then back to the office, make those endless phone calls that area mangers were expected to make, sort out a couple of problems about builders and clients, and then have a meeting with Molly to talk about the new computer system in which we were investing.

Of all my new responsibilities as Area Manager of Gladstone and Richards, giving Molly orders was the scariest. Not that I had the nerve actually to give her orders. I had started by sort of begging her to do things for me, and then decided that that was behaviour unbecoming of an executive. So, I moved on to using a very manipulative girly technique whenever I had to deal with her. That was a dismal failure – Molly hated girlies. So now I tried to do my job as Area Manager and tell Molly what she had to do, while avoiding all eye contact. That seemed to be working for the time being.

I was surprised when Angela Maunsell opened the door of my parents' house. Not that it was too extraordinary that she should be there – she was my mother's cousin, after all. It was the fact that she opened the door dressed from head to toe in red chiffon that had me gobsmacked.

'Well?' she asked, twirling in my parents' hallway. 'What do you think? I can't see getting married in white when you're my age, can you? To tell you the God's honest truth, Ellen, I couldn't care less if we never got married, but Ralph is a bit old-fashioned, and nothing will do him but the whole nine yards. So? What do you think of my wedding dress?'

Angela twirled again, and a cloud of gauzy red fabric billowed around her slight frame.

'You look deadly,' I said, because that was true in every sense of the word. 'Like a total slapper.'

Angela winked and smiled. 'Thanks, love. Did I tell you we're getting married in Rome?'

'No. That's brilliant. When is the big day?'

'November the eighteenth.'

'I hope Ralphie knows how lucky he is to be getting a stunner like you for a wife.'

'Go 'way ou' that! Get into the house and talk to your mother and stop trying to butter me up – I've no money to leave you.'

'Have to keep well in with my neighbours,' I said, walking past her into the kitchen. My mother was standing at the cooker in her regulation uniform – a navy pants, cream sweater, striped apron and oven glove – and a red feather boa.

'Very nice, Ma,' I said, walking over to kiss her on the cheek. Almost every time I stood beside my mother, I was amazed at how much taller than her I had become. I was five foot ten and she was five foot two, but it didn't make much sense to me because I could clearly remember a time when she had looked tall to me.

'Ellen! What brings you to these parts?'

'I had a meeting nearby and I thought I'd just drop in and say hello.'

My mother beamed. I'd been right. She had sensed my presence on her side of town – it was just as well I'd called.

'Cup of coffee?' Angela offered from behind me. She was back in her tracksuit.

'Coffee'd be great,' I said, sitting at the table. 'Where's the dress?'

'In its box. Give me my feathers, Phyllis, before you drop them into that stew you're cooking.'

'Boeuf bourguignon,' my mother said, unwinding the boa from around her neck. 'The old favourites are often the best.'

'Looks like stew to me,' Angela said, taking the length of red feathers and cantering out of the kitchen.

'There's a lovely bit of fruitcake there in the tin on the table,' my mother said.

'I'm grand – full. Just had my lunch, Mam. The coffee'll be perfect. So, how's everybody? Dad? Will? Any word of Alison?'

'Fine, all fine. Alison rang yesterday.'

'How is she?'

'Good. She and Dermot are off to the Maldives during her mid-term. Isn't that lovely?'

'Lovely,' I said, swallowing the jealousy that was rising in my throat.

As well as being super-efficient, my almost-perfect sister was also the jammiest wagon I knew. Everything seemed to go her way. If I was in charge of Alison (which was a thought too absurd to contemplate), I'd make her spend at least half her wages every week on Lotto tickets, because she had such good luck she was bound to win eventually.

At that point, Angela came back into the kitchen and all discussion immediately turned to the forth-coming wedding. As I sipped my grainy coffee and listened to her plans, I wondered whether somebody should warn Rome about what was going to hit it when Angela stepped off the plane.

I stayed talking with my mother and Angela for about half an hour. Then, glad to have performed my filial duties, I set off back to work, my head full, once more, of thoughts on how I could get out of Ruth's party and stay alive. I was really finding the whole thought of that bloody party oppressive and beginning to feel persecuted. Little did I know that within a month, I would be introduced to the real meaning of the word persecution.

# 24

I floated through the rest of Thursday and even managed to slip Molly a few sugar-coated orders before escaping for home. Thursday night was *ER* re-runs night, so I actually cooked a dinner. I opted for pasta with something red and saucy from a jar poured on top, and then smothered it in Parmesan so that really that was all I could taste.

Friday morning at work was bedlam but it was pretty routine bedlam. Things going wrong, Molly being cross with me – the usual. By the time I got into the office, Molly was already there, and not one piece of electronic equipment in the joint was working.

I interviewed no fewer than five IT specialists on the phone to get somebody to fix the chaos that our office had become with the new computer system. Tim and Spencer were going directly to a meeting in Newcastle West, and whether or not it was my responsibility was immaterial. I knew we were all dead if somebody didn't come to fix Molly's computer. Eventually I found a young woman who seemed to know what she was about, and she promised to come as soon as possible and save my life.

'It's all your fault,' I snapped at Spencer ten minutes later as he arrived into my office, looking dapper and yet attractively dishevelled in his cream linen suit.

'I'm sure it is, Ellen, but just for the record – what exactly is my fault?'

'The stupid new computer system. Molly is going to kill me. She thinks it's all my fault that that bloody network is bananas, and really it's all Reval's fault insisting we update our system.'

'It'll be better when it's working – I promise it will,' Spencer said, folding his arms and leaning against my desk. 'Shall I call somebody to come and take a look?'

I shook my head. 'Already done.'

'You're a whiz.'

'What can I say except that yes, I am a whiz.'

Spencer grinned and rearranged himself on the desk. 'Did you decide yet on your costume for Ruth's party?'

'No. I've been thinking about it all right but I haven't had a chance to sort it out. You?'

Spencer nodded and smiled. 'I found this really great place – they do costumes for theatre as well. The girls in that place are some of the nicest, most helpful people I've ever been lucky enough to meet.'

I'll bet, I thought, appraising Spencer's handsome profile as I pretended to fiddle with the drawer of my filing cabinet. I'll just bet they were helpful.

'What's it called? The costume-hire place?'

'Wearing Thin. Isn't that a cool name? Why? Do you think you might use them?'

I nodded. 'I've been trying to think of something to wear that won't make me look like either a transvestite or a prostitute. They might be able to help me.'

'But I thought you had a costume? I'm sure India told me you had.'

'Spencer, ignore my friends – they just want me to look like a fool.'

'You never look like a fool.' His voice did that octave-dropping thing again, and he fixed me with a trance-like gaze. *The Yank has it bad*, I heard Roxy's voice say inside my head. No way, I told it – no goddamn way. I opened the filing cabinet and fiddled with a row of suspended files. Spencer and I were just colleagues – OK, maybe a bit more than that in the Clarion, but that was just one of those things and now it was over. I looked at Spencer under my arm and he grinned. Damn. Was he watching me? Picking up about half the folders from the drawer, I carried them to the desk.

'Well,' I said, with a mock sigh. 'Better get cracking. Lots of work to do. How about yourself? Aren't you and Tim going to meet that crowd in Newcastle West? The health-farm people?'

Spencer nodded. 'I'm just about to leave.'

'Is Tim here?'

'No. I'm meeting him there at twelve.'

I looked at my watch. 'There can be an awful lot of traffic at this time of day – you'd be surprised.' I shuffled my files.

Spencer stood up and walked to the door. 'I was

wondering if you'd like to catch a movie or something tonight, if you're not busy.'

'Oh dear,' I said, scrabbling for a plausible lie. 'I promised my sister I'd baby-sit tonight. Sorry about that.'

'Some other time,' he said, a gentle smile on his lips.

'Definitely – that'll be great. I'll look forward to it. I'll see you tomorrow at Ruth's party.'

Spencer gave a mock military salute and left the room. As soon as my office door closed, I dropped my head onto the desk. OhmygodwhatwasIgoingtodo? *The Yank has it bad, the Yank has it bad,* Roxy's voice repeated. 'Oh shut up, Roxy,' I said aloud.

I lifted my head, feeling better as I managed to weave some kind of an explanation for the earnest look in those eyes. Everybody knew that Yanks were friendly and he didn't know anybody else and maybe he was even hoping for a reprise of last Saturday night's activities. That would be natural enough and would mean that he was just interested in my body. Which was great and exactly how I wanted to keep things between us.

There would be nothing to worry about between Spencer and me as long as we kept emotions out of the picture. Bloody emotions – never did me any good anyway. I was certain that Spencer had no intention of getting emotionally involved with the first woman he'd met when he arrived in Ireland. That line of reasoning cheered me up considerably. I wasn't worried about lust – lust was grand; it was love that caused all the problems.

The IT woman came just as I'd waded through my Spencer-worry and, though I was thrilled to see her, the fact that she looked like a twelve-year-old boy in oversized army fatigues didn't inspire me with confidence. Still, Molly had stuck to her side and that meant she was off my back and I was happy with that state of affairs.

'I think I'll take this opportunity to go through that whole filing cabinet,' I said, as Molly and the combat-clad IT genius looked at me. 'I'll be in my office if you need me.' I ran off and slammed the door behind me, saying a small prayer that they'd forget I was there as they became involved in the intricacies of networks.

And that was pretty much the case. Friday trotted along quite nicely and, apart from treating Molly with kid gloves, I was finding that I really liked my new job as Area Manager. When I'd started, I'd been a little nervous at the thought of all the networking and planning I was going to have to do. Contrary to what I would have expected though, I was full of ideas and already progressing a plan to have Gladstone and Richards as the premier estate agent in town. Which was what I'd said at my interview, pretty much – I was just surprised that I was able to follow through.

I was also discovering, to my surprise, that I was a nifty little negotiator. I had hung up the phone more than once that first week of my new job, amazed that I had actually managed to talk someone into seeing things my way. Pity that talent didn't seem to apply to my personal life. Still, who knew what the future held? Maybe I'd offer my services to the UN, and bring about world peace.

I'd pretty much finished all my work by four and decided to head for Wearing Thin on my way home. If I was going to this party, I was damned if I was going to look like a fool. Even the brokenhearted had to keep up appearances after all.

I pulled out of the car park and into the manic Friday afternoon traffic. As I edged my car, slowly, through the town, I cursed myself for not just leaving it at work and walking to the costume-hire shop. It would have been faster even if the shop had been a couple of miles away. The traffic slowed from treacle to complete gridlock as I drove up O'Connell Street. What the hell was wrong with me that I'd decided to take this route? A sudden, heavy mist descended, making everything look grey and indistinct.

Pedestrians wove their way across the street between the stationary cars, flicking up the collars of their autumn jackets to combat the sudden winter weather. As I fiddled with the radio and cursed the town planners, I saw Roxy. She was standing outside the Augustinian church with her buggy, her two little girls, and a tall, willowy young man.

She had her back to me so I could clearly see the man's face. It was pale and almost pretty – smooth, clear skin; big eyes with heavy lashes; high, delicate cheekbones; and all topped off with shiny black hair that fell onto his forehead as he spoke, causing him to flick his head backwards as if to clear his vision.

Really and truly, he was beautiful – like all the romantic poets I'd ever imagined.

As I watched Roxy and her mysterious friend, the man leaned forward and picked up one of the girls – I wasn't sure but I thought it was Shakira. Roxy became very agitated as the man hugged and kissed the child. Even from the distance, I could tell that Roxy was upset. Not that she was shouting or any- thing – it was more to do with the sudden rigidity in her spine. She looked as if she might actually physically snap in two.

The conversation between Roxy and the pretty man continued, but now Roxy had one hand on the arm of the child in his arms. Though he looked quite harmless, there was something about Roxy that was setting off alarm bells inside me. I opened the window of the car.

'Roxy!' I shouted.

Roxy, the man and the two little girls all turned to look.

'Hey, Roxy! Come on! Your lift is here. Did you forget? I was driving around looking for you every- where.'

I looked around me at the traffic. It was going nowhere, so I got out of the car and walked towards them.

'Will I take the baby out of the buggy? Hey, girls! How are you? Come on. McDonald's will be closed if we don't hurry.'

Roxy looked at me with her big, old-young eyes. 'Sorry about that, Ellen. I had to pick up some medicine for Shakira and there was a queue in the chemist.'

She bent down and whipped Enrique from his bed. He squirmed and wriggled in his sleep as she handed him to me and proceeded to collapse the buggy. All the time, the man stood silently by us. I arranged Enrique on my shoulder and stole a look at the man. He was watching Roxy with a type of intent that made the small hairs on my arms stand up. He was still holding Shakira. Roxy stood up.

'Ellen, I never introduced you. This is my friend, Ellen Grace. Ellen – Teddy Hannon.'

But I'd already guessed. And even though I didn't know any details, there was something in the air around Teddy Hannon that made me understand why he frightened Roxy.

'Nice to meet you,' I said.

Teddy Hannon's eyes flicked in my direction and he nodded.

'Could you carry her over and put her into the back of the car?' I said. 'That traffic will start to move and I'll be lynched if I'm blocking it up again.'

I led the way to my car and Teddy Hannon deposited the little girl he was holding into the back. Roxy ran around like a lunatic, throwing the buggy into the boot, and strapping the other little girl into the car. Then she climbed in herself, and I handed her the still-sleeping Enrique. Throughout, Teddy Hannon stood, silently, beside the car.

'Right,' I said, opening the driver's door. 'See you so. Nice to meet you, Teddy.'

Miraculously the traffic began to move forward as soon as I sat into the car, and I drove off. Roxy chatted to Shakira and Shania, and I watched Teddy Hannon standing like a poet on a cliff, staring after my car as we drove away. Enrique gurgled.

'Thanks,' Roxy said, suddenly. 'How did you know, Ellen?'

'I didn't,' I said, catching her eye in the rear-view mirror. I could see that she was terrified – eyes wide, lips blanched and bitten, face almost grey with fear.

'Are we going to McDonald's now?' Shania asked.

'Oh, I don't think so, love,' Roxy said, looking away. 'Ellen meant later. Didn't you, Ellen?'

'No, I meant now,' I said, changing lanes as I changed my mind about hiring a costume. Stupid party! I'd find something to wear tomorrow. 'I think I could do with a feed of junk food right now – what do you think, girls?'

Shania and Shakira cheered and Roxy smiled at me in the mirror. We drove to the nearest McDonald's which was festooned with Halloween decorations. The girls squealed with delight when a vampire version of Ronald McDonald handed them a couple of Halloween masks. We found a table, fed and watered the girls and rocked Enrique back to sleep before seating ourselves at a separate table next to the children.

'So?' I said, pausing to bite into a Big Mac.

Roxy looked at me and sipped her coffee.

'Are you going to tell me what happened?'

She shrugged. 'Nothing much . . . it's just him. He wants access to the girls.'

I swallowed a lump of meat. 'Well, he is their father, isn't he?'

Roxy nodded. 'Unfortunately.'

'Jesus, he's very good-looking, though, Roxy! I have to hand it to you.'

Roxy finished her entire paper cup of coffee. 'Funny that. He looks ugly to me, now. I mean, I know he's good-looking and all, but when I look at him—'

Her voice trailed away and she looked into the distance, absentmindedly jiggling Enrique's buggy.

'Well, refuse him access if you don't want him to see them,' I said, downing half a litre of Coke. Traffic jams are thirsty work.

Roxy laughed a hard little laugh. 'Easier said than done.'

'Are the girls attached to him?'

'No, they hardly know him. Shania's a bit afraid of him, if anything. I think she probably remembers some of the scenes before he went to prison. I'm not sure – she was only a toddler – but she doesn't like him.'

'Well, I have to admit there is something a bit scary about him all right,' I said. 'Is that why you don't want him having access?'

Roxy nodded. 'I know this is a terrible thing to say but I don't think he really wants the girls. He never had much time for them. It's to do with me. Ever since we first met, Teddy has been kind of obsessed with me. That sounds a bit bigheaded, doesn't it?'

'No.'

'Even if it does, it's true. He couldn't accept it when I left him and even when we were together – before things started to go bad and stuff – he used to scare me sometimes. Teddy is full of talk about destiny and fate and soul mates and all that, and he used to say he and I were soul mates. Meant to be either together or alone but not with anybody else.'

'Sounds romantic in a way.'

Roxy nodded. 'All my friends thought that, and I suppose I did as well – for a while. Then I realised it wasn't just something he said to get into my knickers or whatever. He meant it.'

'So I take it he's not too happy about Pa?'

Roxy laughed and rolled her eyes.

'And Enrique?'

Roxy shook her head. 'Funny thing. He never said one word about him. I thought he'd say something – he has a tongue like a knife, that fella.'

'But he didn't.'

'No. You must have been right about it not being Teddy who broke into my house.'

'Told you, Roxy.'

'Thank God!'

'So, what will you do about the access?'

Roxy shook her head. 'I don't know. I can't bear the thought of him taking the girls off by himself. I might never see them again.'

'What does Pa say?'

'He doesn't know, yet.'

'You should tell him.'

'I will. I know Pa isn't the girls' father, but do you know something, Ellen? He has more time for them than Teddy Hannon ever had.'

Shakira and Shania arrived at our table at that point, sloshing Fanta and ice in paper cups.

'I wanna go trick-or-treating,' Shakira said, climbing up beside her mother. You'd have easily known they were mother and daughter. Shania was dark like her father and had the same delicate features, but luckily she didn't have the insane look in her eyes. Shakira was dark as well, but looked more like Roxy.

'Please,' Shakira said, solemnly.

'Please,' Shania said, looking at me this time. 'I've a witch's costume.'

'Who could refuse such lovely ladies?' I said, standing up. 'Let's go.'

# 25

By the time I dropped Roxy and the kids home, it was almost 6.30 – too late to be hiring costumes. I rang Alison as soon as I got in. Some sort of warped logic: maybe if I made contact with my sister, it would mean I hadn't told Spencer a lie about baby-sitting. . . . I knew it made no sense but I was, somehow, compelled to do it.

'Hey, sis,' I said when she answered the phone. 'How are you?'

'Oh, Ellen—' she said and then burst into loud and pitiful sobs.

'Alison? What is it? What's wrong? Did something happen to Kieran?'

'Oh, Ellen—' she said again and cried harder.

I dropped my handbag onto the kitchen counter. 'Alison, look, take a deep breath and tell me what's wrong.'

'It's . . . it's . . . Der . . . it's Dermot.'

'Dermot? What happened?'

Alison upped the decibels of the crying for a few seconds. I took a deep breath. Bastard! What was that bastard doing to my sister? I was going to get into my car and drive straight to Dublin and beat seven kinds of shit out of him and I didn't care if he was six foot three and a scrum half.

'What did he do to you?'

'Oh, Ellen—' the crying started in earnest again. That decided me. I was going to tell Mam, and even if she did love Doctor Dermot, she wasn't going to let him do the dirty on our Alison like that. Who did he think he was? Bloody mouth-breather. He didn't deserve a beautiful, accomplished wife like my sister. I listened as the sobs subsided and, seeing my opportunity between crying jags, tried again.

'Alison, I'm here. I can come up if you want. Don't worry about a thing. Where's Dermot now?'

'Out. At training.'

'OK, good. And Kieran? Where's Kieran?'

'Playing here at my feet.'

'OK, that's good.' I paused to try to think how I might maintain this improvement. Alison was definitely calming down and I wanted to keep her that way. 'Why don't you tell me what happened?'

'Well, it all just happened a little while ago – that's why I'm still in a state, I suppose. The shock.'

She paused again and I was afraid she might start crying but I could hear her say something to Kieran. Bloody bastard, Dermot! What other woman would have him, the big lump?

'Ellen?'

'Yes.'

'Thought you were gone.'

'No, I'm not going anywhere. You were saying?'

'Yes. Well the phone rang just before Dermot was

to go out and it was Gillian O'Neill and she said . . . she said it and we were just flabbergasted.'

'What did she say exactly?' I said through gritted teeth.

'Oh, that Dermot was to captain the team on Saturday. Can you believe that? I'm so proud, I can't—'

And the tears started all over again.

'You're crying like the rain because your husband was asked to captain some stupid team?' I interrupted.

'Yeeeeeeees.'

'A rugby team?'

'Not just any team. He was asked to act as Captain for Ireland on Saturday,' she said tearfully. 'The regular captain broke his leg last weekend, bungee jumping at a charity event.'

'I thought something horrible had happened to you, Alison. I nearly fainted here at the end of the line and I was ready to get into my car and drive to Dublin to kill your husband because I thought he'd done something to you.'

'Really?' Alison asked, as the tears stopped.

'Yes, really.'

'Oh my God!' she screamed into the phone, as she began to cry all over again. 'That's so sweet. Really, Ellen, I can't tell you how much it means to me that you'd kill my husband.'

Then she had to stop talking as she was too busy crying. I tapped my foot impatiently as I waited it out. What the hell was wrong with my sister? I was supposed to be the sister that was all over the place in our family. She was supposed to be calm and cool and contained and successful. Not bonkers. Eventually the tears stopped.

'Are you OK?' I said.

'Yes, thanks,' she replied, shakily. 'I think it's just the hormones.'

'Hormones?'

'I'm pregnant. Didn't Mam tell you? I was going to call you myself this weekend but I thought she'd have told you already. I'm so sorry . . . I—'

I could hear her voice moving back into bawling gear. 'Alison, Alison, listen to me – it's fine, great, grand. I'm not upset you didn't tell me. Congratulations. Are you still going to the Maldives?'

'Of course we are. I can't wait.'

'That's good. So, when are you due?'

'Next May. I only found out yesterday but I should have guessed – I know it mightn't be obvious but I don't really feel like myself.'

There's an understatement, I thought, but didn't say a word.

'We're delighted. Dermot's so funny – he did a little dance when I told him and now . . . now . . . this—'

'Look, Al – great news but there's my doorbell – got to go. Talk to you soon.'

I hung up opened the fridge and tore a leg off a chicken which was still in its foil bag. Jesus! Alison was pregnant now as well. What the hell was going on? Between marriages and pregnancies that were happening to everyone else but me, I was beginning to feel as if the universe had a grudge against me. At least Doctor Dermot hadn't done the dirty on my sister. That was something, even if she was a bit unhinged.

Joey and I ate the chicken and we settled down in front of the TV. I thought I might do my hand-washing and even sew the hem on the skirt I'd glued the previous week. Might as well, as a bachelor girl with nobody to care about her, I'd have to establish a routine of looking after myself. Get into the groove of what was promising to be the rest of my life.

Before getting down to work, I thought I'd just watch a few minutes of *Dr Quinn: Medicine Woman* – where did that woman get such a good-looking husband? And all that hair? Next thing I knew, it was four in the morning and I was sprawled on the couch and the TV was still on. I staggered into bed, thanking God it was Friday night, and slept the sleep of the innocent until almost ten.

When I awoke, I was feeling pretty perky and, as I lay in bed, turning the events of the week over in my mind, I suddenly thought of Tony Jordan. Maybe he'd be at Ruth's party. She'd said that she'd met him again, hadn't she? And he was a neighbour, after all. I jumped out of bed and ran into the shower. This was ridiculous. Why the hell was I thinking about Tony Jordan?

As the water pounded over me in the shower, I found myself remembering our relationship. If you could call it that. If I was to be honest, I had to admit that it hadn't been a relationship as much as a string of trysts – great trysts, but trysts nevertheless. Great sex. Great fun. Then there was the fact that he'd almost got me killed with his bloody criminal dealings.

I was definitely having absolutely nothing to do with Tony Jordan – that much was for sure. Yes, it was true, he was gorgeous. And it was true that there was a certain air about him – a look in his eye, maybe – that seemed to rock something deep inside me. But it didn't matter. After all, Teddy Hannon was as good-looking as Tony Jordan, and he was a head case.

I dried my hair and found some clothes and the phone book. And then, with a huge mug of cocoa and a plate of butter-dripping toast, I sat down by the phone to find a costume-hire shop. First, I tried Wearing Thin.

> *Thank you for calling Wearing Thin theatrical and party costumes. Your call is important to us. Our business hours are Monday to Friday, 9.30 a.m. to 5 p.m. We're not available to take your call right now. Please leave your name and number and we'll get back to you as soon as possible.*

Damn.

Dripping butter onto the telephone directory, I rang every single number I could find under costume hire. All closed. What the hell was that about? Didn't they think anybody wanted a costume at the weekend?

What if I was staging an important play? This was not good. I'd been banking on being able to hire a costume for Ruth's party. I was not going to go as a fairy – even presuming that my fairy costume was still at my parents' house.

Well, I had tried and there was not a thing I could do about it. I couldn't go now. I had no costume and, worse than that, Tony Jordan was invading my thoughts – Ruth would just have to get over it. I dialled her number with shaking hands.

'Hello?' Ruth's voice said.

'Hi, Ruth. It's me. Listen—'

'Oh Ellen! Ellen, I was just going to ring you. I had a letter from my mother – my birth mother. She sent photographs and everything. Do you know she took photographs of me when I was born? She sent copies to me. Paddy looks just like me – I never realised. I'm so delighted you're coming tonight. I don't think I could go through with the party if you and India weren't here, and Emerson would be devastated if we called it off – he's so looking forward to it. Anyway, I'll show you the stuff. I still don't know if I'll meet her yet – feels weird – but, look, we'll talk about it later. OK?'

'Sure,' I said.

'Talk to you later.'

'Bye, Ruth.'

And she was gone. I lay down on the couch and watched *Little House on the Prairie* and cried my eyes out with Charles Landon. Never was a man born who was so in touch with his crying side. Shit! Now

I had no choice but to go to the party. I couldn't abandon Ruth when she needed me. A telling off would have been fine. I wouldn't have cared if she had been cross with me for not going, but I couldn't desert her when she was so vulnerable. Maybe I could wear civvies – that wouldn't be too bad. I rang home.

'Hello?'

'Mam?'

'Ellen. Good morning, love. I heard you were talking to your sister last night on the phone. Isn't that great news?'

'About the baby? Yes, it's great – really, really great. Mam, do you remember that pink fairy costume I wore years and years ago to a party? I don't suppose it's still around? Probably not, and if it isn't, don't worry.'

'No, no it is. It's upstairs in your old bedroom. Funny coincidence, really. I was talking to Ruth the other day and telling her I found it and washed it – and really, American clothes are great because it still looks as good as new.'

Damn, I thought – it *was* there *and* Ruth knew about it. Damn and blast!

'Why do you ask?'

'Oh, there's a party in Ruth's tonight – fancy dress – I haven't anything else to wear.'

'Drop by and collect it, so, love. Do you still have your key? Will and Shannon have gone on some college trip and Dad and I have to go to a funeral.'

'Who died?'

'Oh, some second cousin of your father's, but it's in Waterford, so we'll be gone all day.'

'I have a key. It's fine.'

'OK so, love. Look, I'd better go. Angela and Ralph are coming to the funeral and we have to pick them up.'

'But Angela is related to you, not Dad.'

'I know. But Ralph loves funerals – says it makes him feel lucky, so they're coming along for the jaunt.'

'Have a lovely time.'

'You too, love. Enjoy your party.'

'Thanks. I'll try.'

But I'm not likely to succeed, I thought as I hung up. Especially now that the fairy costume was looking inevitable.

At about four that afternoon, I let myself into my parents' spookily silent house and trudged up the stairs to get my stupid dress out of the wardrobe. It was exactly where my mother had said it would be. I lifted it out and it rustled in response. Bloody thing! I couldn't believe I had to wear it. I was going to make Ruth pay for this loyalty sometime. Meanwhile, I was in a hurry.

I had slung the offending garment over my shoulder and begun my descent of the stairs when I heard a loud bang. Stopping in my tracks, I listened. Nothing. Must have been Mrs Dooley next door, or a car backfiring. I began to walk again. A sudden crash, like a vase falling, rent the air, followed by what sounded like voices. But there was nobody home. Will was away, my mother had said, and so were my parents. That left only one explanation.

My parents were being robbed. Or I was being stalked by a murderous felon who had followed me and intended to kill me on my mother's new stair carpet. I preferred the former explanation. It was the third bang that decided me. Before I could think better of it, I had bounded up the stairs in the direction of the noise – my parents' bedroom, as far as I could ascertain – and flung open the door.

'OK,' I shouted, as I ran in. 'The police are on their way. Get the hell out of here!'

As the words came out of my mouth, I cursed myself for not having had the foresight actually to ring the police before charging in like McGiver. Now I was going to be raped and murdered and it was too late to ring anyone.

'Ellen—' Will's voice said as he appeared from deep under my parents' duvet.

'Jesus!' I said.

'I know what this looks like—'

'Jesus, Will!'

'Look, Ellen, I can explain.'

A rosy-cheeked blonde girl sat up in the bed beside Will. She smiled and wiggled her fingers at me in a wave. Now I don't exactly have the best memory in the world for faces, but, unless I was having hallucinations, this was not my brother's fiancée.

I shook my head and tutted. 'Will, Will, Will.'

Will tried a smile but I scowled in return and

looked at my watch. 'At least you aren't burglars. Clean up before you leave.'

I turned and left the room, holding my stomach the whole way down the stairs to prevent the guffaw in my throat from escaping. Will was going to have to rethink the whole engaged thing, I thought as I trotted to my car, pink dress rustling like a giant crisp bag. But maybe that wasn't such a bad thing. And I was going to be able to blackmail him merci- lessly for the foreseeable future. And that definitely wasn't a bad thing.

When I got back to my apartment, I had barely enough time to shower and dress. I slapped a load of make-up on in the hope that I'd at least look fairly all right around the face. But when I looked at myself in the full-length mirror on the back of the wardrobe door, I could have cried. There I was, all five foot ten of me, dressed in a calf-length pink satin dress with a pearlised pink gauze overskirt, puffy satin sleeves and a handkerchief hem. In an effort to look less camp and more vamp, I had put on a pair of pink strappy high heels. But they only made matters worse, as they made me closer to six foot one than five foot ten. I was simply too big to dress as a fairy. Instead of looking all delicate and fragile and like I lived in a buttercup, I looked like an extra from *Priscilla, Queen of the Desert*.

I rooted in the bag that had been hanging on the hanger with the dress, and found a diamanté tiara and a diamanté-encrusted wand. Plonking the tiara on my head, I went back to the mirror for another look. I had to laugh. I looked ridiculous – there was no other word for it. I twisted my body, and my pink, gauze wings flopped around with the movement. Still, I thought as I adjusted my tiara, Spencer was going to be at Ruth's, and, if Roxy was right and he was developing any sort of a notion of me, this would definitely cure him. With that thought, I pulled on a short leather biker jacket, picked up my wand and handbag, and left for the party.

## 26

I arrived at Ruth's just in time to see India and family emerge from their car. India was wearing a long black coat that pooled on the ground behind her, and had piled up her hair and somehow painted a white stripe across the front.

'Hey Cruella!' I shouted as I walked towards her, 'You look great.'

She turned and smiled. 'Thanks, Twinkle-toes. So do you.'

'No I don't – I look like a demented drag queen.'

India laughed and shook her head. 'No, you look like the fairy at the top of the Christmas tree.'

'Bloody big Christmas tree.'

'You look lovely, Ellen – stop. I think we're late.'

All around us was a sea of parked cars. How many people did Ruth and Emerson know anyway?

I shook my head. 'Not late, Cruella, darling – we're not late – just making an entrance.'

Tim arrived just then carrying Alyssa in her carseat. 'OK, dear, that's everything. I have the nappy bag here. Yes, that's it. I think I have it covered.'

Alyssa looked edible in a fleecy, spotted Dalmatian sleeping suit, complete with a hood that had tiny ears on top. Tim himself was dressed in a long, brown work coat, and a matching cloth cap – and he had a pink, purple and green spotted nappy bag slung diagonally across his chest.

'Oh my God! How cute is that baby?' I whispered, unable to resist stroking Alyssa's fat cheek.

Tim grinned. 'Isn't she something?'

'She certainly is,' I said. 'Cuter than any puppy dog.'

'More like a bag of cats than a puppy dog,' India said, smiling at her daughter. 'I think we'll have to take the doctor's word for it – Alyssa has colic.'

'Aw, poor Alyssa,' I said, kissing her gently on her sleeping forehead.

'Poor me, more like,' India said. 'I've spent most of today jiggling her around – don't wake her up.'

I saluted India and we made our way towards Ruth and Emerson's open front door where long beams of yellow light streaked out onto the gravel yard in the autumnal evening. It was a clear but cool night, and I was glad of the warmth of the leather jacket, and past caring how ridiculous I looked. Loud rap music shook the leaves on the rhododendron by the front door as we went in. I looked at Alyssa and then at India. She shook her head.

'That won't wake her,' she said. 'Once she actually goes to sleep, she stays asleep. All that crying is pretty exhausting for her as well as for me. We'll find some-place a little quieter than just here and she'll sleep for a couple of hours.'

I shook my head in amazement and watched as

Alyssa glided past the throngs in the narrow hallway and slept soundly on. The world of babies. Mysterious wasn't the word for it.

While Tim and India went in search of a quiet space for Alyssa, I went in search of Ruth. I soon found her in the kitchen, wearing a full nun's habit, complete with wimple and rosary beads. She was balancing Paddy – dressed only in a lion-skin patterned nappy – on one hip, as she rooted in the freezer for something.

'Hey, Missus,' I said.

Ruth grinned at me from under her arm. 'Aw, look at you – Tinkerbell.'

'Shut up, Sister Ruth – I can't believe they'd let a slapper like you wear that, even for fun.'

Ruth straightened up and began to fill a big glass bowl with ice cubes from a plastic tray. 'Haw-haw, very funny.'

Emerson came into the room wearing a loincloth and sandals, and took Paddy from Ruth's arms.

'I'll take him into the party for a while, Ruthie. Will I put a sweater on him?'

Ruth nodded and waved at Paddy as he left the room with his dad.

'Tarzan as man and boy?' I asked.

'Bingo,' Ruth said, filling a glass with water and taking a long drink. 'Though I think the sweater may ruin Paddy's outfit. Still.'

'So,' I said. 'How are you?'

Ruth grimaced and adjusted her wimple. 'Not too bad but a bit confused. And as if I didn't have enough problems the bloody corkscrew broke a couple of minutes ago. Why can't life ever be simple?'

I shook my head. 'Don't know. Seems to me just when you think everything is sorted out, the whole arse falls out of the world.'

'And ties you up in knots.'

'Exactly.'

'Knots of confusion,' Ruth said.

'You say it, sister.' And then, as if to prove my point, the back door opened and in walked Tony Jordan. My heart jumped against my ribs as if I'd received an electric shock, and I wasn't sure why. I'd known he'd probably be at the party, so what the hell was going on? He was dressed in a white frilled shirt, tight black pants and a short black jacket with bright silver buttons. A wide brimmed black hat complete with a red ribbon was perched on the back of his head.

'Ellen!' he said, a smile spreading across his face.

'Tony,' I said, unable to stop myself smiling back. My stomach squeezed and, for a tiny fraction of a second, I had the sensation of falling as I looked into Tony Jordan's eyes.

'I found the corkscrew, Ruth. Here it is,' he said.

Ruth grabbed the corkscrew that he tossed in her direction. 'Jesus, Tony! Lethal weapon here. Be careful.'

Tony smiled at Ruth and then looked straight back at me, and my head filled with memories of us kissing and kissing and kissing, and then I realised he was speaking. To me.

'Sorry?' I said.

'I just asked how you were.'

'Great. Great. Never better. You?'

'Terrific.'

'Great.' I twirled my wand in my hand. 'Nice costume – who are you supposed to be? Speedy Gonzalez?'

'Very funny – I'm supposed to be Zorro. Who are you? Shirley Temple Bar?'

'Haw-haw,' I said as we grinned at each other. I could hear Ruth clinking glasses and ice and bottles and I figured I should help, but I couldn't seem to take my eyes off Tony. His brown eyes were looking at me with such intensity, it felt like being touched, and my breath was beginning to feel as if it was caught in my chest. The back door opened again and a set of car keys came sailing through the air.

'Tone – the keys for the jeep,' Wolfie said. 'Ellen – good to see you. You look great.'

'As man-fairies go, Wolfie,' I said, hugging him. 'You make a pretty enormous schoolboy – I'd say the teachers wouldn't give you too much hassle.'

Wolfie laughed. 'This was actually my school uniform – can you believe that? My mother still had it. How do you figure?'

'Mothers, hah?'

'Mothers,' Wolfie agreed.

'I'd better bring this wine out to the party, now that we have a corkscrew, thanks to Tony,' Ruth said, attempting to lift a large crate full of bottles.

'Hang on a minute, Ruthie,' Wolfie said, picking

the crate up as if it was a bag of crisps. 'I'll give you a hand.'

And then they were gone. And Tony and I were alone in Ruth's kitchen, and somebody in the other room had changed the music to Marvin Gaye.

'Nice party,' Tony said, moving to stand by the sink.

I nodded.

He folded his arms across his white, ruffled chest. 'How have you been?'

'OK. You?'

Tony smiled. 'Didn't we just have this conversation a minute ago?'

I nodded.

'Ruth said you've had . . . a bit of hassle . . . broke up with your boyfriend?'

I nodded and looked down at my pink sandals. 'That's life.'

'That's life,' Tony echoed. 'Would you like a drink? There seems to be lots of stuff here. Juice? Wine? Fizzy water, flat water – whatever you like.'

'Fizzy water.'

Tony poured me a glass of water and walked over to where I stood. I took the glass from his hand, struggling to avoid touching but it was a waste of time. He touched me. Lightly. On the face.

'You look incredible,' he said.

'Like I said, for a man-fairy.' I tried to smile but my face muscles were paralysed and, no matter how much I wanted to, I couldn't stop looking at him.

He shook his head. 'Just amazing. Every time I

see you, Ellen, I get a shock – it's like I can't remember the reality of you and then I see you and—'

I kissed him. Long and hard and on the lips, cursing the glass of water in my hand. As we separated, he looked at me and took the glass from my hand, and he kissed me. My hands stretched across his back, and my body felt as if it might explode with pleasure. My head knew all the reasons why I shouldn't be doing this, but there were no messages that weren't sexual getting through from my brain to my body. As we finished kissing, Tony pulled me close and held me to his chest and kissed my head.

'Great wings,' he mumbled into my hair.

'Nice ruffle. Boy George,' I said as I inhaled the smell of him.

Tony laughed. 'I've missed you so much, Ellen. I know how things were and I know how we finished, and anyway, you were involved with somebody else, and I was . . . well, on the run . . . but all that time, I could never get you out of my head and—'

I looked up at him as he spoke and, before I could help myself, I kissed him again.

'Jesus, Ellen!' he said as we came up for breath. 'You're still just the most—'

'Unbelievably good surprise kisser?'

Tony laughed. 'Definitely one of your strong points – the surprise kissing. Can I ask you a question?'

I nodded.

'Did you miss me at all?' Tony stepped back and I looked at him and thought about Andrew and how much I'd loved him and all the hopes and heartache.

I searched Tony's olive-skinned face, and something that I'd never let myself admit rose to the surface.

'Yes,' I said, because suddenly I knew it was true. I had. There was just something about Tony Jordan. Something more than you could explain away by talking about handsome faces and pheromonal urges. 'Yes, I did miss you, Tony.'

And then, I'm sure we would have kissed again – and who can know what else would have happened? – except that the back door opened and a tall, blonde woman in a blood-red dress and masses of diamanté appeared in the kitchen, and ran up to Tony and wound her arms around him.

'At last, sweetie. I thought I'd never get here. Have you been here long?'

Tony looked at the woman and looked at me and I felt as if I'd been punched in the stomach. The woman reached up and kissed his cheek.

'Hello,' she said. 'I'm Nikki, Tony's fiancée, and you are?'

'This is Ellen,' Tony said.

Nikki reached out her left hand and pulled it back as quickly, but not before I'd seen the cluster of diamonds on her engagement finger.

'Ooops, wrong hand,' Nikki said, offering me her right one. We shook hands and I wondered if Tony had produced those diamonds from the china cat's arse in his other life as a thief.

'Nice to meet you, Ellen,' she said, beaming at me.

'You too, Nikki. Is that Ruth calling?' I said in a

loud voice that hurt my own ears. 'See you around, Tony.'

'I don't . . . it—' Tony said as I walked towards the door. 'Ellen?'

But I was gone. Out into the thronged hallway, my cheeks on fire, my heart pounding like a kangaroo's foot, and my stomach clenched with embarrassment. Brilliant! I was obviously never going to learn. Just as I was beginning to see the light at the end of the tunnel after Andrew – what the hell was wrong with me?

I watched the garishly dressed crowd of strangers that surrounded me and it was as though I was separated from them by a pane of glass. I was an alien. A weird, needy girlie who wanted to be loved so badly that anybody would do. Even a crook with a harlot for a girlfriend. What was it with me?

I found a table of wine bottles and desperately peered into each of them, searching for anaesthesia. But they were all empty – Ruth's bloody alcoholic friends had obviously polished them off. How could I leave without upsetting Ruth? Because I had to leave. I couldn't stay after I had humiliated myself so badly. I poured myself a glass of cranberry juice, but as soon as I swallowed the first mouthful I wanted to puke. Then again, that might have been due to the sheer stomach-crunching reality of what I'd done.

I closed my eyes and tried to wish it all away like I used to when I was a kid – but it was no good. I was an adult, and that wishing thing didn't work anyway – if it did, I'd be at home snuggled into the sofa, watching a movie, with Andrew. I wouldn't be alone.

My eyes filled with tears, and a hand grabbed my arm.

'Ellen?' a voice said from behind me.

I swung automatically towards the voice, pink gauze rustling as I moved.

'Spencer! Oh my God, Spencer! What do you look like?'

In spite of the fact that my world was in smithereens, I roared with laughter. Spencer was standing behind me, wearing a white, powdered wig, a blue brocade jacket, plain blue knee breeches, long, white socks and pointy, black, buckled shoes. His face was powdered as white as that of Will's girlfriend, Shannon. He had a pink rosebud mouth painted over his lips and a black, heart-shaped beauty spot on his cheekbone. He rolled his eyes. I bit my lip and tried to stop laughing.

'Louis Quatorze?' I asked, swallowing a laugh.

Spencer sighed. 'I think so. A French courtier of some description, I guess.'

'And did you do the make-up yourself?'

Spencer shook his head. 'Part of the service. When I hired the costume, I made an appointment to be dressed at seven o'clock tonight. I thought it would be fun . . . not just funny.'

I laughed again, in spite of myself. 'Sorry, Spence.'

'Don't worry about it – I should have known that as they were theatrical costumiers, something outrageous like this would happen. Do you think men in France really dressed like this?'

I nodded.

'Even the lips and the beauty spot?'

'Maybe not for everyday wear,' I said. 'But it's really not too bad. Very *Dangerous Liaisons*. That's what a costume party is all about. Have a look at me, for pity's sake.'

Spencer smiled and reached out a hand to ruffle my overskirt. 'I think you look great. In fact, I think you look like Xena the Warrior Princess would look in a pink fairy dress. Pretty damn sexy!'

'Thanks, Spence, and *I* think *you* look like John Malkovich – pretty damn sexy as well.'

We smiled at each other. Spencer was a really nice man, I thought. Good and kind and friendly and very, very handsome – even in a wig and white face powder. And he was all of those things and seemed to like me, and I had just been humiliated by Tony Jordan and needed to be around somebody who liked me better than they liked stupid bitches in red dresses. Anyway, it was only fun, wasn't it? What could be so bad about that? No need for anybody to get hurt. I was just looking for a bit of distraction and Spencer was new in town, not to mention the fact that he was obviously a commitment phobic if he'd been engaged six times.

'Ellen?'

'Yes?'

'You OK?'

I nodded.

'Would you like a drink?'

I looked at him. 'Coffee, maybe?'

Spencer smiled and raised his eyebrows. 'Coffee?'

I stared at him. Really, that painted-on rosebud mouth was a very sexy look – it was a pity it had gone out with the French Revolution. I nodded. 'I think I could do with a cup of coffee right about now.'

'OK – well, as usual, I think I know where we can get real good coffee,' Spencer said.

I shrugged into my leather jacket that I'd been trailing along behind me since I'd arrived at Ruth's. 'I have a new espresso machine,' I said. 'And I'd love to make you coffee. What do you think?'

Spencer fixed the collar of my jacket and straightened my tiara. 'Will Ruth mind if we leave?'

I shook my head as I considered his question. Would Ruth mind? Well, maybe she would – it was true that she was upset and all that. However, I couldn't bear to watch Tony and that simpering blondie woman all evening after I'd been such an idiot. Not to mention the fact that Spencer was so handsome and so interested and that the sexual energy between us could have run a small power station.

'I'll apologise tomorrow,' I said. 'That is, if you think you'd like some coffee?'

'You must be kidding,' Spencer said. 'No "ifs" about it.'

'I like a decisive coffee-drinker,' I said, grinning and beckoning him to follow.

Spencer and I left the party then, and I arranged with him to follow my car back to my apartment building. As I drove home, I blocked out all thoughts that weren't sexual. Even so, the drive cooled my ardour considerably. By the time we were standing side by side in the apartment's underground car park, waiting for the lift, I was no longer filled with desire. Instead, I was sort of mortified. My God! What had I been thinking? What was I doing inviting this man back to my apartment for sex just because I was angry with another man? That couldn't be all right. I was going to have to have a very serious look at my life. The lift doors opened and we stepped in together.

Maybe I'd really just make coffee and we could chat for a while and he'd go home. That was an idea. After all, I hadn't (luckily) said, *How about we go back to my place for a quick shag?* And though it certainly was what I'd been thinking and probably what he'd understood me to be saying, I hadn't actually said it. Spencer was an honourable guy. He'd be happy to drink his coffee and leave if I made it clear that that was what I wanted. The only problem was I didn't actually own an espresso machine, so it would have to be instant coffee. Still.

'Ellen?'

I turned to look at Spencer who was leaning against one of the stainless-steel walls of the lift.

'Penny for them?' he said.

I smiled. 'Oh, I don't know—' I began, but he leaned forward and kissed me gently on the lips, and the explosion of sexual energy that that chaste kiss unleashed was so huge, I could almost hear it.

'Sorry,' he said. 'You were saying.'

I shook my head and moved close to him, kissing him as I pressed him against the wall, and, within seconds, we were in a bad movie scene where the couple have sex in the elevator. Except that we didn't quite have sex – not that I wouldn't have – my apartment building is simply not tall enough. The doors opened on the third floor and I ran Spencer down the hall and through my front door in a flurry of bodies and lips and hands. I slammed the front door behind us and, without bothering to turn on the light, we pulled at fabric until all around was a sea of blue brocade and pink chiffon, and all I could think about was the overwhelming desire of the moment. It was incredible. After we'd had sex just inside my front door, we moved to the bedroom, where I fell asleep almost as soon as my head hit the pillow.

I woke up in the middle of the night to find Spencer looking at me in the dark. He smiled as he saw that I'd opened my eyes.

'We didn't have any coffee,' he said.

'Mmm,' I agreed, stretching. 'Sorry about that. And it gets worse, Spence – I don't have an espresso machine. I mean, I *am* planning to buy one, but I'm afraid I don't have it just yet. Sorry.'

'So you brought me here under false pretences?'

I nodded. Spencer grinned and kissed me. I kissed him back and rolled on top of him and pretty much let myself slide, once more, into a delicious sexual oblivion.

When I awoke in the morning, Spencer was still

asleep, traces of white make-up evident in his hair-line. It was my turn to watch him as he slept. My heart felt heavy in my chest as I looked at his boyish profile. Big business tycoon, and he still looked about twelve when he was asleep. Poor old Spence – I really kind of liked him and hoped that that was all he felt for me – kind of liked me. I was sure it was – he hardly knew me after all.

Wide awake, I decided to get up. It was seven o'clock and just light. The sky outside my apartment window was grey and cloudy, and promised nothing except rain. I closed the curtains and made myself toast and cocoa and turned on TV. A documentary on dolphins took my attention and I half-watched as I ate. Just as the dolphins were swimming with a woman in a floral swimsuit, I heard a gentle tapping at my front door. Angela. I didn't want to answer but I knew she could probably hear the TV from outside the door. Anyway, maybe something was wrong. I opened the door and a gigantic bunch of assorted flowers was pushed into my face.

'I'm sorry,' Tony's voice said from behind the flowers.

I stepped back and he lowered the flowers. He was still wearing his Zorro costume, except that now it was wrinkled and the collar of the shirt was wide open. His eyes were red-rimmed, and stubble shaded his jawline.

'I'm sorry,' he said again, and I became conscious that all I was wearing was a long green T-shirt that I'd found in the laundry basket as my toast was cooking.

'Why?' I asked. 'Why are you sorry, Tony?'

'I brought her to the party on purpose. I knew you'd be there and I knew you'd broken up with your boyfriend—' He paused and took a deep breath. 'Does that make any sense?'

I shook my head.

'OK,' he said. 'I'll start again. I brought Nikki to the party because I knew you'd be there and . . . I don't know . . . I thought maybe you'd be jealous . . . maybe I hoped you'd be jealous and then . . . then when we were in the kitchen, I realised it was a mistake, but it was too late. So, I'm sorry. I never meant to hurt you – that would be the last thing I'd ever do.'

'Oh,' I said, anger rising in my chest. Who the hell did he think he was that he imagined he had the power to upset me? Bastard! I hated him. Game-playing bastard. 'Are you apologising for bringing your fiancée to Ruth's party? Jeez, Tone. Don't apologise for that. We all brought somebody along to Ruth's party.'

Tony looked at me and I leaned against the door-jamb. 'She's not my fiancée.'

'That's not what *she* thinks,' I said. 'But look, we all say things we don't mean when we're looking for a convenient shag, don't we?'

'Ellen, listen to me—'

I stepped back and let out a scream as something sharp stabbed my bare foot.

'Bloody tiara,' I said, kicking the offending object across the floor. We both looked down at the tangle of clothes still on the floor inside the door and, camp as they were, somehow it was obvious that half the clothes belonged to a man.

'Well, well, Ellen,' he said, focusing on Spencer's shoes. 'I see I'm wasting my time here. See you round.'

Tony turned and walked away, the flowers dangling from his hand. I slammed the door. What the hell was that all about? Who did he think I was? Bastard! I ignored the memory of the look of hurt in his eyes. I was damned sure he'd soon find succour and comfort. He'd soon get over it. He didn't care about me and I'd made a complete fool of myself with him, but now it was fine.

Boy, was I glad I hadn't sent Spencer home. That had shown Tony Jordan I wasn't just another idiot girl, sitting around waiting for him to bestow his handsome presence on me. Not that he'd ever said anything like that, but it was the case, I just knew it was. I had no intention, anyway, of ever letting myself be vulnerable again like I had been with Andrew. It simply wasn't worth it.

Then the tears came. Hot, stinging tears, flowing down my face from that bottomless pit that had appeared inside me after Andrew had left. I hated them and I hated the feeling of emptiness inside me that invariably accompanied them. I pulled jeans and underwear out of the same clothes basket in which I'd found my T-shirt, shoved my feet into a pair of trainers, and picked up my leather jacket from the clothes pile on the floor.

I scribbled a note to Spencer, telling him I'd been

called away on family business, and to eat anything he could find, and that I'd see him on Monday at work. Then I ran out the door in case he woke up. I couldn't handle trying to fob him off and convince him I was fine, just fine – especially as I was crying like the rain. It might be hard to convince him.

In the foyer near the front door, a bunch of flowers was upended in the tall aluminium rubbish bin. Were they the flowers that Tony had had in his hand? I didn't know and I didn't care.

By the time I emerged from my building, the rain had started. It was a heavy drizzle at first that gradually built into a more robust cold, pelting rain as I walked by the choppy river. The weather had all the trademarks of winter. Autumn was over. No more sunny afternoons and rosy sunsets. No more not-too-hot-not-too-cold weather. It was winter now. Hard. Cold. Definite. No ifs or buts. I was glad. I was sick to death of the twilight zone anyway.

There was no doubt in my mind as I walked through the rain and watched the seagulls whirl hopefully overhead that I was finished with all the messy stuff in relationships. Maybe it wasn't sweet and pleasant and warm and cuddly to decide you were finished with love and all that shit. Maybe it was even a pity. But I knew that that was the decision I had to make if I was to survive. I simply could not manage all the emotion bouncing around. It would kill me.

I bought a Kit-Kat in a filling station, and returned to the river bank where I fed it to the seagulls. As the grateful scavengers gobbled down the chocolate biscuit, my way forward became increasingly clear. I'd do my job and get all the love I needed from my friends and family. I'd go out and have fun and try not to become a bitter old spinster. But even if I did, I didn't care. I was resolved. I was finished with love for good and glory, and I was about to begin a totally new chapter in my life. And I was going to start just as soon as I could stop crying.

# 27

On Monday morning, I finally reached a small personal goal of mine; I arrived at the office first, before Molly even, and opened the front doors with my barely used key. The place felt eerily quiet as I made coffee in the kitchen and brought the steaming cup into my office. I swivelled on my chair until I faced the window, and sipped coffee as I watched O'Connell Street come to life.

The city looked great at this time of the day, and I noticed in the quiet, still morning how this street had changed since I'd started working for Gladstone and Richards. Most of the beautiful Georgian houses had been restored, with the exception of two directly across the road from us. But even they were now being renovated and had been cordoned off by a builder over the weekend. I didn't fancy a building site across the road from me for the next few months, but at least once the houses were done, that would be it.

I sipped more coffee and heard voices in reception. Molly and Ryan? Molly and Spencer – that's who it was. God, I'd never learn. I heard his footsteps approaching my door. I swivelled back to my desk and picked up the phone.

'Of course, no problem,' I shouted into the phone as Spencer knocked and opened the door. He smiled at me in a kind of lovelorn way. Jesus!

'I'll look it up right now for you,' I said to my imaginary client, and rooted around my desk for something that resembled a file. Spencer leaned on the doorjamb and I smiled at him and pointed to the receiver. He shrugged and closed the door. I dropped the receiver into its cradle and then picked it up again and dialled Ruth's number. I'd put off ringing her to apologise about walking out of the party. The phone rang out. Nobody home. I rang her mobile and she answered immediately.

'Deserter,' she said.

'I'm sorry, Ruth. I'm really sorry.'

'It was Tony, wasn't it?'

'No. Yes.'

'I'm just outside your offices. I'm calling in actually and I've two lattes in a paper bag—' she said and hung up before I could respond.

I could hear her in reception making hello noises to everyone. She waltzed into my office wearing a beautifully tailored, rose-coloured suit and stiletto boots.

'You look great. Where did you get that outfit?' I asked as I stood up and took a coffee from her.

'I know that trick, Ellen Grace. Butter me up now after running out on me on Saturday night!'

'No, seriously, Ruthie. That colour is gorgeous on you.'

'Emerson bought it for me in Paris. So, spill.'

I looked at Ruth, trying to decide whether I'd give an edited version of the events of Saturday night.

She narrowed her eyes and stared at me as she sipped her coffee. 'The truth, the whole truth. I'll know if you're lying.'

I laughed. 'Tony and I . . . I kissed him in your kitchen . . . well, no, we kissed and—'

'Kissed, as in lightly on the cheek, or kissed as in snogged the faces off one another?' Ruth asked.

'Snogged the faces.'

'Oh, I see. And then?'

'And then his fiancée appeared out of nowhere and wrapped herself around him.'

'Nikki, the flight attendant. Tony introduced us. What a bloody talker – she never shut up for the whole night.'

'He had the cheek to . . . well, to kiss me, and all the time he had a bloody fiancée. I can't believe I was such a sucker.'

'Are you sure he's engaged? He never said a thing to me.'

'I saw the ring, Ruth. Anyway, I couldn't stay after that – it was too mortifying. I'm sorry about walking out, Ruthie. I knew you wanted to tell me about your mother. Tell me now.'

Ruth shrugged and sipped coffee. 'It'll hold. So, go on. What happened?'

'No, you tell me about your mother. This other stuff is just trivial shit.'

'No,' Ruth insisted. 'You tell me first. Then, I'll tell you.'

'OK – I was so mad, Ruth. Mad with Tony, mad with myself. I really had no choice but to leave. I mean, imagine how mortified I was when I realised he'd actually been there with his future wife.'

'He likes you.'

'Oh, please! He likes anything remotely female. It's just a bloody game with him. Colin Farrell wouldn't get a look in. And anyway, you're forgetting one important little detail – he's engaged.'

'He asked me where you'd gone.'

'Oh, that was big of him.'

'He left shortly after you.'

'With Nikki?' I asked triumphantly.

'Yes, but I don't think Nikki was his main concern. Anyway, there must have been something in the air because Spencer did a disappearing act too—' She looked enquiringly at me. I felt hot colour flood across my cheeks.

Ruth whistled. 'You didn't, Ellen?'

I bent my head and examined a scratch on the desktop.

'Ellen, Ellen, Ellen. Will you ever learn?'

I shrugged. 'I like Spencer.'

Ruth laughed. 'Three-horse race,' she said.

'What do mean?'

'Andrew, Tony and now Spencer. Three-horse race.'

'Andrew is well gone and, for the record, so is Tony Jordan. And Spencer is . . . well, we're just friends, so there's no horses and no race.' I gulped some latte.

'Do you have sex with all your male friends?'

'Look, I like him. I'm attracted to him, I mean who wouldn't be? But I'm not in the market for a serious relationship – no way.'

Ruth stood up and dusted down her short skirt. She walked to the long picture window overlooking the street, and looked out.

'And that's fine, as long as both of you understand the boundaries. Be careful, Ellen. That's all,' she said, her back to me.

'I'm fine – nothing to worry about at all,' I said.

'Jesus Christ Almighty! I don't believe it!' Ruth said.

'Why not?'

'Not you, eejit,' she said, pointing out the window and laughing at the same time. 'The bloody scene across the street. I'm not able for it!'

I walked to the window and searched the street for the source of Ruth's amusement and disbelief. A truck had pulled up outside the cordoned-off derelict buildings. Two workers in yellow hard hats were lifting something heavy from the rear of the truck. They had their backs to us, and the taller man's jeans had dropped slightly to reveal a classic builder's crack. I laughed.

'It's not that funny, Ruthie. A builder's crack – dime a dozen in Limerick,' I said.

'Yeah, but Wolfie's? I don't think so,' she said and fell into hysterical laughter.

I looked again at the workers in the luminous hats, just as one of them turned around and stared directly at our building. I nearly fainted as I recognised the face, and I dived away from the window and stood against the wall. Tony bloody Jordan!

'Jesus!' I said, looking at Ruth who was laughing as she struggled to open the sash window.

'Don't open it, for God's sake!' I said through gritted teeth. But Ruth didn't hear me. She was too busy wolf-whistling and gesturing out the window. I could hear Tony Jordan's low, soft laugh and I could imagine him smiling that melt-your-insides smile as he waved at Ruth. Bastard!

Ruth closed the window, and wiped tears of laughter from her eyes.

'Oh Ellen, that was so funny. You can unglue your-self from the wall now – they've gone into the building. That was such a laugh.'

'No, it wasn't,' I said as I peeked carefully out the window. I read the writing on the side of the dark blue truck. '*Jordan Properties. Restoration, Renovation, Rejuvenation*' proclaimed the slogan in elaborate gold lettering. Bling, bling. Wolfie's doing – definitely Wolfie. My brain whirred into action as it assessed how this new information about Tony would affect my life. I'd need a disguise to go in and out of my offices for starters. This was bad. I'd have to see him every day for God knows how long. Before I had even voiced this thought to Ruth, she was shaking her head in disbelief.

'It'll be a long winter,' she said and burst out laughing again.

'It's not funny,' I said as my mobile rang. I answered it and glared at Ruth.

'It's me, Ellen. Roxy.'

'Hi, Roxy. What can I do you for?'

'I'm in a terrible rush. Enrique's screaming his head off upstairs. I just wanted to know if you could call around as soon as possible? I got a date for the christening and I wanted your advice before I go booking anything.'

'No problem, Roxy. But I don't know if I'll be any help.'

Roxy laughed. 'I'm having a big do – Pa and I decided. And you are the godmother, after all, but the godfather is a bit on the small side – he's Pa's brother and . . . look, can you call and I'll tell you all about it?'

I watched Ruth as she stood at the window, still laughing softly. I threw her another dirty look.

'I can call this evening after work – how's that?'

'Perfect. See you then, Ellen.'

'Bye, Roxy.'

'And Ellen . . . are you still there? Thanks. For . . . for everything.'

'No problem,' I said but the line was already dead.

Ruth had positioned herself opposite me again and was flicking through photos that she'd taken out of her handbag. She handed me a black-and-white picture of a pretty young girl with a tiny baby in her arms.

'My mother with me,' said Ruth, all traces of earlier laughter gone from her face and voice. I studied the faces that seemed to stare out at me from another era.

'Wow,' I said. 'How weird is this?'

'You tell me,' said Ruth, handing me more snaps of a tiny baby that looked exactly like Paddy. She finally handed me a recent studio portrait of a middle-aged blonde woman in a low-cut, royal-blue, sequined top. I felt like I was looking at the future. Ruth – in about twenty years' time. It was uncanny. But what was more uncanny was that I imagined I knew this woman. I felt like I'd met her before.

'Jesus, Ruth – it's unbelievable!' I stared at the picture, and then I looked at Ruth. One tear had escaped from her eyes and was sliding down her face unchecked. I stood up and, making my way around the desk, I knelt down in front of her and hugged her to me.

'It's OK,' I said. 'You're entitled to be freaked out. It'll be OK.'

'I think I want to meet her,' she said into my hair. I pulled away and met her eyes.

'Are you sure?' I asked.

Ruth pulled away and wiped her eyes with her sleeve. 'I don't think I'll ever be sure. But after seeing the pictures, I just feel like I know her already – like I have some kind of connection with her.'

'Well you're the absolute image of her, Ruthie. I feel like I know her too. But often reunions like these . . . they just don't work out like you think they will.'

'I know that, but I think I need to do it anyway.'

'I'll come with you – that's if you want me to.'

'Would you?'

'Sure.'

'I might meet her on my own but if I thought you were near – a shout away even – it'd be great.'

'I'll be there, Ruth. I promise.'

'Thanks, Ellen.' Ruth stood up and reached for her handbag. She smiled at me. 'You didn't finish your story. The boys interrupted us.'

I stood up too and shrugged. 'Nothing to say except I'm guilty as charged. Oh and Tony called to my apartment on Sunday morning with flowers.'

Ruth stared at me. 'She tells me the interesting bit just as I'm leaving! So, what happened?'

'Nothing. Just the usual stuff that Tony is so good at. I didn't fall for it though. No siree.'

'What exactly did he say?'

I rolled my eyes.

'Did you hear him out?'

'Nope. I threw him out.'

'He really has a thing for you, hasn't he?'

'Has he? I don't think so, Ruth. Tony's not my type – definitely not. I don't do fiancés.'

Ruth laughed. 'Tony is any sane girl's type – trust me. And all this fiancé stuff? I'd like to hear that from the horse's mouth.'

There was a knock on the door just then and Molly came in. She held a huge hand-tied bouquet of flowers in her arms.

'For you,' she said as she laid the flowers on my desk. She looked Ruth up and down, then nodded at her and sniffed before strutting out of the room.

Ruth picked up the tiny white envelope that had fallen onto the table and handed it to me. 'Isn't that so sweet, so romantic?' she said as I opened the card.

*Love Spencer* it said in black ink. I smiled and passed the card to Ruth.

'Maybe he's my type,' I said.

'Be careful, Ellen. That's all I'm going to say to you – be careful.' And she left the room.

I went to the small office kitchen, searched for and found a big glass vase. I carefully arranged the flowers, stood them on top of the filing cabinet and sat at my desk and admired them. I didn't care what Ruth thought – Spencer was my type – no strings.

# 28

I was last to leave the office that evening. I had been delayed doing the final paperwork on Spencer's new penthouse apartment. He planned to move in within a matter of days, and so I had to use all my negotiating skills to cajole the solicitors into action. It seemed to have worked because I finally got word that Spencer could collect his key on Wednesday.

As I walked out onto the wide, stone steps in front of our building and turned to lock the office doors, I thought I smelled burning. I looked around and saw black smoke billowing from the rear of the derelict site across the road. I ran down the steps of Gladstone and Richards and noticed that Tony's Range Rover was gone but the truck was still parked outside. The front door was open, and I guessed that Wolfie was probably still there. I debated with myself about whether to go in and warn him. Just then, the smoke seemed to thicken and billow up, and that decided me.

The derelict house was surprisingly bright inside, and I followed the increasingly strong smell of burning until I stood in the kitchen at the rear of the property. I could see thick black smoke coming from the corner of the small, enclosed yard.

'Wolfie, Wolfie,' I called, suddenly worried by the silence. Jesus! Maybe I should have called the fire brigade first. I couldn't care less about Tony Jordan's building sites but a burned-to-death Wolfie was another matter entirely.

'Wolfie,' I shouted as panic gripped me. I could feel adrenalin pumping through my body. I turned around and noticed that somebody big was standing in the doorway. I looked up into the melt-in-your-mouth eyes of Tony Jordan. He was leaning against the doorjamb, a small smile playing on his lips. I glared at him and pointed over my shoulder at the smoke.

'I thought . . . the smoke . . . I thought Wolfie was here and the place was on fire—' I said in my best all-business voice. I knew by his face that the 'fire' was not a fire at all, and that I looked like a complete eejit, running around, shouting hysterically. Colour flooded my face but I stared defensively at him and folded my arms across my chest.

He locked eyes with me. Gorgeous, chocolate eyes that made my stomach feel funny. Jesus Christ! What was I thinking? I concentrated hard and gave him my best condescending look. He smiled slightly.

'Ellen, what a surprise,' he said, and even though he was halfway across the room, I could have sworn that I felt the heat of his body.

'I have to go,' I said.

'So soon, Ellen? It was just starting to be fun. You know how I love surprises.'

'Very funny,' I said and tried to stare him down.

What was it with this guy? Even when I hated him, I was afraid I'd morph into a reckless sex maniac.

He smiled and seemed to take a step closer to me. I jumped back, knowing that proximity to Tony Jordan was never a good idea.

'You're very jumpy, Ellen. I don't bite, I promise,' he said, his dark eyes crinkling at the corners with amusement. He was laughing at me, the bastard! He walked past me suddenly, and picked up a hammer at the far side of the room.

'So there's nobody on fire. Goodbye, so,' I said taking my opportunity now that he was out of the doorway.

I could hear him chuckling as I hurried through the hallway.

'See you tomorrow,' he called as I reached the front door.

'Not if I can help it,' I muttered to myself and made my way to my car.

Roxy had dinner ready when I arrived at her house, and I sat at the small kitchen table with her and her beautiful children. We had stew, and it was the simplest and most delicious meal that I'd had in ages. The little girls were delightful company after a hard day at the office. Roxy looked like their big sister in tight-fitting low-slung denim flares and a ribbed jumper. Her hair was pulled from her face in her trademark ponytail and she wore no make-up. She talked animatedly about the christening.

'Imagine I couldn't get a date until 10 December. Mind you, it was probably my fault because I wanted it on a Saturday. Anyway, Ellen, the church is all booked. That just leaves the reception.'

'Reception? Enrique's not getting married, just christened,' I said and mopped up the last of my gravy with a piece of bread.

'I know but the big do is Pa's idea. He says he wants everybody to know how much he loves Enrique. I think it's sweet,' said Roxy. Shania and Shakira had finished their dinner and were pouring salt onto their plates.

'Anyway, I think I'll book the Regal. What do you think? And Mam said she'd do a huge buffet but I said no – we'll let the hotel do it. Oh, and I know exactly the christening robe I want for him. It's cream – much better than white with his skin colour.'

'Slow down, Roxy! I'm getting lost already,' I said, laughing at her enthusiasm.

Shania and Shakira began to argue over the salt-cellar.

'Stop it, please – ye'll wake the baby,' said Roxy, and ordered them into the living room to watch a video. Shakira jumped from her chair and ran off. Shania refused to budge. Crossing her arms defiantly, she glared at her mother. I tried not to laugh.

'Shania, behave yourself. I'll give you one last chance to go with your sister.'

'I hate you,' said the little girl, her eyes mutinous.

'That's fine. Now, off you go,' said Roxy.

'Slut!' said Shania and both of us looked at her, astonished at that word coming out of her tiny rosebud mouth.

'Where did you hear that?' asked Roxy, her voice almost a whisper. The colour had drained from her face and she'd dropped the saltcellar onto the table.

Shania didn't answer. She just sat there, arms still folded, eyes fixed on a spot on the wall behind her mother's head.

'Where did you hear that?' asked Roxy again. This time her voice was loud and deadly.

Shania knew she was on thin ice. Her bottom lip quivered and her huge, blue eyes filled up with tears. 'Daddy called you that, not me,' she said, running to her mother and throwing her small arms around Roxy's legs.

Roxy hugged her and took her into the living room. When she came back, she looked at me and burst into tears.

'She's only a kid, Roxy. They say stuff like that all the time,' I said, reaching out to hold her small hand in mine.

She shook her head and sniffled. 'No, it's him. It's Teddy Hannon. Oh Ellen, I'm so scared.'

'Scared of him? Don't be, Roxy. That's probably what he wants.'

'I know but he has access to the girls and he's poisoning them against me and I don't know what to do. And sometimes he looks at me . . . and—'

I rooted in my handbag for a tissue and handed one to her.

'And?'

Roxy shrugged. 'It's the way he looks at me sometimes.'

'He can't hurt you, Roxy, and he won't hurt his own children. Don't upset yourself imagining the worst.'

Roxy looked at me and wiped her eyes again and smiled. 'Ah well, he can go to hell. I don't want to be wasting my life worrying about stuff that might never happen.'

She stood up and began to clear the table. I joined in and, by the time the kitchen was sorted, Roxy had returned to her usual cheerful self.

It was late when I left and Roxy walked me to the front gate. Just as I was saying goodbye, we heard a rumpus coming from Maurice McMahon's house next door. The front door opened and a figure came dashing out, Maurice following in hot pursuit.

'Don't you ever darken my doorstep again. Shame on you with your dirty money. I'll never sell my house, no matter what ye offer,' shouted Maurice. The man fiddled with the gate which seemed to have stuck. He wore a dark suit that looked too small for him. When he managed to open the gate, he turned back to face Maurice.

'You'll be sorry. Very sorry,' he said, pointing a finger at Maurice, who seemed to be hyperventilating. I thought I'd better intervene.

'What's the problem?' I asked and the man turned around to face me. We recognised each other instantly.

'You,' I said.

'You,' he said and sneered at me.

'Up to your old tricks again then – threatening and mugging people? I think we should call the guards,' I said.

He laughed and spat at my feet. 'You're good at that, bitch,' he said and walked away.

The three of us watched him disappear around the corner.

'You know him, Ellen?' asked Roxy.

Maurice was still breathing too fast.

'Well, sort of. He used to wear a hoodie all the time, so I didn't recognise him at first in a suit. He threatened me last year when I was sort of seeing this guy – Tony Jordan—'

'Tony Jordan? *The* Tony Jordan? Tall, dark and dangerously handsome?'

'You know him?'

'My mother knows him really well. And I've been in love with him since I was about three,' she said.

'The cheek of him – offered me cash if you don't mind, for the house. And then threatened me when I wouldn't sell. He won't be back here in a hurry, I can tell you. A bloody lackey for Sarsfield Properties,' said Maurice, fully recovered now from his encounter. He seemed pleased with himself.

'Maybe you should tell the guards about this,' I suggested.

'I sorted him out. We don't need any guards,' said Maurice, looking as though he'd enjoyed it all. He'd get great mileage out of this at the pigeon club.

'Tell them anyway,' I said and fished in my handbag for the keys of the car.

'You and Tony Jordan? You and Tony?' repeated Roxy. I opened the car door, and having climbed quickly in, drove away.

By the time I got home, I was convinced that Maurice was in more danger than anybody realised. They had no idea what Hoodie and his boss, Robert White, were capable of doing. After all, they had kidnapped Will, tried to kill me and Tony Jordan, and gatecrashed Angela Maunsell's seventieth birthday party, brandishing guns.

I knew I wouldn't sleep unless I spoke to Hilary Thornton. I rang the police station but she was actually off duty for once, and I couldn't persuade them to give me her home number, so I went to bed and dreamed of fat men with guns.

Next morning, that feeling of unease was still with me, so I rang the police station before I went to work.

'Good morning, Ellen,' Hilary said as soon as we were connected.

'Robert White and his henchmen are up to their old tricks.'

'What do you mean?'

'I met that Hoodie guy last night – he was threating poor Maurice MacMahon, an old man. Those people will stop at nothing to get what they want.'

'Maurice MacMahon? Wasn't he the man who had his house vandalised a little while ago?'

'Yes, and I meant to ring you at the time. Do you know about Sarsfield Properties?'

'Somebody mentioned the name all right – what about them?'

'They're the developers who are trying to build a hotel and leisure centre at the back of Maurice's house. He's leading the residents who are objecting. Last night, I overheard Robert White's lackey threaten Maurice.'

'What did he say?'

'He said that Maurice would be sorry if he didn't sell them his house.'

'Really? Would you be willing to make a statement to that effect?'

'Definitely. I'm not afraid of those bastards.'

'When can you come in?' Hilary asked.

I checked my watch. 'How about now?'

'See you in twenty minutes.'

I finished dressing and went straight to the police station to give my statement. Afterwards, as I drove to work, I was proud of myself for doing the right thing – those thugs deserved whatever they got. But, somehow, alongside the feelings of virtue was the worry that I might have drawn that shower on me once again.

# 29

It was Thursday by the time I'd finished the paperwork for Spencer's new penthouse. I'd spent the
previous few days ducking in and out of the office
so that I could avoid meeting Tony Jordan. Spencer
was in Lahinch with Tim Gladstone, looking at a
new apartment complex that we had been asked to
sell. I'd stayed behind to hold the fort. We had a
number of really important projects on the go and
I wanted to oversee them personally.

Ryan had been rather sullen with me since his
return from Scotland, but he seemed to be clinching
deals with no problems, so I wasn't too worried about
it. Anyway, he was probably happy enough in the
Hebrides – at least he'd have had lots of time to consider his investments and his bloody 'portfolio'.
Molly, on the other hand, was a different story.

The computer problem was sorted out, so she'd
thought up a new torture for me. There was a vacancy
now for my old job, which Ryan would probably get.
The problem was Ryan's job. Molly had the perfect
candidate – her niece, Renata O'Brien.

I tried to avoid the Renata subject, but with interviews looming the following week, it was getting

more difficult. Besides singing Renata's praises at every given opportunity, Molly was also killing me with kindness. I presumed this was to sway me in favour of hiring Renata, and I must admit it did make life very easy, but I knew in my heart that Renata wouldn't get the job. I wasn't going to tell Molly that until I absolutely had to, though.

Andrea, the other junior, had just arrived back from a training course in Dublin. With a couple more years' experience behind her, she was going to be excellent at her job. The one thing that annoyed me about her was her unswerving adoration of Spencer. But she really was good at her job, so I could forgive her even that.

I loved being Area Manager, but my work day was longer – there was no question about it. I also seemed to be taking work home with me and I kept promising myself I'd stop once I'd reduced the backlog. I was beginning to forget what Jerry Springer looked like, not to mention my family. So, on Thursday evening, I decided that after I'd met Spencer to give him the keys of his new apartment, I'd go and have dinner with my family. Will would be there too, so at least I'd have someone to share the bad food with.

I ducked out of my office at six o'clock, and drove past Tony Jordan's building without looking over. Having pulled into Steamboat Quay, I waited in the small riverside pub where I'd arranged to meet Spencer. I ordered a Coke and sat in the window seat, reading a newspaper that had been left on the table. After a few minutes, Spencer arrived.

'Ellen,' he said. 'Sorry I'm a little late. Traffic was crazy in Ennis.'

I looked up at him and smiled. Jesus he was very good-looking all the same. He didn't smile back, just examined me with his eyes. My body started to tingle and I could feel the sex-maniac monster that lived inside me spring to life.

'Have you time for a drink?' he asked. And then he smiled. Tiny dimples appeared at each side of his mouth. Cute. Very cute.

I didn't answer. I just took the keys of his penthouse and handed them to him. A look of understanding passed over his face.

'I have an idea. I won't be long,' he said and strode to the bar. He came back straightaway with a bottle of Moët et Chandon in his hand.

'It's chilled already. Will you christen the new pad with me?' he asked, his head tilted to one side in a pleading fashion.

God, he was so cute tonight! To hell with it! I couldn't resist, and anyway we were friends, so what was the harm in one little drink? And it was nice to be with a man who adored me. So what if he sprinted every time he saw a bride waiting at the altar? I'd done a bit of that myself. The last thing I wanted was that kind of commitment. We were well-matched.

I smiled and nodded. 'Just one drink. I'm going to see my family later,' I said.

And really that's what I thought at the time. So how did I end up naked with Spencer in his hot tub, sipping champagne and watching the Limerick skyline? We'd barely managed to close the door of the apartment before our clothes had come off and we'd had sex on the pristine white carpet of the living room. We hadn't even bothered to turn on lights, but muted light flooded through the screen doors that led to the deck. The light was mottled and had made the sex strange and erotic.

Afterwards, we had moved to the rooftop garden and sat in the cool night air with our coats on, and nothing underneath. We had laughed and drunk champagne from the bottle, and Spencer had managed to turn on the hot tub. Then, we had dropped the coats and climbed into the delicious warm water.

I climbed onto Spencer's lap and kissed him hard on the mouth. Water bubbled around us and I could feel my body kicking into sexual overdrive yet again. I had turned into a sex addict but I didn't care – it felt great. Michael Douglas had the same problem after all, and he seemed to be doing all right. My mobile phone rang and I remembered that it was in the pocket of my coat, which was thrown in a heap on the ground.

'Ignore it,' said Spencer and we kissed. The phone stopped ringing and then started all over again. There's something about a ringing phone that almost compels you to answer. I leaned over the edge of the hot tub and rooted in the pocket of my coat for the phone.

'Ellen, the chicken fajitas are ruined and the guacamole has turned brown,' said my mother. Spencer licked the lobe of my ear as I answered.

'I'm really sorry, Mam. I got delayed and—'

'And you couldn't ring?'

'I was very busy. I'm sorry. Really, I am.'

'What's that noise in the background, Ellen? Is there a kettle boiling?' asked my mother.

'I'll call tomorrow, I promise,' I said. Spencer's hands were all over me at this stage.

'Your brother wants to talk to you,' said my mother and Will came on the line.

'You knew it was chicken fajitas, Ellen, and you didn't warn me,' he said in a low voice so that our mother wouldn't hear.

I laughed. 'See you, Will,' I said and hung up, dropping the phone onto my coat.

'Now, where were we?' I asked Spencer.

I kept my promise and called to see my parents the following evening. I'd been in brilliant form all day and I'd decided that sex in large doses with no strings attached was an excellent ingredient in my life. And I was now able to handle being around Spencer during work hours, except the once when he came into my office and stood over me with the plans for the Lahinch apartment complex on the desk in front of us. I had an unbelievable urge to have sex with him right there on the floor, but I managed to control myself.

I felt wonderful that Friday, and even when I came face to face with Tony Jordan as I left work that evening, it didn't spoil my mood.

'Ellen,' he said, his face deadly serious. He had dark circles under his eyes.

'Tony, how are you? Lovely day, isn't it?' I sang and sailed past him to my car. I'd parked it on the street earlier instead of our car park. I could feel his eyes on me as I opened the car door, and my stomach did an involuntary somersault. I put it down to wind and waved at him as I pulled away, and he stood there, his face all moody and serious. Jesus! Who did he think he was – bloody Heathcliff in *Wuthering Heights*? Give me Spencer any day. No strings, no complications, just pure, simple sex.

I was spared having dinner in my mother's house as it was Bingo night and she always had dinner early on Bingo night. But she'd made a salad for me, which was edible – even my mother couldn't spoil a salad. We chatted as I ate.

'Angela's getting married in Rome – did she tell you that?' asked Mam as she scrubbed an already spotless cooker-top.

I couldn't remember who had told me so I said nothing.

'Less than two weeks' time. It's all sorted. Your dad and I are going out with them, for a couple of days,' she said as she continued scrubbing.

'Cool! Rome is meant to be beautiful,' I said. 'That'll be a nice break for you.'

My mother stopped her scrubbing and looked at me. 'I know, but who'll look after everything here? And then there's poor Alison – she'll be back from her holiday – and there's Will.'

'Stop it, Mam, for God's sake. They can look after themselves – they're not children.'

'You're right, love. And I can make dinners for Will and freeze them – he'll be fine then.'

I smiled at my mother. 'Good idea – he'll be happy once he has your dinners.'

'Did I tell you about Madame Leonora?'

'Who?' I asked, wondering if this was some cousin I was supposed to know.

'We're going to see her next week, Angela and myself. She's a fortune teller. Angela calls her a clairvoyant. Anyway, we're going to see her next week. Why don't you come, Ellen? She might be able to tell us if there's a tall, dark stranger waiting in the wings for you.'

I was tempted – it really did sound like fun. 'What night are you going?' I asked as I ate the last of my coleslaw.

'Wait! I'll get the newspaper – there's a full-page ad. Everybody's talking about her, you know,' she said and went to look for the paper.

Dad came into the kitchen just then and I got up and kissed his cheek. He seemed thinner and older than when I had last seen him, which was only a couple of weeks ago. He smelled strongly of cigarettes.

'Back on the fags, Dad?' I asked as he poured himself a cup of tea. He'd had a heart attack a couple of years ago and the doctor had ordered him to stop smoking. Dad blamed the string of telly chefs who had pushed my mother's cooking over the edge from just plain bad to exotically inedible. He looked like he could do with the break in Rome.

'Heard you're off to Rome,' I said. 'It'll be a grand break for you.'

Dad smiled. 'I know. How are you, Ell?'

I looked at my father, and saw concern in his eyes. And love.

'Great. I love the new job except I never get to see anyone any more,' I said. He nodded agreement.

'Don't work too hard, love. Nobody will thank you for it in the end.' He stirred sugar into his tea. My mother came back into the kitchen, carrying the newspaper in her hand.

'There,' she said. 'Tuesday night in the George. Can't you come, Ellen? We'll have a laugh.'

I looked at Madame Leonora's full-page ad and nearly fainted.

'Oh, Jesus!' I said.

'There's no need to take the Lord's name like that, Ellen,' said my mother.

'What's wrong, Ellen?' Dad asked.

I picked up the paper and stared at the studio portrait of Madame Leonora. The picture was in colour and she stared out at me with Ruth's big blue eyes. Jesus! Ruth's mother was a clairvoyant. I wondered if Ruth knew, and if not, should I tell her?

'So, will you come?' asked Mam as she put on her coat for Bingo.

'Are you all right, Ellen? You look like you've seen a ghost,' said Dad.

'I'm fine, I just remembered something to do with work – that's all. Anyway, I think I'll give Madame

Leonora a miss this time,' I said, still staring at the picture. 'Can I keep the paper, though?'

Both my mother and father looked at me quizzically.

'If you want to, but it's last night's paper.'

'That's OK,' I said, folding the newspaper and putting it in my bag.

# 30

I cleaned my apartment on Saturday, and Joey followed me around, rubbing himself against my legs. I felt he'd noticed my absence since my promotion and was trying to make me feel guilty. It worked and I gave him a full tin of salmon for his lunch.

The doorbell rang and interrupted my cleaning.

Somebody stood at the door, face obscured by the largest bouquet of flowers I'd ever seen.

'Ellen Grace?' asked the voice behind the flowers.

'That's me,' I said and signed for the delivery and thanked the young man. I laid the enormous spray of roses on the worktop and opened the card. *Love Spencer* the card said. I smiled and went in search of a vase big enough for the flowers. Spencer was sweet. That was true. And a very attentive lover – that was also true. The love bit on the card bothered me a little, but he probably just meant it generally. All in all, this Spencer thing was working out grand. We had an arrangement that suited both of us, and, for once, I felt quite happy with the state of my life. I rarely thought of Andrew now, and Tony Jordan was almost married. Everything was turning out just fine. The phone rang.

'Ellen, it's Spencer.'

'Hi, Spence. I just got your flowers. Very nice. It'll be my turn the next time to send you some.'

He laughed. 'Glad you liked them. I was passing the florist on the way home from the market and I saw the roses and I thought of you.'

I didn't answer.

'Anyway, I got the ingredients for a meal and I thought maybe we could eat together tonight.'

I watched Joey stretch out on the windowsill, his belly full of salmon.

I'd promised India I'd call over tonight but she wouldn't mind if I cancelled. I could ring her and tell her about Ruth's clairvoyant mother at the same time.

'I'd love to. What time?'

'You would? That's so great, Ellen. Eight o'clock? I'll pick you up – I'd like that.'

'Great. See you then,' I said and hung up.

I dialled India straightaway.

'Hi, India. How are you?'

'Great. How are you? I haven't seen you since the party.'

'You know how it is. God, I haven't a minute with this new job.'

'Hmm. Just the job keeping you busy then?' asked India in a sweet voice.

'Ruth's been talking,' I said.

'Hmmn. And my husband.'

'Tim?'

'I think that's his name.'

'What has Tim been saying?'

'That you and a certain American hunk are a hot item.'

'Tim would never say that. He'd never use the words "hot item" or "hunk".'

India laughed. 'Well that's what he meant. So?'

'So nothing.'

'Ellen?'

'OK, OK – we're just friends, that's all.'

'Friends are never described as hot items.'

I decided to change the subject. 'How's Alyssa?'

'Still an insomniac, but a very cute one. That's what's keeping her alive.'

'I need your advice, Ind. I discovered something about Ruth's birth mother. She's famous.'

'Don't tell me. She's Mary McAleese?'

'No, fool.'

'She's Margot – or better still, she's Twink!'

'She's Madame Leonora, the clairvoyant.'

'Never heard of her but I don't believe it – Ruth's mother's a fortune teller?'

'Honestly.'

'I was talking to Ruth earlier and she said nothing.'

'That's because she doesn't know. I said her mother was the clairvoyant, not Ruth.'

'My God! Are you serious?'

'Yes. I saw a big ad in the paper.' Joey had woken and was circling my legs again. Poor Joey – he was really feeling neglected.

'Are you sure it's her?'

'Certain. Look, India, about tonight—'

'Yes?'

I laughed. 'Spencer asked me over for dinner—'

'Don't mind poor me. You go and have dinner with the gorgeous Spencer and I'll watch a rerun of *Hart to Hart*.'

'I'm sorry, India.'

'Don't be. We'll meet for lunch during the week – how about that?'

'Brilliant. Wait, India. I need your advice about Ruth. How will I tell her about her mother?'

'Just tell her. The more information Ruth has before she meets her, the better equipped she'll be. Information is power. That's the first rule of working a successful court case.'

'Thanks. See you during the week.'

'Bye.'

I put down the phone and thought about what India had said. She was right – I'd have to tell Ruth. If information was power, then Ruth would need the extra help. After all, her mother was a clairvoyant, and if she was any good at it, she knew all about her daughter's life already.

I didn't phone Ruth until that evening. She picked up the phone on the first ring.

'Ellen?'

'It's me, but how did you know?' I asked.

'Telepathy,' she said.

'Wow,' I said, thinking this clairvoyant thing must be in the genes.

'Or caller display. I was just going to ring you,

Ellen. I discovered something about my birth mother.'

'I think I know,' I said.

'Madame Leonora. I saw it in the paper.'

'Yeah – mad, isn't it?'

'Insane. And do you know what's madder? I went to see her years ago, Ellen – the year I did my Leaving. You couldn't come because you had a basketball match, remember?'

'Jesus, that's right. You went with Anne Hayes, and Madame Leonora told Anne she'd marry a tall, dark stranger.'

'That's right, and we fell around the place laughing when she married Paul Ryan – five foot seven, red-haired and the boy next door!'

We both laughed. 'It must be really strange, Ruth,' I said, knowing this was the understatement of the year.

'Weird out, Ell. I think—' Her voice caught in her throat.

'Don't be upset, Ruthie. So she's a clairvoyant. I mean she could have been something way worse, like . . . like a life consultant, or a lap dancer, or an accountant even.'

'It's not what she is really. It's the fact that I met her and didn't know she'd given birth to me.'

'I know. I understand.' I checked my watch – Spencer would be here in half an hour and I hadn't even showered yet. But Ruth sounded so upset.

'Could you come over, Ellen? I'd love a good heart to heart, and Emerson has to film some stupid thing in the dark, and Paddy's asleep—' her voice trailed off. I didn't know what to say and the silence grew.

'You probably have plans. I'm sorry. I didn't think.'

'It's just that Spencer is cooking a meal for me . . . I mean, for us – him and me, and—'

'No, forget I even mentioned it. Emerson said he wouldn't be long anyway. I'll let you go. You probably want to beautify yourself.'

'No, I've plenty of time yet,' I said, feeling guilty.

'Bye, Ellen. We might meet up next week.'

'Definitely. I'm supposed to have lunch with India some day. I'll organise it, say, for Wednesday – how's that?'

'Grand. You ring me with the details. Thanks, Ellen,' she said and hung up.

I replaced the phone in its cradle and bit my nail. Maybe I should have gone out to Ruth's but I was so looking forward to the night ahead. Anyway, she'd be grand. Emerson would be home shortly.

Spencer surprised me. His living room was filled with candles – which was nice – but it was also full of furniture, which was amazing. Only two days earlier, there hadn't been a stick of furniture in the place. Now it looked like something out of *Image Interiors*.

'Jeez, Spence. The place is looking great. How did you do that in two days? Did you hire *Changing Rooms*?'

'Apartment outfitters,' Spencer said, handing me a glass of wine. Soft music played in the background – something French that I didn't recognise.

'Have we got those in Limerick?' I stroked the back of the huge cream leather couch as I walked around the room.

'I never have a problem finding things that I want in Limerick,' he said, his voice doing the octave dropping thing that made me nervous. The aroma coming from the open-plan kitchen was gorgeous, and made me feel hungry. Spencer looked earnestly at me, his green eyes worryingly soft and warm.

'Well!' I half-shouted, 'What delicious repast have you prepared for us this evening?'

Spencer laughed. 'A Thai banquet for your pleasure, madam. Step right this way.'

I followed Spencer to the table, which was pulled over to the screen doors. The city spread out in front of us, lights twinkling. This was a great way to spend a Saturday night.

And then Spencer surprised me yet again. He could cook. I mean, really cook. I felt as if I was in a five-star restaurant as dish after dish appeared on the beautifully laid table. I ate everything he put before me, which seemed to delight him.

Afterwards we sat on the leather couch, sipping wine and talking about our childhoods. I was in the middle of some stupid story about how I had run away when I was seven after a fight with Alison, when I caught Spencer looking at me in a strange way. My voice trailed off and I didn't finish the story. He stroked my cheek lightly with his finger.

'Ellen, you're beautiful.'

I laughed. 'Bet you say that to all the girls.' I said

as I had a mental picture of Spencer's four fiancées, lined up at the altar, watching him run like the hammers of hell.

'No, I don't. I've never felt like this before. Never,' he said, leaning towards me. Then he kissed me on the lips. Bet you have, I thought – bet you have, a whole bunch of times before, and I put my arms around his neck and pulled him closer to me.

I awoke in Spencer's king-size bed, with the sun streaming in the window. Spencer stood in his boxer shorts at the far wall. He was doing t'ai chi and looked like a Greek god. He didn't know that I was awake, and I watched him in fascination. What a fine body. Better than Andrew's and at least as good as Tony Jordan's. I could have stayed there all day, wrapped in silk sheets, watching Spencer. He finally stopped and looked over and caught my eye. I threw back the sheet and patted the empty space beside me. Spencer smiled and leapt back into bed for an Ellen session of t'ai chi.

We finally got up at around midday and I took a shower in the ensuite bathroom. It was white marble with a double shower, and was the same size as my living room. Afterwards, I opened the closet to search for another towel. Inside were matching his and her towelling robes and slippers. For some reason, I found them really disturbing. I knew that they were just bathrobes but they seemed to scream 'marriage' at me silently. Or at the very least, 'serious relationship'.

I closed the closet door quickly and leaned against it, as if I was trying to keep the bathrobes from stepping out to join me. I heard Spencer knocking softly on the door, and then he came in, his hair still damp from an earlier shower, or else vigorous sex with a t'ai chi twist. I still had my back thrown against the closet.

I pointed to the closet. 'Robes,' I said. 'Matching ones. Oh, and slippers too. Did they come with the penthouse?'

Spencer laughed and shook his head. 'No. I bought them yesterday in that cool store – I can't remember the name of it. I just thought they might come in handy if you decided to sleep over.'

I looked at his face in an effort to read his intent.

He reached out his hand and stroked my bare shoulder and then bent down and kissed me lightly on the lips.

'OK?' he asked.

I nodded.

'Hurry up and get dressed. Brunch awaits you on the terrace,' he said, smiling as he left the room.

I arrived home on Sunday evening, absolutely exhausted. I was worried that Joey might be fretting even though I'd rung Angela Maunsell earlier to go into my apartment and feed and water him. I waited for the lift, as the thought of four flights of stairs was more than my body could endure. The lift doors opened and there in front of me stood Nikki, the flight attendant.

She floated out of the lift in a midnight-blue

tailored suit, complete with a chiffon scarf tied casually around her neck. Her blonde hair was poker straight – hair that straight took hours of work. Her make-up was flawless, and I felt naked with my scrubbed face and sticky-out après-shower hair. I decided to be friendly so I smiled hello at her. She looked me up and down and smiled back, but there was a question in her eyes.

'I'm Ellen Grace – Ruth and Emerson's party? We met at the party.'

'Did we?' she asked, her accent overpoweringly posh.

Bitch, I thought to myself. And anyway, what the bloody hell was she doing in my apartment block? I nodded goodbye and skirted into the lift just as the doors were beginning to close. I got madder and madder as the lift ascended to my floor. Why did I bother saying hello at all? Maybe Tony had said something to her to turn her against me? Or maybe I was so insignificant that she actually had completely forgotten me?

Angela Maunsell was just coming out of my apartment as I fished for the key in my handbag, making me jump with fright.

'Jesus, Angela! You scared me.'

'Sorry, love. Joey was miaowing to be let in so I went and let him in the door of the balcony. Is that all right?'

'Great, Angela – you're a star. Hey, Ang, did we get a new tenant recently? Blonde hair, tall? I just met this one in the lift—'

Angela nodded her head. 'You mean Micki or is it Nikki? Micki I think. I knew her mother well – a lighting bitch if there ever was one. And do you know what? She's the same – that Micki one. She pretended she didn't know me in the lift last night. Imagine that!'

'So she's renting an apartment?' I couldn't believe my bad luck. Tony's fiancée ends up in my building. Weren't there loads of other bloody apartment blocks in Limerick that she could go live in?

Angela pointed up to the ceiling of the narrow hallway. 'Penthouse,' she said, nodding her head knowingly at me.

'Penthouse here? We have a penthouse in this apartment block? First I heard of it.'

Angela laughed. 'That's what she called it last night. 'I've moved into the penthouse oportmont, octually,' said Angela, imitating an over-the-top posh accent. But I must admit, it did sound like Nikki.

'And do you know where they're from, those Cussens? From the arsehole of Treaty Heights, that's where,' said Angela triumphantly.

I laughed out loud. One thing I knew for sure – Angela Maunsell called a spade a spade, and if you claimed to be anything other than what you were, she wouldn't be long giving you a reality check. I was still laughing when we said our goodbyes.

# 31

But I wasn't laughing the following morning. I was late getting up, and stumbled around trying to find clean underwear and tights without holes. I had to settle for a pair of tights that had no holes from the knees down. I decided to wear flat shoes and hoped that my pinstripe skirt would cover the holey parts. I grabbed a slice of bread and hastily buttered it before dashing out the door in the direction of the lift. I had a really important meeting in Ennis at 9.30, and I'd never make it if I wasn't on the road by eight, at the latest.

I got into the lift with the slice of bread jammed whole into my mouth, as I had to use one hand to press the lift button and the other to carry my two-ton briefcase. I dropped my briefcase on the floor and, chewing on the bread, I pressed the ground-floor button and made eye contact with my fellow travellers. And then I froze like a rabbit caught in car headlights as I looked into the perfectly groomed faces of Tony Jordan and his fiancée.

'Morning, Ellen,' he said. He wore a gorgeous tan-coloured suit and smelled of expensive after-shave. No building site for him, this morning. So now I had to face him at home and at work. Was he trying to ruin my life?

'Mnmnn,' I said, through a mouthful of half-eaten bread. Nikki looked me up and down again, and then leaned against Tony. He didn't acknowledge it but gazed levelly at me, like it was perfectly OK to stare because we were in a lift and there weren't many things you could look at in a lift. I was glad when we reached the ground floor. I ran from the lift and out into the car park of our building, then jumped into my car and drove away.

As I pulled into the heavy morning traffic, I noticed that the holes in my tights had already made their determined way down below my hemline, and I reminded myself to buy a new pair before the meeting. And I reminded myself also not to be perturbed by Tony Jordan. He was entitled to sleep with his fiancée, and she did happen to have moved into my building. All of that was logical. What wasn't logical was the effect proximity to Tony Jordan had on me. The minute I looked into those huge mocha eyes, every logical thought seemed to desert me.

I mean, I had a fine-looking boyfriend in Spencer, and he was great in bed, so why were my insides doing a back flip every time Tony Jordan's bloody eyes met mine? Bastard! I'd buy dark mirror glasses like Wolfie's, and wear them winter and summer. That would be the end of the eyes. And anyway, Tony Jordan probably did the eye thing with every girl. I'd hit the nail on the head when I compared him to Colin Farrell. More women than sense – that was his problem. I decided that the next time I met him, I'd be polite, but under no circumstances would I make eye contact with him.

The week flew by after the Tony-in-the-lift encounter, and I didn't see him again, thank God. Spencer and I saw each other every day at work, though, and ended up doing something together every night as well. I don't know how it happened, and I didn't think anything of it. It was like the natural progression of a friendship, really.

We spent Tuesday in Lahinch, negotiating the apartment deal, which was bubbling along nicely. We finished early and had a fabulous meal in a seafood restaurant that was perched literally on the shoreline. Afterwards, we walked hand in hand on the expansive golden beach and watched the surfers trying to catch some waves. It was a magical day away from the real world.

On the way home, when I checked my phone, I discovered a missed call from Roxy, and I meant to ring her back but somehow it got away from me. There were also missed calls from India and Ruth, but they hadn't left messages, so I figured it was nothing urgent.

When we returned to Limerick that night, we fed Joey and caught a movie in the Cineplex. The following night, I was to meet Ruth and India for drinks, but cancelled at the last minute when Spencer and I decided to go bowling. I thought India was very cool with me on the phone, and I tried to think of something I'd done to annoy her. Maybe she was tired, and the baby was cross again.

By the weekend, I'd decided to throw a few clothes in a bag and stay over at Spencer's for a couple of days. It would save all the back-and-forth stuff, and Will had agreed to drop in and feed Joey. I did feel guilty about poor Joey, but after an Indian take-away, a DVD and a bottle of wine on Spencer's now-familiar leather couch, Joey was a distant memory.

We hardly went out for the whole weekend and, by Sunday evening, we had established a nice simple routine for ourselves – sex, food, wine and movies. But I decided to go home that night despite Spencer's protestations. I needed clothes and I also needed space, and time to catch up with my own life.

Ryan had been given the nod for promotion to senior estate agent, so that left us with a vacancy for a new junior. Juniors were the hardest work because they had to be constantly babysat. Andrea was excellent though and promised me she'd help once the new recruit started work.

I had to sit in on interviews all day Monday, but it turned out to be fun as Spencer was on the inter-view panel too. And Spencer had an unbelievable effect on all the female interviewees, including Renata O'Brien, Molly's niece, which I found highly amusing. If I asked the questions, their answers were articulate and coherent. If Spencer asked the ques-tions, they turned into mumbling, blushing girlie girls.

After a while, I no longer found it funny – I found it downright annoying.

How did they expect to get on in the cut-and-thrust world of property if they were reduced to idiots by the first pretty face that presented itself? I wanted to give the job to the first girl who came through the doors and took Spencer on. And that's exactly what happened.

Her name was Donna and she was young, enthusiastic, intelligent and confident. I could smell a good estate agent in her. She was pretty but not over-produced, and Spencer had about as much effect on her as Bobby Davro would have on me. She got the job, and while Molly freaked, I hid in my office, checking my e-mails.

The phone rang as I skimmed through my mail.

'Ellen?'

'Will. What do you want?'

'Just ringing to see how you're keeping – that's all.'

I laughed. I knew this boy too well to believe that. 'I'm fine, Will. Now, do you want to hear all the minute details of my life? OK, let's see—'

'You win. Have you a loan till my allowance next Friday? There's this great gig in the college—'

'No problem, but you'll have to call in here, Will. Or wait. I'm meeting Ruth and India for a drink after work in the Blue Bar. Do you know it?'

'Brilliant. It's on my way to Shona's house.'

'Shona?'

'Long story, Sis. You don't want to know. Thanks

for the loan,' he said and hung up. Shona, I thought, as I began answering e-mails. I wondered was that the name of the girl I'd caught him with in our parents' bed. I decided that when I met him that night, I'd warn him about getting engaged. At the rate Will was going, he'd be giving Spencer a run for his money in the serial fiancé department.

I didn't have any appointments for a while so I decided to ring Roxy. The phone barely rang before she answered.

'Roxy?'

'Yes. Who is this?'

'It's me, Ellen. Look, I meant to ring you back but I was up to my eyes. So? How are you?'

Roxy didn't answer.

'Roxy? Are you still there?'

No answer.

'Roxy?'

It was then I heard her crying softly.

'Roxy? Roxy? What's wrong? Is there something wrong?'

'Teddy was here and . . . and . . . Pa's gone to Russia . . . and ohhhhh, Ellen—'

'What about Teddy?'

'I think my nose is broken.'

'I'll be right there.'

I hung up the phone and ran from my office and straight to my car, for once not noticing whether or not Tony was around. I knew that Teddy Hannon was bad news. There was just something about him – something almost evil. I pulled up outside Roxy's house, full of trepidation. How badly had he hurt her? Maybe I should have called the doctor as well.

I ran up the short path to her house and rang the bell. The door opened a crack and I could see one of Roxy's eyes. She stepped back and let me in, immediately locking the door behind me. She was wearing a red tracksuit, and her blonde hair hung loose around her shoulders. She held a wet towel over one half of her face.

'Where are the kids?' I asked.

'Enrique's asleep and my mother took the girls for the afternoon. Good job, too.'

'What happened?' I asked.

Roxy took the towel down from her face. My breath caught in my throat. Her right eye was so swollen it was almost closed, and a thin trickle of blood ran from her nose.

'Jesus, Roxy!' I said, putting my arms around her. She bawled against my shoulder. As I held her tiny frame, I wanted to find Teddy Hannon and beat the crap out of him. Bastard!

'Where did you say Pa is?' I asked.

'Russia,' Roxy said, the tears subsiding. She dabbed at her nose with the towel. 'Let's make some coffee,' she suggested.

I followed her to the kitchen where she began to clean off the worktops like a maniac.

'He came at lunchtime and I even made him coffee and then he started . . . the usual Teddy shit – you know – how much he loves me and how he can't live without me.'

Roxy scrubbed the sink with a brush. 'I ignored him at first. He doesn't love me – he doesn't know what the word means, and then I just said it straight out – that I was with Pa and I was happier than I'd ever been, and that was that. He went ballistic.'

The kettle boiled, and Roxy made two cups of coffee and handed me one. I took it and tried to think of something to say but I was way out of my league so I kept my mouth shut for once.

'He screamed at me – all this horrible stuff. And then before I knew it, he punched me in the face and he was gone. I'd have thought it was just a nightmare except for the blood.'

'You have to report this to the police,' I said.

'No.'

'You have to – Pa is away. You have to protect yourself and the kids.'

'Pa'll be back next week, and I know Teddy Hannon – he'll be very scarce now for a while. That's what he does.'

'Listen to me, Roxy. You have to go to the doctor. Then you should go to the police, and I'll talk to my friend – she's a solicitor.'

Roxy shook her head.

'You have to think of the children,' I said. 'Somebody who'd do something like this is capable of anything. Get him out of your life once and for all.'

Roxy looked at me, her eyes full of tears. 'You're right,' she whispered. 'I do have to think of the children.'

'Get the baby, and get your coat. I'll drive.'

Roxy nodded and left the kitchen. I pulled my phone from my bag and rang India.

'Ellen – don't tell me you're cancelling again.'

'I need your help, India. Roxy's just had the crap beaten out of her by her ex-husband. What does she need to do to get protection?'

'She needs to go down to the courthouse,' India said, immediately moving into professional mode. 'She has to get a protection order. It's a temporary order, and she'll have to go to court in a couple of weeks to get a proper restraining order, but it'll protect her in the short term.'

'So, who does she see in the courthouse?'

'The court clerk – he'll set it all up for her.'

'Thanks, India. See you later.'

'Bye, Ellen – good luck with that.'

Just as India hung up, Roxy came into the kitchen, carrying a sleepy Enrique. She had washed the blood from her face and tied up her hair.

'Ready?' I asked.

She nodded and we left the house in silence. Luckily her doctor lived close by and we were in and out in no time.

'What did he say?' I asked as we sat back into the car.

'He told me to go to the guards and to get a protection order,' she said.

'Let's do it,' I said and drove straight to the local garda station where a kind officer took Roxy's statement. After that, we headed for the courthouse. By the time I'd navigated all the traffic, Enrique was beginning to lose his patience. As I parked outside the newly restored stone building, I could see that Roxy was losing her nerve.

'Look, Enrique's jaded tired. We'll go home – I'll do it tomorrow,' she said.

'Ah no, sure we're here now,' I insisted. 'I'll walk around outside with Enrique and you go in and get it over with.'

Roxy took a deep breath and looked at me. 'I'm scared.'

'I know but you have to do it anyway,' I said. I leaned over and hugged her. 'Go on – you'll be grand. Enrique and I'll go for a walk.'

'OK,' she said in a small voice, opening the car door and stepping out. I watched her disappear through the huge doors. Enrique squealed in his car-seat.

'All right,' I said. 'I promised you a walk.'

I got out and unstrapped the baby. Snuggling him against my shoulder, I strolled around the cobbled forecourt of the courthouse. Three guards – one particularly cute – were smoking surreptitiously around the side of the building. I was trying to dream up a reason to chat to the handsome one when Teddy Hannon strode past like an apparition. Just as he walked in front me, he turned his head to stare straight into my face, lifted his hand, and shot me with an invisible gun. And then he was gone.

My legs began to shake uncontrollably and I had to lean against the cut-stone wall for support. That couldn't have happened, could it? Not in plain view of loads of guards. Teddy Hannon hadn't threatened me. That kind of thing didn't really happen. My heart pounded in my chest and I found it hard to breathe. I wanted to tell the guards but what exactly would I tell them? A man I barely knew had made some sort of a hand gesture as he walked by? You can't be arrested for that. I didn't know what to do. But one thing I did know for sure was that he was following Roxy and that I wasn't going to tell her.

My breathing had just about returned to normal when she came out of the courthouse. 'So? How did you get on?' I said too brightly.

'Fine. I have to go to court in two weeks' time. I'm glad I did it.' She took Enrique from me and kissed the top of his head. She looked tired and defeated.

'Come on. I'll bring you home,' I said.

Ruth and India were perched on high stools in what looked like deep conversation when I arrived at the Blue Bar that evening. I was late. The girls fell silent as I approached, and I got the distinct impression that they had been speaking about me. I kissed each one on the cheek and sat down on a stool beside them. Maybe I was paranoid. Just tired and paranoid, that was it.

'How did Roxy get on today?' India asked.

'India told me – is she all right?' Ruth asked.

'She's fine and she got on grand,' I answered.

'Did they give her a protection order?' India said.

I nodded. 'She has to go to court in a couple of weeks' time.'

'You look shattered,' said Ruth.

I laid my head on the bar top and pretended to fall asleep. 'Hard day. Hard few weeks actually.'

'All that sex must be very tiring,' said India, and I sat up straight immediately and looked at her.

'What do you mean?' I asked.

'Is your mobile working?'

'Well, it was the last time I checked.' I signalled the barman for a bottle of water.

'So does it only register calls from handsome American men?'

I looked at India and then at Ruth who had her head down and was playing with a beer mat.

'What's up, India? Why don't you come straight out with it?' I asked.

'Well, there was the lunch date last week that never happened. And drinks on Wednesday night – side-lined in favour of bowling. Not to mention calls and texts that weren't returned. Will I continue or would you like Ruth to add to the list?'

My temper was rising and I tried to control my voice.

'Well, I beg your pardon for having a life, India. Both of you have families now so things have changed a lot. And I'm sorry but that doesn't make your lives more important than mine. I can't drop everything and come running.'

'I never expected you to do that.'

'Yes, you did. I've been playing chief gooseberry

around the two of you for a long time now and –
hey! – suddenly I'm having a little fun and getting
on with my life, and somehow I'm doing something
wrong.' My voice was unsteady but there was no way
I was going to cry.

'You're not being reasonable, Ellen.'

'No, India. I'm daring to disagree with you and
you think that's unreasonable.'

India looked away. 'I didn't drop my friends the
minute a man came into my life.'

'Didn't you?' I asked.

'Stop, please – both of you,' said Ruth. 'Screaming
at each other in a bar won't solve anything. Both of
you are right.'

India and I looked at Ruth, waiting for her to
explain how both of us were right.

Ruth fiddled with the beer mat as she continued.
'Our lives have changed – all three of us. And India,
you and I have families now, and it's impossible to
hang out together the way we used to.'

'Well, at least I try to maintain our friendship!
Ellen, on the other hand, makes lunch dates and
doesn't bother to turn up.'

Ruth put up her hands. 'No, stop it, India. All of
us have done that at some stage. And Ellen has a
new boyfriend now and is in the first flush of love.'

'No, I'm not,' I said too loudly. 'We're friends. We
hang out together – that's all.'

'Well, Tim says Spencer is in love,' said India, her
eyes narrowed, waiting for my reaction.

'So, Tim is a love expert now, is he?' I asked her.

'No. He's Spencer's friend though,' said India.

'We're friends – that's it, end of story,' I said as my phone began to ring. I rooted in my handbag for it, spilling my water as I did so. Water dripped in a puddle onto the shiny wood flooring.

'Shit!' I said, and answered my bleating phone.

'Ellen, it's me, Spencer. Are you still in the Blue Bar? My meeting has finally ended and I was going to call by. We could get something to eat and maybe catch a movie.'

My mind whirred into action. I didn't want the girls to know who was on the phone after all the love stuff. But, on the other hand, I was fed up with noodles and Joey and Jerry Springer. Spencer was much better company than any of those.

'Great, how long will you be?' I asked, and watched India and Ruth exchange knowing glances. Well, fuck them! They were off home to cute babies and adoring husbands.

'Fifteen minutes, max. See you then, sweetie,' said Spencer and hung up.

I shrugged as I dumped my phone into my handbag. 'Are ye going to kill me now? For God's sake, lads! If you were me and your choice was between falling asleep with Jerry Springer and Joey or the delectable Spencer, which would you pick?'

India and Ruth stared at me for a few seconds and then all three of us burst out laughing at the same time.

'Mad bitch!' said Ruth.

'Right back at ya,' I said.

Just then, a tall man came into the bar, smiling broadly as he searched the bar with his eyes.

'What a looker,' said Ruth.

'Don't you dare, Ruth Burke. That's Will, my baby brother,' I said and waved at Will as he made his way towards us.

'Oh my God! Will! I didn't recognise him.'

'Liar. Keep your beady eyes off my brother.'

'Hi, Ell! Hi, girls,' he said and smiled shyly at them.

'Will Grace, you've grown into a fine handsome man,' said Ruth.

Will was mortified and tried to smile his way through it.

'Leave him alone, you,' said India. 'How's college, Will? Are you enjoying the course?'

'Not really, but the social life is cool,' said Will, and laughed and shuffled his feet. I knew what that meant. My brother wanted to be gone.

'Come on. I'll walk you to the door,' I said and stood up. Will nodded goodbye to India and Ruth amidst appeals from them to stay for a drink. Didn't they understand that the company of people years older than you was absolutely no fun when you were nineteen?

We walked out into the dark, cold evening, and I gave Will some money.

'You're the best, Ell. Really you are. I'll give it back to you on Friday, I promise.' He mock punched me as he headed off to meet Shona. I watched his tall, angular frame saunter down the road, and, even though he looked like a man, I knew in my heart he was still the boy Will, my baby brother.

'Will,' I called. 'Come here a minute.'

He turned around and gestured to his watch, but walked back anyway.

'Whassup?' he asked. 'More money is it?'

I laughed. 'Nope. I was just thinking about . . .you know . . .your engagement and stuff—'

'I meant to ask you about that, Ellen.'

'What do you mean?'

'Well, I was wondering, like, do you know how to get . . . em . . . I'm trying to think of the word – unengaged – that's it—'

I laughed with relief. 'Would this have anything to do with Shona – is that her name? The girl in Mam's bed?'

Will smiled at me. 'That was Ciara, Ell. Shona's just joined the band. She's the new drummer and she's a babe and a half.'

'And what about Shannon?'

Will shrugged. 'Being engaged wasn't for me, Ell. No, siree! So many girls, so little time – you know how it is.'

'Just be careful, Will,' I said.

'I'll probably be just like you, Sis, still stringing them along as I hit thirty.' He winked as he left me, his words echoing in my mind.

I walked back to the bar. India was gone, but her cream trench coat was still on the stool so I knew she hadn't gone far.

Ruth looked at me as I sat on my stool and picked up my now flat fizzy water.

'Are you all right?' she asked.

'Yeah. It's just something Will said – it bothered me, that's all.'

'Like what?'

'Ruthie, do you like being married?'

'Jesus, Ellen, what a question!'

'Well, do you?'

'I like the regular sex – that's good. And Paddy's cool too.'

'Seriously, Ruth.'

Ruth laughed. 'Why, Ellen? Are you thinking of getting married? And if so, to which of your three men?'

'I don't have three men. I don't really even have one man,' I said and glanced up as Spencer came into the bar, looking great in jeans and a long leather jacket. He beamed at me and I waved. India had come back from the loo and didn't reclaim her seat. Instead, she leaned against the bar and watched as Spencer approached. He kissed the girls and, standing behind my stool, he kissed the back of my neck. I put my arms behind and hugged him in a backwards kind of way and we both laughed. India and Ruth nodded sagely at each other. I knew what they were thinking but I didn't care.

'I booked Tosca's,' said Spencer to me as he nuzzled my ear.

'Great,' I said, still holding onto him.

'Sorry, ladies – if I'd known, I would have tried for a table for four. Wait, I'll try anyway,' said Spencer and reached into his cool Matrix jacket for his phone.

Ruth and India began protesting together.

'Don't Spencer. We're just leaving anyway – babies and dinners to see to,' said India. Ruth nodded agreement, and they both stood up and put on their coats.

I stood up too.

'Ellen, Friday is D-day, by the way – five o'clock in Café au Lait. Can you make it?' asked Ruth as they were leaving.

'D-day?' I said.

'Yep. Our appointment with the clairvoyant.' said Ruth. 'It doesn't matter if you can't make it. India said she'll come.'

Spencer was still nuzzling my neck and I half-heartedly pushed him away. 'I'll be there, kiddo. Count me in,' I said and hugged both my friends goodbye.

'So, Ellen, you're going to see a clairvoyant?' asked Spencer after he had ordered two glasses of white wine.

'Sort of,' I said.

He laughed. 'How do you sort of see a clairvoyant? Anyway, if you are going, could you ask one question for me?'

I looked at him nervously. Spencer sipped his wine. 'Would you ask should I sell my Microsoft shares soon?'

I laughed and my phone beeped. I rooted for it and saw that there was a new text message from Ruth.

*The man is in love, mark my words* it read. And then I heard Roxy's voice in my head again, saying over and over, 'The Yank has it bad.'

# 32

I was passing Hollyfields on Thursday on my way back to the office and I decided to call in to see Roxy. I pulled up outside her house and noticed that Pa's van was still missing. And then I noticed Maurice's garden. Well, I noticed what was left of Maurice's garden – it was completely submerged in about five tons of gravel.

'Jesus!' I said aloud as I walked along Roxy's path. I knocked on her door and she opened it almost straightaway. She wore a beige fitted coat and high, tan stiletto boots.

'Ellen! Come in,' she said.

'I'm sorry, Roxy. You're just on your way out,' I said.

'Shakira finishes playschool at twelve,' she said and shrugged. She looked gorgeous except for her black eye.

'How are you feeling?' I asked.

'OK. Pa's coming back on Saturday night.'

'What exactly is he doing in Russia? I never got to ask you.'

'Picking up timber for his brother-in-law, Rhino.'

'Do you want a lift?' I asked.

'No, I'd be faster walking. Why don't you walk with me, or have you forgotten what your legs are for?' she said. I laughed and followed her out the door.

'So, what does Rhino do?' I asked.

'He's a builder and he's getting into those timber-framed homes.'

'Did you tell Pa what happened?'

'No. I'll tell him when he comes home.'

'And is there any sign of Teddy?'

'No. He won't come within a mile of me for weeks. I don't need to worry about him until court.'

Roxy latched the small garden gate and we walked past Maurice's house. 'Did you see that?' she asked, nodding towards his garden.

'He must be planning on building something very big,' I said.

Roxy stopped pushing the buggy and looked at me. 'Ellen, why would he dump that gravel onto his prize roses?'

'You mean, somebody—'

'Exactly.'

'Did he call the guards?' I asked.

Roxy shrugged. 'They won't do a thing without proof, and the dogs on the street know who's doing it. Lousy, isn't it?'

'Yes, it is.'

'Did I tell you about the pigeons?'

'No.'

'Three of his best pigeons had their necks broken, and he found them lying in a row on his Welcome mat.'

'Jesus! And the guards? What did they say?'

'Same thing.'

We'd reached the playschool. Small children clamoured at the glass doors, waiting to be picked up. I could see Shakira's face break into a huge smile when she caught sight of her mammy. She ran out the door into her mother's outstretched arms.

'My mammy, my mammy,' she chanted, and suddenly I thought of Katie and Buzz Lightyear, and tears sprang to my eyes.

Shakira held my hand as we walked back towards the house.

'Are you still going ahead with the christening?' I asked.

'Damn right, I am.'

'Good.'

Roxy laughed. 'I don't know if I'd have any choice anyway.'

'Why?'

'It's turned into Event of the Year. It's so long since we had a family get together that everybody's decided this one should make up for the lack of parties.'

'Jesus! What about the cost?'

'Don't you know about my money, Ellen?'

'No. Why? Did you win the Lotto?' I asked, joking.

'I did, actually. Last year.'

'Seriously?'

Roxy laughed again. 'Don't go thinking millions now, Ellen. Think a few hundred thousand.'

'Cool. So that's how you bought the house?'

'Yeah. And I've the rest of it invested. I knew if it

was lying around, I'd only be dipping into it all the time. But I'm happy to give the family a big party. It's the least I could do.'

'And what about Teddy? Does he know?'

'You must be joking. Nobody knows except my mother, Pa and now you.'

We'd reached Roxy's house again. Maurice McMahon was standing at his front door, looking at the mound of gravel in his garden. He looked old and beaten and I felt terribly sorry for him. I waved at him and he waved back.

'Are you coming in for a cup of tea, Ellen?' Roxy asked as we reached her gate.

'Please, please, please,' squealed Shakira, tugging my arm as she did so.

I checked my watch. 'Not today, Shakira, honey. I have to go to work.'

Shakira looked crestfallen but cheered up immediately when I produced a euro from my pocket. 'That's for your piggy bank,' I said, and she nodded earnestly at me and clutched the coin for dear life.

'Roxy, I'm going to ring that detective, Hilary Thornton, about Maurice. It's a crazy situation,' I said as I opened the door of my car.

'Try if you like, Ellen, but I don't think there's anything they can do without actually catching someone red-handed.'

We said goodbye and I pulled away from the kerb, searching the area with my eyes as I drove. I had a feeling we were being watched, but then again, maybe it was just paranoia after poor Maurice's troubles.

But I did ring Hilary Thornton just before I left work that Thursday. I rang the garda station and discovered that luckily she had just started her shift. I walked to the window of my office as I waited for her to come on the line. I could see Wolfie across the street, loading tools and stuff into the truck. I looked around for Tony's black jeep – something that I did subconsciously almost every day now. It was parked beyond the truck, in all its gleaming glory. I'd have to duck out tonight.

'Ellen Grace, you again, I'm getting worried, hearing from you so often. Please tell me that your life is quiet and peaceful and that you're just ringing me to see how I am,' said the voice on the telephone line.

I laughed at the detective's reference to all my problems of the previous year. 'My life is hectic, but I've no dead bodies or kidnappings to report – at least not yet, anyway.'

'Not yet. Now why do those two little words worry me so much?' she asked.

I saw Tony coming out of the derelict building, wiping his face with a red hanky. He wore faded torn jeans and a sea-green sweatshirt.

'It's about my friend, Roxy Dawson, and her neighbour, Maurice McMahon.'

'Uh uh. So what about it?'

'Well, I called today and poor Maurice has suffered another string of intimidating stuff, and well . . . everybody knows who it is – Robert White and that bloody Sarsfield Properties – and we all know they want Maurice's house, so why the bloody hell are they allowed to get away with it?' I asked.

Tony was leaning against the truck now, talking to Wolfie.

'Do I tell you how to sell houses, Ellen?'

'Pardon?'

'You heard me.'

'No, but—'

'Do you think we're doing nothing? That we're sitting back twiddling our thumbs and drinking bad coffee?'

'No, I—'

'We're doing everything possible to catch the criminals. This is a democracy – we need proof, and we don't have any proof linking Sarsfield Properties to the incidents reported by your friend.'

'I know. I didn't mean that you weren't doing your job.'

'I appreciate your concern, Ellen. Really, I do. But trust me – we're doing everything we can. I promise you.'

'I believe you, Detective. And I didn't mean to criticise you.'

'I know. We're monitoring the situation, and, sooner or later, we'll catch them.'

'Thanks,' I said.

'Look, if I tell you something – can you keep it to yourself?'

'Sure.'

'CAB is about to go after Sarsfield Properties.'

I roared with laughter.

'Why is that so funny?' Hilary asked.

'Well, Robert White thinks I was the one who shopped him to the Criminal Assets Bureau two years ago – he sent me that letter bomb to thank me.'

'I remember that.'

'Why CAB?' I asked.

'Because the best way to get these guys is in their pockets. If the CAB people have sufficient reason to suspect dirty money, they can freeze bank accounts and make life very difficult for those involved.'

'Excellent. So that's about to happen to Sarsfield Properties?'

'You didn't hear that from me,' Hilary said. 'One other thing, Ellen. I have seven daughters.'

I wondered how this concerned me. 'That's nice,' I said.

'It's hard work most of the time. Anyway, one of them is called Shona and she just joined your brother's band. Will – that's his name, isn't it? Wasn't it Will who was kidnapped that time?'

'Yeah.'

'Shona's a drummer – or thinks she is at any rate. Well, I hope Will keeps an eye on her. Seventeen is an awkward age. Goodbye, Ellen,' she said and hung up.

I'd have to warn Will to stay away from Shona Thornton, I thought as I continued to look out the window at Tony Jordan.

And a few minutes later, I met him face to face, only inches away from me. I'd sneaked out the front door, and had just turned the corner and was walking into our small car park when I crashed slap bang into Tony's chest. I dropped my briefcase and my car keys.

'Hey, Ellen – look where you're going. You might crash into the wrong person someday,' he said, bending to pick up my car keys. I was bending too, and I raised my eyes and looked at his. Big mistake.

'I just did,' I said, and both of us straightened up together as if it was some secret dance that only we knew the steps to. He handed me the keys and our hands forgot to separate again. I was mesmerised by his face and couldn't think of a single thing to say to break the spell.

'Ellen,' he said. At least I thought he did. It was barely a whisper. Just then, out of the corner of my eye, I noticed that Spencer was standing on the footpath, obviously on his way into the car park. I didn't know how long he'd been there. I pulled my keys from Tony's hand.

'Thank you,' I said. Spencer had walked over and I reached up and kissed him on the mouth.

'Spencer, this is an acquaintance of mine - Tony Jordan,' I said, without making eye contact with Tony. 'And this is Spencer Alexander the Third.'

The two men shook hands. I smiled at Spencer. 'Let's go. We'll be late,' I said, and walked towards my car, Spencer following.

'Late for what, Ellen?' he asked as I climbed into the car.

I shrugged at him. 'Dinner?'

'My place or yours?'

'Your call.'

'My place, Ellen. I couldn't face noodles again.'

'See you there.'


Friday was D-day for Ruth. I'd actually written it in my diary, just in case I forgot. Anyway, the important thing was that I remembered – I was in enough trouble with Ruth and India, and forgetting a biggie like this was just a non-runner. Spencer was in Dublin and was staying overnight, so at least he wouldn't be distracting me. I rang Ruth after lunch to firm up our plans.

'Hi, Ruthie.'

'Hi, Ellen. I'm as nervous as hell. I'm tempted to open the bottle of Johnnie Walker in the press – talk me out of it like a good friend.'

'Don't open the whiskey, Ruth.'

'How about the vodka?'

'No alcohol. Look, when it's over, the three of us will go for a few drinks – how's that?'

'Good, but could we go beforehand?'

I laughed. 'Stop, Ruth! You'll be grand. What do you want us to do? Will we just hang around outside?'

'I was thinking you should come in and have coffee. Don't sit too near us, but within seeing distance. I'd like that. And my birth mother doesn't know ye so it'll be fine.'

'Sounds like a good plan. I'll ring India and tell her. So you'll arrive at Café au Lait at five, and we'll come in around quarter past. How's that?'

'Perfect. Wish me luck, kiddo.'

'Good luck, Ruthie. We'll be rooting for you.'

'I know that. See you later,' she said and hung up.

India and I met at ten to five and watched from across the street as Ruth went into the café. Shortly after, we saw Madame Leonora go in. She looked nothing like the picture in the ad, and she was tiny – smaller than Ruth. She wore a fake-fur coat, a Russian-style hat, and huge, hooped earrings. India and I felt like private investigators – India had even worn a trench coat. We stayed across the street, watching the café as if something was going to happen there. By the time we decided to go in, we were both frozen.

We chose a booth near the door, having already spotted Ruth at a table near the back. A waiter came, and we ordered lattes and chicken wraps. I was hungry, as I'd worked through lunch. I knew that if we were going for drinks, I might not get the opportunity to eat until much later. I tried surreptitiously to watch Ruth with her mother as India and I ate.

Madame Leonora had taken off her coat. She wore a skin-tight cerise-coloured sweater and matching skirt. Her hair was pulled back in a neat chignon – a must really if you're a clairvoyant. Ruth looked lovely and was very conservatively dressed in a tailored pinstripe suit and gorgeous ankle boots. I made a mental note to ask Ruth where she had bought the boots.

Ruth seemed relaxed, and they both poured over something that looked like photographs – probably of Paddy and Emerson. I said as much to India, who had her back to the proceedings. We decided then that India should be the one who got to go to the loo so that she could sneak a proper look.

It was half past six by the time Ruth and her mother stood up to leave. I was on my third latte and was feeling the effect. India was still breast-feeding so had wisely switched to water. They glided towards us, Ruth ahead of her mother.

'Ellen, India – I'd like you to meet Kathleen Brennan,' Ruth said, stopping in front of our table. India and I stood up like first years when the teacher came in. My heart was pounding. I was terrified that I'd do it all wrong and mess up Ruth's important day. We shook hands with Kathleen Brennan and sat back down. Ruth's mother smiled broadly and the resemblence to her daughter was startling.

'I've asked Kathleen to join us for a drink in the Blue Bar,' Ruth said.

'Great!' India said and jumped up from her seat.

'Brilliant!' I said, following suit.

The four of us walked from the restaurant. India and I were the nervous wrecks – talking too fast, bumping into things, laughing inappropriately – while the main protagonists, Ruth and Kathleen, were cool and composed.

The Blue Bar was just around the corner from Café au Lait. I'd left my car in our car park, knowing that it would be relatively safe there if I decided to have more than one drink – which, let's face it, was very likely if I was with Ruth.

As soon as we arrived in the bar, Kathleen excused herself and went to the loo.

'Well?' India and I chorused. Ruth hushed us and went to the bar where, within seconds, she'd lined up three drinks for herself – two of which she downed without a pause. She reminded me of a cowboy in the Wild West, lining up whiskies after a particularly tough shoot-out.

'Kathleen Brennan?' I said and all three of us laughed.

'She seems nice,' India said as she signalled to the barman.

I nodded.

'She is nice,' Ruth said. 'It went much better than I expected.'

And that was all we got to say as, at that point, Kathleen Brennan came floating back to join us. India ordered drinks for everybody and we went to sit in a quiet corner. At first, it was a bit awkward, as we all obviously struggled for things to say. Then I accidentally discovered that Kathleen was as big a Jerry Springer fan as I was. We swapped Springer stories for a full ten minutes, which somehow made everybody relax. After finishing her Margarita, Kathleen put on her coat and fumbled with her huge handbag.

'It was lovely to meet you, girls,' she said, smiling. 'But my show in the George starts at eight, so I need to go and get ready.'

Ruth stood up to accompany her mother. India and Kathleen shook hands. Then I reached out my hand towards Kathleen. She took it in both hers and clasped it to her chest, then closed her eyes and moaned softly. Ruth sniggered and I looked away.

'There's somebody here,' Kathleen said.

I looked around at the crowded pub.

'Oh no! Oh no! Oh no!' said Kathleen – who was rapidly morphing into Madam Leonora in front of my eyes. She swayed from side to side and I considered pulling my hand away, except that she was gripping it as if her life depended on it.

'Ellen!' she said in a husky voice, 'Someone you love is in grave danger. A dark shadow is gathering force and will burst upon your life. Beware of the man whose name begins with T, or maybe it's an R. Anyway, his heart is black and his unhappiness will destroy the light.'

Madame Leonora loosened her grip on my hand, and I pulled it away and pushed it into my jacket pocket.

'Well,' she said, sounding like Kathleen Brennan again. 'Better be off. See you all soon, I hope.'

Then she and Ruth disappeared, and I plonked onto my seat and drank a full glass of wine.

'Holy shit!' I said.

India laughed. 'And she didn't even charge you for the consultation.'

'Very funny, India.'

'It must be Tony Jordan,' India said as Ruth rejoined us.

'What? My mother is predicting that Tony Jordan is trouble? Ruth said. 'I could have told you that.'

'Tony Jordan is nothing to do with my life any more, and anyway, he's hardly the only person I know whose name begins with T, is he? And anyway, let's face it – she was a bit vague – either T or R. That covers about quarter of the people I know.'

'Like who, for instance?' Ruth asked, swigging whiskey from her glass.

'Like you,' I said.

'Very funny, I'm not a man.'

'Well, there's my Dad, Tom. There's my cousin, Terry.' I looked at India. 'There's Tim . . . and last, but not least, there's Ryan Ferry my arch enemy at work.'

'My money's on Ryan,' Ruth said. 'Your dad doesn't look to me like the grim reaper.'

'Yes, and I believe you sent Ryan to the Hebrides, Ellen. Is that true?' India asked.

I shrugged. 'An area manager's gotta do what an area manager's gotta do.'

'Bitch!' Ruth said, smiling and rattling the ice cubes in her glass. India and I looked at each other and then all three of us fell into a fit of uncontrollable laughter. Tears streamed down my face and everybody in the bar seemed to be looking at us.

We had a brilliant evening. Ruth told us all about her conversation with her mother. She seemed happy but a bit cautious, and I was glad. Who knew where it was all going to go? We broke up at nine o'clock. I felt light-headed – probably from the five glasses of wine I'd consumed – and was dying to get home and into bed. Ruth was worse than I was as we left the bar. And that was definitely as a result of drinking like a cowboy.

I almost left my briefcase behind me in the bar, but thanks to India's sobriety, she remembered and ran back to get it. She also drove us home, even though I lived only ten minutes away and was insisting that I'd be fine walking home alone. But India was having none of it. When she dropped me at my building, I almost tripped over my stupid briefcase as I was getting out of the car. Ruth was skitting at me in the front seat, and I stuck my tongue out at her as India pulled away.

I went into the building, just as the doors to the lift were closing. I ran, almost tripping up again, and pressed the up button. Miraculously, the doors opened. I stepped inside and put the briefcase on the floor, then straightened up and looked directly into Tony Jordan's delicious eyes. My face began to flood with colour, but at least the lift was dark.

'Fourth floor?' he asked, his fingers poised over the buttons.

'New job?' I asked and smiled at him.

He laughed then and pressed the buttons and stood next to me. Somewhere from deep within my alcohol-swamped brain, I remembered the eye thing and Tony, so I fixed on a grease mark on the stainless-steel wall in front of me. I could hear him breathing beside me but kept my eyes locked straight ahead. He smelled of alcohol or else I had surpassed myself in the drinking stakes. But I was dead proud that I didn't let him do the eye thing to me. Jesus! When he did that, it was like having sex with him.

The floors whizzed by. Neither of us spoke but it felt like an electrical storm in the tiny lift. Finally we reached my floor, and I stepped carefully out of the lift and walked down my corridor as the lift door closed softly behind me. Off up to his dumb fiancée, I thought, as I rooted in my bag for my keys. I could hear Joey mewing inside. That was good – Angela had let him in and probably fed him as well. It was nice of her, considering that she was still on her honeymoon.

I found my keys and staggered slightly as I pushed them into the lock. I giggled to myself and turned as I heard the lift doors open again. And there was Tony Jordan, walking down the corridor with my briefcase swinging from his hand. I'd just turned the lock on the door and it swung open. Tony put the briefcase down near my feet. I could see the top of his head as he bent down. He got up slowly and looked straight into my eyes.

'You forgot this,' he said, never taking his eyes from mine.

It sounded like the sexiest thing anyone had ever said to me.

'Did I?' I said, my eyes still locked to his.

'Yes,' he whispered and bent down until his mouth was near mine. And then we mauled each other, stumbling in the door of my apartment. Joey jumped on me as we came into the living room, and I pushed him away with my arm. I ripped Tony's shirt from him, and we fell against the coffee table, knocking over the lamp in the pitch-black room.

'Jesus Christ!' said Tony as he pulled clothes from me.

'It's OK. It's only a cheap lamp from Dunnes,' I said.

Tony laughed and kissed me on the mouth. Suddenly there was soft light from the overturned lamp. Tony had managed somehow to switch it on. We were lying on the floor now, naked.

'I want to see you. I want to see your face,' he said.

'Me too,' I said and kissed him back, and we lost ourselves in delicious sexual re-acquaintance. Afterwards, we lay on the couch, with a quilt thrown over us. My body tingled with the aftermath of incredible sex. Tony was the best lover – he'd won that competition hands down. And I never tired of looking at him. It felt great to lose myself in his eyes, and not have to hold back. And, I concluded, he had the longest eyelashes I'd ever seen. I held his face in my hands and licked his lips.

'You taste like a brewery,' I said.

'Nice. Very romantic, Ellen,' he said and kissed the top of my nose. I hugged him closer to me.

'Wolfie's birthday,' he said, his hands slowly moving down my body.

I stifled a groan of pleasure. 'When, tonight?'

'No, today. We went for a drink after work. And for the record, you smell like a wine cellar,' he said, kissing my neck. 'Lucky I like wine.'

'Ruth's mother—' I said, joining in the hands-exploring-body expedition that was going on under the quilt.

'Ruth's mother's birthday? Nice,' he mumbled as his mouth sought lower regions of my body.

I groaned out loud this time, not caring who heard. 'No, Ruth's mother is a clairvoyant,' I said and sank into another tantalising sexual tryst.

He made coffee afterwards, walking naked around my tiny kitchen. I lay back on the couch and blatantly admired him. He knew he was gorgeous though. Otherwise, he'd be hiding bits of himself. He brought coffee over to me and sat on the floor, below me, holding the cup to my lips.

The coffee was hot and I spat some out, making him spill the hot liquid on his naked thigh. We both laughed. He stopped suddenly and looked at me.

'Where to now, Ellen Grace?' he asked, and traced my facial features with his finger.

'How about the bedroom?' I said.

'Always the smart mouth. That'll get you into trouble sometime,' he said and reached up to kiss me.

'So,' he said when he finished the kiss. 'What do we do now?'

'Before or after your wedding?' I asked, looking down into the mocha eyes.

He laughed. 'Smart answer, again. OK. Let's try one more time. How do you feel about me?'

I knew he was serious this time. 'You first,' I said.

'I'm mad about you, Ellen, and I don't think that will ever change. What about you?'

'What about you and your fiancée?'

Tony laughed and climbed back onto the couch beside me. I covered him with the quilt. He had muscles in his back – I'd never noticed that before.

'My fiancée. My fiancée isn't my fiancée and everybody knows it except her. And don't look at me like that, Ellen. I've told her as much. She knows in her heart it's true.'

'So, why are you always at her place?'

'What should I be doing? Waiting around for you to feel the same way as me?'

'And what about the engagement ring? I saw it myself.'

Tony laughed. 'That's her grandmother's ring.'

'I thought the diamond came from the stash that was up the china cat's arse.'

Tony laughed again. 'No more diamond robberies, Ellen. I'm legit now, I'm an honest builder.'

It was my turn to laugh. 'Well, you must be the only honest builder in Ireland.'

'So? How do you feel about me?'

I kissed him instead of answering. Suddenly there was a noise at the front door. We both sat upright and looked in its direction. The door swung fully open and Spencer stood there, my briefcase in his hand, and a miserable look on his face.

'I'm sorry. The front door was open and the briefcase was . . . I'm sorry. I'd no idea you'd company, Ellen,' he said, walking backwards while he spoke.

'Spencer . . . Spencer, wait up—' I said, as I

scrambled over Tony. Spencer shook his head and turned and vanished out the door.

'Jesus Christ!' I said, searching in the tangle of clothes for underwear. I dressed hurriedly, swearing all the time. Tony said nothing, just watched me steadily, his hands behind his head.

'Ellen, answer my question. How do you feel about me?' he asked as I struggled to put on shoes.

'Not now, Tony. It'll wait. Spencer's . . . Spencer's upset,' I said and ran towards the door.

'Stay,' said Tony from the couch.

'I can't. I have to talk to Spencer,' I said and ran out the door and down the corridor. I skipped the lift and took the stairs, two steps at a time. I caught him just as he was leaving the building.

'Spencer – wait . . . I didn't mean—' I said to his back. He kept walking.

'Spencer, please,' I said, shivering in my trousers and skimpy top. I hadn't had time to find my coat.

He stopped and turned to face me. He was crying.

'I'm sorry,' I said.

He shook his head and wiped his eyes with the back of his hand, breathing deeply as he did so.

'I'm so sorry,' I said again.

'Sorry that I walked in or sorry that it happened?' he asked. I could see the hurt in his face, and I could hear the murmur of it in his voice.

'Spencer, look. I thought we had a . . . well . . . a casual thing going . . . I didn't . . . Jesus! I never meant to hurt you,' I said. My teeth were beginning to chatter from the cold.

'Goodbye, Ellen,' he said and walked quickly to his car.

'Spencer, don't leave like this, please,' I said but he was already in his car. I watched him drive away, wheels screeching like something from *NYPD Blue*.

I went back into the building and took the lift to my floor, preparing in my head what I'd say to Tony. I knew now how I felt about him. And I think I probably knew deep down, from the very first time I ever met him.

There was a connection between us that was incredibly powerful, and also very special. While I could love other men, there would always be something lacking. With Tony, I got the whole deal, including the passion. I reached my apartment and braced myself. The door was still slightly ajar, so I pushed it in and walked into the living room.

'Tony,' I said. But the room was empty. He'd folded the quilt and laid it on the couch. His clothes were gone. I ran to the bedroom, but I knew in my heart it would be empty. And it was, except for Joey, sitting on a pillow, staring unblinkingly at me.

'Oh, Joey,' I said and burst out crying as I snuggled up next to him.

I awoke with a jump. I'd fallen asleep on my bed, fully dressed, one arm curled around Joey. Something had woken me but I didn't know what it was. I sat up and looked around the room. Light was beginning to creep through the blind as dawn broke over the city. I began to remember bits of last night and groaned aloud. I also remembered bits of the fabulous sex.

Tony Jordan – bastard! Couldn't even be bothered waiting for me. The phone rang suddenly, piercing the eerie dawn silence. I jumped and realised that that was the sound that had woken me minutes before.

I scrambled into the kitchen and picked up the phone.

'Hello?' I said, wondering who was calling me at this time of the morning. And then I thought of Dad. I hoped it wasn't about Dad.

'Ellen? India here. Sorry to disturb you at this hour.'

'What's wrong, India? There's something wrong, isn't there?'

Fear gripped me like a vice.

'It's Spencer. He's been in a car crash—'

'Ah, Jesus! No. Please, no.'

'He has severe concussion, and a fractured—'

'But he's alive – please tell me he's alive?'

'He's got a fractured collarbone. But they're more worried about the concussion. The left lobe of his brain is swollen.'

'How did it happen, India? Does anybody know?'

'We thought you might be able to fill in the blanks.'

'Me?'

'Well, Tim said he was calling to you after they came back from Dublin. Then hours later, he crashed his car into a wall near the Raheen roundabout.'

'Jesus! I don't believe it.'

'His blood alcohol was sky high, Ellen. That's the unbelievable part. Spencer would never ever drink and drive. Would he?'

'Oh God! I don't believe this.'

'Well, that's the story so far.'

'Should I come down to the hospital – the Regional, I presume?'

'That's your call, Ellen. Tim is with him now, and they said no visitors under any circumstances, so maybe you should leave it for a while.'

'Will you ring me if there's any news?'

'Of course. They said it's a miracle he's alive at all. His seatbelt saved him. Drunk as he was, he put on a seatbelt. Look, I'd better go. Alyssa is crying for breakfast. I'll call you later, OK?'

'OK, India, and thanks.' I hung up the phone and sat at the kitchen table, allowing a train of events unfold in my head – from the time Spencer had left me the previous evening. Poor Spencer – he could have been killed stone dead. But the one consolation in it for me was that he'd worn his seatbelt. If he'd meant to kill himself, if I'd driven him to it, then he wouldn't have worn his seatbelt. I had to believe that. Slowly Kathleen Brennan's melodramatic performance in the Blue Bar floated back into my head. *Beware of the man whose name begins with T.* Looked like she'd been right.

# 33

I spent the weekend hiding in my apartment, eating junk food, and trying not to think about Spencer and Tony. So, instead, I found myself thinking about Andrew. I couldn't have that. By Sunday, I was running low on my ability to ignore the huge wave of disaster that was my life. I cleaned the apartment, did all my hand washing, disinfected Joey's litter tray, sewed all my glued-up hems, and polished my shoes. When I ran out of things to clean, polish and sew, I decided to bake fairy cakes.

I rummaged in the presses in the vain hope that I'd bought a bag of flour and forgotten about it. It didn't seem to be the case. I could have run out to the local shop at that point, but my flour search had yielded a full bottle of vodka. I was surprised to find it, but then I remembered bringing it with me when I moved from Andrew's house. If it was going to be a contest between fairy cakes and vodka, the vodka was going to win hands down.

I found two litres of orange juice, a pint glass and *Titanic* on TV. Then Joey and I curled up together on the couch. Joey fell asleep and I got shit-faced. As Rose and Jack fell in love and conquered the odds to be together, I just knew that I had to get in contact with Tony Jordan. I found my phone in my bag and scrolled down until I reached his number. I wanted to hear his voice but what would I say? I'm sorry I ran away but Spencer was on his way to getting drunk and almost killing himself. I couldn't say that. OK – maybe I could say something else. Or maybe not. I'd text him.

*Tony where did you go?*

I looked at the blurry words on the tiny screen of my phone. I couldn't send that. It made no sense. Fumbling with the menu buttons, I tried to delete the message but accidentally pressed send instead. Shit! I filled my glass with vodka and orange juice and tried to fool the phone into thinking I wasn't waiting for a reply. I needn't have bothered. The bastard never replied.

By the time the movie was over, the bottle of vodka was half-empty and I was lying on my back on the floor, crying fat tears.

'D'you see that, Joey?' I slurred, sniffing loudly. 'See that? If she really loved him, she'd have jumped into the sea with him. Now, that's what I'd have done. Poor Leo. I think he got a raw deal with that auld Kate one. Selfish bitch!'

I tried to focus on the TV. The credits were rolling. God! I truly hated that *Titantic* theme.

'D'you know something, Joey? My life is shit, and it's worse it's getting.'

Then I rolled over and fell asleep. Sometime during the night, the cold woke me. I somehow found my way to the kitchen where I dosed myself with Solpadeine, and then staggered into bed.

The phone rang at six o'clock in the morning, and I awoke with a pounding headache and a knot of terror in my stomach. What if there was more bad news about Spencer? I stumbled into the kitchen, stubbing my toe and stepping into Joey's bowl.

'Goddamn cat!' I muttered, swearing that I was finally going to get a cordless phone I could bring into the bedroom at night.

'Ellen?'

'Hello?'

'Ellen. It's me, Roxy. Sorry to call you so early.'

'That's OK – are you all right?'

'No, no, I'm grand. We're all grand. There's just been a bit of an . . . incident. Maurice's house. A fire.'

'Oh my God! Is he all right?'

'He's fine. The house isn't even all that bad – a lot of broken windows and smoke damage and stuff, but it's still standing. No, it's just the guards are gone—'

'The guards?' I asked.

'Yeah – they were here – and Maurice kept telling them he was fine and there was no need to be fussing and no way would he let them bring him to hospital. So they're gone and now he's not great. Grey-looking and his breathing is bad, and I want to bring him to hospital but the van won't start—'

'I'll be there in five minutes.'

I hung up and ran into the bedroom where I pulled on a pair of jeans, a sweater and a pair of boots.

Then I ran out the door, pausing only to grab a warm jacket. The morning was bright but freezing. Blue cloudless sky, white hoar frost on the bare trees and tops of walls, and that almost liquid feeling of cold that enters into your lungs every time you take a breath.

As I drove to Roxy's house, through the quiet early-morning town, I tried to figure out what could have happened. It had to be malicious if poor Maurice's house had been set on fire. First Acorn House, and now Maurice's house – either Sarsfield Properties were responsible, or else that particular part of town was unbelievably prone to spontaneous combustion.

As soon as I pulled up outside the house, and before I had had time to switch off the engine, the front door opened. Roxy appeared with a very frail-looking Maurice by her side. Her hair was streaming down the back of her red, puffy jacket, and though she was smiling and waving at me, even from that distance, I could see the lines of strain and the remains of Teddy Hannon's handiwork.

The Maurice who was shambling down Roxy's garden path was like a facsimile of himself. An empty copy, devoid of energy. There was none of the usual I-could-fight-the-world-and-come-back-for-seconds look, which I associated with Maurice. Instead, his face was cadaverous and yellow, and his right hand was pressed against his breastbone, as if he was swearing an oath. Or struggling for breath.

I jumped out of the car and opened the passenger

door. Roxy lowered Maurice into the front seat and then climbed into the back herself. Maurice held himself tautly upright, and his breath came in short, laboured pants. Roxy leaned forward and fastened his seatbelt. I was suddenly so frightened that we wouldn't manage to get Maurice to the hospital fast enough that I could hardly breathe myself.

'So? How are ye all this morning?' I asked, pretending normality. I strapped on my own seatbelt and started to drive away, half registering the smoke-blackened front of Maurice's house out of the corner of my eyes.

'I see Pa's back,' I said.

Roxy nodded. 'I think the journey might have been too much for the van.'

A heavy silence descended.

'God! It's cold, isn't it?' I said, moving into motor-mouth. 'But at least the sky is blue and that makes such a difference, doesn't it? I love that sort of high sky. But sure, no wonder it's cold. It's November. We won't feel Christmas coming, hah?'

I shut my motormouth long enough to steal a side-wards glance at Maurice. He was still working hard at it, but at least he was also still breathing. Roxy caught my eye in the rear-view mirror and smiled. She winked with her good eye.

I silently thanked God that there was a hospital less than five minutes' drive from Roxy's house. Every traffic light went with me, and there was still very little traffic so we were soon there. I pulled into the car park and Roxy helped the fragile Maurice out of the car.

'I'll just park the car and then I'll come in,' I said. Roxy smiled and nodded.

'Thank you, Ellen,' Maurice breathed, and struggled for a smile to give me.

'No problem, no problem at all,' I said, as we made eye contact. 'See you in a minute, Maurice.'

Roxy and Maurice moved slowly towards the hospital entrance, and I drove around the back of the building and found a legal parking spot. Hospitals are probably the only place I bother to search for proper parking places – even I couldn't bear to block an ambulance. I walked back to the building and through the long terrazzo corridors to the A & E unit. Roxy was standing by a vending machine, drinking steaming coffee from a paper cup. There was no sign of Maurice.

'They're very quiet, thank God,' Roxy said in answer to my unasked question. 'They've taken him off already to do some tests. Would you like coffee?'

I nodded and Roxy pounded coins into the slot.

'Cappuccino?' she asked.

I nodded again and we both watched the frothy milk and water squirt into its paper receptacle. I picked up my cup of coffee as soon as the machine seemed to have finished.

'What happened?' I asked.

Roxy sighed. 'He was fine – he really was. Maurice has more smoke alarms in his house than bulbs, so the fire wasn't too bad when he woke up.'

'Just as well,' I said.

'Yeah, really. He did the right thing – came into our house to call the fire brigade because the phone is in his front room, and that's where the fire was the worst.'

'Maurice has his phone in the front room?'

Roxy nodded. 'He was great. Really, really sharp – did all the right stuff and was like a twenty-year-old running around giving orders to the firemen. You know what Maurice is like.'

'Definitely,' I said, trying not to think of the frail old man who had sat in my car, struggling for breath, just a few minutes earlier. 'That man could boss in the Olympics.'

Roxy grinned and took a mouthful of coffee. 'Well, anyway, the fire was put out fairly fast. Though the place is destroyed from smoke and water, it wasn't too bad, and then, when Maurice and Pa and me were drinking a cup of tea in my kitchen, a guard came.'

'Why?'

'The firemen called the police. They said they wouldn't know for sure until they send in the experts but they thought the fire was probably started by a petrol bomb.'

'Oh shit!' I said.

'Yeah, fucking hell! I can't believe it. But that's why they called the guards.'

'And what did the guard say?'

'Just that. Just the stuff about maybe it being a petrol bomb. And the guard was lovely and wanted to take Maurice down here to be checked out, but no way would he go. He said he was fine. And he was, Ellen – he *was* fine—'

Roxy's eyes filled with tears and I put my arm around her shoulders. 'Oh, love, don't, it'll be all right. I promise – everything will be all right. You've had a terrible week. Maurice will be fine, and, anyway, he's in the right place now, isn't he?'

Roxy nodded and sniffed. 'I hope so. He seemed grand, and then everybody was gone, and Pa was making a bed for him in the spare room, and he sort of collapsed in the kitchen in front of me. Couldn't breathe and all that stuff, and I roared for Pa, and Maurice wouldn't let me call an ambulance. Then the van wouldn't start, so I called you—'

Roxy started to cry in earnest, and I put my scalding yet entirely tasteless coffee onto a plastic chair and hugged her tightly. As she sobbed against my chest, I wondered what all of this could mean. It had to be Sarsfield Properties. After all, with that shower of shits they had working for them, anything could happen.

CAB would want to hurry up and shut down Sarsfield Properties and arrest the thugs doing their dirty work for them. They were the very ruthless so-and-sos who'd have shot me or Will in a minute to get at Tony Jordan the previous year, and everyone – including the police – knew that they had murdered Jerome Daly, even if it was impossible to prove.

And now they were trying to terrorise an old man into selling his family home. I was beginning to lose my patience with the whole lot of them. Roxy stopped crying and took a deep breath.

'OK, she said. 'OK, that's it. Enough crying.'

She fished a tattered tissue out of her jacket pocket and blew her nose. 'I'm sorry about that, Ellen. I'm just upset but—'

'Don't worry about it,' I said.

'It's just I hope . . . you know . . . I hope he's OK. I really like Maurice, and the kids love him and he reminds me of my grandad.'

'Is your grandad still alive?' I asked, passing Roxy a packet of tissues from my handbag.

She blew her nose again. 'No. But I totally loved him – he was like Maurice – a cranky auld bastard on the outside. My grandad was cross as a bag of wasps on the outside but he'd give you the coat off his back at the same time.'

Just then, the doors to the interior of A & E opened and a much healthier-looking Maurice than the one who'd sat in my car was striding in our direction. Roxy shouted his name and ran forward to give him a hug. Maurice smiled and hugged her in return. A pale woman with a scraped-back blond bun and green eye-shadow was walking behind him.

'Well, have a good rest now, Mr McMahon, and maybe call your doctor tomorrow and have him check you over,' she said, looking from me to Roxy and back as she pushed bunched-up papers into the pocket of her white coat.

'What was the matter?' Roxy said to no one in particular.

'Well, we think it was probably all too much for him,' the woman said, pausing to smile at both Roxy and me. 'Dr Fenton. Pleased to meet you.'

'Roxy Dawson and Ellen Grace,' I said, shaking the doctor's cold hand and nodding towards Roxy. Roxy shook her hand as well.

'I'm right as rain now. Right as rain,' Maurice said.

'Of course you are, Mr McMahon, but still now, don't forget what I told you . . . a man your age—'

The doctor's voice trailed away as Maurice glared at her. Roxy winked at me.

'I'll have you know, Doctor, that I have no intention of resting – I have work to do.'

'But—' the doctor began. Maurice waved a hand imperiously.

'I never felt better. That must just have been my childhood asthma putting in an appearance. But now I'm fine. Storm in a teacup.'

'You're fine?' Roxy asked.

Maurice nodded. 'Fit as a fiddle. They'll have to go a long way further than a bloody petrol bomb before they can stop Maurice McMahon.'

I smiled but my stomach squeezed. What Maurice didn't realise was that they probably would go a lot further before this whole thing was finished. The thought made me furious.

'Shall we go now?' Maurice asked as Roxy linked him. They both looked at me. I shrugged.

'Take care of yourself, Mr McMahon,' the doctor said, jamming her hands into her pockets and smiling an empty, irritated-looking smile. I figured she'd probably have liked to thump Maurice herself, and was getting her fists out of harm's way. And I didn't blame her. I was sure he was a nightmarish patient. Still, I was actually delighted to see the return of the pompous Maurice. That meek, frightened man I'd driven to hospital was a hundred times scarier for me. Maurice raised a hand in a farewell salute to the doctor, and he and Roxy started for the door.

'Does he need any medication or a prescription or anything?' I asked the doctor who turned as though to leave.

She shook her head.

'Inhalers or anything?' I asked. 'For asthma?'

Dr Fenton smiled, and her washed-out blue eyes became warm for the first time. 'It was a panic attack. Pure and simple. A panic attack. And to be honest with you, if someone petrol-bombed my house, I'd have one too. That did happen, didn't it? The petrol bomb?'

I nodded.

'I don't know why he's so upset that he's upset – if you know what I mean,' she said. 'Anybody would be upset under the circumstances.'

'But not Maurice the People's Champion,' I said, shaking hands with her again. 'That's the thing, you see. Thanks for everything, Doctor. Take care.'

I stood in the corridor, watching Dr Fenton walk away, and wondered if there was any point in running after her to ask about Spencer. Maybe she'd know how he was. But then maybe I'd have to go see him, and I wasn't ready to face that particular ordeal. Instead, I trotted out to the car park after Roxy and the Saviour of the Little Ones, concentrating on bringing them home in one piece.

# 34

I dropped Roxy and Maurice off and drove home and showered and dressed properly before heading into work. I dreaded the thought of going into the office, but I really had no option. I was sure that the atmosphere would be unbearable, though. Just as I was ready to leave, the telephone rang. It was Ruth.

'What the fuck is going on, Ellen?'

'I beg your pardon?'

'You heard me. Is it true that Spencer walked in on you and Tony Jordan in bed?'

'No. It was the couch. And anyway, it's none of your business.'

'Jesus Christ! What are you playing at, Ellen? First you led Andrew Kenny up the bridal path, and now that poor fool of a Yank. Have you no heart?'

'I never led anybody anywhere they didn't want to go. Spencer knew the score, Ruth. He knew we were just having fun.'

'You know in your heart that that isn't true, Ellen. A dog with a mallet in his arse could tell he was in love with you.'

I didn't answer.

'You know I'm right, Ellen. You used him and now

he's in hospital after drinking his brains out and driving at a wall.'

'That had nothing to do with me.'

'Oh no! I suppose the sight of the woman he loves rolling around naked with another man is something you'd expect him to take in his stride.'

'Piss off, Ruth!' I said and banged down the phone. I picked up my keys and my briefcase and stormed out of the apartment. It was so unfair. It wasn't my fault if Spencer Alexander the Third had lost his marbles, for God's sake. How was it that I was responsible? I never asked him to fall in love with me, did I? I never promised him anything, so it wasn't fair that everybody – even my supposed friends – seemed to think I was somehow to blame for his accident.

As if my morning wasn't bad enough, just as I arrived into the Gladstone and Richards car park, my phone gave a message alert. Somewhere in the dark recesses of my memory of the night before, I remembered having accidentally sent Tony a message. I laid my head on the steering wheel, afraid to look. Fuck! I couldn't even remember what I'd said in the text. Maybe it wasn't that bad, after all. Maybe it was about the movie. I sat up and picked up the phone off the passenger seat. Taking a deep breath, I opened my new message.

*Spencer out of danger. Broken collarbone. Thought you'd have called to find out. India*

Great! Now India hated me as well. I had no boyfriend. No friends. No prospect of living happily ever after. At least I still had my job. Tim was speaking with Molly in reception. They were hovering over an enormous get-well card, and laughing quietly as I came through the doors. They turned to look at me.

'Morning,' I said, a cheesy grin plastered on my face. I wasn't to blame. I wasn't to blame. I wasn't to blame. Molly and Tim nodded politely and I swept past as quickly as I could without breaking into a run. I closed the door of my office behind me and took a deep breath. Just as I exhaled, the telephone rang.

'Ellen. A Mr Harrison for you,' Molly's voice icily announced, 'he rang my switchboard twice.'

'Thanks. Hello? Mr Harrison? Ellen Grace speaking. How may I help you?'

The telephone receiver was silent.

'Hello?' I said again. 'Hello? Can you hear me?'

I looked at the receiver in that insane way everybody does when you can't hear anything. Still dead air.

'Hello?'

'Ellen Grace?'

'Yes. Mr Harrison? There you are! I thought we'd been cut off. Now, how can I help you?'

'Keep your fucking nose out of things that don't concern you or you'll be sorry.'

'I beg your pardon?'

'You've been warned. I won't warn you again.'

The telephone receiver beeped as the connection was broken. I dropped the phone back onto the desk. Oh, my God! What was that about? Who'd ring me and threaten me like that? Sarsfield Properties? Teddy

Hannon? I stood up and walked to the window and opened the blinds with shaking fingers.

What did that mean – *you'll be sorry*? I took some deep breaths as I tried to make sense out of what was happening. Sarsfield Properties were trying to get Maurice to sell up so that they could build a big entrance to their stupid, stupid hotel. They were already intimidating him and now they were trying to intimidate me. What was the point of intimidating me? I had nothing to do with their hotel. Unless, of course, they'd had a visit from CAB and were blaming me again.

I scanned the activities across the road. Two men in yellow hard hats were erecting scaffolding along the front of the building. I craned my neck but there didn't seem to be anyone else around. Not that I was looking for anyone in particular.

I walked back and forth across the small floor of my office. As I paced, a bubble of anger began to rise in my chest. Who did these people think they were? They were really the lowest of the low, and most of the reason they were successful was to do with the fact that they managed to intimidate their victims into silence.

Then a picture flashed into my head of Teddy Hannon's almost pretty face and the imaginary gun he had pointed at me. Roxy was wrong – he *was* around. He must have been following us the day we went to the courthouse. Bastard!

I didn't want to think about any of it, so I opened my filing cabinet and pulled out the file on a proposed new housing estate. The builders had asked me to have a look at the plans and the projections, after I'd talked them into making Gladstone and Richards the exclusive agents.

For all the thanks that was getting me around the office at the moment, I might as well have been filing my nails since my promotion. I flipped open the file and took out the architect's drawings of the finished product. A tree-lined road with neat gardens, small pigtailed girls on tricycles, and a man who was the spitting image of Andrew Kenny swinging a baby in the air outside his architect-designed house. For God's sake! I slammed the drawing shut and grabbed my bag. I needed to go for a drive to clear my head.

The whole reception area of Gladstone and Richards was deserted as I hurried through. I cantered around the corner to the car park avoiding looking at Tony's building. But as I pulled out in the BMW, into the stream of traffic, I couldn't resist a quick glance. Still nobody I recognised – though the scaffolding guys would have warranted another look if I hadn't been so distracted.

I made painfully slow progress through the town, deciding to go visit Maurice and Roxy before I did another thing. As I pulled up outside Roxy's house, I saw a pick-up parked in front of Maurice's, and guessed from the fact that all the doors and windows were thrown open that Maurice had the renovation crew in already. You had to admire the man's spunk. I knocked on the door, still wondering if I should tell them about the phone call, or if that was just going to frighten them. I was so preoccupied with that that I didn't hear the door open. Mind you, I heard my name being spoken. There was only one person who spoke my name exactly like that.

'What are you doing here?' I asked.

Tony Jordan stepped back into Roxy's hallway. Oh God! What I wouldn't have given to know what I had said in that text.

'Are you coming in?' he asked.

I nodded and followed him to the kitchen. Roxy was sitting at the table with a sleeping Enrique snuggled against her, and Maurice was standing at the sink, scrubbing the bottom of what looked like a chip pan.

'Good morning, Maurice,' I said, rushing to stand beside him – and as far away from Tony as possible. 'How are you feeling now?'

'Never better. Never better.'

'I see you've started the clean-out of the house already.'

'Indeed I have. No point in letting the grass grow under your feet. And poor Roxy and Patrick can't be expected to put up with me for too long.'

'You're more than welcome to stay here as long as you like, Maurice,' Roxy said.

Maurice turned around and shot a look of pure adoration at Roxy. 'I know. Still, better off in my own house. And Tony says the whole job'll only take a couple of days.'

'You'll be back home by Friday at the latest,' Tony said.

'You're doing Maurice's house?' I asked, before I could stop myself.

Tony nodded. He was wearing a torn red sweat-shirt and a pair of Levis that were coated in plaster dust, and he still managed to look undeniably gorgeous. Looking at him made my heart ache. Why did I always make such a mess of everything?

'Well,' he said, looking at everybody except me. 'Better get back to work. Wolfie'll be looking for me. So, you're sure you want that same green for the hallway, Maurice?'

'Certain. Eau-de-Nil – water of the Nile – Julia loved that colour and it's very relaxing, you know –she'd never have the hallway any other colour while she was alive, and I like it too—'

Maurice paused and looked out the window into Roxy's back garden. The steel wool he held in his hand dripped soap, and his thin shoulders heaved slightly.

'So that's it, Tony, please,' he said, with a definite nod of the head as he resumed scrubbing the black-ened pot base, 'Eau-de-Nil.'

'No problem,' Tony said. 'We'll have everything back to normal as soon as possible. See you later.'

Roxy laid a still-sleeping Enrique in a Moses basket on a stand in the corner of the kitchen.

'What time is it?' she asked, distractedly. She walked out of the kitchen and we could hear her open and close the front door. When she came back into the room, I could see that she was preoccupied by something.

'Everything all right?' I asked.

'Just thought I heard the doorbell.'

Shakira and Shania came arguing into the kitchen, dressed in matching pink fleeces, and jeans with flowers embroidered up the legs.

'Stop it this minute,' Roxy said, halting the little girls in their tracks.

'She took the pink slides,' Shakira said, pointing at two plastic slides with diamanté trim that were pinned askew in Shania's hair.

'I like them. They're mine,' Shania said. 'Here.' She threw a large purple butterfly-shaped slide at her sister who looked as though she was about to burst into tears.

'I don't like that one,' Shakira complained, her voice trembling with emotion.

Roxy tutted loudly. 'Oh, for God's sake, give it over!' She rummaged in her handbag and produced two identical pink slides, then she pulled Shakira towards her and pinned back the front of her long dark hair.

'There,' she said. 'Now stop fighting and run and get your jackets. Your aunt will be here in a minute.'

The placated girls ran out of the room and I looked at Roxy.

'Teddy's taking them for the day. His sister, Fiona, is collecting them.'

'The whole day?' I asked. 'Are you sure that's a good idea?'

'Only until four.'

'It's not a good idea, Roxy.'

Roxy shrugged. 'What can I do? He *is* their father and he's never done anything to hurt the kids. Teddy's mad stuff is all about me.'

'Does he know about the protection order?'

'He must know now – I told his sister when she rang about the kids. She'll do all the collecting and dropping off. The kids love her.'

'I still think you shouldn't let him near the kids.'

'Easier said than done,' Roxy said, walking over to stand by the sleeping baby. She reached into the basket and smoothed his hair. The doorbell rang. Roxy jumped away from Enrique and disappeared into the hallway, calling the girls' names as she ran. Maurice and I stood like statues, pretending not to listen.

'Good morning, Roxy. Girls,' a woman's voice said, softly. 'All ready?'

The girls murmured something in reply.

'Fiona,' Roxy's voice rang out, louder than normal. 'Bring them home at four. I'm expecting them at four.'

'See you, Roxy. Come on, girls.'

Then there was the sound of kissing and hugging and small voices saying goodbye to their mother, and Roxy issuing instructions to the girls. The front door closed. Maurice attacked his now-shining pot with the steel wool, and I opened my handbag and pretended to look inside.

'Well,' Roxy said, as soon as she returned to the kitchen. 'That's that, I suppose.'

I nodded, not knowing what to say that might

reassure her. 'I'd better go and do some work, I suppose,' I said, closing my bag. 'See you later, Maurice. Roxy.'

They both waved and I left the house and headed straight for my car, keeping my eyes determinedly on the front of the beemer. Tony Jordan was everywhere. Across the road from my office. In and out of my apartment building. And now, working next door to Roxy's house. The bloody man was haunting me.

I decided to take a drive out to see that new housing development. Andrew Kenny was hardly going to be there even if he was in the architect's drawing. I'd been once before but I've found that it's always worth visiting an area a few times when I have to sell houses there. That way, I get a feel for the place and can make a better pitch to customers.

The houses were being built on the Clare side of town. Fifty houses, nicely spaced out and well designed – if they stuck with their plans. The site was empty that morning. A couple of diggers were sitting idly in a corner of roped-off site, and I could see where they'd just begun to dig the foundations. I parked my car on the road and walked onto the site. The day had changed. It was cold and grey and threatening rain, and a magpie chattered like a rattle at a football match. I walked slowly around the perimeter, avoiding the churned-up mud-tracks that had been made by the diggers.

As I pulled my coat close to my body, I wondered who the hell that had been on the phone earlier. And what exactly did they hope to achieve by threatening me? I shivered at the thought that somebody might want to hurt me. None of it made any sense, but thinking about it spooked me enough to send me running back to my car.

I had lunch at a pub on the outskirts of town, and then decided to visit my old pal, Davina Blake, to discuss the annual property fair that was due to be held in January. I didn't really feel all that comfortable dealing with Davina most of the time – she'd been Andrew's girlfriend while we were split up the first time, and that made things awkward between us. But there was so much tension at the office at that moment, that a couple of hours spent with Davina would be a relaxing break in comparison.

# 35

By the time I left Davina's office, I had a pain in my facial muscles from the effort of insincere smiling. Nevertheless, we'd managed to get through most of our work and – more importantly – it was 4.30 and I could head home, in all good conscience, without going back to the office. Things were bad when hanging out with my ex-boyfriend's ex-girlfriend was the best the day had to offer. I was driving across Sarsfield Bridge, cursing myself for taking such a congested route when my phone rang.

'Ellen?'

'Roxy – are you OK?'

'No, Ellen. The kids aren't back yet, and I don't know what to do.'

'What time is it?'

'Almost five. They were due back at four.'

'Look, Roxy – I'm sure it's fine but I'm finished work for the day – I'll swing by as I'm passing, OK?'

'That'd be great, Ellen.'

'See you in about ten minutes.'

'See you then.'

Half an hour later, I was still only twenty feet further on than when I'd spoken to Roxy on the phone, and I was on the verge of losing my mind. According to the car radio, a truck had jackknifed on the Dublin road, and that was having a knock-on effect throughout the rush-hour traffic. It was almost six by the time I arrived at Roxy's, and I expected that everything would be sorted out by then. Instead, I found a demented-looking Roxy pacing the front garden.

'Ellen!' she said, running to meet me as soon as I stepped out of my car. 'Oh, Ellen, what will I do?'

I took her by the arm and walked back into her front garden. 'It'll be fine, Roxy. Did you ring Fiona?'

Roxy nodded her head. As I looked into her eyes, I could hardly bear the look of fear. Her thin body trembled, and her shoulders were bowed with terror.

'Her phone is turned off. I tried about a hundred times.'

Miraculously, right at that moment, a cab pulled up in front of the house. Teddy Hannon, Shakira and Shania stepped out onto the pavement. Roxy vaulted over the garden gate and picked up her two girls in one armful. Teddy Hannon smiled at the scene, clearly happy to have caused her so much grief.

'Run in home, girls,' Roxy said, kissing both of them on the cheek. 'Pa has ice-cream.'

The girls whooped and ran past me into the house. Roxy stood up and looked at Teddy Hannon.

'Don't ever do that again,' she said.

He tilted his head to one side. 'Sorry?'

'You heard me, Teddy. In future, bring them home when you say you will or . . . or—'

'Or what?'

Roxy shook from head to toe, and she wrapped her arms around herself. Teddy Hannon leaned back on his heels and smiled a languorous smile. 'I got your little message by the way. You shouldn't have gone to all that trouble.'

'What are you talking about?' Roxy asked.

'The invitation from the court. I'm really looking forward to that – every man deserves his day in court.'

'And every woman,' Roxy said defiantly.

Teddy Hannon stared at her, a smile playing on his lips. 'Can't wait. Meanwhile – these are *my* children and I'll see them if and when I want. And neither you – nor anybody else – will stop me.' He paused and leaned close to her, grabbing her arm. 'Listen to what I'm saying.'

Roxy tugged at her arm. 'Get off. Let go.'

Teddy smiled and moved in close to her face as if he intended to kiss her. Roxy craned her neck away and tugged furiously, but he was obviously a lot stronger than he looked.

'Fiona will collect the children on Wednesday.'

Roxy pulled again at her arm but Teddy's fingers were locked tight. She looked at the pavement.

'Let go,' she said.

His face contorted momentarily and I was positive he was going to hit her. I strode as quickly as I could to where they were standing.

'Let her go,' I said as I approached.

Teddy Hannon looked at me. 'Excuse me?'

'Let her go,' I repeated, anger beginning to win

the battle with fear. 'Let go of her arm. And, by the way, there are ways to stop you seeing your children. I wouldn't be quite as cocky and self-assured, if I were you.'

Teddy Hannon dropped Roxy's arm and moved to stand in front of me. I could smell a faint minty smell from his breath.

'This is family business,' he said.

I pulled myself up to my full five foot ten and looked him in the eye. His eyes were the palest blue I'd ever seen, and his lashes long and luxuriant. I'd have loved to punch his soft-looking face.

'It's police business, actually, and Roxy could have you arrested right this minute. You're in breach of the protection order. If you don't get the fuck out of here right now, I'm calling the police,' I said, pulling my phone out of my handbag. Teddy Hannon smiled broadly, glanced at my phone and then straight into my eyes.

'Wednesday, Roxy,' he said, never taking his eyes from my face. 'Have the girls ready. Looking forward to our next meeting, Miss Grace.'

Then he turned and got back into the cab, and Roxy and I watched as they drove away.

Roxy was shivering from head to toe. So was I. I knew a threat when I heard one. A cold drizzle had begun to fall, and there was a smell of winter in the evening air.

'You really should consider not letting him have the girls any more,' I said as we walked together back into the house.

'Teddy isn't like other people. You try to keep him happy because otherwise . . . well, otherwise—' Her voice trailed off and I didn't need to ask her to elaborate. I could imagine what she was suggesting.

Shakira and Shania were propped at the kitchen table, and Pa was squirting chocolate sauce into two big bowls of ice-cream. Maurice was holding Enrique.

'Can't you give the child a small taste of ice-cream?' Maurice said.

Pa shook his head and handed the bowls to the girls. 'Jesus, Maurice! He's only a few weeks old – d'you want to give him the colic?'

'In my day,' Maurice said, jiggling the baby who was draped across his forearm. 'We gave babies everything that was going and it never did them one bit of harm.'

'How's it going, Ellen? Would you eat some ice-cream?' Pa said.

'Don't mind if I do,' I said, pulling out a chair and sitting down at the table beside Shania.

Pa scooped ice-cream into a bowl. 'Do you want some, Rox?'

Roxy shook her head and took Enrique from Maurice. She buried her face in the back of his downy baby head.

'You OK, love?' Pa asked her as he handed me the bowl of ice-cream.

Roxy smiled and nodded, though it was clearly not the case that she was OK.

'Daddy gived us chewing-gum,' Shakira said, smiling at her mother.

'Shakira!' Shania said, poking her in the side, 'Don't say that. Mammy doesn't like chewing-gum.'

Roxy looked at me and then back at the girls. 'Did you have a nice time with Auntie Fiona?'

Shania wiped her chocolate-sauce mouth with the back of her hand, nodding her dark head all the time. 'She's cool. She's bringing us to a restaurant next day. Isn't she, Shakira?'

Shakira nodded, her spoon poised mid-air.

'Well,' Roxy began. 'I'm not sure you'll be able to go that day – it's a bit busy. I have to bring the baby for his injections, and you two are supposed to go to Nana's and—'

Shania sighed loudly. 'Please. Please, can we go? Daddy said we can, and Fiona.'

Shania's eyes filled with tears, and both girls looked at their mother.

'We'll see. Take your ice-cream into the sitting room and watch TV,' said Roxy.

The girls cheered and ran off, clutching their bowls. As soon as they had left the room, Pa turned to Roxy.

'What happened? Where was he?' he asked.

Roxy shook her head.

'Teddy Hannon is a bastard – playing power games,' I said.

'I know the power game I'd play with him, if I had my way,' Pa said. A hard, determined look I'd never seen before transformed his face. 'I told you, Rox – me and Rhino and Jimmy would sort him out once and for all.'

'More violence isn't the solution,' Roxy said, walking over to Maurice and taking Enrique from his arms.

'I don't know, dear,' Maurice said. 'Sometimes that's all people like him understand.'

'I just wish it would all go away,' Roxy said, on the verge of tears.

'Roxy's right – let the courts sort it out,' I said, putting my arm around her.

'Well,' Pa said. 'They'd better, because if they don't, I won't be waiting for permission.'

Roxy looked at the floor and kissed Enrique's head.

'Listen, I need to lie down,' she said. 'I've an awful headache. Do you mind, Ellen?'

'Not at all – don't let me keep you up. I'll just finish this ice-cream and head on home myself.'

Roxy smiled a thin smile as she walked from the kitchen with the baby in her arms. 'Thanks, Ellen. Talk to you soon.'

I finished my ice-cream, said goodnight to Pa and Maurice and the girls, and set off for home.

Joey was waiting inside the front door for me as soon as I went into the apartment. He mewed accusingly.

'I know,' I said, opening a tin of cat food. 'I realise it's half seven and you're starving, Joey, but there was an emergency.'

Joey looked at me as if he didn't believe me and rushed past me to get at the food as soon as I put it in his bowl. I knew that the ice-cream Pa had given me was probably not quite enough by itself for dinner, so I cooked myself a frozen pizza. I took it and a huge glass of cranberry juice with me to watch *EastEnders*. I couldn't get Roxy and Teddy Hannon out of my head, though. And now that I had the time, I found myself thinking about Spencer too.

After *EastEnders*, I flicked from channel to channel, trying to find something to watch. There was no way I was allowing myself too much time to think. I finally settled on *Sleepless in Seattle* – I reckoned that that should probably keep me from dwelling on the Spencer thing. I wondered how he was. How could it all have got so far out of hand? I didn't want to think about him and what everybody believed I had done to him. But I couldn't help it. Suddenly, there was a knock at the door.

I stepped over my dinner debris and padded in my bare feet to the door. As I put my hand on the handle, I remembered Teddy Hannon and paused – what if it was him? I peered through the spy hole and saw the top of Angela's mauve-grey head, and beside her the tanned brown pate of Ralph.

'Welcome,' I said, throwing open the door and hugging both of them. 'Come in and tell me all about Rome and how married life is treating you. And any other scandal that springs to mind.'

'You're very thin,' Angela said, squeezing my arm as they came into the apartment.

'A bottle of real Italian vino,' Ralph said, winking at me.

'Thanks a million,' I said, accepting the tissue-wrapped bottle from Ralph. 'Sit down and I'll get a couple of glasses and we'll open this lovely wine.'

'I'd prefer a cup of tea, if you don't mind, love,' Angela said, settling herself on the sofa.

'No problem.' I looked at Ralph. He sat into the corner of the sofa beside his wife, arranged his chest, and smiled at me.

'Tea would be great,' he said.

Angela nodded. 'I know that wine is lovely and everything, but it all starts to taste like vinegar after a while, and you can't get a decent cup of tea in the whole of Italy.'

I walked over to the galley kitchen and switched on the kettle.

'So?' I said, as I leaned against the worktop and waited for the kettle to boil. 'How have you been? What have you been up to? Tell me all about the wedding. I haven't had a chance to get the gory details from you yet.'

Angela and Ralph exchanged a smile.

'Well,' Angela said. 'The wedding was lovely. Quiet. We met a lovely boy – John – curate from Donegal somewhere. Lovely boy entirely – wasn't he, Ralph?'

Ralph nodded. 'Lovely. Great man for the Wolfe Tones songs.'

'And then we went to that Lake Garda place for the honeymoon. Very nice – not warm but then I suppose it is the winter. And it was very quiet – no bit of nightlife there this time of year.'

The kettle boiled, so I made tea and carried a

tray over to Angela and Ralph, and placed it on the coffee table.

'So that's it,' Angela said. 'We're settling into married life, and, well, I suppose the really big news is that we're having a baby.'

# 36

'What?' I said, spilling the tea all over the tray.

'Ha-ha,' Angela said. 'Knew that'd get you.'

'Angie,' Ralph chided gently.

'A baby?' I said, mopping up the mess with kitchen paper.

Angela and Ralph nodded.

'But . . . but . . . but—' I said.

Ralph laughed. 'You're an awful woman, Angela Maunsell. My daughter, Susan, is an Irish-dancing teacher, and some of her students have to go to Boston to a big championship. Susan has a baby – well, she's a year old now – and there's no way she can bring her to Boston, and that husband of hers—'

'Is a waster.' Angela finished his sentence for him.

'I wouldn't say that exactly, love, but they're separated and he can't mind the baby, so we offered.'

I filled cups with tea and handed them to Angela and Ralph.

'Jesus! Sure, you're great,' I said.

'It's only for five days,' Angela said.

'Still,' I said.

'We'll love it. I always wanted children and it never happened for me. Hubert – God rest his soul – used to say there were enough babies in the world and it was as well not to be adding to the overpopulation problems. But I didn't feel that.'

'And how many children do you have, Ralph?' I asked.

'Six. Susan is the youngest and the only girl, and also the only one who lives in Limerick.'

'The baby is a dote,' Angela said. 'Emma is her name. Wait till you see her, Ellen. I can't wait.'

'When is she coming?'

'Wednesday,' Ralph said, winking at Angela. 'Give us a chance to recover from the honeymoon.'

Angela poked him in the side with her elbow but grinned broadly. I smiled at their antics. How lucky they were to have found each other, I thought, as we drank our tea and Angela told me all about the Vatican and the Coliseum. A lot luckier than me, anyway – that much was for sure.

I went to bed almost as soon as Angela and Ralph had left, and cuddled up with Joey, struggling not to think about how lonely I actually felt. I didn't care about any of it. I was happy to be on my own. Really I was.

Next morning, I had a meeting at 9.30 with a client in a new apartment building in town. I needed to collect some documents in the office, and really, really couldn't face Molly and the Spencer-support club, so I went into the office at 8.15. Gladstone and Richards auctioneers don't normally open for business until nine, so I was fairly confident that the place would be empty. I let myself in the back door. The building had that silent but alive hum that all empty buildings seem to have.

'Morning,' a man's voice said as I walked into the foyer.

My rape and murder flashed before my eyes, followed by the eulogy at my funeral.

'How are you?' the voice asked.

'Andrew?' I said. 'What the fuck are you doing here?'

Andrew smiled and placed the briefcase in his hand at his feet. 'Oh, that's a lovely reception.'

'Sorry, I'm sorry. It's just that you put the heart crossways in me.'

Andrew smiled again, and the sight of his smile had a domino effect inside me, waking up all the emotions I'd buried.

'I know. Sorry to startle you – I didn't expect anybody to be in at this hour.'

'Well,' I said. 'There is always a possibility that Molly will be in – I told you before that I suspect she sleeps in the office.'

'But not you, Ellen.'

'No,' I said, and the air between us was heavy with things that couldn't be said. 'No, Andrew – not me.'

'I had to come,' Andrew said then, switching into professional mode. 'With Spencer's accident and everything – head office needed someone to come over and sort out his stuff for him.'

'He's going back to America?'

Andrew nodded. 'He's out of hospital – did you know that?'

I shook my head.

'Well, he is. He was discharged yesterday, and he seems to be fine. There's some Reval work here that needs tying up, and neither Tim nor you could do it. And under the circumstances, Spencer wasn't up to it himself – so, they sent me. How's the new job, by the way?'

'Grand. When is Spencer going home?'

'To the US? Friday.'

'Friday?'

Andrew nodded. 'With me.'

'Is he fit enough to fly?'

'His doctor says he's fit to travel though the airline aren't as sure – they made him sign a disclaimer. He's just determined to get home.'

'Oh.' I walked to Ryan's desk and pulled out his chair and sat down. His precious portfolio was open in front of me. 'How's Katie?'

'She's fine – good. Settled in really well.'

'And you?'

'I'm not too bad. A lot better than I thought I'd be. I love my new job and I even quite like Austin.'

'That's good.'

'And how about you, Ellen? How are you?'

"I'm OK. Great. Fantastic.'

'Good, good, and everything is going all right for you?'

'Never better,' I said, with oodles of bravado.

'There's something I want to—' Andrew began just as the back door opened.

'Andrew? Andrew! Andrew! Oh, my goodness!

What a lovely, lovely surprise,' Molly sang at the top of her voice.

She rushed towards Andrew and hugged him as if he was her long-lost son.

'Molly! How are you?'

Molly patted her head. Even though the wintry gale whipping up outside had not dislodged a hair, she still did her mandatory check. Then she slipped off her white woollen coat and draped it over her forearm. 'Look at you, Andrew. You look terrific. Life in the States really suits you, I can tell.'

She was right. Andrew did look terrific. His skin was honey-coloured and he was wearing an open-collared white shirt under his pale-green linen suit. His hair was shorter than usual, but he still had the same beautiful mouth.

'I'm good, Molly, thanks. Settled in well. You're looking pretty good yourself.'

Molly smiled and touched her fire-engine red nails to her matching lipsticked mouth. 'Andrew!'

'No, no. I mean it, Molly – it's younger-looking you're getting.'

I stood and picked up the file in front of me and went into my office as the flirting continued apace. Molly's high-pitched voice rattling on and on. Andrew's soft voice, teasing and laughing and flirting. My heart beat in my chest as I closed the door and sat down at my desk. Jesus! Andrew! I couldn't believe it.

I took deep breaths to calm down and then opened the folder I was holding. This wasn't mine. What the

hell? I flicked through the documents. Oh my God!
This was Ryan's portfolio and I'd accidentally taken
it off his desk in my confusion. I knew it was wrong
but I couldn't resist having a closer look. Which was
how I discovered that Ryan was a partner in Sarsfield
Properties.

'Holy shit!' I said out loud, as I read a letter to
him that listed the partners. It was from a solicitor, and it was some legalese or other about incor-
poration. None of it made much sense to me, except
for the fact that Ryan was the silent partner in
Sarsfield Properties. I wondered if Ryan was
involved in all the harassment of Maurice? He probably was – he was certainly a big enough shit to
do something as horrible as that. I decided that *he*
was probably the one who had made that threatening phone call to me. It was all beginning to
make sense.

I looked at my watch and saw that it was after
nine. I'd better get going. I opened the filing cabinet
and fished out the documents I needed for the
meeting.

What a morning! It was only nine o'clock and
already I'd discovered that Ryan was involved in
shady dealings. But that wasn't a patch on the shock
of seeing Andrew standing in the front office.

I collected my bag and folders and made my way
back through the reception area, dropping Ryan's
portfolio on his desk as I passed. Tim had arrived
by that time, and there was a small crowd gathered
around Andrew. He raised a hand and waved at me

as I passed. I returned the wave, and almost broke into a run in my anxiety to escape.

I drove to my meeting, struggling all the time to keep Andrew out of my head. I had sworn that I was finished with men, and I had every intention of keeping that promise to myself, especially after the fiasco of last weekend. They were just way too much trouble and, sure – yeah, the sex was good, but the price was too high for my liking.

There was Spencer – who I'd never intended would fall in love with me – almost killing himself when he discovered . . . well, that I didn't love him in return. Then there was Tony Jordan – always bloody Tony Jordan – popping up all over my life like a plague of mushrooms, and now – as if things weren't messy enough in my love life – Andrew was back.

I stopped my car right outside the new apartment building. I had no time to dwell further on the state of my emotional life because I saw Henry Tuohy – the owner of the building – waving at me. Henry was a nice man and not too bad-looking if you like short, balding, chubby men in their mid-thirties, with clear blue eyes and infectious laughs.

'Great to see you, Ellen. I see they came to their senses in that place at last and made you the boss,' Henry said as soon as I came within shouting distance.

'Not quite the boss yet,' I said, smiling. 'So, how are you, Henry?'

'Not too bad, not too bad. The twins haven't slept in a week. Rita is trying to get her stained-glass studio up and running. I'm lying awake at night, worrying that I'll never shift the apartments in this place and I'll lose all my money. But other than that, I'm fine – thanks for asking.'

'You're a big whinger, Henry Tuohy,' I said, punching him in the arm. 'Show me the apartments and we'll make a plan. Otherwise, we won't ever sell them.'

Henry and I proceeded into his empty building that was so new it still smelt of plaster dust and builders' sandwiches. I followed him around, writing down details and impressions, and reassuring him that they'd be queuing up to buy apartments in this river-view, central-location 'des res'. When we finished, I declined Henry's offer of coffee and, after we had shaken hands, walked back down the short stretch of street towards my car.

The weak, wintry sun was glinting off the bonnet of the beemer, and, while I like to think of myself as fairly detached from material things, I couldn't help a small pang of pride that that car was actually mine. I pointed my electronic key ring towards the car, and it gave a satisfying clunk as it unlocked. I dreaded the thought of going back to the office. What the hell was I going to find? Maybe Spencer would be there as well, and they could all line up and point out my faults and failings. Just as I reached out to open the car door, I heard my name.

'Yes?' I responded turning towards the voice. Henry Tuohy was trotting down the pavement towards me. I took a few steps in his direction, and, as I did, a sudden loud noise erupted behind me, and a wind like the hurricanes you see on TV whooshed past my ears and made me fall forwards. I think I might have blacked out then because it all became a bit confused, with noises and feet and Henry Tuohy's voice calling my name. I struggled out of the darkness I was in and forced myself to focus on Henry's moon face.

'Ellen! Ellen! Are you all right?'

I nodded my head and closed my eyes for a second. Next thing I knew, there was a woman pulling at my eyelids and asking me my name and age and address and stupid questions like that. Gradually I felt myself float back into my usual state of consciousness, such as it is.

'What happened?' I managed to ask Henry who was still crouched beside me, holding my hand.

'Your car blew up,' he said, simply.

I turned my head to look in the direction Henry was looking, and saw that there was a fire engine on the street, and that a tall fireman was pumping some sort of foamy stuff all over my poor, poor BMW. I couldn't see the car clearly, but I could see enough of the smoke that was still seeping from under the bonnet to know that Henry was telling the truth.

'Why?' I asked, turning back to Henry and struggling to my feet.

Henry shrugged and shook his head while he helped me up. My legs felt like cooked spaghetti under me, but at least I was standing. Then, out of the smoke – literally, like in a scene from *Terminator*

*II* – appeared the matronly police detective who I'd come to associate with times of great disaster. Hilary Thornton.

'Ellen,' she said, smiling as soon as she saw me.

'Detective.'

'Are you OK?'

I nodded.

'Sure?'

I nodded again.

'In all my years in the force, I've never known anyone to be involved in more unfortunate incidents than you. I mean, kidnapping, letter bomb and now this.'

She fixed me with her matronly smile and I burst into tears. Hilary Thornton put her arms around me as I cried. When I finished, she gave me a large, cotton handkerchief to blow my nose.

'You see,' I said, as the full realisation hit me. 'You see, I had my hand on the door, and then Henry called me and I stepped back. And if I hadn't . . . if I hadn't—' I began to cry all over again. Hilary Thornton muttered something suitably reassuring and waved away anyone who approached. When I stopped crying, I saw that Henry was gone. I didn't blame him. I was a bit dangerous to be around.

'Will you come down to the station with me and make a statement?' Hilary Thornton asked.

I nodded and blew my nose again. She helped me into the back of a garda car which started moving as soon as the doors were shut. It was driven by a young man with bristly black hair climbing up over the back of the collar of his blue shirt. On the short drive to the garda station, my head was spinning with what might have happened.

It had to be Sarsfield Properties, but why the hell were they always trying to blow me up? It must be the statement I'd made to the guards about Hoodie threatening Maurice. Robert White probably blamed me for CAB getting involved. Still, blowing up my lovely car was below the belt.

Hilary Thornton took me to a small room with a big desk, two chairs and a photocopier.

'My office,' she said in an apologetic voice. 'Well, it's not really my office, but my real office is being painted, and this is all that's available at the moment.'

'It's fine.'

'Tea? Coffee?'

I shook my head.

'OK. So – tell me again what happened, and, this time, I'll ask you questions and take notes, OK?'

'OK.'

So I told Hilary Thornton the same story that I had told her twenty minutes earlier, except this time I managed not to cry. She jotted down notes as I spoke, and asked only a few questions. We were finished in ten minutes.

'I know who it was,' I said as soon as she stopped writing. She looked at me and pushed her reading glasses low on the bridge of her nose. 'Sarsfield Properties. It has to be them.'

Hilary made a face.

'You don't believe me?'

'No, Ellen, I do. I mean, I see how you think that, but I just don't see it. Foncie and Majella Ryan are Sarsfield Properties – along with that Ferry guy that works for ye.'

'Ryan Ferry – I just found out.'

'That young fella is engaged to Vanessa Ryan.'

'Go away. Imagine marrying Ryan – yeuch!'

Hilary smiled. 'I know that that lot might be criminally annoying, but I just don't see them doing something like this.'

'But what about the henchmen,' I said, standing up and pacing the small office. 'And all the things that have happened to Maurice – you know, his house was set on fire on Sunday night?'

Hilary Thornton sat back in her chair and nodded.

'So, go pay them a visit,' I said. 'A small bit of police harassment goes a long way. It might rattle them at least.'

'There is just no evidence to link them to any of it. Get me evidence and I'll gladly visit them.'

My eyes filled with tears. 'I could have been killed back there – or at the very least, maimed – and you just sit there and say there's no evidence?'

'Unless the forensic lads turn up something.'

I sniffed back the tears. I was damned if I was starting that blubbing all over again.

'Are you finished with me?' I asked.

Hilary Thornton nodded. 'I'll get someone to drive you home.'

'No need. I want to walk. Thanks.'

I was so furious at the impotence of the police

that I wanted to break something. But it was a garda station and I knew that even though they couldn't get the guys who'd tried to kill me, they'd be well able to arrest me for damaging government property. I waved Hilary Thornton goodbye and stormed along the carpeted corridors, past men and women in navy uniforms, and out into the drizzling day.

The street outside the garda station was full of cars and people going about their business and, as I made my way between them, I could hardly believe that I'd almost been killed. But it was true. If Henry hadn't called me, and if I hadn't stepped away when I had. . . .

I marched along the busy street as if I knew where I was going, but it was entirely aimless. As I walked, a volcano of anger was beginning to erupt inside me. I was sick and tired of being helpless in this whole situation. I pulled my mobile out of my bag and dialled India's number. The phone rang and rang. I was just about to hang up when I heard her voice. Alyssa was screaming in the background.

'India?'

'Ellen? Hello, how are you?'

India's voice was stilted and formal, and I knew she was still angry with me about Spencer. But, right then, I didn't care.

'Is Alyssa all right?'

'She's fine.'

'India, I'm sorry to disturb you, but I've a favour to ask.'

'Go ahead.'

'Do you remember the research you did when Roxy bought the house?'

'Sure.'

'And you found out that Sarsfield Properties own the land behind her house.'

'I remember.'

'Where would I find them?'

'Who?'

'Sarsfield Properties. Do they have offices? Is there some place I could go to talk to them?'

'Why?'

'Oh, just stuff. Is there?'

'Hold on a minute – I wrote all that information in a notebook, and I think I put it in the desk in the study – hold on.'

I leaned against a shop window and watched the passers-by as I waited for India. In the distance, I could hear her talking to her baby, and doors opening and closing.

'Hi, Ellen?'

'Yes, I'm here.'

'Sarsfield Properties don't really have an office as such – the address is Onedin, The Sanctuary. That's one of those very exclusive residential developments off the Westlink road. It must be their home.'

'Thanks a million, India. Talk to you later.'

I hung up then, before India could ask me more questions about why I wanted the information and what I was going to do. I didn't know the answers to those questions and I didn't want to start thinking about them. Without planning to, I found myself walking over Sarsfield Bridge, along the Ennis road, and turning onto the Westlink road. I was just going to look. That was all. Just walking and thinking. Merely satisfying my curiosity.

I knew where the Ryans' house was – I wasn't an estate agent for nothing. I'd never sold one of those houses, but I'd wanted to, because the commission would be good and fat. The drizzle turned into rain as I walked, and I pulled my jacket close around me. Inexplicably, I began to think of Spencer. Why had I ignored all the signs? Everybody was right – I had strung him along – not consciously, but still I'd done it. Guilty as charged.

I hadn't meant for him to get hurt, though. That had never been part of the plan. I remembered the stories about Spencer as serial fiancé, and knew that somewhere I'd banked on that. Spencer wanted the same things as me. Distraction. Fun. Sex. Whatever. He was a goodtime boy, and I'd been hoping that if I'd been using him – and I had – that he had just been using me right back. But somewhere, deep inside me, I'd seen what Ruth and even Roxy had recognised.

For some reason, Spencer had fallen in love with me, and I'd told myself he hadn't, because . . . well, because if I'd admitted it to myself, I'd have had to stop using him, and I hadn't wanted to do that. My heart was heavy as I faced up to the Spencer thing, so I was quite cheered to see the big, decorative sign announcing 'The Sanctuary'.

I turned into the cul-de-sac of individually built

detached houses. Or perhaps a better word might be mansions. Each house stood on a quarter of an acre of landscaped gardens, and each was designed and finished to within an inch of its life.

Onedin was impossible to miss. It was a huge, mock-Georgian house, double-fronted, and painted white with grey quoin stones. Four large wrought-iron lampposts flanked the driveway. As I stood in the rain, staring at the house, I wondered what I was going to do now.

These people had burned down Acorn House, harassed Maurice, defaced Roxy's house, and now they'd blown up my lovely BMW and tried to kill me. How was I supposed to deal with them when the guards said that *they* couldn't? This was a total waste of time and energy, walking the whole way out here in the rain. Who the hell did I think I was?

I suddenly felt exhausted as I reviewed all the things that had happened. Exhausted and a bit afraid. I'd go home. Actually, I'd go home to my mother and tell her what had happened, and she'd make me something inedible to eat, and tuck me into bed, and I'd sleep for a couple of hours, and, when I woke up, everything would look a lot better.

I readjusted the collar of my jacket to stop the rain from dripping down my neck. As I turned to leave the cul-de-sac, a large hand grabbed my shoulder.

'What the fuck are you doing here?' a deep man's voice grumbled into my ear as I swung around.

## 37

Robert White's ugly face and garlic breath pressed in on top of me. I hadn't seen that hideous mug since he'd followed Tony into my parents'garden during the trouble a couple of years before. He'd threatened me, and Andrew had hit him across the back of the head with a shovel. I'd forgotten that, and the memory of him crumpling onto the ground made me smile.

'What are you smiling at, you slapper?' he said, squeezing my arm tightly.

'Let go!' I screamed.

'Oh, shut the fuck up, will you? Oy! Take her there and bring her inside.'

Robert White let me go, and both of my arms were grabbed and pinioned behind my back. I craned my head around to have a look. Oh shit! Hoodie. He grinned at me.

'I had a visit from the guards,' he said, as we made our ungainly way up the driveway of Onedin. 'Told me they heard I was harassing old men. I wonder who could have told them that—'

'How would I know?' I said.

'You're too much fucking trouble,' he said, his eyes darkening with anger. 'From the very beginning, you were too much trouble, and you're still too much trouble.'

My heart thumped against my ribs as the large, red front door was opened by a small, grey-haired woman.

'Are Foncie and Majella in?' Robert White asked in a high-pitched, polite voice.

'Sitting room,' the woman said, pointing to a door on the left, before disappearing through a door on the right. I couldn't believe she was gone. My one chance and she'd dematerialised. What the hell was I going to do now? The three of us crossed the big, square hall, and Robert White knocked on the door, then opened it without waiting for a reply. Hoodie dragged me with them into a huge sitting room. It was as big as the average parish hall – high ceilings, banks of windows along one wall, flanked by heavy, red velvet drapes, a fireplace big enough to fit Hoodie up the chimney, and three islands of red brocade-upholstered sofas and dark-wood coffee tables.

A tall, middle-aged man, with a stomach as flat as an ironing board and hair the colour of cotton wool, was standing staring out the windows. A plumpish woman – who looked to be the same age – lay on a sofa. She had a pretty, girlish face, elaborately streaked blonde hair, a pink Juicy tracksuit, bare feet and cerise-painted toenails. They both turned their heads to look at us as we came into the room.

'What the fuck's going on?' Robert White asked in place of a greeting.

The man at the window turned and regarded him before answering. He took a long draught from the glass in his hand and then smiled. 'You heard?'

'Damn fucking right, I heard, Foncie. What do you think you're playing at?'

Foncie shook his head. 'Nothing. We have no control over it.'

'But what about my money?' Robert White asked.

'I told you at the start. I never tried to fool you.'

'Yeah, but it was supposed to be all right – I was supposed to get an eighth of the hotel.'

'But no money,' Foncie said. 'I've no money, Robert – I suggest you get in the queue with the rest of the people who are looking for a piece of me.'

Robert White's face was red, and he looked as if he might actually physically explode. Everybody was looking at him, and I thought that maybe it might be a good time to make a break. Hoodie had let go of my arm but he was also blocking the door. I wondered if they'd be able to catch me if I sprinted across the room and out the window beside Foncie Ryan.

'Those fuckers in CAB,' Robert White said, pulling a packet of cigarettes from his pocket and lighting one. 'There should be a law against them.'

Majella tutted and waved her hand in front of her face, looking at her husband, but he was still busily staring at something outside the window.

'Great idea,' she said.

Robert White looked at her.

'CAB can do what they like,' she said, swinging

her bare feet onto the floor. 'And do you know something? I think this is a punishment.'

Her husband looked at her. 'A punishment?'

Majella walked over to stand in front of Robert White.

'Give me one of those,' she said, pointing at his cigarette.

Robert White fished in his pocket and held the cigarette packet towards Majella. She took one, lit it with his lighter and walked back over to her sofa.

'Majella!' Foncie said. 'I can't believe you're smoking. What will your trainer say?'

Majella laughed. 'I don't think he'll give much of a shit when he finds out I can't pay him the money I owe him for the last six months.'

Foncie sighed and shook his head.

'You've other money,' Robert White said, walking up to stand by Foncie. 'Everybody knows you're loaded – I think you're just trying to pull a fast one.'

Foncie looked at his wife, and they both laughed. A cloud of cigarette smoke swirled around the three of them.

'It's all gone, Robert,' Foncie said. 'We mortgaged everything to get the money to buy that land in Hollyfields.'

Majella laughed and flicked cigarette ash. 'The whole kit and caboodle. And we deserve it.'

Foncie looked at her.

'I mean it,' she said. 'We never carried on the way we've been carrying on for the past two years. We never mixed with—' Majella pointed at Robert and

Hoodie. 'We worked for our money and then when we were offered the land. *You'll be rich in no time,* they all said. Gerry Hayes told us there might be a problem with the access but no, we wouldn't listen. Greed, Fonce, pure and simple.'

Foncie gave another loud sigh. His wife threw her cigarette butt into the gigantic fireplace, then walked over to him and wound her arms around his waist.

'We'll be fine, love,' she said, looking up into his face as if they were alone in the room. 'We have our health and we have each other, and the kids are all done for. We'll survive this – we've survived worse.'

Foncie put his arms around his wife and they held onto each other looking a little like passengers on the *Titantic* and, for all that they'd done to me, I couldn't help feeling sorry for them. Robert White tutted angrily to himself and lit another cigarette.

'Well, you can be as lovey-dovey as you like, but you still owe me money. When I took on this job last year, Gerry Hayes told me I'd get an eighth of the hotel.'

'But there won't be a hotel,' Foncie said, leaning his chin on top of his wife's head. 'I'm not lying to you, Robert.'

'Well then, Foncie, you'll just have to find another way to pay me for my work.'

Foncie shrugged. 'Don't know what that'll be.'

Majella pulled away from him and turned towards Robert White. 'I'm glad we can't pay you. I'm ashamed we were ever mixed up with you in the first place. I think it's right that you not be paid for whatever it is you did.'

'Very fucking easy for you to say,' Robert White said, stepping closer to Majella. 'Sitting here in your big house, trying to pretend you don't know what's being done in your name.'

'Exactly,' Majella said, smiling at him. 'I'm ashamed to say that that's true. You know what they say? If you lie down with dogs, you get fleas.'

'The fucking most annoying thing of all is that if you hadn't been so fucking squeamish, I'd have solved this problem weeks ago, and then everything'd be fine.' Robert White's temper was rising again.

'Maurice would never have sold his house to you,' I blurted out before I could stop myself.

'Who said anything about selling?' Robert White asked, laughing loudly. 'Hah? Who said anything about selling?'

Hoodie joined in the raucous laughter and my skin crawled at the sound.

'Fucking psychopath,' I said.

Everybody in the room was looking at me. I pulled at my wet hair and shrugged. Maybe if I made a dash for the door now? But Hoodie was still bang in the middle of my path to freedom, and probably not amused enough to be off his guard.

'Who are you?' Majella asked.

'Ellen Grace,' I said, stepping forward. 'Area Manager with Gladstone and Richards.'

'Have the courts sent you already?' Foncie asked.

'No,' I said. 'My car blew up and the guards said

they couldn't do anything and I knew it was Sarsfield Properties and I was upset so I came here but I'd have gone away – I swear – but then these two dragged me in.'

'God Almighty!' Foncie said, looking at his wife, who shook her head and walked over to the sofa where she shoved her feet into high-heeled sandals.

'Your car blew up?' she said, walking towards me. I nodded. 'And you think we had something to do with that?' I nodded again. She looked at Hoodie and Robert White.

'I don't know nothin' about that,' Hoodie said.

'Like you'd admit it,' I said.

'So you want to leave?' Majella Ryan said to me.

'Yes, of course I do.'

'Off you go, so, love.'

I looked at Foncie and then back at her and they both smiled politely and I moved towards the door. Robert White and Hoodie looked at each other. Hoodie shook his head at me. 'You're not goin' nowhere, love.'

'I beg your pardon,' Majella said, walking towards me. She stopped at my side. My God! The woman was tiny – just about up to my shoulder even with her high heels on. 'I just told this young lady—'

'Ellen,' I supplied.

'That's right, Ellen. I just told Ellen she could leave, so step out of her way and let her leave the room right now.'

Hoodie folded his arms and shook his head. 'No can do.'

'Oh fucking yes can do,' Majella said, standing in front of him. 'This is still my house. Foncie? Foncie?'

'Move out of the girl's way,' Foncie said.

Hoodie produced a small, silver gun that looked like a cigarette lighter, but I was pretty sure he wasn't about to light a fag. He smiled at us.

'You don't give us orders no more,' Robert White said, moving towards us. 'I have a bit of bad news for you, Foncie. I've a reputation to look after, and nobody – and are you listening to this? Because I mean absolutely no-fucking-body – messes with Robert White.'

'I know, but I told you, I've no money,' Foncie said.

'So, I suppose I'll just have to get the payment some other way, won't I, Alphonsus?'

'What do you mean?'

'Well, I haven't decided yet, but I can promise you this – I will get payment of some kind.' He looked at Majella and she pursed her lips defiantly. Then he pointed at me. 'As for that bitch? We'll see about her as well – she's a pain in the arse.'

Robert White pulled a gun from his pocket. Suddenly, the door flew open and Hoodie spun across the room and sprawled onto a brocade sofa. A tall, red-haired policeman strode into the room.

'What's this?' he said in a Kerry accent. 'Put away that gun, Robert, before you hurt yourself.'

Two more police officers followed him into the room and disarmed and handcuffed Robert and Hoodie.

The Kerry guard looked around him as if he was at a dinner party. 'Grand house you have here,' he said. 'Lovely quiet area.'

'At least the cavalry got the timing right,' Foncie said to the policeman, who laughed and pushed his hands into his trousers pockets.

'But how?' Majella asked her husband. 'Who called them?'

Foncie smiled and squeezed her shoulders. 'I didn't want to say anything to you, love – worry you more.'

'What do you mean?'

'Well, I had a feeling that these fellas would turn up sooner or later and that they wouldn't be too happy with applying to the courts for payment. So, I told Winnie to call the police if two thugs turned up – and she did.'

Majella hugged her husband, and frankly I felt like hugging him myself.

The two uniformed giants escorted Robert White and Hoodie out of the room.

The red-haired Kerryman looked at Majella and Foncie. 'Oh, yeah – listen, lads, those CAB fellas are looking to have a word with ye.'

'I knew that would be the case,' Foncie said. 'Don't worry. We won't make a run for it or anything.'

'And are you going to arrest Ryan Ferry?' I asked.

The policeman looked at me. 'The CAB boys might want a chat with him, right enough.'

'Ryan doesn't know anything,' Foncie said.

'But he's a partner in Sarsfield Properties, isn't he?' I said.

Foncie laughed. 'Ryan's grandmother left him a lot of money, and he was looking for an investment, and it seemed like a good idea at the start.'

'There goes his portfolio,' I said.

Foncie Ryan shrugged.

'I'll be off so,' the policeman said. 'We never took a statement from you, young lady. Would you mind telling me your name?'

'Ellen Grace.'

'And what are doing here, Ellen?'

'It's a long story, Guard, but Hilary Thornton knows all about it.'

'Does she now?'

'She does. Can I go home? I'm wrecked – I've had a very hard day.'

The guard looked at me and finally nodded. 'You're a bit exhausted-looking, all right. Go home and get some sleep and you can come down to the station tomorrow to give a statement. How's that?'

'You'll have to get me a room of my own in that place,' I said.

I left immediately. The rain had stopped and, declining offers of lifts, I set off walking towards home. And my mammy.

# 38

My mother was sitting at the kitchen table, looking at photographs of Angela's wedding, when I let myself in the back door.

'Ellen! How are you, love? Look, here's a photograph of your father and me at the Trevi Fountain. I didn't realise he'd lost so much weight. I'll have to feed that man up. So? How are you?'

I sat down heavily on a kitchen chair and leaned my elbows on the table as I tried to look at the photographs.

'Not great,' I said.

'Are you sick?'

'No.' My attention was momentarily taken by a photograph of Angela and Ralph on horseback.

'Ellen?'

'Sorry, Ma. No, I'm not sick. I'm fine. And don't be upset now because I'm fine and there's no reason to be upset but . . . look, there's been a bit of trouble. There was this crowd and they wanted to buy Maurice McMahon's house so they could make a road into their hotel – well, the hotel isn't built yet but they were afraid to start until they had it—'

I paused and looked at my mother. She was

thumbing the corner of the photograph envelope and looking at me with big, confused eyes.

'Do you follow what I'm saying?' I asked.

She shook her head.

'OK,' I said. 'OK – it's very simple. Acorn House was supposed to be demolished to make room for a road into this new hotel and leisure centre in Hollyfields. But then An Taisce came along and put a preservation order on it and it couldn't be knocked down.'

'OK, love.'

'Anyway, everybody thought that Acorn House would be demolished then but it went to court and the owners – a crowd called Sarsfield Properties – were told to rebuild it because of its historic importance.'

'Have you eaten?'

I shook my head and immediately regretted it as my mother jumped up and opened the fridge.

'Ah no, Ma. I'm grand, really.'

'It won't take me a minute to fry up a few sausages for you. Go on with your story.'

I sighed and watched my mother pulling pans and oil and fish slices out of cupboards, and I wasn't sure I was going to have the energy to eat, but I'd have to try.

'OK,' I said, leaning my tired head into my hands. 'OK. Where was I?'

'They had to rebuild the house.'

'That's it. Anyway, if they couldn't knock Acorn House, they couldn't get proper access to the hotel unless they were able to buy and knock this one other house.'

'Could they not go in a different way?'

'No. The river is at the other side of the site. Anyway, the other house had to be purchased or they couldn't build because they wouldn't be keeping the terms of their planning permission.'

'And who owns that house?'

'A man called Maurice McMahon. You don't know him, do you?'

'No.'

'Well, Maurice is a cranky old bat and he had no intentions of selling his house to anybody. Plus he was leading the residents in a protest against the new hotel and leisure centre.'

'So, that was that, was it?' my mother asked, plonking in front of me a plate of sausages and rashers that were floating in a bed of grease.

I picked up a knife and fork and began trying to cut one of the rubbery rashers. They were cooked with love, after all – that should do me.

'Thanks, Mam,' I said, trying a smile.

'Enjoy,' my mother said, and sat back down beside me.

I chewed and managed to swallow the piece of rasher. 'All sorts of odd things started to happen to Maurice. His windows were broken; his house was set on fire; one of the biggest crooks in town turned up at the door in a suit and offered him money – that kind of thing.'

'And where do you come into this?'

'How do you know I come into it at all?'

My mother raised an eyebrow. 'I know you, Ellen

Grace, and, as sure as God made little green apples, you're involved in this somehow.'

'Well, not really,' I said. 'I mean, I did tell the police about Hoodie.'

'Hoodie?'

'The thug I told you about.'

'Love and honour of God!' My mother clutched the front of her chest as if she was going to keel over from the weight of what she was hearing.

'I knew you'd be upset and there's no need – nothing happened to me . . . well, until today—'

'Jesus—'

'Calm down, Mam.'

'Just tell me, Ellen.'

'OK. Today – this morning – my car was blown up. I wasn't even scratched though. Look at me – I'm fine.'

'Jesus, Mary and holy Saint Joseph! What will become of you? After all the other carry-on and now this.'

'It's a different thing – well, not entirely different, but not the same either. The guys who blew up the car were arrested today, and they were the same gangsters who did all that stuff, last year. But now the guards have them. And this time, they have people to testify against them, and it'll all be fine. Just fine . . . really, really fine—'

Big tears slid down my face onto my plate as the day's events washed over me. I could have been killed. I had no intention of saying that out loud to my mother but it was true. If Henry Tuohy hadn't called me . . . I laid my head on the table and sobbed. My mother came over and wrapped her arms around me.

'Shh, love. Shh. You're fine now. Come on, up to bed with you and you can have a rest, and then I'll cook you a lovely dinner and everything will be just fine, OK?'

I let my mother lead me up the stairs to my old bedroom and put me to bed. I knew she was no match for underworld thugs, but somehow it didn't matter. I still felt safer in my old bed than I'd felt in a while. As I drifted off to sleep, the scene of the explosion replayed in my head, along with a mish-mash of faces. Majella and Foncie, Robert White, Ryan, Tony, Spencer, Andrew. And then – out of the blue – Teddy Hannon. But that was a whole other set of problems, wasn't it? Today I had to recover from exploding cars and thugs threatening my life.

In my parents' house, I slept like the proverbial baby, until ten o'clock next morning, when I awoke to see Andrew Kenny standing at the foot of my bed. I was sure I was dreaming, so I turned over and snuggled down for another forty winks.

'Ellen?' he said. Unusual – dreams didn't ordinarily sound quite as real.

'Ellen?' he said again. 'Are you awake?'

I rolled over onto my back and opened my eyes fully.

'Andrew?'

He smiled at me and sat at the end of the bed. 'I heard you were blown up?'

I nodded.

'Are you OK?'

I nodded again.

'What happened?'

'Oh, it was a big rigmarole, but at least this time it was about work and not my stupid personal life.'

'So I believe. Sarsfield Properties?'

'Yeah.'

I stretched. 'How are you, Andrew?'

'Fine,' he replied, standing up and leaning over me in the bed, causing a virtual avalanche of memories for me. He bent down and kissed my cheek gently.

'I . . . I—' I began but I couldn't find any words that would explain or make anything better. 'When are you going back to Austin?'

'Friday.'

'Oh, right. You told me that.' I sat up in the bed and pulled the covers up to my chin. Oh my God! I was sure my breath was stinky and my hair was sticking out at right angles around my head. 'Well, thanks for coming to see me.'

'You're welcome, Ellen. I'm glad you're not injured.'

'Thanks.'

'Goodbye.'

'Goodbye.'

Andrew stood in the doorway of my bedroom, and we stared at each other as if neither of us could bear to break the contact. After what felt like a very long time, he raised his hand and stepped into the hallway, gently closing the door behind him. How come I had made such a balls of my life with this lovely man? What was wrong with me?

My head hurt and my body ached. I crawled into the shower and dressed in yesterday's clothes. By the time I reached the kitchen, there was no sign of my mother, but she'd left me a note to tell me she'd gone shopping. Glad of the reprieve, I wrote her a note in return, rang Molly to say I wouldn't be in, and left.

I had no car now the beemer was dead and gone, so I had to walk back to my apartment. Would Tim replace the car? It was a company car, after all, and not my fault that those hooligans had blown it up and I was sure it was well insured. I walked through the dark, winter morning, and tried not to think about what had happened. It was impossible. Joey assaulted me as soon as I opened the door.

'Shit!' I said, running to find cat food. 'Animal welfare will be on to me.'

I gave Joey a whole tin of cat food and searched in my phone book for my Uncle Gerry's telephone number. The fastest way I could get wheels under me was Uncle Gerry and the insurance company would pick up the tab. Since I'd been given a company car, I'd stopped needing the services of my Elvis-impersonator, car-dealer uncle.

Uncle Gerry answered the phone. 'Graceland Motors. Best deals on wheels. Gerry speaking.'

'Don't be giving me your sales guff.'

'Ellen? How are you? How's that big, beautiful car?'

'Blown up.'

'Jesus!'

'So, I'm back in the market for one of your cars for at least a couple of weeks.'

'Say no more, Ellen – I've the very car for you.'

I dreaded already what he had in mind for me. My last car from Uncle Gerry was the lipstick-pink Hyundai, and the one before that had spontaneously combusted. I had every reason to be worried.

'Let me see – the lads are working on it at the moment. Four o'clock – how's that? I'll drop it to your office.'

'No, bring it to my apartment, please. I'm not at work today.'

'Great stuff. See you at four.'

By the time I'd finished arranging a temporary set of wheels, it was nearly noon. So, I made my regulation pot of noodles and threw myself onto the sofa with Joey to watch Jerry Springer. I'd been neglecting Jerry of late, what with temporarily having a life and all. I'd also been neglecting noodles, I realised, as I stuffed my mouth. All that wholesome, delicious food that Spencer had been so fond of cooking was no substitute for a bowl of noodles and a mug of cocoa.

There was an excellent fistfight on Jerry, complete with throwing chairs and restraining bouncers. This was quality viewing, really. How could people criticise something that was capable of taking all of your attention even when your life was a heap of shit like mine?

I thought about waking that morning and seeing

Andrew sitting at the end of my bed, and how comforting it was to have him around again. There was no denying that I had a soft spot for Andrew. He was like noodles and cocoa and Joey and trash TV – warm and comfortable and loving, and hard to imagine being without.

Lovely thoughts if only I wasn't also half in love with Tony and having sweet and lovely thoughts about my time with Spencer. I was ridiculously confused, and everything that happened seemed to add to my confusion rather than clear it up. It was time I took control of my life.

I changed my clothes and called a cab. Within ten minutes, I was standing nervously outside Spencer's apartment building. Before I could think too much about it, I rang his buzzer.

'Yes?' Spencer's distinctive voice said over the intercom.

'Hi, Spencer. It's me, Ellen.'

'Door open.'

Spencer's voice disappeared and the red front door of the building made a loud noise. I walked straight in and climbed into a waiting lift. I had no idea what I was going to say to him but I knew I couldn't leave things the way they were.

The lift deposited me on the top floor, and I could see Spencer standing in the doorway of his apartment. From the distance, he looked like an extra on *ER*, with a huge plastercast on his right shoulder and arm. Up close, he looked like a man who'd been hurt in every way. His face was pale and there were dark circles around his lovely green eyes.

'Hello, Ellen.'

'Spencer.'

We walked in silence into his apartment.

'I know you're going back on Friday,' I blurted out. 'So I wanted to come and see you and say . . . say . . . sorry.'

Spencer walked to the huge glass doors and looked out. Rain pelted on the glass, and the city looked menacing and dark. I stood behind the cream couch, fingering a gold, velvet throw and looking at his broad back.

'I know I hurt you,' I said. 'All I can say is that I didn't mean to. I told myself that we had an under-standing – that we were just having a good time.'

Spencer didn't answer and didn't turn around.

'Oh, Spencer! I don't know how to make it up to you. All I can say is that I am really and truly sorry.'

My eyes filled with tears and I swallowed them back. That was that so. At least I'd apologised. I turned to walk out of the apartment.

'Ellen.'

I turned around. He was looking straight at me.

'I loved you,' he said.

Tears coursed down my face. 'I know,' I said. 'I'm sorry.'

'I never loved anybody before. I mean, I thought I did, but I didn't. Not really. I saw us together forever – marriage, kids . . . hell – even grandchildren.' He laughed wryly and looked at the floor.

'Spencer—'

'No, Ellen, listen. I know they call me 'the run-away groom' at work, and it's true – I've done my fair share of wooing and using. Like you, I didn't mean any harm. I just never knew what it felt like to be on the receiving end. I suppose I should thank you for teaching me that – but I can't.'

Spencer and I looked at each other for a few seconds. There was nothing else to say.

'I'd better go,' I said.

He nodded, and I walked towards the door.

'There's just one thing,' I said, my hand on the door handle. 'You're a great guy, Spencer.'

Then I left, immediately, before the tears that were already flowing down my face moved into high gear. I decided to walk back home in the hopes that it would clear my head. The rain had stopped, though it was still cold and grey. Town was busy – crowds of people jostling on the footpaths, cars splashing rainwater as they drove in interminable lines of traffic.

I stopped crying and blew my nose. I was glad I'd gone to see Spencer, even if I'd had to listen to the truth. It was what I needed to do. I was replaying the conversation in my head when I accidentally slammed into a woman walking in the other direction.

'Sorry,' I said.

'Ellen! Ellen! I'm so glad to see you. I was going to call Ruth and ask her for your number.'

I focused on the vaguely familiar woman in the grey fur hat standing in front of me.

'Kathleen, how are you?' I said, as I recognised Ruth's birth mother.

Kathleen Brennan grabbed my hand and squeezed it tightly.

'There is danger – grave danger, Ellen. A malevolent force is abroad and nothing will sate it except to have its way.'

Kathleen Brennan had closed her eyes and slipped into clairvoyant mode. I needed that like a hole in the head in the middle of O'Connell Street. And especially as I didn't understand a word she was saying. She squeezed my hand again.

'I saw it this morning. The dark forces coming together – an eruption of some sort, I can't say exactly what. And I saw the numbers 105 – clear as day. Do those numbers mean anything to you?'

'No. Unless . . . oh my God!' A tremor ran through me from head to toe. 'It was about five past ten yesterday when my car was blown up. That might be 105 – ten five.'

Kathleen Brennan opened her eyes and gave me a satisfied nod. Then the trance came back in full force. Her eyes closed, she swayed from side to side, and, I swear to God, she was humming a tune. She dropped my hand from hers and suddenly her eyes flew open.

'Death is his intention. A loved one could die in the marble hall.'

I almost laughed, as the song, 'I Dreamt I Dwelt in Marble Halls', started up inside my head. Kathleen's face changed and she became an ordinary middle-aged woman again. Apart from the mad Russian hat.

'OK,' I said, cheerfully. 'Lovely to see you, Kathleen. I'd better get going. Take care.'

'No, Ellen – *you* take care.'

I waved at Kathleen and hurried on home. I didn't want to miss Uncle Gerry's arrival. By the time I reached my apartment block, it was almost four o'clock, so I decided to wait outside the building. I stood there shivering as a freezing wind whipped up off the river. Clusters of people hurried along the street, anxious to be out of the miserable weather. It struck me that I could have managed without a car until the beemer was replaced. That was a novel thought. It had never even entered my head before.

I did live and work in town, after all, and could easily have walked to the office. Mind you, I'd need a car for meeting clients or viewing properties. Just as I was making up excuses to myself for why I was so lazy, I heard a car horn and immediately regretted not buying a bicycle to get me over the hump.

Right there at the entrance to my building was a huge gold jeep with my Hawaiian-shirt-clad Uncle Gerry behind the wheel. The jeep looked like something that might be living in a rapper's garage on *MTV Cribs*.

'Holy shit!' I said, waving at Uncle Gerry. He waved back and stopped the engine. What the hell was I going to do with this for the next couple of weeks? It made the pink Hyundai look restrained and classy.

'It's a Big Horn,' Uncle Gerry said, leaping from the jeep like a man half his age. All that rock 'n' rollin' at Elvis conventions was obviously better than any gym membership.

'Oh,' I said, because it was clear by the way he was looking at me that a response was necessary. That was enough response for Uncle Gerry. He rubbed at the gold paintwork and gave me a broad smile, then leaned back into the cab of the jeep and flicked a switch.

'There,' he said, pointing downwards.

I couldn't see anything.

'I thought the pink would be good for you as you're a girl.'

And then I saw it. A long strip of pink neon light ran all around the bottom of the Big Horn. Jesus! I was going to look like a right fool driving this yoke. I smiled weakly at my uncle.

'Told you I'd see you right,' he said. 'There won't be another estate agent in this town driving one of these.'

Only drug-dealers, I thought. No other estate agent would be seen dead in one of those. But I couldn't say that, so I said, 'Great, great. I should need it for only a couple of weeks. I'll talk to Tim and he'll get the insurance company to fix you up for the car hire. Thanks a million.'

Uncle Gerry nodded. 'If you can't do a turn for your own flesh and blood, what good is any of it? This baby'll take a while to shift – it's only a very particular type of customer will be looking at anything as up-market as this. So, I'll keep it on the books and if anyone wants to look at it, I'll send them around to you. How's that for a deal?'

Uncle Gerry winked at me.

'Thanks again.'

'Ellen, enough auld talk out of you. Give me a lift back to Graceland and we'll call it quits. OK?'

I smiled at my uncle then. Why was everybody related to me bonkers? Not that it mattered. I loved them anyway. Uncle Gerry threw me the keys of the jeep and I nervously drove to his garage. By the time I dropped him off, I was beginning to like driving the jeep.

I was so high up that I imagined I'd not only be able to see everything I needed to see on the road, but also I was hoping to be able to get a gawk into other people's cars. Power. I liked it.

Maybe Tim would consider buying me a Big Horn instead of a new BMW. Who knew what clientèle might be attracted if the Area Manager had a more hip vehicle? The Big Horn had tinted windows and chrome interior trim, and an incredible sound system. I had the feeling that I might need to buy a few rap albums to do it justice. All I was short was the bouncing hydraulics wheels. With those I could have been the coolest estate agent in the 'hood.

I was loving the jeep so much that I took it for a short drive out the Cork road. It bombed along the new road effortlessly, and the feeling of contained power under my foot every time I accelerated was magnificent. No wonder men loved cars so much. It

would have been nice to have driven the whole way
to Cork but I decided I'd postpone that pleasure for
another day, and reluctantly turned the jeep after
about ten miles and headed for home.

As I reached the outskirts of town, my mobile
rang, and I pulled onto the hard shoulder and stopped
the jeep.

'Hello?'

'Ellen? Ellen, are you OK?'

'Roxy?'

'Oh, Ellen, you are OK.'

'Of course, I am. Why wouldn't I be OK?'

'Oh my God! I don't know what I'm going to do
– he's taken them and I don't know where he is and
he said he blew up your car and I thought that you
were . . . you know – dead.'

'Who? Who said that?'

There was a silence on the other end of the line
and then the sound of a loud sob.

'Teddy.'

## 39

'Are you telling me that Teddy Hannon has taken the girls?'

'Yes.'

'He's trying to torture you. Calm down.'

'No, Ellen. He rang me. He's not even due back with them until six. He rang and said he's not bringing them back.'

Roxy's voice broke up and I listened, my heart thumping in my chest. I heard the sound of a deep breath.

'Then . . . then he said all this shit about them being *his* children and that they have a right to be with their father and I'm just a slut, not fit to raise them—'

'Did you call the guards?'

'Not yet. I just hung up from talking to Teddy.'

'Ring the station and ask for Hilary Thornton.'

'All right.'

'And I'll be straight over.'

'Thanks, Ellen.'

I put all the things she had said out of my head and hung a right. Fucking Teddy Hannon! He was probably just trying to freak Roxy out. If he was the one who had blown up the car, then Robert White and Hoodie were telling the truth, for once. I was starting to realise that Teddy Hannon made Robert White and his cronies look like the Legion of Mary.

I pulled up outside Roxy's house and ran in through the open front door. She was pacing the kitchen, her blonde hair loose and curling down the back of her green fleecy tracksuit jacket, her face gaunt with terror. Pa was holding Enrique. Roxy ran to me and hugged me as soon as I came into the room.

'I'm so glad you're all right,' she said, her voice breaking as the tears began to flow down her face.

'Did you call the police?' I asked.

'I did,' Pa said. 'I asked for that woman.'

'Hilary Thornton?'

Pa nodded. 'She's away.'

'Shit!'

'But I told them anyway and they said they'd send somebody out. They kept saying, "Oh, it's a domestic" and "We get that all the time" and "He'll probably bring them back later and it'll all be fine."'

Roxy blew her nose noisily. 'They don't know him. Pa told them who Teddy was and that he'd been in jail and all. But they just think he's one of the ordinary scumbags they deal with every day. They don't know what he's capable of.'

The kitchen door opened and we all jumped with fright. Tony Jordan and Wolfie walked in.

'Jesus, Ellen!' Wolfie said, walking straight over to me and hugging me against his enormous chest. 'You

OK? Maurice told us what happened. That bastard took the kids and blew up your car?'

'I'm fine,' I said, looking at Tony. He was staring at me as if he'd never seen me before, and, given our track record and my recent brush with death, I was glad the room was full of people.

'You were lucky,' Tony said. 'He meant to kill you.'

'But why?' I asked.

'Because he's a mad bastard and you stood up to him,' he said.

'So he tried to blow me up to teach me a lesson?'

'No,' Roxy said. 'He tried to kill *you* to teach *me* a lesson.'

A muscle at the side of Tony's face jumped and he stared out the kitchen window. 'And he definitely has the girls, Roxy?'

'Yes,' she said, plaintively.

'Where's he holding them?' Tony asked.

'He won't say. Just rang to tell me he has them.'

Tony and Wolfie looked at each other. 'He wouldn't – you know – hurt them, Roxy, would he?' Wolfie asked.

'He could do anything,' she said.

'They're his kids,' Tony said.

Roxy shook her head. 'Teddy has all this mad stuff about soul mates and how we're really soul mates and he never really had much interest in Shania and Shakira other than as his possessions. Ellen was right – I should never have let him have access.'

'You thought you were doing the right thing,' I said.

Roxy shook her head. 'I'm a bad mother.'

I went to her and wrapped my arms around her. 'No one could ever accuse you of that. You're a terrific mother.'

'We need to find him,' Tony said. 'Don't worry, Roxy – Wolfie and I still have loads of contacts, so we'll drive around and find out what we can. And then we'll make a plan. How about that?'

Roxy nodded.

'Have you called the police yet?' he asked.

'I called them,' Pa said. 'They'll send someone out later.'

'It'll be too late,' Roxy said in a flat voice.

'OK,' Tony said. 'We'll go and have a look around.'

'I'm coming with you,' Roxy said.

Tony shook his head. But Roxy shook hers as well. 'No, Tony – I'm coming with you or I'll lose my mind. Pa will mind the baby. Won't you, love?'

'No problem,' Pa said.

'And he can talk to the guards as well. Can't you, Pa?'

'Also no problem.'

Tony and Wolfie looked at each other and then back at Roxy. Pa coughed loudly and cleared his throat. 'You can't expect her just to sit here,' he said. 'What would you do, Tone?'

'I'm going as well,' I said, walking over to stand beside Roxy.

'Jesus, Mary and Joseph!' Tony said.

'You sound like my mother,' I said, and a quick grin flitted across his face.

'Come on, so' he said, starting towards the hallway. 'Call us if there's any news, Pa.'

'Will do. Best of luck,' Pa said, his voice calm and clear.

Wolfie, Tony, Roxy and I filed out of the house and walked towards Tony's jeep.

'Who owns the Big Horn?' Wolfie asked, in what can only be described as reverent tones.

'Uncle Gerry,' I said with a sigh, and they all looked at me. 'It's on loan.'

Tony opened his jeep and sat in behind the wheel, and the rest of us climbed in. The evening was about to turn from cold to absolutely freezing. Roxy shivered as Tony started the engine, but refused Wolfie's offer of a jacket.

'I'm grand,' she said, shaking her head and trying a weak smile. 'Let's just go.'

So we did.

# 40

As we pulled out of Hollyfields, Roxy's phone rang.

'Hello?' she said, and then was silent as she listened.

Her body tensed. Wolfie and Tony were talking quietly in the front of the jeep and I tapped their shoulders and pointed to Roxy.

'Where are you?' Roxy asked. 'OK, OK, I'm listening. Right now? You want me to go there now? OK. OK. Ten minutes.'

Roxy took a breath. 'Teddy? Teddy, are you there?' She looked at me. 'He's gone.'

'What did he say?'

'He said I'm to come to the Regal. Room 105. Now.'

'You can't do that,' said Wolfie.

Roxy ignored him and continued to look at me.

'So?' I said.

'So, I'm going. What else can I do?'

'Call the guards,' I said.

'No,' Roxy said. 'He told me to come alone and I'm going alone.'

'No way, Roxy,' Wolfie said. 'We'll go and get the kids.'

'Stop the car, Tony,' Roxy said. 'I know you mean

well, Wolfie, but I'm going alone and that's it. Please stop.'

'I'll drive you to the Regal,' Tony said.

'But I'm going in by myself,' Roxy said.

'I know but I'll drive you. It'll be faster.'

Roxy leaned back in her seat and stared out the window, and I wished I knew what to say to her. I could see from her face, though, that all she was focused on was the girls. Everything beyond that was a distraction that she didn't want. It was a ten-minute drive to the Regal and nobody spoke. Tony pulled into the hotel car park and stopped outside the entrance. Roxy immediately opened her door.

'Wait, Roxy,' Tony said quietly.

She turned her head to look at him.

'We need a plan,' he said.

'I have a plan. I'm going to Room 105 and I'm getting my girls.'

'He won't let you take them.'

Her face collapsed. 'I don't care. I have to try.'

'I have an idea,' Tony said.

Roxy looked at him, and tears rolled down her smooth cheeks.

'I know the layout of this hotel – I wasn't a burglar for all those years for nothing.'

Roxy gave him a thin smile.

'There's an extension at the rear of the hotel, and Wolfie and I can climb it. All the upstairs rooms have windows at the back. We'll find 105, no problem. All we need you to do is to keep Teddy in the room and keep him talking.'

'But what will you do then?' Roxy asked.

'We'll kill the fucker,' Wolfie said.

Roxy looked alarmed.

'No, we won't,' Tony said. 'But we will overpower him while you take the girls and get the fuck out of there.'

'I don't know. Teddy could do something mad if it goes wrong.'

'He could do something mad anyway,' I said. 'It's worth a shot.'

'Do whatever you want as long as it doesn't endanger my children,' Roxy said getting out of the car.

Then she ran up the front steps of the hotel and disappeared through the revolving door into the lobby. Tony and Wolfie simultaneously threw open their doors and jumped out of the jeep. I jumped out as well. Tony held out the keys.

'Park it, Ellen,' he said. 'Then wait in the lobby. If we're not out with the kids in ten minutes, call the guards.' They ran off around the back of the building before I could even answer. I sat into the jeep, found a parking space, and dashed into the hotel.

The foyer was wide and tiled in white marble with a glass atrium as a roof. The reception desk ran along the left-hand wall, while a huge fire roared up the chimney in the carpeted seating area on my right. Facing me, on the back wall, were three old-fashioned lifts with wrought-iron gates.

A spattering of Yanks sat at tables, drinking Irish coffees and reading the complimentary newspapers.

What would I do? Where would I sit? How long exactly had Tony and Wolfie been gone?

I sat down at an empty table and, picking up *The Irish Times*, began flicking through it distractedly. I looked at my watch – it was 8.15 exactly. I guessed that Tony and Wolfie had been gone for five minutes and decided that I'd call the police at 8.20 on the button.

I tried to concentrate on an article about Gabriel Byrne, but every noise made me start. I couldn't bear to think what might be happening in Room 105. Just as I gave up on Gabriel and turned to an article on property prices, the centre lift at the end of the lobby opened.

Teddy, Roxy, Shakira and Shania appeared. My heart leapt. Teddy was smiling and talking, and carrying Shakira in his arms. Roxy was paler than I'd ever seen her, and her expression was frozen like a mask. She held Shania's hand as they hurried towards the door. None of them saw me, and I knew they were going to be gone before Tony and Wolfie turned up. Dropping the newspaper on the ground, I ran straight at them.

'Surprise!' I shouted into Teddy Hannon's face. Taking advantage of his momentary shock, I grabbed the child from his arms and deposited her on the floor.

'What the fuck!' he said.

Out of the corner of my eye, I saw Roxy snatch Shakira and run away with the girls. At that point, Tony appeared around the corner at the end of the lobby, his face red with exertion and fear. Wolfie followed. Thank God, I thought – it's over. Everybody's safe.

Suddenly, Teddy Hannon grabbed me. He swivelled me around until I was facing forward, and his arm was like a vice around my throat. A small revolver in his other hand pressed against my temple.

'Gee, look, honey! They're making a movie,' a woman in an Aran cardigan said loudly.

'Let her go, Teddy,' Tony said, as he approached.

Teddy Hannon laughed and turned, pulling me with him until we faced Tony. 'And who exactly are you? Bruce Willis?'

'Let the girl go,' Wolfie shouted as he ran up behind Tony.

Teddy Hannon tightened his grip, constricting my throat until I could barely swallow. I wriggled to try to free myself but that made his grip tighter so I stopped. I could smell soap and shampoo, but the fact that he was a clean psychopath wasn't really very consoling.

'Oh, I have it now,' he said. 'The Dynamic Duo – Batman and Robin.'

I squirmed again and Teddy pulled me closer to his body. My handbag bit into the flesh on my shoulder.

'Where's Roxy?' Teddy asked.

'Look—' Wolfie began.

'Back off unless you want me to shoot her right now. I already tried to kill her once. I assure you it won't bother me to kill her if you fucking keep walking towards me.'

Wolfie stopped.

'What do you want?' Tony asked.

Teddy sighed. 'Good question. What do I want? What do any of us want? I want my wife. Is that unreasonable? Is it wrong for a man to want to be with his wife? I think not.'

'Let her go, Teddy,' Roxy said in a quiet voice as she appeared out of nowhere and stood in front of us.

Teddy's grip loosened slightly and, before I could think about it, I elbowed him in the solar plexus.

'Fuck!' Teddy said, doubling over. A shot rang out as I threw myself away from him. I crashed into a coffee table and fell inelegantly onto the ground. The contents of my handbag spilled as I fell, and I landed hard on my make-up bag. A number of tampons and two lipsticks rolled past me on the marble floor.

'Oh my God!' said the American woman who'd been shouting about movies earlier. 'What's this movie gonna be called?'

'But, honey, there's no camera,' a man who seemed to be her husband said as I was scrambling to my feet.

The woman screamed. 'Oh my God! Then she really is shot.'

I didn't feel shot, but the front of my blouse felt damp. I wiped my hand across it and nearly fainted when I saw that my palm was covered in blood. I looked down at my make-up bag and then back up at Tony as he shouted my name.

Teddy grabbed Roxy by the wrist and dragged her towards the door. Tony started towards me.

'No, I'm fine,' I shouted at him. 'Get Roxy.'

'But—'

'Halloween party. Fake blood. Get Roxy.'

Tony and Wolfie set off after Teddy Hannon who was just about to step through the revolving doors. Wolfie barrelled at them and sort of rugby-tackled Roxy, pulling her from Teddy's grasp. Teddy fell to the ground as Roxy and Wolfie rolled across the floor.

'Mammy!' a child's voice pierced the air.

Shania appeared around the end of the long reception desk.

'Let my mammy go!' she shouted as she ran across the white marble floor.

'Shania! Get back!' Roxy screamed, scrambling to her feet.

Teddy Hannon lunged forward towards the child. But Tony reached her first and threw her through the air into Wolfie's arms. Then time slowed down. Teddy and Roxy stood, like players centre stage, with every eye in the place fixed on them.

'It's over,' Teddy said quietly, as he lifted his right arm and pointed the gun at Roxy. And then he could have backed towards the door and tried to escape but he didn't move, and I knew then that Roxy was going to die. I looked across the foyer at Tony and we locked eyes just before Tony sprang at Teddy and clotheslined him back against the revolving doors. A shot cracked loudly and Tony staggered backwards. The door revolved and Teddy disappeared.

Wolfie and I ran to where Tony lay. Black-red blood

pooled on the white marble floor. I skidded to my knees beside him.

'Not fake, Ellen,' he said, smiling weakly as his eyes closed.

'No,' I screamed, pulling off my fleece jacket and ramming it up against the spreading redness on Tony's chest.

'Ellen—' Wolfie said.

'Call an ambulance, Wolfie. Quickly!'

Wolfie ran away.

'Tony,' I said. 'Open your eyes.' Miraculously he did as I ordered. 'I love you, Tony. Don't die.'

I leaned down and kissed him on his white lips.

He smiled. 'Best surprise kisser,' he whispered, and his eyes closed again. I was going to scream but somebody pulled me away. Before I knew it, Tony was on a stretcher and I was running after the knot of medics clustered around him.

I climbed into the ambulance behind them. A nurse asked me Tony's details while a doctor and two other nurses huddled around the stretcher all the way to the hospital, shouting medical jargon at each other as they pulled and dragged at Tony's unconscious body. It was an episode of *ER* but without the luxury of being able to flick over to Jerry Springer.

The ambulance pulled up outside the hospital and the medics jumped out, shouting information to an equally frantic reception committee of doctors and nurses. I followed the stretcher down a maze of corridors until it disappeared through double doors that slammed in my face and wouldn't open no matter how hard I pushed.

I slumped onto a chair a little way down the corridor and stared unseeing at the pristine white wall in front of me. Events of the past hours kept playing in my head and I imagined I could hear the sound of the gun over and over again. And I could see Tony's red blood on white marble. He was going to die. My gut instinct told me he was going to die in a sterile operating theatre in Limerick. I'd never see him alive again. Never see those incredibly gorgeous eyes or kiss his mouth. I loved him. I knew that now with a certainty I'd never felt before in my life, and that's why he was going to die on me.

# 41

'Are you OK?'

I looked up to see a beautiful woman's face close to mine. Her eyes were brown and her curly blonde hair was tied in a loose ponytail. She wore a blue, short-sleeved top and white pants, and her nametag said she was called Jenny Collins.

'I'm fine,' I said.

'Did you cut yourself?'

'No. Fake blood. It was in my handbag since Halloween and I fell on it.'

Jenny Collins smiled and sat on the chair beside me.

'My friend . . . he was shot. Gone in there. The doors are locked. How do I find out about him?'

Jenny Collins stood up. 'I'll go. Stay there. What's his name?'

'Tony Jordan.'

Then she tapped a code into the number pad by the double doors. The doors opened in a ghostly slo-mo way, and Jenny Collins disappeared. What was behind those doors anyway? I wished I'd asked her.

I closed my eyes for a second. When I opened

them, Wolfie and Roxy were hurrying along the terrazzo corridor. I jumped up and ran towards them. Wolfie grabbed me and hugged me.

'Where is he?' he asked.

I pointed at the doors.

'And?'

I shook my head. 'A girl – a nurse or something – is gone to find out.'

'Where are the girls, Roxy?' I asked.

'With Pa. They're fine.'

'And where's Teddy Hannon?'

'He got away, but he's a dead man. I'll find him,' Wolfie said, and his face contorted into a frightening version of himself that I'd never seen before.

'The guards are looking for him,' Roxy said. 'Maybe they'll find him.'

Then the doors opened and Jenny Collins emerged. I felt Wolfie and Roxy tense beside me. They knew she was the messenger. When I saw that she had a doctor in tow, I knew the news was bad. The doctor was a tall Asian man who looked to be in his mid-forties.

He smiled at us. 'Are you Mr Jordan's wife?'

I shook my head.

'Oh,' he said. 'I wonder if you could tell me how to contact Mr Jordan's family.'

My knees buckled and Roxy grabbed my arm. Wolfie wrapped a big muscle-bound arm around my shoulders and pulled me close so that I was able to lean against him. Tony was dead. Tony was dead. Tony was dead.

'We're all the family Tony has,' Wolfie said.

The doctor smiled and extended a hand to Wolfie. 'Hello. I'm Dr Mistry. Pleased to meet you.'

'Bobby Wolfe. And these are Tony's friends – Ellen Grace and Roxy Dawson.'

Roxy and I shook hands with the doctor, and my heart felt as if it had stopped in my chest. What was I going to do now? How could I stay alive?

'Mr Jordan is very ill,' Dr Mistry said. 'We've removed the bullet but he lost a lot of blood. That jacket around his chest saved his life. We've moved him to Intensive Care.'

'But he'll be all right?' Roxy interrupted.

Dr Mistry looked at Roxy. 'Well, he's critical at the moment. The next twenty-four hours are crucial.'

'But he's alive,' I said, because I couldn't believe it.

'Yes. Would you like to see him?' Dr Mistry asked.

'Could we?' Wolfie said.

'Just two of you and only for a few minutes.'

'I'll wait here,' Roxy said.

Wolfie and I followed the doctor through the doors and into a quiet corridor. We walked in silence behind him until he stopped outside a glass door.

'He's not awake. Two minutes. That's all.' The doctor smiled and motioned towards the room. Wolfie looked at me and stepped forward to open the door. I felt he was afraid that if he paused at all, he might change his mind and run away.

Tony lay on the high hospital bed in the centre of the tiny room, surrounded by a tangle of machines.

It was as if the drips, tubes and monitors were the only things holding him in the world. Wolfie walked up to the bed and a loud sob broke free from his large chest.

'Fuck it, Tone!' he said, walking away to stand in a corner of the room.

I leaned over Tony and kissed his blanched cheek. His face was a perfect serene mask – his long, black eyelashes tipping the top of his cheekbones, the beginnings of stubble shading his chin. I was overwhelmed by how fragile he looked. Tony was always so big and strong and capable and now. . .

Behind me I could hear the quiet sounds of Wolfie's crying and the rhythmic whirr of machines. There was a light tap on the door, and Dr Mistry beckoned us to leave. Wolfie and I obediently left the room and walked side by side back along the corridor.

'The canteen is still open. Why don't you go and have something to eat?' suggested the doctor as he let us out the door.

'Can I stay?' I asked.

'If you like, but I'm afraid you'll have to stay in the waiting room. It's just there to the left.'

'Thanks for everything, Doctor,' Wolfie said. 'And look, mind him, will ye? Please.'

The doctor smiled. 'Of course we will.'

The doors whooshed closed. Roxy was still standing directly outside.

'Well?' she asked.

'He's not too bad,' I said, loudly. 'Pale but calm

and – you know yourself – there are machines and tubes and all of that. But Roxy, I think he'll be fine.'

I looked at Wolfie whose eyes were full of tears. Roxy put her arm around him – as far as it would go.

'I don't know, Ellen,' he said. 'He looks very sick to me.'

I shook my head. 'No, Wolfie. He's fine. Really, he's fine. It'll be the same old Tony in the morning – wait and see.'

Wolfie widened his eyes to stop the tears.

'I'm going to stay,' I said. 'Why don't you two go on home?'

'But Ellen—' Roxy began.

'No, really, it'll be fine. Pa and the kids will be worried about you. The girls have had a traumatic experience – go on home. You too, Wolfie.'

'I suppose you're right. If you don't need me here—' Roxy said.

'I'll be back in a while,' Wolfie said. 'I'll drop Roxy home and then I'll be back.'

'Hasta la vista, baby,' I said but nobody smiled.

Roxy hugged me and then she and Wolfie left. Jenny Collins – who turned out to be a nurse – brought me a couple of blankets. I left one on a chair for Wolfie and settled myself into an armchair. I thought I'd just doze for a few minutes. It had been a long, long, long day.

I awoke with a start to the sound of Wolfie's snoring. I looked at my watch. Five o'clock. How was Tony? He was still alive anyway, as nobody had

come to call us during the night. That was a good
sign surely. I went into the corridor and noticed that
there was a bell beside the entrance to Intensive Care.
I tried it. A plump nurse opened the doors.

'I'm just enquiring about Tony Jordan,' I said.

'Are you his wife?'

'No – his girlfriend.'

'He's very ill but has been stable through the night.
Would you like to see him?'

I nodded and followed her to Tony's room. He
looked exactly as he'd looked the night before. I
approached the bed and kissed his forehead. I took
his hand gently in mine.

'Tony,' I whispered. 'It's me, Ellen. Can you hear
me?'

Suddenly, a loud alarm ripped through the silence.
What the hell was that? Where was it coming from?
Surely that was too much noise for an Intensive Care
Unit? I realised that the alarm was coming from a
machine behind me. I turned my head to look, just
as a nurse and a doctor ran into the room.

'He's crashed,' the nurse said to nobody in particular as she dragged a trolley of resuscitation
equipment close to the bed.

I stepped back into a corner and looked at the
heart monitor. The black screen had a row of
luminous green numbers along the left-hand
side, and a long, flat green line along the bottom.
You didn't need to be a doctor to know what a flat
line meant. I shouldn't have spoken to him. I
shouldn't have come back into his life. I was a

Jonah – being involved with me just brought everybody bad luck.

The nurse stripped the sheet away from Tony's body, and the doctor called the *ER* catchphrase.

'Clear,' he said as he applied the electric paddles to Tony's chest. Tony's body jerked in the bed. We all looked at the heart monitor. It was still showing a long, green flat line. The doctor repeated the procedure. This time, the line on the monitor kinked. My own heart was about ready to stop.

The doctor and nurse stepped back from the bed and we all watched the monitor again. Gradually, Tony's heart established a rhythm. The emergency seemed to have passed. The nurse noticed me then and came over to where I was standing.

'We need to make Mr Jordan more comfortable. Why don't you go to the canteen and get some coffee? You can come back in later.'

I nodded and left and made my way back to the waiting room. Wolfie was awake.

'Ellen?'

I stood there in the middle of the floor, my mind and body frozen. Gradually the freeze changed to a numb feeling, and then to an unbearble pain.

'He's dying,' I said, and a huge sob tore up my throat and out my mouth, and I bawled. 'Tony's heart stopped and they had to start it again, like on *ER*, and what if it doesn't keep going?'

Wolfie jumped up and folded me into his arms, and I cried and cried and cried. He stroked my head and I could hear his heart beating, and it reminded me that Tony's had stopped, and that made me cry more. Eventually the tears subsided and I plonked onto a chair.

'Tony's a fighter,' Wolfie said, sitting opposite me.

'I hope so. It was horrible when his heart stopped. I was so afraid.'

'But it did start again, didn't it?'

I nodded.

'So, it'll keep going now,' said Wolfie. 'I know it will.'

The door of the waiting room opened and Jenny Collins appeared with a tray.

'Tea and toast,' she said, putting the tray on a small table.

'Thanks,' Wolfie said. 'You're a star.'

She smiled and left. Wolfie poured the tea and I drank a full cup, but I couldn't face the toast. I listened to the sounds of the hospital waking up – trays banging, footsteps along the corridors, a distant floor-polisher whirring. Ordinary sounds really – surely Tony couldn't die when everything in the world was carrying on as normal?

# 42

I spent the rest of the morning sitting on a chair in the corner of Tony's hospital room. The machines did their work and made their noises, and Tony lay as still as a statue. As the morning wore on, a strange feeling of calm grew in me. I didn't understand it but it was real and had something to do with being with Tony. In spite of the circumstances.

At around lunch time, Wolfie came into the room to stand vigil. Ruth and India were waiting in the corridor when I came out of Intensive Care. They were crying but I was still calm.

'It'll be fine,' I said.

'Oh Ellen,' Ruth said and threw her arms around me. She was so tiny – funny, I hadn't noticed that in ages. India came to stand beside us, and put her arms around both of us. She was crying too.

'At least you weren't hurt. That guy could have shot everybody in the hotel,' said India.

I started to laugh and they both looked at me. 'It's just—' but I couldn't finish the sentence as a fit of wild, uncontrollable laughter possessed me. I took a deep breath and tried again. 'There was an American woman and she thought we were making a movie in the hotel and . . . and—' I started to laugh again. India and Ruth looked at each other and then back at me.

'You had to be there,' I said.

A few moments later, my mother, father and Angela Maunsell arrived. Mam and Angela had brought my toilet bag and a change of clothes and a bag of scones and apples.

I went and had a shower, which made me feel half human. By the time I got back to the ICU waiting room, it was beginning to look like a Grace family get-together. Will had turned up, along with Ralph and Roxy, and, most surprising of all, Andrew.

Tears welled as soon as I saw him, and he walked directly to me and held me in his arms. I put my arms around him and breathed in the smell of him, which was so familiar and comforting. It was a balm to my heart.

'Will we go and get some coffee?' Andrew suggested.

I nodded gratefully and we jumped ship, leaving the assorted friends and relatives to themselves. Andrew bought two large cappuccinos in paper cups, at the restaurant, and then led the way into the hospital grounds. We sat in silence on a low wall and sipped our coffee. It was a clear, cold day. The sky was high and blue and dotted with fluffy white clouds that belied the northeasterly wind. I shivered in the wind and hugged my warm paper cup. Andrew put his arm around my shoulders, and I leaned into him.

'Thanks for coming,' I said. 'Do you know something, Andrew? You're always there when I need you.'

'Like the *Golden Pages*.'

I laughed. 'No, I mean it. I really appreciate it – you know that, don't you?' I turned my head towards him and our faces were inches apart. He kissed me lightly on the cheek.

'I love you, Ellen.'

I didn't answer.

'Don't worry. I'm not about to revisit any of our more painful conversations,' he said. 'But there is something I want to say to you, if it's OK with you.'

I shrugged and nodded. He took a deep breath.

'When I left for America, I was devastated. I felt as if my heart had been cut out, and, for the first few weeks, everything was a blur.'

'I'm so sorry, Andrew.'

'No, no, no. Listen. You see, the thing is, I've met someone – Claudia – I work with her in Austin—'

'You didn't let the grass grow under your feet.'

Andrew laughed softly. 'You'd be one to talk, Ellen Grace. I love you, you know, with all my heart. But now I think I understand what went wrong between us. I think that instinctively you knew there was something missing. I'm sure of it because of Claudia.'

I took Andrew's hand in mine. 'I love you too, Andrew. You'll always be one of my best friends. I hope everything works out with you and Claudia.'

'Thanks. And how about you? Is Tony Jordan the man for you?'

'I don't know. The way it is now, who knows what will happen? Tony might not even survive.'

'Poor Ellen.'

'No, funnily enough, I'm OK. I realised something this morning while I was sitting with Tony – what will be, will be. I can't determine what will happen but I can accept it.' I started to laugh.

'What?' Andrew said.

'Que sera sera,' I sang. 'I'm turning into Doris Day.'

Andrew hugged me and stood up. 'I have to go back to the States tomorrow – unless you need me to stay.'

'No, I'm fine. Best of luck with everything – especially Claudia – and give Katie a hug for me.'

'Will do.'

He bent down and kissed me lightly on the lips. Then, with a wave, he walked away across the hospital car park. I sat on the wall for a few minutes, thinking. Andrew was gone from my life now, and it looked like his life was finally working out. He was happy. I was glad.

The question was, was *I* ever going to be happy? I shivered inside my thin sweater and wrapped my arms around myself for warmth. Sure, I was able to have relationships and even able to be in love. But there was something about total commitment that terrified me more than I'd ever cared to admit. All the time, there was a part of me afraid that there might be a better party down the road. Suddenly everything was clear and I couldn't really see what had caused the confusion in the first place. The biting wind became too much to bear and I went back into the hospital building.

Ruth was the only person left in the waiting room. She looked exhausted.

'Are you OK?' I asked.

She jumped up and hugged me. 'Am I OK? Jesus, Ellen! I should be asking you that.'

I hugged her back. 'I met your mother in the street yesterday – God, was it only yesterday? She told me a load of stuff. More about the danger and the man whose name begins with T.'

'She is a performer, Ellen.'

'I know but lots of it happened. Kathleen predicted the whole Teddy Hannon thing, and even – oh my God! – she said it would happen in a marble hall. *And* she predicted that the number 105 would be important and that was Teddy Hannon's hotel room.'

Ruth grimaced. 'Lucky guess.'

I shrugged.

'Oh yeah,' Ruth said. 'I knew there was something else. A policeman was here. They arrested Teddy Hannon at the airport.'

'That's good news, but don't tell Wolfie where they're holding him.'

As if on cue, the door opened and Wolfie came in. 'Do you want to go in for a while, Ellen?'

I nodded. 'How is he?'

'He's still the same. But at least he's holding his own – that's what the nurse said, anyway.'

'That's good,' Ruth said.

I gave her a quick hug. 'I'll talk to you later,' I said and left.

I pulled the chair close to Tony's bed as soon as I arrived in his room. Wolfie was right. No change. I held his hand in both of mine and, suddenly exhausted, laid my head on the bed. I was too tired to think any more. I'd just rest my eyes for one minute.

I dreamed I was walking on a beach with a huge elephant and a tiny Jack Russell terrier. Someone was playing circus music, and my mother was calling me for my dinner, and pulling me by the hand. I opened my eyes afraid of what my mother had cooked. Slowly I realised where I was. Intensive Care. But why was my mother still pulling my hand? It wasn't my mother. I sat up. Tony's eyes were open and he was looking at me.

'Tony,' I said, and he blinked. 'Oh Tony, you're OK. You're awake.'

I covered his face in kisses, carefully avoiding the tubes. He gave a sleepy smile and gently squeezed my hand. I stroked his face.

'Tony Jordan, will you marry me?'